The House on Bellevue Gardens

RACHEL HORE

**SIMON &
SCHUSTER**

London · New York · Sydney · Toronto · New Delhi

A CBS COMPANY

First published in Great Britain by Simon & Schuster UK Ltd, 2016
This paperback edition published 2016
A CBS COMPANY

1 3 5 7 9 10 8 6 4 2

Simon & Schuster UK Ltd
1st Floor
222 Gray's Inn Road
London WC1X 8HB

www.simonandschuster.co.uk

Simon & Schuster Australia, Sydney
Simon & Schuster India, New Delhi

A CIP catalogue record for this book
is available from the British Library

Paperback ISBN: 978-1-4711-3079-3
eBook ISBN: 978-1-4711-3080-9

Excerpt from *The Poetry of Robert Frost*, edited by
Edward Connery Lathem. Published by Jonathan Cape.
Reprinted by permission of the Random House Group Limited.

Typeset in the UK by M Rules
Printed and bound by CPI Group (UK) Ltd, Croydon, CR0 4YY

Simon & Schuster UK Ltd are committed to sourcing paper
that is made from wood grown in sustainable forests and support the Forest
Stewardship Council, the leading international forest certification organisation.
Our books displaying the FSC logo are printed on FSC certified paper..

David's

'Most people in our culture have lives clogged up with superfluities: habits, activities, goods. Most of us are bound hand and foot, not physically but by our dreams, our prejudices, our fears.'

GRETA MCDONOUGH, *THE CLARY GHOST*

'The foxes have holes, and the birds of the air have nests; but the Son of man hath nowhere to lay his head.'

ST MATTHEW

'Home is the place where, when you have to go there,
They have to take you in.'

ROBERT FROST, *THE DEATH OF THE HIRED MAN*

Hidden behind a busy street in north London, Camden way, is a tranquil garden square. You might pass it without suspecting its existence. Its terraced houses are white-iced like giant wedding cakes. At some point in its history an unknown individual named it Bellevue Gardens. Many of the houses have been divided into flats. Their glory days are long past, but once they were the homes of well-to-do middle-class families whose fathers were lawyers or bankers, whose children played on the trim back lawns or in the square's wild garden, under the vigilant eyes of their nannies, whilst their mothers took tea in one another's drawing rooms and organized dinners or charity whist drives and changed their gowns several times a day. The bourgeois world of an age long gone.

There's not much more to say. In the Eighteen Nineties, Oscar Wilde visited friends at Number 13. A blue plaque states that a famous Edwardian actress once lived at Number 34. A row of three houses on the north side still bears scars of the Blitz – misshapen chimneys, patchwork roofs, angles twisted out of true.

Sometimes, when Leonie Brett arrives home late on a warm summer's night, she finds it easy to forget the ranks of parked cars, the distant grumble of London traffic, and imagines instead sparks flying from horses' hooves as they strike the flagstones, bright clinks of harness and the rumble of carriage wheels. The music and laughter drifting through an open window might be a party from another century, when young girls with stars in their eyes danced in white dresses with coloured sashes, as fresh and lovely as flowers.

Despite its current shabbiness, Leonie believes that her house, Number 11, must once have been the most splendid in the square. It stands at the centre of the left-hand terrace, its single doorbell an indication that it hasn't been turned into flats. It also has a grandiose portico, which makes it look particularly welcoming. She remembers one day, over forty years ago, sheltering under this from the rain as a frightened runaway, of setting her bags down in the hall and wandering the spacious, high-ceilinged rooms with their neat square fireplaces and shiny parquet floors. How grand the house was then, with its ornate mirrors and damask sofas, its heavy mahogany furniture, such a nuisance to polish. There used to be old paintings on the walls, but over the years these have gone to pay bills.

The kitchen is still the heart of the house, but now splashes of paint and tea stains mar the lovely oak table, and candles jammed into empty wine bottles that drip stalactites of wax. The garden was landscaped in an Italianate design. Now it's a blissful wild paradise, with only a series of hedges to remember its formal past.

How safe the place made her feel, how quickly it became home. Over the decades her feelings for it have grown deep roots. Through everything that's happened since she arrived, the tears, the joys, the things lost and the things found, all the people who have come and departed, it's still her sanctuary, her foxhole, and she hopes it will be always.

One

Leonie

2015

It had been a day of memories, so many of them crowding in, a day of laughter, but sadness, too. It was always like that with Trudi, Leonie reflected as she walked home from the tube station. She loved seeing her old friend, which happened only infrequently, Trudi being always impossibly busy, off visiting her married daughter in New York or holidaying in Florida, but her company, though invigorating, could also be exhausting.

As she turned down the street of shops and offices that would bring her eventually to Bellevue Gardens, Leonie smiled at the thought of something said once by one of Trudi's ex-husbands – there had been three of them. It was that Trudi saw herself as the star in her own show, and everyone else was simply the audience. He had spoken with bitterness, and although it wasn't the full story – Leonie had usually experienced Trudi's considerate and generous side – there was more than a grain of truth in it. Trudi had always been a drama queen.

Even now she was in her seventies her life lurched from intrigue to crisis – or so she liked to make out. Today, for instance, at lunch in her Chelsea duplex, with its wonderful views over the river, Trudi, her green eyes bright with excitement, had told her that her new downstairs neighbour – who with iron-grey hair slicked back *must* be a retired gangster – had been sending her flowers and chocolate truffles from Fortnum's, and simply *wouldn't* be put off. When Leonie enquired wickedly whether Trudi had tried hard enough, her friend's green gaze turned dragonish. 'And how is that old crosspatch you keep in your basement? Really, darling, you and your lame ducks.'

'They're not lame,' Leonie retorted. 'They walk perfectly well.' Except Bela, perhaps, the ageing Kashmiri lady who shuffled about in slippers because of her bunions. 'Some of them are down on their luck, that's all.'

Leonie frowned as she walked along. Although she and Trudi were still very fond of one another, it was funny how differently their lives had turned out since the time they'd shared lodgings together with another girl over a shop on the Edgware Road all those years ago. There was Trudi, well-heeled and well-travelled, recently installed in her new luxury apartment overlooking the yachts of the marina, and here was she, Leonie Brett, rounding the corner into her Georgian garden square, as she must have done thousands of times before, and never tired of doing, coming home to the house she had shared with so many friends over the years.

This evening the square was scorched by the flames of

a spectacular sunset. So beautiful. She stopped to admire the shapes of the budding plane trees against the sky, the stately houses glowing a peachy orange in the dying sun. It was always so peaceful, this secluded square. From the garden in the middle came the lush warbling of a blackbird, no doubt assuring the other avian residents that everything was all right with their world.

As she crossed the road towards Number 11 her heart gave a little jolt of satisfaction to see its bohemian tattiness; the house was like a louche Cinderella between more splendidly attired sisters. The neighbours – mostly young professionals who had snapped up the converted flats – might frown at its dilapidated paintwork and the weeds growing from its gutters, but she loved the house with all its faults. It had become her home at a time of crisis in her life and, in turn, she'd opened it to others who'd needed a safe place.

She squeezed between two closely parked cars and paused on the pavement in surprise. For a fox was trotting along towards her, a vixen by the slightness of her. It stopped dead a few feet away, its obsidian eyes shining in the gathering dusk. For a lasting second they stared at one another, the lady and the fox, before the animal turned tail and fled.

There were far more foxes than she remembered there being in the past. They played extravagantly and noisily at night and left their toys on the lawns, old shoes, bits of tennis ball, once a pigeon's wing. Gardens were their playgrounds, dustbins their food baskets, burrows under sheds or brambles their homes. Just as her house had been a bolthole for many people. Leonie watched with sadness the vixen's brush vanish through the railings of the square's garden. It was as though the beautiful creature with its wildness had taken something of hers with it, and for a moment she thought of her grandson Jamie. Another wild creature who'd run from her and disappeared.

She searched her handbag for her keys as she climbed the steps of Number 11, scooped up a plump packet propped in the porch, and wrested open the door. Oh the sense of relief that always arose when she stepped inside. She sniffed the air as she pressed the door shut behind her. She loved the old-wood-and-polish scent overlaid by the fragrance of the lilies in their vase on the heavy hall stand and, today, a strong top note of turpentine.

Studying the label on the parcel she saw it was for Bela's husband, Hari. More of his bewildering range of health supplements, no doubt, by the lumpy feel of its contents. She set it down on the stand and leafed through the fresh pile of mail. The electricity bill and some circulars, a letter for Peter, the 'crosspatch' who occupied the basement flat, and, as ever, post for inhabitants long gone. A clothes catalogue for Jennifer, the resting actress with her silent small daughter, who had moved to Cornwall a year ago. A postcard of the seafront at Frinton for sweet old Norman, who'd retired from his hospital portering a few weeks back and gone to his brother's in Newcastle. She set these aside for forwarding and looked for something from Jamie. It had been her birthday last week and she'd hoped that he might have remembered. Perhaps he had, she tried to reassure herself, but the effort of getting together a card and a stamp was more than she could expect of him.

She sighed and turned over a stiff manila business envelope, then tutted under her breath on seeing the solicitor's name printed across the top. It would be another complaint from next door. She knew what it would say. A structural repair to the party wall, blah, blah, blah, and how would she pay for that, she'd like to know? She swept the other unwanted post into the top drawer and slammed it shut, but the manila envelope she dropped down the back of the stand in a gesture of defiance. Out of sight, out of mind, she told her reflection in the mottled mirror. Yet as she hung her coat on a hook and went through to the kitchen something troubled her. I'll think about the letter later, she told herself. It was her tried and tested way of dealing with impossible problems. Sometimes if you left them to stew for long enough they solved themselves one way or the other. As she filled the kettle, her thoughts moved again to Jamie. Sometimes they didn't.

Rosa

When Rosa stepped down from the coach into the early morning gloom of the coach station forecourt, the hot stench of diesel fumes and the grinding of engines reminded her of home and the terminus she'd started from twenty-six hours ago. Dragging tiredness and anxiety about the task ahead gave her a feeling of unreality, as if she was having a bad dream.

The driver was hauling luggage from the dark belly of the vehicle, and she waited patiently until he lifted out the small wheeled case that had belonged to her mother. She took it from him and exclaimed in surprise.

'There's something the matter?' he said in their own language.

'It's cold, that's all.'

He gave a smoky laugh. 'All part of the great British welcome. That tunnel went under the sea, don't forget.'

'Yes, of course,' she stammered. She thanked him and moved quickly away, drawing her handbag more securely across her chest and examining the confusion of people and vehicles all around. On the far side of the concourse, beyond the barriers, a familiar symbol on a door met her eye. Tipping the case up onto its wheels she made her way towards it.

Once inside the washroom, she joined a queue of women and children, just off the morning coaches, heavy-eyed from lack of sleep. When a cubicle became free, she locked herself in, dug wipes and clean underwear from her case and freshened up as best she could.

Afterwards, at one of the basins, the tang of toothpaste stinging her to full wakefulness, she looked into the mirror, and for one disturbing moment fancied it was her brother who was staring back. Her eyes, like Michal's, were deep-set, a sea captain's blue, only today, instead of their usual grave expression, it was his heart-tugging vulnerability she saw. The rest of her features – wide mouth, defiant chin and short, straight nose – were reassuringly her own. She stroked concealer over the shadows beneath her eyes, but others were waiting for the basin, so she bit her lips into redness, feathered her dark fringe with quick fingers and gathered her possessions. A final glance in the mirror at Michal's pleading eyes. I'm coming to find you, she promised him silently before moving away.

Back in the arrivals hall, she studied the signs until the words *Exit* and *Underground* asserted themselves, then steered her case in the direction indicated and joined the flow of humanity swimming towards daylight.

Outside, it was the cleanness of the London street that impressed her first after the grimy part of Warsaw she'd left behind. She liked the gracious silhouettes of the old buildings here, their subtle greys and browns, pushing up into a sky washed the airiest of blues. Across the road, a cream-coloured limousine slid away from the kerb to expose a colourful shop front, where tight bundles of daffodil buds stood in buckets beneath trays of dewy apples, oranges and bananas. She was hungry suddenly. Breakfast had been a cold-meat sandwich, eaten hours ago as the coach waited at Calais. She thought of the chocolate in her shoulder bag. Once that was gone she'd have to break into her carefully hoarded cash. London, she knew, was expensive.

She unfolded a scrap of paper she'd taken from her coat pocket then crossed the road at the lights. As she followed the signs to the Underground, her trepidation mounted. It couldn't be long now, then she'd find out. Find out what though? Something at least. That would be better than the silence, the terrible uncertainty she'd endured for so many months.

Sitting in the swaying train as it rushed north through the tunnels she cast covert glances at her fellow passengers. A girl in a black headscarf was bending over a pushchair. A scholarly-looking Asian man had to stretch full height to reach the handrail overhead. Sitting next to her was a grandmother as round as a hen cuddling a toddler who watched Rosa with eyes like dark stars. A pair of pale-faced youths in tracksuits lounged against the end wall of the carriage, like a couple of panthers. It astonished her that so many different people could be confined together in this small space, yet not speak to or show curiosity about one another. Instead the youths listened through ear-buds to music only they could hear. Some passengers read the blue-topped newspapers tossed about the carriage. Others stared at their smartphones. She checked her own phone again in case Michal had replied to the text she'd sent at Dover, but it wouldn't connect down here in the blue-white glare, hundreds of feet below London.

The train stopped at half a dozen stations before the name she was searching for glided into view. She waited for the doors to spring open then lifted her case through and manoeuvred it along a passage with white-tiled walls, up several echoing flights of stairs, and out between the jaws of a ticket barrier.

At the station entrance she stopped and stared in confusion at the busy road junction. No signs were visible. Should she turn left or right? 'The High Street, which way?' she asked the bored-looking attendant at the barrier. The woman pointed towards a map screwed onto the station wall.

It took twenty minutes to walk to her father's house. The road took her up a hill past modern apartment blocks with threadbare communal lawns, then a row of box-like shops and a church of dark brick, its stubby tower a far cry from the ethereal English spires she'd seen on the television. Rosa recognized none of it, but then she'd left London more than twenty years ago now, when she was still small. A red-and-blue swing in a garden overgrown by brambles. Rough wooden steps disappearing down into cold and damp-smelling darkness. A tortoiseshell cat which glared at her with yellow eyes before leaping through a cat flap. These were her only memories of the house.

A wheel on her case kept sticking, making it prone to flipping over at kerbs. She was light-headed with lack of sleep and hunger, and nervous anticipation had settled as a tightness in her throat, so her heart seemed to beat faster at every step. When she reached the turning she needed, left, into a street of pastel-painted houses, she rested on a low wall for a moment to catch her breath and eat the last bit of chocolate. Nearby a pigeon picked at the remains of a chicken drumstick in the gutter and her stomach turned.

She took a sip of water from the bottle in her bag and

her courage began to return. Not long now, she told herself, as she set off once more. Not long and then she'd know.

Her hope faded at each of three side roads before it finally rose at the sign for Dartmouth Street. She paused to look down it, searching for anything familiar. Was she imagining she'd seen that curve of semi-detached houses before, warm red brick with white-painted first-floor balconies? She set off, noting the numbers as she went.

Number 28 was exactly like its neighbours, except that its balcony was green instead of white, the paint blistering, and it still possessed a scruff of front garden where others had concreted over theirs for their cars. There was no one about. Apart from the rumble of a plane far overhead it was curiously peaceful.

The dainty metal gate moved stiffly at her hand. Striped curtains at the sash window prodded a distant memory and her confidence rose. Then fell. Something wasn't right. Runnels of dirt streaked the window. Now, as she cast her eye, signs of neglect were everywhere. The grass was overgrown, a pot plant on the window-sill inside long dead. She pushed a bell and waited in the shallow brown-tiled porch. No one answered so she pressed it again and rapped on the door with her knuckles.

After a while she pushed open the letterbox and peered through. Envelopes and papers were strewn over a dirty brown carpet. So many, they must have lain there a long time. Probably, she was shocked to realize, her own letter was among them. Not simply unanswered, then, but unopened.

She withdrew, the flap of the letterbox snapping at her fingers. All her hope, all her energy was gone and she slid down the wall onto the cold tiles, nursing her hand, her mind a blank. That there would be nobody here at all was the last thing she had expected. Had she come so far for nothing?

At a metallic sound she started, thinking it came from inside the house, but it was from next door, the other half of the semi. She peered out to see its door open and someone step outside, a youngish man with a cheerful pink face and receding sandy hair. Everything about him was ordinary: his jeans, a soft grey jacket, the T-shirt straining over his slack belly. 'See yer then,' he called to someone inside before pulling the door shut. A key in his hand, he walked round to the driver's door of the compact silver car nosed up against the house, then noticed her, with a frown of mild surprise.

'Good morning,' she said.

'No one lives there, love.' He sounded kind, but puzzled.

'Dexter. Do you know Mr Dexter?'

'Haven't ever seen anybody,' he said, louder this time. 'We been here since the summer and . . .' He spread his hands and shrugged to indicate nothing and nobody.

She gazed up at the empty house, as though seeking confirmation. When she turned back to him he was staring at her curiously.

'Hang on, there was someone a few months back. A young lad, looked a bit like you, come to think of it.

He came two or three times. I told him there weren't anyone, but he didn't get it.'

She caught the gist of what he said. 'Maybe my brother, Michal.' Her voice trembled. 'He don't speak English like me.'

'Your brother, that makes sense, yeah.'

'Where he go after?'

'No idea. Sorry.' He pointed the key at the silver car, and its lights flashed obediently.

'Try asking the other neighbours?' he said, opening the car door. 'There's an old girl across there might know. Sorry, got to go now. Fetch my kid.'

She nodded and watched him get into the car and drive away. The street was quiet once more.

Following his advice she crossed the road and pressed both the doorbells of the house he'd indicated, but no one replied. Retracing her steps she tried her father's other neighbour, but the girl with a baby who opened the door knew no more than the young man had, so Rosa returned to Number 28 and sank down on the doorstep, wondering what to do next. Her father wasn't here, hadn't been for months, it seemed. What had happened to him? Her brother had arrived, the man next door said, but then gone away again. Where? And why hadn't she heard from him?

Springing to her feet she pushed at the front door in frustration. It did not give. Next she tried lifting up the window sash. Once that had failed, she rattled the handle of the high wooden side gate. Even that was firmly locked, and barbed wire coiled cruelly along its lintel.

Increasingly desperate, she scanned the front garden for something with which to break a window. There was a shard of roof tile lying in the grass. She picked it up, but then the prickly feeling that she was being observed made her glance over at the house opposite.

In an upstairs window, she caught a movement. The bulky figure of a man was standing, watching her. He was drinking from a mug and held a phone pressed to his ear. She put down the tile, seized the handle of her case and left, setting off in the direction she'd come. She had no idea whether the man had been calling the police, but he might have been. Breaking in had been a stupid idea. Suppose the house wasn't her father's any more? She could have got into serious trouble.

In any case, she must decide what to do with herself now. The mission that had brought her here seemed to have ended before it had begun. She had no fall-back plan at all. She'd assumed that her father would be there to welcome her and she would stay with him. How could she have been so naïve?

Loitering outside the Underground station in the hope of finding people to ask about somewhere to stay, Rosa caught sight of a café a few doors down and, with a sudden longing for somewhere warm to sit and think, went to explore.

The Black Cat Café was small and cosy-looking, with hatched windows, and a cat-shaped sandwich board outside proclaimed it was *Open all day*. It was part of an attractive brick terrace of shops of the same vintage as the station. The glass had misted up, but Rosa could still see inside. Customers occupied some of the dozen wooden tables and chairs. Others were queuing at the counter, above which was a notice listing prices. The wooden fittings and the pleasant homeliness reminded her of the café, run by a friend of her mother's, where she'd worked for a while after leaving school. It seemed entirely natural for her to push open the door and step inside.

At once, delicious scents of sugar and cinnamon wafted around her, and a pleasant hum of conversation competed with the cheerful hiss of the coffee machine. A curvy young woman with rosy cheeks and dark hair tied in a ponytail under a snowy cap nodded at her from behind the counter. She left her case beneath coats thrown on a row of hooks next to the door and joined the short queue. As she waited she read a handwritten note taped to the till. *Part-time help wanted. Must have experience. Ask Karina.*

When her turn came she ordered coffee and a pastry and took the tray to a table where a wizened old man sat turning the pages of a newspaper with bold black headlines and lurid pictures. The coffee was wonderful, creamy, mellow and reviving, and the pastry tasted of the sweet syrupy almond cakes her mother loved. Rosa ate and drank as slowly as she could, wanting to string out the moment. It felt safe and warm in here, and she enjoyed watching the woman at the counter banter with the customers and soothe an elderly lady who had got in a muddle with her change. Yes, she liked this place. It would be sensible to stay round here, find somewhere to live, while she searched for Michal and her father.

She dabbed up the last almond flake from her plate and licked the froth from her coffee spoon. When a break came in the queue she took her dirty crockery to the counter.

'Thanks.' The woman received the tray from her with a pleased expression.

'No problem.' Rosa gave her a guarded smile. 'I would like to speak with Karina.'

'You are speaking to her. I'm Karina,' the woman replied, assessing her with shrewd brown eyes.

Rosa pointed to the note on the till. 'I have experience,' she said. 'I worked in a café like this at home for some years.'

'Did you?' Karina dried her hands and picked up a biro. 'What's your name, then?' she said, drawing a notepad towards her. 'Can you come back for a chat at five?'

Rosa nodded. She could come back any time.

Stef

One week later

I don't want this any more, cried the voice in her dream and Stef surfaced from sleep to hear the crash and grind of the dustcart edging its way along the street outside. She rolled over, felt cold air rush in under the duvet and realized he wasn't there. When she looked at the clock by his side of the bed, the figures glowed *8.04*. He'd have gone. Usually his alarm roused her at 6.30, and she would lie with eyes closed, listening to the hum of the shower, the mysterious thuds and rustles as he dressed, the smart clip of his shoes on the kitchen tiles, shortly to be followed by the soft thump of the front door closing, and silence. Then she could relax. Today she must have slept through all this instead of pretending to. These days she both longed for him to leave and feared it. He took with him all the tension, the need for her constantly to be alert, yet left alone in the flat she felt undone, all sense of purpose lost. She'd pull the duvet tighter round her and go back to sleep. After all, there was nothing else she wanted to do.

There was something different about today, though. Something in her mind had shifted. Exactly what, she couldn't say, but it had to do with the dream. She couldn't remember what it had been about, except there had been a lot of struggling and shouting. Perhaps the shouting was the bin men calling to one another as she'd flailed towards consciousness.

With a sigh, she rolled out of bed and padded to the bathroom. Which was redolent of him, still damp and warm, with the musky scent of aftershave hanging in the air. Wrapped in the silky white dressing gown he'd bought her, she passed through the hall to the kitchen, where she ran scalding water into a mug from the spigot at the sink. The sterile convenience of the metal-and-granite design denied her even the cosy ritual of boiling a kettle. She was glad, however, as she swirled the tea bag by its string, of the heated tiles under her feet. She dropped the tea bag into the waste caddy by the sink, reached across to the window and pushed aside the blind.

The kitchen was at the back of the building and looked out onto other apartment blocks like it. This flat was one of the biggest, he always said with satisfaction, on the first floor with a good view of the communal gardens. At the far side she could see a young man in a boiler suit hoeing dark compost into a flowerbed with quick, impatient movements. Between the buildings a cloud-veiled sun glimmered in a sky of dishwater grey. Seagulls glided on an updraught, making her think of the river beyond. She imagined the fresh wind and the surge of the tide. Perhaps she would walk there today, but the thought faded before it took root. Too much effort. She dropped the blind and turned back to the kitchen and the oppressive silence of the flat.

After pouring a bowl of sugary cereal she carried breakfast into the living room and set it on the glass coffee table, next to a neat line of remote controls. The second one she picked up and pressed caused the television to flicker on and she snuggled cross-legged on the sofa, nursing one of the hard cushions and sipping her tea. On the screen a brightly dressed blonde woman outside a sun-baked villa prattled into a microphone about a tennis star's adultery. Never heard of you, Stef breathed as the man's portrait flashed up. She waved the remote control. The picture morphed into grainy footage of some wary-eyed youths being loaded into the back of a van, but she'd missed what the item was about and instead she thought about her mother and how long it was since they'd spoken. Her mind wandered so often these days, she could hardly concentrate. When she next paid attention to the television three women on a purple sofa were engaged in earnest discussion. Then one said something that made her lean forward and listen. *I don't want this any more.* Those were the woman's words. Now she remembered. Those same words had formed in her mind as she'd woken from her dream. *I don't want this any more.* This time when she reached for the remote, it was to raise the volume.

As she listened, she ate her cereal, hardly noticing its empty sweetness.

Rosa

It was half past eleven that same morning, and Rosa, who had been working at the Black Cat Café for five days, was topping up the bowl of egg mayonnaise in the chilled counter. She glanced up when the door opened. A woman she hadn't seen before came in. She looked neither young nor very old, but there was something neat and elegant and certain about her that drew Rosa's eye.

'An Americano with milk but no sugar,' the woman said to Karina, 'and a toasted goat's cheese panini.' Her voice was pleasantly husky, with a little catch to it. She pronounced her words very clearly.

'I'll bring it over if you'd like to sit down,' Karina said as she gave the woman her change.

'Thank you.'

The woman picked *The Times* out of the rack, settled herself at a table by the window and took a pair of glasses out of its case. Rosa wiped the edge of the mayonnaise bowl and couldn't help watching her as she replaced it in the counter. What lovely hair the woman had, a silvery ash-grey, cut in a shoulder-length bob. The cerise of her cardigan might be faded, but it fitted her narrow shoulders perfectly and her navy-and-white scarf was knotted over her collarbone as though it belonged there. She didn't think that they were expensive designer clothes, yet the clever way the outfit had been put together showed she had flair.

'Thanks, that looks lovely,' the woman said, smiling up at Karina when she placed her sandwich in front of her.

Rosa pushed the plastic egg tub back into the big fridge and started to slice tomatoes, listening to Karina chat away as she emptied the grounds drawer of the coffee machine. Karina, who had invested all her savings in the café, was moving into a rented flat with her boyfriend Jared.

'How long will you stay at that hostel?' she asked Rosa. 'Is it all right?'

Rosa frowned. 'It's ... fine, but some of the people there are not ...' She screwed up her face. It had been after giving her the job that Karina had phoned the council for her and got the address of the accommodation. It was only ever meant to be temporary, so she'd need to find somewhere else very soon.

'Everywhere's so expensive, isn't it?' Karina said, cutting open a bag of lettuce. 'When you've finished the tomato, table six needs clearing.'

Rosa traipsed to and fro with dirty crockery, then reached to retrieve a tray a customer had left propped against the window. Near by, the stylish woman shifted her paper and said, 'I'm not in your way, am I?'

'No, no. It is good.' Rosa felt warmed by the woman's smile.

Instead of returning to her reading, she lifted her spectacles onto her head and said, 'I haven't seen you before, have I? Are you new?'

'Five days,' Rosa said, stopping wiping the tray to hold up her fingers.

'Not long then. Are you enjoying it?'

'Yes, I like. I am lucky there is work.'

'I suppose so. Have you been in London long? Forgive me, it's your accent.'

'Seven days only.' She wondered where this conversation might be leading and the woman must have caught her wariness for she said, 'I'm sorry, how rude of me. My name is Leonie. Leonie Brett.' She offered her hand. 'I come here quite a lot. It's my treat before I go shopping.'

'Yes. I am Rosa,' she said, shaking it. 'Rosa Dexter.'

'Nice to meet you, Rosa.' Her fingers felt cool to Rosa's touch. Cool and gentle, but there was a firmness there, too. She could sense the woman sizing her up, but somehow she didn't mind.

'Rosa, I don't mean to intrude, but I couldn't help hearing. Do you need somewhere to live? It's simply, well, my house is half a mile down that way.' She pointed. 'Bellevue Gardens, do you know it?' Rosa didn't. 'It so happens I unexpectedly have a spare room and you're welcome to come and look at it.'

'You have somewhere for me to live?' Rosa could hardly believe it. 'Thank you.'

'Well, I have somewhere you might like to live. Of course, it may not be your cup of tea, and you'd want to meet my other lodgers, but the offer's there. People say the rent is very reasonable.' She named a sum which did indeed sound astonishingly cheap.

'Thank you. Thank you very much,' Rosa said, hardly able to breathe. She wondered if there was a catch, but the woman seemed genuine enough.

She saw Karina frowning at her, so she moved away and started wiping another table with a cloth. This gave her time to think. After a moment she straightened and said to the woman, this Leonie Brett, 'I would like very much to see your house. When may I come? I finish here at four today.'

'Then come after work,' Leonie Brett said, and wrote down an address on a paper serviette, and drew a simple map.

When Rosa took the serviette from her their eyes met and once again she sensed the woman's friendliness. And something surprising. Respect.

After all her experiences, Rosa knew she should be careful, but Leonie Brett, she felt, was someone she might dare to trust.

Stef

When the studio discussion was over Stef switched off the television, rose, put down her cereal bowl and went to the window. Outside, the gardener had finished hoeing, and was forking up debris into a wheelbarrow. Everything appeared so normal and quiet, and yet her mind was in turmoil. She knew what she had to do, but for some minutes she could not do anything. It was as though her limbs would not obey. And then, slowly, she took her crockery through to the kitchen, washed it in the sink, dried it and put it away, then mopped up some grains of cereal that had skittered over the worktop. The empty surfaces gleamed back at her. Now there would be no record of her presence. It was as though she had never been here. She'd erased herself. The message was clear and it was enough. It was time to go.

She walked back into the bedroom, showered and dressed, then wandered round the apartment collecting up her possessions and stuffing them into the holdall she found in the hall cupboard. There wasn't much, she was surprised to realize. Most of her things would have been packed up with the rest of her childhood home and were probably in boxes in her mother's new house.

She straightened the duvet and gave a last glance

round the bedroom. It was as it had been when she'd first walked into it six months before. His black-and-white-striped duvet cover, the framed nude, sketched in a few charcoal strokes, hanging above the bed. All was tidy, except ... She bent to pick up a big black portfolio case from under the bed and something small and metallic bounced across the wooden floor. She knelt down to reach for it. A pin badge like a bottle top. How did that get here? She held it in her fingertips, remembering where she'd bought it. Camden Market, several years ago. There was a symbol on it. A girl's face smiling out of the centre of a flower. 'Genuine Swinging Sixties,' the stallholder had insisted. She'd given him £5, a rip-off, but she'd wanted it. Now she fastened the badge onto her jacket. Then picked up her holdall and the portfolio and let herself out of the flat. She double-locked the door and, after a moment's hesitation, posted the key through the letterbox. She'd left no note, but what could she write? He'd know why she'd gone. Or if he didn't he should.

Outside, it was chillier than she'd expected and the sun dazzled her eyes as she walked quickly up the street, dodging the wheelie bins the dustmen had strewn about the pavement. Where should she go? She thought through the options. There weren't many. She'd almost decided when—

'Watch out!' said an old man. She'd nearly stepped on his dog, the size and colour of a large rat.

'Sorry,' she threw behind her as she dodged past. She felt as though the apartment had a force field and, if she didn't hurry, she'd be pulled back into it and lose the strength to get away. She dared not look back at the man and his dog because, if she did, she might be frozen in her tracks like that woman in the Bible story. She thought of the way Oliver would fix her with a searching gaze and say he needed her, couldn't live without her. No, she mustn't dwell on that or she'd return and be lost all over again.

It wasn't far to the river along streets busy with people and traffic. The bridge, a graceful curve in the distance, was noisy close up, buses and lorries inching their way, bumper to bumper, to and from Westminster. Traffic fumes burned her throat. She waited at the lights, then, when they changed, the crowd swept her forward into the road. A van was blocking the crossing so people had to flow round it. A big hairy man in front of her banged the van's flank with his fist. The driver lowered the window and swore at him. 'Excuse me,' she said to the hairy man, twice, until he moved to let her pass.

From the refuge in the centre of the road she had to wait once more for the lights. Ahead, a bus swept past the crawling traffic and slowed for the stop on the bridge. She suddenly knew where she wanted to go – she wanted her mum. She couldn't see the number, but it might be the bus she needed. Seconds ticked by. Come on, she thought. At last the cars stopped, lined up, engines revving impatiently. She moved forward. 'Sorry,' she gasped, dodging past people to get to the bus. It was hers, she saw, the one for the coach station.

She had almost reached the opposite pavement when

she saw him waiting near the bus queue, his back to her, the clipped dark hair hardly touching the crisp white collar, the heavy silver watch peeping from under the cuff of the hand that held his attaché case. She stopped still in the road. Her last sight was him turning towards her, horror dawning on his face. *It wasn't Oliver*, was all she registered before the blow came, then she was flying through the air.

Rick

On any normal Monday morning, Rick wouldn't have been anywhere near the accident. He'd have been safely asleep in his bedroom in the house in Bellevue Gardens, the grimy duvet pulled over his head to shut out the daylight glowing through the scrap of curtain. But last night he'd had a call from his sister. She was 'desperate'. Claire was often desperate. Her plans had a habit of falling into disarray. This time the babysitter had let her down at the last moment and would he come instead? He'd responded grumpily as he'd hoped to have a quiet evening toying with the story he was writing, and, much as he loved them, his two young nephews always ran rings round him. He knew, however, that Claire rarely went out socially in the evenings so he obliged, though the journey to her flat south of the river was two bus rides away and he hadn't yet had any supper. Claire had returned late from her evening out, as she often did, despite her promises, and a little the worse for wear, so somehow he found himself getting the boys up for breakfast and walking them to school. After that, there was nothing for him to do but get the bus home again. Thank heavens it was his day off work.

Waiting to cross at the lights, the only reason he noticed the girl standing next to him was that she had the same pattern on her holdall as Claire had on her washbag, one of those pretty flowery jobs once seen mostly on curtains and little girls' dresses but which had spread to everything from raincoats to tents nowadays.

The girl looked nervy, thin, not his type at all, although he'd be hard-pushed to say what his type was as it was a while since he'd dated anybody. Not this fair-haired elfin sort with an anguished expression at any rate, he thought as the lights changed and the crowd rushed forward. He was more at home with definite people like his sister, who knew what they wanted and told him what to do. Even though marriage hadn't worked out for Claire, she was still good at getting on with life and was on speaking terms with the boys' father. If only Liam didn't have to travel for work and could help with the childcare more often.

'Excuse me,' the nervy girl said in a pale voice. She wasn't talking to him, he realized, but to the big hairy ape arguing with a van driver. Rick smiled at her briefly to indicate she should go ahead of him past the van. She had brown eyes, he noticed, as they waited in the central refuge, not blue as he'd somehow expected with that hair. 'Tawny' was the word that came to mind for her hair, but perhaps 'tawny' was too dark. He liked the sound of the word though, sort of warm and darkly golden. 'Honey' might be more accurate. Rick liked to squirrel away words and phrases. There was always a time when they came in useful. The girl darted ahead in the direction of a waiting bus, the holdall and a large portfolio case hampering her efforts. She wore skinny jeans and a pair of little pink pumps with no socks. Must be cold, he thought. Then, why's she stopped, the idiot? Hadn't she seen?

'Hey!' He could hear his own voice as if from a long way off. And all of a sudden, he was running after her.

The cyclist had jumped the lights and sped up the bus lane, then swerved out to overtake the waiting bus. Later, a policeman told Rick that the young man had a bet on with a colleague to get his time down. Thirty minutes to the office from south Wimbledon was the aim. All three of them went down in a screaming tangle on the road.

Faces, voices, pain, confusion. Then relief as the bike was lifted from its resting place on Rick's chest by a burly labourer in a fluorescent waistcoat, who hoisted him to his feet. His ribs hurt, but he hardly noticed and brushed off the man's cheery 'All right, mate?'. Behind him the cyclist sat on the kerb, cursing 'stupid airheads having a picnic in the middle of the road', but it was the girl Rick was worried about. She was lying half on, half off the kerb, unmoving, eyes closed, and a plump black woman with turquoise nail polish was bent over her, checking the pulse in her neck. Near by a dapper man in a City suit was speaking urgently into his phone. Passers-by hung about in various states of shock or curiosity. All around, the traffic was at a standstill, people gawping from their vehicles. 'It's a new bike,' the cyclist moaned. 'Look at it. Do you *know* how much those gearboxes cost?'

The workman tried to make Rick sit down on the pavement, but he shook his head and instead bent down painfully beside the girl. There were streaks of oil across her face, like claw marks. 'Is she all right?' he asked the woman with the turquoise nails.

'She's breathing, if that's what you mean,' the woman answered. 'You know her?'

'No, no. I was simply trying to—'

'That ambulance coming?' She turned her head to address the man in the suit.

'Yah, think so,' he said, staring uncertainly at his phone. The labourer was gathering the girl's luggage together.

A police constable joined them, hunkering down next to Rick. 'What's happened?'

'She's hit her head, poor duck,' the woman told him.

As the constable spoke urgently into his radio Rick stared at the girl's still face and felt sadness well up inside him.

The ambulance came at last and Rick travelled with the girl the short journey to the hospital. The paramedics thought he might have cracked a rib and should be examined and Rick was grateful for the excuse to go with her. They left the unharmed cyclist talking to the policeman.

On the way, Rick lay quietly on a narrow stretcher and watched the male paramedic tend to the girl, adjusting her oxygen mask, checking a hand-held monitor. She was beginning to come round, her lashes fluttering. When she opened her eyes properly, her gaze darted about the vehicle, anguished, confused, but after the young man spoke gently to her, they closed again. Rick saw tears creep from beneath her eyelids and he longed to reach out and reassure her.

'You feeling comfortable, mate?' the paramedic cocked his head to ask. Rick nodded and lay back, staring at the ceiling of the vehicle, wondering if he should call Claire but not prepared to reach into his back pocket for his phone in case it hurt to move. He was more aware of the pain now, where the bike handlebar had driven into his chest. It was hot and sharp, worse when he breathed in.

The X-rays showed he'd indeed chipped a rib. There would be considerable bruising and he should move carefully, but otherwise he could go. The police constable had arrived and taken his statement, then he was alone in Accident and Emergency reception, of no further interest to anybody. He tried the double doors back into the treatment area, but they were secured by some electronic system.

'Can I help you?' He turned and recognized the nurse who'd taken down his details when he'd first come in.

'I'd like to see the girl I came with in the ambulance. How is she?'

The nurse hesitated, then said, 'The blonde one with the head injury? She'll be fine. That is, she's come round

OK, and she's had a couple of tests. Just to make sure there's nothing wrong.'

'Please, can I see her?' He had to, it was the decent thing. He also felt guilty. He hadn't reached her in time and, actually, he might have made the accident worse by getting in the way so the cyclist hadn't been able to take evasive action. Well, that's how he had explained it to the policeman. He hoped he wouldn't regret telling the truth. The cyclist might be the litigious sort.

'Are you a relative?' the nurse wanted to know.

'No,' Rick admitted. 'I've never seen her before today. It's just ... I feel responsible for the whole thing. Would you ask if I could see her? Please? My name's Rick, I expect you remember.'

'I can't be expected to recall everyone's name.' She looked annoyed, then gave in, which Rick found people often did with him. 'Wait here, don't move,' she ordered, and the doors opened like magic for her to go through.

Stef

Stef lay still, the ceiling of the cubicle coming in and out of focus. Her head hurt, though they'd given her painkillers and the agony was settling into a dull ache. She must have struck her head against the kerb when she fell, the doctor had told her. As he spoke she had noticed how the light shone through his hair, short and spiky, like a cat's fur. She couldn't remember falling. She'd had an accident, apparently. A cyclist had ridden into her. All she could think of was her mother's black cat, curled on the storage heater, its fur fluffing up in the hot air. That was in the old house. Her family had just moved to a new one in Derby. No storage heaters there apparently. She tried to imagine the cat balancing on a radiator.

'Do you remember what happened?' the doctor interrupted, frowning.

She tried shaking her head and regretted it.

'What do you last remember?'

She considered. Getting up this morning? Turning on the telly. That was all. She'd been alone. Oliver had gone to work. He always left early. 'I don't know.'

'Who is the current Prime Minister?'

'*What*?'

'I'm testing your memory.'

'It's OK, I know the answer to that.' And she told him.

He sighed. 'Can we call someone for you? Your mum? Boyfriend?'

She thought of Oliver, visualized the back of his head, short black hair trimmed just above his collar. The man near the bus stop who'd turned round hadn't been Oliver after all, but a stranger. She tried to imagine Oliver in a place like this. The harsh lights, this claustrophobic room, nurses and doctors popping in and out. He'd hate it. Hospital. Somewhere he had no control, where there was mess and uncertainty and lack of privacy. She could imagine his discomfort, his frustration. No, she didn't want Oliver here. She knew this now with a strengthening certainty.

'My mum's in Derby, but I don't know her new

address. Her number's in my phone, though.' Her phone was in her handbag. Her holdall was beside her bed, her cardigan draped over it, her pink pumps, splattered with dirt, under the chair, the portfolio against the wall near by, but when she'd asked no one seemed to know where her handbag was and she couldn't remember her mother's mobile number. A nurse was dispatched to find out from the ambulance driver if he'd seen the handbag, and she'd waited, but the woman hadn't returned.

She was sitting up in the bed drinking sweet tea out of a throwaway cup and wiggling her toes, which peeped from under the blanket, when the curtain was swished back and a different nurse came in, a doubtful expression in her eyes.

'There's a young man wants to see you. He says he was involved in your accident.'

Oliver was her first thought and she must have seemed alarmed for the nurse hurried on. 'You don't have to see him, if you don't want to. He says his name is Rick.'

Rick? She didn't know anyone called Rick. 'The man on the bike?'

'I don't think so. Is that a no, then?'

'Yes. No, I mean, wait.' This accident. She needed to know what happened. 'Do I look really bad?'

The nurse's smile reached her eyes as she scrutinized Stef. 'You'll do.'

'Hi.' A boy her own age hovered at the entrance to

the cubicle and Stef whisked her toes back under the blanket.

'Hi,' she replied. Nice, but shy, was her impression. The sort of guy she could talk to without worrying whether he found her attractive. Which was a relief when she must look a mess, with a bump on the back of her head and her face stained with dried tears. But then he didn't seem that great either. Overlong hair the colour of sandstone, tied in a loose knot behind, a parka jacket with a ripped pocket. His eyes were a soft blue, however, and there was a whimsical quirk to his full lips.

'I was really worried about you back there, lying in the road. How are you?' There was a slight twang to his speech, Irish or something.

She screwed up her face and leaned back against the pillows. 'OK, I suppose. My head hurts. Did you see what happened? It's going to sound stupid, but I . . . can't remember.'

'I did see. I was behind you, crossing at the lights. You went running off after a bus, but then you stopped in the middle of the road, like you'd changed your mind, and this cyclist came out of nowhere. I tried to get to you, but I couldn't. Just made matters worse. Maybe he'd have missed you if I hadn't got involved. That's what my mam's always saying. Don't interfere, Richard, you always make things worse.'

Irish, definitely the slightest twang. 'Richard?'

'She's the only one who calls me it. Everyone else uses Rick. Though my sister Claire says Ricky, which sounds like a little dog's name.'

'I'm Stephanie. Stef.'

'Hi, Stef.' He nodded as though he liked it, and sat down without grace on a plastic bucket seat that squeaked when he edged it nearer the bed. 'So how long do you think they'll keep you in?'

'I don't know. They won't let me go yet because of the concussion. They say someone's got to come and fetch me. The trouble is, there isn't anyone.' She didn't say the full answer which was *There isn't anyone I want to come and fetch me.*

His face darkened in a frown. 'Where d'you live then?'

'Lambeth. I know it's not far, but it's . . . not my place, it's someone else's.'

'And the someone else can't come?'

She drew her knees up under the blanket and hugged them. 'He doesn't know where I am and I can't go back there. Please. Don't ask.'

'OK,' he said slowly.

'And I've lost my mum's number. She and my step-dad live in Derby. They moved house last month and I haven't been there yet. There's not much room for me, anyway, by the sound of it.' She turned her face from him and pinched the bridge of her nose to stop the threatening tears. It was ridiculous, she never cried, it must be the shock of the accident.

'I see,' he said, though the uncertainty in his voice told her that he didn't. 'So you're like, homeless.'

'I suppose I am in a way.' They sat together in silence for a bit.

Finally he stirred and seemed to come to some

decision. 'I'll tell you what,' he said. 'I want to help. I feel it's my fault, you see, all this, what's happened to you.'

'That's silly,' she said. 'It sounds like it was mine. Sometimes I forget what I'm doing, but I don't know why I stopped in the road like that. Everything's muddled. I can't even remember where I was trying to go.'

'Don't worry. I'm not trying to kidnap you or anything.' He gave a clownish smile. 'If you like you can come back with me. Where I live, see, there's a spare room come up. I'm sure Leonie – Leonie's the woman whose house it is – would let you stay a night or two. Maybe longer if it worked out.'

Although she knew she was taking a risk, there was something about Rick that made her believe him. Perhaps it was the way he seemed worried about her, the kindness with which he'd sought her out. She'd lost confidence in her judgement of people just as she had about everything else.

'I'm not sure,' she said, not wanting to offend him.

'It was only an idea,' he said quickly, lowering his eyes to examine his hands, and she could tell he was disappointed. His nails, she saw, were bitten right down to soreness, awaking in her a mixture of distaste and tenderness. Maybe he could at least help her get out of the hospital. She supposed that if it came to it she could simply walk out, but the staff would get stressy and she didn't like upsetting people, didn't have the strength.

At that moment the nurse with blue-black hair and coffee skin who'd gone to find out about Stef's handbag appeared through the curtain to the cubicle. 'The ambulance is out on a call and we haven't been able to speak to the driver yet,' she said, barely acknowledging Rick.

'My phone was in my handbag. You didn't see what happened to it, did you?' Stef appealed to Rick.

Rick shook his head. 'I'm sorry. I should have noticed, but I didn't.'

'We'll keep trying,' the nurse said.

She was about to retreat, when Stef made up her mind. 'Nurse, this is Rick. I'm going to go home with him, is that all right?'

The nurse gave Rick a surprised up-and-down look, then pursed her lips. 'I'll speak to the doctor. And we'll hear back from the ambulance driver soon, I expect.'

'I don't mind waiting,' Rick said to Stef, grinning. 'It's not like I have anything else to do today. Well, not really.'

He waited outside the cubicle whilst Stef was examined once more by the doctor and then tidied herself up. Half an hour later the nurse came along with a packet of painkillers and told her that the bag had been found, but it couldn't be returned to the hospital that day. Tomorrow, maybe, she'd need to telephone first. How can I telephone without my phone, Stef wondered, but at least her bag was safe.

'Where are we going?' she asked Rick when the nurse asked for an address.

'Bellevue Gardens in Camden,' Rick said, and spelled it so the nurse could write it on a form.

Bellevue. Beautiful view. Promising, Stef thought. If she didn't like it she didn't have to stay, but for the moment it was somewhere to go. She had lived in London for over a year and it wasn't that she didn't have friends in the city. Still, there was nobody she could think of she knew well enough to ask if they had a spare bed.

The bus dropped them by a cluster of shops near a tube station and, with Rick carrying Stef's holdall, they walked down one busy road and left into another, then turned right into a pleasant square of white-terraced houses with a wild garden at its centre. Lining the pavements were great trees coming into leaf, which looked as though they'd thrust their way up between the stone slabs. Cars were parked nose-to-tail along the kerbs, but all was peaceful, and only birdsong and the sounds of children, playing unseen in the garden, reached Stef's ears. Rick said hello to a cheerful couple who were unloading boxes of plants from the back of a jeep.

'It's amazing, isn't it?' Rick said as she stared up at the houses, which she thought were like aristocrats from another century, outraged aristocrats, perhaps, for sometimes their elegant Georgian frontages were compromised by a satellite dish or a plastic window box. 'They're mostly flats now, but they were originally for posh families with loads of servants. Ours is still a proper house, though. Here we are.'

He set down the holdall outside Number 11 as he riffled in his rucksack for his keys. They'd stopped outside a house plum centre in the middle of its row. It was pretty despite the damaged plaster and the weeds growing from its gutters, the steps up to the front door and another flight down to the basement fringed with tubs of plants, some coming into flower, but higher up, chunks of stucco were missing from the wall. Far above, what looked like a small tree was growing out of the balustrade, thrusting boldly towards the sky. A sash window on the ground floor was open and the sound of a radio orchestra wafted out into the square.

Stef followed Rick up to the front door and waited whilst he unlocked it, admiring the heavy metal bell pull and the grand brass letterbox. The door swung in on squeaking hinges and she found herself standing in an airy hallway, warm and streaked with light from the late-afternoon sun streaming in through the fanlight. Doors led off to the left and back, and an elegant stair-case climbed to the floor above and down, she assumed, to the basement.

'We'd better find Leonie.' Rick laid down her bag on the scruffy carpet under a coat stand and wandered off towards a door at the back of the hall. 'Are you coming?' he said, pushing it open, and she put down her portfolio and followed him down several steps into a big kitchen.

Here they had clearly interrupted a conversation, for the words 'a bit of peace' drifted away into the air. They were uttered by an old man with furious eyes beneath a shock of white hair. His was one of three faces that looked up at their entrance. The second belonged to a dark, solemn young woman sitting at the wooden table before a mug of tea and the third to a tall, graceful, fine-boned older lady with neat ash-grey hair, who was filling another mug from a battered silver teapot by the range.

'Hello,' the older woman said in a cheerful voice. She set down the teapot and eyed Stef curiously.

'Leonie, this is Stef,' Rick said. 'She's been in an accident so I brought her home.'

'You poor thing,' Leonie said, gazing at her in pity. 'What kind of accident?'

'It was my own fault,' Stef said in a shy voice. 'I wasn't looking where I was going.'

'One of those bloody cyclists not looking, you mean,' Rick said. 'Going through a red light an' all, he was, when he went into you.'

'Come and sit down, Stef,' Leonie said, pulling out a chair. 'Tea? Or maybe something stronger. Peter, where's that brandy you opened last night?'

'There's plenty left, if that's what you mean,' the old man said, scowling at her.

'Oh no, tea will do fine,' Stef told them before sitting down gratefully opposite the solemn dark girl, who had not spoken yet.

'Must be getting along.' The old man left the room, clumping up the steps to the hall, and the atmosphere lightened. Stef's eyes met those of the other girl, who gave her a serious smile.

'Stef, Rosa, Rosa, Stef,' Leonie said, setting a mug in front of Stef. 'Rosa, this is Rick. Rick's in the room next to yours. Stef we haven't met before today, Rosa, but she's obviously a friend of Rick's.'

'It's very nice to meet you,' the dark girl said, looking from one to the other. Her voice was soft but steady, with purring R's. 'Mrs Brett says I can stay here.'

'For heaven's sake, call me Leonie,' she said with a laugh. 'I'm not a hundred and two.'

Rosa smiled, but Stef saw that Rick's face had fallen. He was gazing unhappily at Rosa as Leonie explained that she'd met Rosa in the café where the girl was working and she had nowhere to go.

Leonie broke off, glancing at him shrewdly. 'Something wrong, Rick? You are a bit pale.'

'A mere matter of a cracked rib. The cyclist got me too.'

'Oh Rick. Dear oh dear.'

'I'm feeling bruised, that's all, you mustn't worry about me.' He assumed the look of a martyred saint, one hand on his ribs, eyes gazing heavenwards.

'Don't put on the noble act, you ought to be lying down.'

'Later. I'm more concerned about Stef's head.'

'Of course.' Everyone looked at Stef, who touched the bump on the back of her head and grimaced. It was hot and throbbed.

'The thing is, I was wondering, now that Norman's gone . . .'

'Rosa's having Norman's room, Rick. It's all agreed.'

'Oh, right then.'

Leonie turned troubled eyes on Stef. 'I'm sorry,' she said. 'I don't know what Rick promised, but . . .'

'Please, don't worry,' Stef said, but an unsettled feeling started to grow inside. The room wasn't available. Where would she go? How stupid, not to remember anything, even her mother's new address, though Derby would be a long way to go tonight. There must be someone to ask in London. Not Oliver's friends, naturally, but maybe a girl from her catering days ...

'Couldn't she have Jamie's room for a night or two?' she heard Rick ask and was horrified to see an expression of dismay cross the older woman's fine features.

'It's still Jamie's room,' Leonie said weakly. 'He'll come back. Though I suppose ...'

There was an awkward silence. Stef, bewildered, wondered who on earth Norman and Jamie were, but didn't like to ask.

'What about the attic then?' Rick said quickly. 'Isn't there some sort of bed in there?'

'There's the futon thing Jamie's friend slept on at Christmas. Yes, we could do that, then she could stay longer. Would you mind, Stef? The room's full of junk and a little dusty, but nothing a good vacuum wouldn't put right.'

'I'm sorry to be such a nuisance,' Stef said. 'I'm sure there's someone else I could contact. It's just I lost my phone so I'm a bit stuck till I get it back tomorrow.'

'She doesn't have anyone's number,' Rick patiently explained.

'And I don't really do Facebook much. Silly, isn't it?'

'No, of course it isn't.' Leonie seemed to have come to a decision. 'You can stay in the attic for as long as you like, but are you well enough to be climbing all the stairs?'

'I'll help her,' Rick said.

'Thank you so much, Mrs ... I mean Leonie,' Stef breathed.

'Don't thank me till you've seen the room.'

The attic room wasn't as bad as she had feared. It was full of the usual things that accumulate in old houses. Flea-market furniture. A broken standard lamp, empty suitcases, packing crates, but an old futon folded out into a perfectly acceptable bed. Stef watched, feeling too weary to help much, as Leonie made it up with linen sheets worn soft with age and a duvet whose cover was patterned with tiny green flowers.

She retired to bed early, without washing or cleaning her teeth, because the bathroom was down on the floor below and her head ached so. The sheets smelled faintly of something herby and for a while she lay awake in the twilight, listening to the faraway sounds of traffic and wondering what Oliver was doing. Was he home yet? Was he sad or angry to find her gone? What would he do? To banish these thoughts she turned over and watched the efforts of a moth crawling up the window, which had no curtains, and the curious silhouettes of the attic junk all around. The kindness of Rick and Leonie, and the calm of the enigmatic dark girl, Rosa, roused tender feelings of gratitude in her and for a brief period she wondered what it would be like to feel safe. Tonight was the closest she'd come to it for a long time and, cradled in that comfortable knowledge, she finally fell into a deep sleep.

Leonie

A sound in the room and she came to full wakefulness. It was early morning. She lay in the greyness, tense, listening, her hearing suddenly acute. For a while there was nothing, then the noise came again, a rustle followed by a sort of scuttering. Not another mouse, she thought with a sinking heart.

There had been a brief period a couple of years ago when the house possessed a cat, a scraggy creature with only one ear. Jamie had rescued it from a man who'd been trying to drown it in the canal. Kurt, named for a dead pop idol, had not proved a success, being barely house-trained and with a habit of bringing live mice into the house so that Leonie's nights were broken by the sound of them scurrying about inside the walls or pattering across the floor. Once she felt one run over her in bed and her scream woke half the household. When Bela started to have asthma attacks, it was the cat that got the blame, and Leonie's dwindling stock of patience ran out. She borrowed a plastic pet carrier and delivered Kurt to a local cat shelter. She felt mean about ejecting him, forlorn that Jamie was upset, and guilty about foisting the half-feral animal on the cranky woman at the shelter. She gave her £50, which she could ill afford, but it was the only thing to be done. After the cat's departure Bela's breathing almost magically improved and Peter relished a ghoulish few days setting traps for the remaining mice. For Jamie the loss of Kurt was one more brick in the wall of resentment he was building around him.

Jamie. Leonie wondered where he was now. Staying with one of those awful friends of his, she supposed. The ones that smoked dope and took goodness knows what else . . . Her train of thought was broken by another rustling sound followed this time by a chirping cry. It was a bird. This realization was confirmed by a whirring of wings and a rattle of falling debris. Not in the room, then, but in the chimney.

The bedside clock read 5.20. She pushed herself up to sitting and in the first glimmering light of dawn stared over at the grate as if expecting the bird to appear, but of course it didn't, the flue had long been bricked up, probably in the Fifties after the Clean Air Act had banished coal fires from the smoggy capital. There was just a vase of dried flowers in the fireplace now.

The bird twittered again. Poor wretched thing. Leonie swung herself out of bed, her feet finding her slippers, and wrapping her dressing gown around her went to examine the fireplace using the torch she kept by the bed. The flue was well and truly blocked up. There was nothing she could do.

She stood listening to the chirping for a moment. The growing daylight must have stirred the bird. It didn't sound too distressed, but still it troubled her. The chimney pots were supposed to be covered over so that birds didn't drop down, but perhaps this pot was damaged, the cover blown off by one of the recent gales. Since no one had been up to examine the roof for a while she couldn't tell. 'I'm sorry, I'm sorry,' she whispered to the bird and perhaps it heard for it fell silent. She shivered in the cold morning air and returned to bed. There she lay, unable to sleep again, wondering how long the creature would have to suffer there. She jumped at a sudden battering of wings. Perhaps it was trying to fly up towards the daylight and would work its way out to freedom?

She snuggled down and tried to drowse, but the periodic sound of the bird prevented sleep. Its distress coloured her thoughts and fuelled other concerns. If the chimney needed fixing, then what about the roof? There was the leak in the attic ceiling, of course, but that only made itself known when the rain was torrential and prolonged. And the crack in the wall of Peter's bedroom, the one presumably the neighbours were complaining about, well the insurance should pay for that, but there was quite a hefty excess on the policy and she had no idea how to cover it. It would have to be done somehow, she couldn't have her house fall down. It was all such a worry, and there were so many people who depended on her. Two more now. Rosa and Stef. Perhaps they'd only be here for a while. Rosa had intimated that she'd be likely to go home to Poland once she'd located her brother, and Stef? Well, there was an unusual girl, pale and fragile enough to be blown away in the wind. Leonie felt for her. Something was wrong there. She wondered what. If Stef was going to stay in the attic for any length of time, something must be done about the leak in the ceiling. And so she was back to worrying about the roof, and the bird, now shuffling about in the debris at the bottom of the chimney. Something was stirring in the house. She felt it in her bones. Something wasn't right.

Two

Stef

Stef woke to greyish daylight and for a moment didn't know where she was, and when she turned her head a pain like liquid fire shot up through the back of her neck. Slowly, very slowly, she sat up, and when the colours stopped swirling behind her eyes, she focused on the mug of tea that someone had left on the floor beside the mattress. The mug was lukewarm to the touch and the tea stronger than she liked it, but she drank it anyway and fumbled for the painkillers the hospital had given her. After she'd swallowed a couple she slept again and woke feeling more refreshed. The soft knock on the door that had woken her came again, then the door opened and Rick's concerned face blinked at her through the gap.

'Can I come in?'

'Hang on. Yes.' She sat up to see that he had brought breakfast on a tray. 'Oh, thank you.'

'Leonie did it all, but she said I could bring it to you.'

'That's very kind.' She watched him set up the tray on its folding legs beside her mattress. There was orange juice, fresh by the look and scent of it, muesli and a pretty jug of milk, a rack of wholemeal toast with tiny dishes of butter and marmalade and a pot of tea.

'She hoped tea was all right. Or there's coffee if you'd like it.'

'Tea's fine,' she said, breathing its spicy fragrance as she poured it into a delicate white mug. The aroma of coffee would have undone her. On the rare occasions Oliver brought her breakfast, the coffee strong and trea-cly the way he loved it but she didn't, it was invariably to say sorry. It was his prized possession, that coffee machine, the thing he joked he'd rescue ahead of her if there was a fire.

Rick sat back on his heels, his hands resting on his thighs, and smiled at her. His hair looked freshly washed, but he must have towelled it dry and forgotten about combing it, because errant strands had escaped the confinement of the elastic band and stuck up around his face, giving him an absent-minded appearance.

'Don't worry, I won't stay and watch,' he said as she sipped the tea, nursing the mug in both hands. 'I have to go to work, in fact I'll be late if I don't go now, but I wanted to see how you were.'

'Better,' she said. 'Just a bit of a headache.' She started buttering toast.

'Did you sleep well?'

She nodded, but it hurt her neck so she stopped. 'What about you?' she remembered to ask as she licked marma-lade off her finger.

'A bit uncomfortable here,' he said, touching his

ribcage. 'I'll leave you then.' He rose to his feet in an awkward movement, but then hovered, uncertain, his hands in the pockets of his jeans. 'Leonie says come down when you're ready, there's no hurry. I'll be back late afternoon.'

'OK,' she said through a mouthful of toast, the butter deliciously salty on her tongue.

After he'd gone she realized she'd been so absorbed in her own problems she hadn't asked him what work he did.

When she took the tray downstairs there seemed to be no one around. A newspaper lay on the table, its pages lifting in the breeze from the back door, which stood open to a rickety conservatory, from which a French window leading to the garden was also ajar. Through the window above the sink she saw a vista of trees, and grass strewn with wormcasts. She laid down the tray on the worn wooden draining board and went to glance at the newspaper. It was one of the free ones Oliver always brought home, removing it from his briefcase and adding it to the neat pile in the recycling box. She never used to read it, it always contained bad news. Today, her eye was drawn to a photograph at the bottom of an inside page. It showed the aftermath of a cycle accident. Her patterned holdall lay next to the fallen bicycle for all to see, upside down by the comatose body of— The shock bolted through her limbs and for a moment she couldn't take it in. It was her. She forced herself to read the accompanying paragraph. There was her name,

Stephanie Anderson, and she read with growing outrage the cyclist's account of the accident. *Pedestrians don't look out for cycles*, he said. There was no mention of his having sped through a red light. She was glaring angrily at his whining words when there came a noise and she turned to see the door from the hall swing open.

She expected to see Leonie, but instead a shy, diminutive Asian man entered with a bulging supermarket carrier in his hand. He appeared surprised to see her then a troubled look crossed his face.

'I am sorry if I intrude,' he said, quivering on the threshold. He was old, she thought, but she couldn't tell how old, with silvering hair cut short above his neat ears and a narrow face with a sensitive expression.

'No, really you're not,' she said nervously. 'I was wondering where Leonie was.'

'Probably she is in the garden,' he said, stepping down into the kitchen and nudging the door shut. 'She often is.' He went over to a tall fridge that was grumbling to itself in a corner, opened it and started to transfer the contents of his bag to the shelves. There seemed to be rather a lot of yoghurts, Stef noticed, fascinated, and when he turned back into the room she blushed, as it was obvious she had been staring.

She muttered an excuse and escaped out through the back door. She liked the old conservatory, which was lined with terracotta pots of succulent plants and furnished with comfortable-looking rattan chairs, silver with age. It smelled pungently of geraniums. The cool breeze came from the French window at the far end. She stepped through it onto a terrace of crumbling crazy paving, astonished to discover how long the garden was. It went back and back, its overgrown lawn rolling down between laurel hedges, like a series of terraces. At what she imagined was the far end were trees, and beneath them, a wooden shed. As she watched, the figure of Leonie, bearing a garden rake, crossed in front of it, on her way to somewhere out of sight behind the laurel. Stef began to walk down the central path, her pumps soon wet from the heavy dew.

Half of the area by the shed, she discovered, had been turned into a vegetable garden, a mess of ragged plants, though Leonie was working away at it. She had cast aside a heap of plastic netting and bamboo canes and was now busy raking up dead vegetation. One long dark stripe of bed was already newly planted with seedlings, however, and the scent of earth woke something in Stef from long-ago childhood. She breathed it in with pleasure.

'It's clever of you to find me,' Leonie said, stretching her back and resting her rake against the fence. 'How do you feel now you're up?' She gave Stef a smile that said she cared about her, and Stef thought how charming Leonie looked with her small turned-up nose and laughing eyes. Today the older woman wore a gilet over a striped navy-and-white top and jeans, and had a red-and-blue cotton kerchief tied about her throat, which gave a jaunty touch.

'OK, I suppose. I've still got a bit of a headache, and my neck's stiff.'

'Sounds as though you should lie low today.'

'Mmm,' Stef said, twisting her fingers together. 'I've got to get my handbag from the hospital.'

'Can't someone fetch it for you? Rick, maybe, when he gets in from work?'

Stef considered this. 'Maybe.' Part of her wanted to hide here and rest, but that meant she'd have time to think and she feared that. It would be better to be doing things.

'What do you grow here?' she said, curious.

'I try most things. Potatoes do well, brassicas too, you know, cabbages and greens,' she added, seeing Stef's puzzled expression. 'I'll be putting in some courgettes here, onions and lettuce when the seedlings are ready. Oh, and there are raspberries over there that need tidying up from last year.'

'It's a big garden, isn't it?' Stef turned to study the house and for the first time saw the whole row of white house backs stretching out on either side, the mid-morning sun dazzling off the windows. Number 11 was undoubtedly the scruffiest. The ones either side were painted like new, and the top of a modern conservatory peeped up next door above the fence.

'Too big for me to manage, but I love messing about out here and Rick or Hari sometimes mow the lawn, but otherwise it's a matter of fire-fighting.' She lowered her voice, her face glowing with annoyance. 'The people over this side are complaining about this house needing renovation. It does, I agree, but I can't afford it. They send me solicitors' letters about it, for goodness' sake.

Why not talk over the fence? I'm afraid I lobbed a particularly fat slug over just now, to relieve my feelings.'
Leonie seized the rake and began to sweep up leaves.
She looked so cross that Stef dared not smile at the slug
story. She'd sounded as though she really cared about
what these people said.

'I think your house is lovely,' she said. 'And it's so nice
of you to have me.'

'Oh, don't worry about that.' Leonie gathered up a pile
of debris in her gloved hands. 'I adore having people
around. No point in having such a big place to myself,
is there?'

'I suppose not,' Stef admitted, whilst wondering who
was related to who in the house. That girl Rosa had
called Leonie Mrs Brett. Was the old man her husband?
But her mind was drifting now; she was worrying about
the handbag and what to do about Oliver. Was he upset
that she'd gone? Did he miss her? She felt a rush of longing for him suddenly, then, after it ebbed, a dull sense
of misery.

In the end she felt well enough to ring the hospital from
the house phone and fetch the bag herself. Rick wasn't
due back until the afternoon from whatever job he did,
and she felt she couldn't sit around doing nothing for
hours. She borrowed some money from Leonie for the
bus and got off at the stop before the bridge where the
accident had happened. She walked across it to the
hospital, feeling very odd as she passed the exact spot.
There was no sign of anything to do with it today and

the traffic was moving easily. She stopped and watched a handful of people crossing at the lights, trying to work out how she could have been so stupid as not to notice the cyclist. Something came back to her. She'd been convinced that the man she saw had been Oliver and the world had narrowed down, yes, that's what had happened, narrowed right down so that her only concern had been that he might see her. Her fear had caused a kind of madness.

She stood for a while to stare down at the river. Alive to the cries of the seagulls overhead, the chill breeze that made her shiver, she felt her fear at least for the moment retreat. She tried pretending that yesterday had been a bad dream.

At the far end of the bridge it felt odd to be turning right towards the hospital again instead of staggered left towards home. Not her home any more, she told herself fiercely as she walked. Oliver's. She'd never really felt it had been hers. It was somewhere she'd lived for six months, that was all.

It didn't occur to her to look for him now. He would be at the office. She pictured him, jacket arranged over the back of his chair as he sat studying a slim computer screen, a frown on his neat, dark features. Or else standing at the window with a takeaway coffee, staring unseeing at all the other glass-and-metal edifices thrust up against the skyline, maybe speaking into his mobile. Was he even thinking about her? She knew all too well his ability to focus entirely on his work, but she remembered, too, how he would sometimes wake her in the night and stroke her face and beg her to hold him. As she hurried towards the hospital, head into the wind, her eyes teared up at the memory of his tender mouth, kissing her in the half-darkness.

In Accident and Emergency, she had to wait her turn to speak to a receptionist and tried not to watch a cleaner mopping up splashes of blood from the floor. Once again her thoughts turned to Oliver. She'd met him nearly a year ago. She'd taken a job with a small and very exclusive catering company that provided corporate lunches for City boardrooms. She hadn't liked it much. It meant wearing a pert white cap and frilly apron, and she felt self-conscious as she helped serve at table, and she hated the way some of the guests looked at her, or rather, round her, as though she didn't matter, as they carried on with their conversations. The women could be the worst, hard-faced, impatient, and sometimes the men would accidentally on purpose brush against her, which made her appear clumsy.

On the day she met Oliver the disaster was her fault, she knew it really. She was tired and hadn't been concentrating. The pink slice of lamb in hot herb butter simply slid out from between the tongs onto the paunch of an American businessman who had reached for his mineral water at the wrong moment. His shout of dismay drew the attention of the whole table and she mumbled apologies as she scooped up the meat as best she could and dabbed at his shirt with a napkin. It was the dark-haired young man sitting on his far side who had risen to the occasion, leading the protesting guest out, bidding Stef's boss to fetch a damp cloth, dispatching an intern to buy a new shirt in time for the man's next appointment.

Afterwards, when she'd been clearing up in the little galley kitchen, her eyes rubbed red, her expression stony, he'd come to find her. 'To see if you're all right.' She'd given him a wan smile and nodded, muttering her thanks, and turned her attention back to stretching cling film across a serving dish. When she glanced round he was still there, waiting, concern in his hazel eyes and the lines of his brow, his lips parted to reveal even white teeth. He was so close to her in the small room she could see the shadow of beard beneath his clean-shaven skin, the glisten of perspiration above his upper lip. But when he spoke again, it was not about the incident at all.

'Could I have some of that delicious-looking pud before you put it away? I missed it because of you know what.'

She laughed despite herself and obliged, watching him eat the creamy roulade with a schoolboy ecstasy. Before long he was teasing her about the way to a man's heart being through his stomach, and she was flirting with him whilst her colleague barged about crossly, fer-rying the trolley of leftover dishes down to the van, and throwing her black looks for not helping.

By the middle of the afternoon, Oliver had her mobile number and she had got a final warning from her boss.

Walking back across the bridge from the hospital, her handbag intact and the wind from the river lifting her hair, she felt a moment of freedom. He didn't know where she was. He couldn't contact her because her phone was dead. Halfway across, she stopped to gaze down at the water surging between the piles of the bridge, like liquid pewter, and placed the phone on the stone parapet, tempted, just for a moment, to tip it over the edge. The exhilaration of cutting herself off from her old life flared, but in the end she couldn't do it. Her mother's number was there, for one thing. And it wouldn't solve anything, not really. She couldn't cut him off for ever.

Back at Number 11, she rummaged in her holdall for the charger, and plugged it into a yellowing electric socket in the skirting board of her attic room. She listened, as the phone charged, to the soft plink of the messages flying in like missiles from the ether. *Oliver, Oliver, Oliver,* read the column of texts. She listened to a series of increasingly worried-sounding phone messages. *Where are you? Call me. Are you all right?*

Her fingers trembled as she tapped in a text. *I'm fine, Oliver. I'm sorry to worry you. I just need some time by myself.* She was about to press send then hesitated, and added *Luv Sx.* After it had gone she turned the phone off in case he rang, afraid to speak to him in case he tried to talk her into coming back. She missed him and the sound of his voice breathy in her ear might yet undo her.

She badly wanted to ring her mum, but that meant turning on the phone again. Why hadn't she copied down the number? She sighed. She'd have to put if off until later.

She left the phone to charge and went downstairs. Again the kitchen was quiet and empty, only the tinny sounds of the radio could be heard from some unseen room. She was standing uncertainly, wondering what to do with herself, when a door at the far end of the kitchen opened and the radio grew louder as Leonie drifted in, holding her hands out before her like Lady Macbeth. Instead of blood, however, her fingers were smeared with something white; chalk perhaps.

Leonie

'Hi.' Leonie smiled at Stef as she rinsed the white pastel from her hands. 'How did you get on at the hospital?'

'I've found my bag.' The girl came nearer, her arms folded round her waist as though she was cold. 'Everything was still in it, which was amazing.'

'Very lucky.'

'Thank you again for having me last night. I really appreciate it.'

'Don't keep thanking me. It was no trouble. I apologize that it was only the attic. I hope you weren't too bothered by the dust. You don't suffer from asthma, do you?'

'No, it was actually very comfortable.' Stef appeared troubled and Leonie wondered what the matter was. There was something so fragile and waiflike about the girl. She must have been twenty-five or -six, but seemed younger. Leonie's heart couldn't help but go out to her and, as was her way, she longed to make things better.

'Do you have any plans?' she asked lightly, drying her hands on a towel hanging from the Aga.

The girl's troubled expression intensified. 'Not really.'

Leonie waited, eyebrows raised.

'You see ... I was living with my boyfriend and ... I had to leave.' She looked away as though she was struggling not to cry. 'Anyway, I haven't anywhere to go at the moment. I mean, my mum ... I could go back to Derby, I suppose, but I don't think she has room and, anyway, it would feel like going backwards.'

'You want to be in London?'

'Yes.'

Leonie studied her. Surely the girl had friends, somewhere to go. There was something unusual about her. She seemed so alone.

'I don't have a job at the moment, and ... I haven't seen anyone much, friends, I mean, for a while. I know this must sound pathetic, but I don't quite know where to start.'

'And you've been in an accident. You poor thing. Don't be too hard on yourself.' She thought for a moment. There wasn't really room for another lodger, but maybe, if they cleared the attic and gave it a proper clean ... 'Why don't you stay on here for the time being. Until you've got yourself sorted out.'

'Really? Could I?' Stef's enormous brown eyes were full of relief. 'That would be brilliant. The only thing is, well, I can't afford to pay you very much. I'll go and sign on until I find a job, but—'

'There's no hurry for all that,' Leonie said quickly. 'It's not much of a room, I can hardly charge you more than a little for it. Everyone buys their own food here—'

'Of course, we can work something out. Oh, thank you so much.' Stef spoke with such spirit that Leonie realized there must be another side to her. She thought about this as she lifted the lid from a ring on the Aga and placed the kettle on it.

'Were you painting or something just now?' Stef asked, her voice lightening.

She was coming out of herself. Leonie was pleased. 'Yes. I'll make us coffee then I'll show you. Do you mind instant?'

'I prefer it. Honestly.'

'Good. I love the real stuff, but it doesn't like me these days. I have to ration it or I don't sleep. Biscuit?' She opened a storage tin and watched with amusement as Stef delved into it, and bit into a chocolate bourbon with evident pleasure.

It's as though she's coming back to life, Leonie thought as she made the coffee. She remembered that feeling so well. When she'd first come here, all those years ago, she'd been a pile of misery, lacking the energy to do anything much. But with the passing of time she'd revived, like a plant given water. Time and space and freedom and kindness, that's what she'd needed. And she'd found it here at Number 11. She smiled at Stef and Stef smiled back tentatively in return.

Stef

Stef followed Leonie through the door the older woman had emerged from and was surprised to find herself in a long, light-filled, high-ceilinged room that looked out to the front of the house. Jazzy piano music tinkled from the radio on the mantelpiece, which somehow suited the bohemian ambience. The room was comfortably furnished in a cheerful manner, with threadbare old sofas draped with throws, great colourful abstract paintings on the walls, and a huge vase of dried flowers and peacock feathers, artfully arranged, standing on a bookcase. Leonie set down the tray next to a laptop on a rustic-style coffee table. 'Come and see,' she said, and Stef followed her across to the window, where a canvas stood on an easel by a table heaped with pastel crayons, rags and bottles and bits of paper covered in pencil sketches. Other, scrumpled pieces had been tossed onto the dustsheet spread on the wooden floor.

'This noble fellow is Arthur,' Leonie announced, and Stef squeezed herself round the easel to see the drawing set on it. She was surprised to see that Arthur was not a person, but a hound, a big smooth-haired hunting dog, standing in what appeared to be a stable yard – the piece was unfinished – but this was no ordinary pet. It held itself so proudly. Leonie had captured something of the animal's vigour and wildness. Its pale eyes gleamed with mischief. 'He's gorgeous.'

'He is rather splendid in a heraldic sort of way. Arthur's a Weimaraner. Just missed best of breed at Cruft's a couple of years back, apparently.'

She must have been working from the photograph that was clipped to the top of the drawing. Half a dozen other prints of the beast spilled from a paper packet on the table.

'Do you always do dogs?'

'Cats sometimes, and occasionally horses, but dogs are what I'm asked for most. The thing is, it's a regular source of income, and, believe me, that's important since I'm not Tracey Emin.' She indicated a stack of framed canvases against the skirting board. 'I had some of my non-animal stuff in a show recently, but it was the first for ages and I didn't sell many.'

'May I see?' Stef asked tentatively.

'Why not?'

Stef swept her long hair over her shoulder as she sank down and began to flip through the canvases. There were abstracts among them, like the ones mounted on the wall, which didn't speak to her particularly, though she liked the bright colours and swirling shapes that suggested perpetual movement. More interesting were a pair of oils of a girl not much older than Stef staring out of a window. The sun was shining in one picture, in the other it was twilight. She was lovely: light-boned with a fall of fair hair and blue eyes smudged black with make-up. There was something immeasurably sad about her expression, bitter even, and Stef wondered whether this was why the pictures hadn't sold. She turned and looked up, but couldn't think of a way to say this that wouldn't offend. 'I like these,' she said simply.

'Do you?' Leonie's face lit up. 'They're of my daughter, Tara. I put them in the show, but they weren't for sale, just to show the sort of thing I can do. No, I'd never sell those.'

Stef replaced the canvases. As she rose to her feet her eyes met those in a portrait hanging on the wall above, which she hadn't noticed before. It was a pastel sketch of a young man sitting astride a kitchen chair, his arms folded across its back. His face was an arresting one, all dark hair and eyes, like that of a cheeky youth in an Italian Renaissance portrait, but a very modern black bike jacket was draped about his shoulders. He stared out of the sketch at Stef, moody, challenging. 'Who are you looking at?' he seemed to be saying.

This time, when she turned back to Leonie, she was surprised to see the expression on the older woman's face. Sadness, but a sort of pride, too.

'Peter drew that. It's Jamie,' Leonie said, her voice abrupt with emotion, and she bent to hide her face, gathering up the litter of paper on the floor.

Jamie. That was the boy whose bedroom Stef couldn't have. She wondered who he was and where he'd gone.

'Let's drink our coffee,' Leonie said, stuffing the wastepaper into a nearby bin, 'then we'll sort out your bedroom. There are some cupboards up there where we can move some of the stuff. Rick can give us a hand when he gets back, if he feels up to it. I hope you don't mind the odd spider.'

'Not really. Where does he work, Rick?'

'At the supermarket near the tube station. He's on shifts. I can never keep track, but it's mostly mornings.'

'His room's below mine, isn't it? How many bedrooms are there here?'

'Goodness. Well Peter's is in the basement, then mine

is on the first floor at the back. Then there's Hari and Bela's next to mine, Rosa's, Jamie's, Rick's on the floor above. And now you right upstairs in the attic.'

'Have you lived here long then?'

'I was left this house by someone who was very special to me,' Leonie said, her eyes soft, her expression far away, and for a moment Stef glimpsed something of how beautiful Leonie must once have been.

'Was it a relation?' Stef prompted, because Leonie seemed lost in some world of long ago.

'What? No, not family. A friend.' She sighed. 'I didn't think I deserved the house though. That's why I've always shared it. I thought that way I'd get to keep it. And then I'd be safe.'

'Safe?' Stef asked her. 'What do you mean? Surely no one's going to hurt you?' Leonie seemed such a together sort of person. What did she not feel safe about? It was she, Stef, who didn't feel safe, and it alarmed her that Leonie might not be the rock she had believed her to be. She had no idea what to do with her life, how she'd manage. She needed someone like Leonie to tell her.

'Oh dear, I shouldn't say these things to you. You're young, everything's still in the future for you.'

'I hope so,' Stef sighed, clenching her knuckles, though the nails dug into her palms. 'It doesn't feel like that at the moment. I can't see which way to go.'

'No, but it'll come. I didn't really mean anything terrible by it, only that if you love people – real deep down love is what I'm talking about – then you're never safe.'

'Because they can hurt you.' Stef's voice was dull.

'If you're unlucky about whom you love, yes. People can be cruel, terribly cruel. I suppose sometimes they can't help being like that, but I wasn't really talking about ...' She sighed, before adding, 'It's the fear of losing them that I mean.'

Stef nodded. She knew about that, too. How you could still love someone who was unkind to you. How at the same time you couldn't bear to lose them. She didn't like the thought of where this might lead her. 'Tell me about the person who gave you the house. I'd love to know what it used to be like. '

'Would you? Ah, now that is interesting.' It seemed that Leonie was strong again.

'It must be really old.' Stef glanced about at the plaster moulding on the ceiling, the old mantelpiece with its scrolled corners. An electric heater stood in the fireplace.

'Georgian, 1820ish. Yes, this house has stood here nearly two hundred years now, I believe. Think of the things it must have seen.'

'The parties,' Stef breathed, imagining the room full of gorgeous dresses and sparkling jewellery, the ladies flushed with the excitement of the dancing and the admiration of the gentlemen.

'Yes, parties,' Leonie laughed. 'We've had marvellous parties here in the past, with lots of lights in the trees. So much fun! There was a fountain in the garden then, so pretty, and a mossy statue of Diana, which vanished one night. Part of the kitchen was a dining room then, and George – that's the name of my friend – used to throw these wonderful dinner parties with silver cutlery and crystal glasses and what there was of a Wedgwood dinner service. We always had to toast the Queen. George was quite a royalist, you know. He liked all the ceremony.'

Stef listened as she sat sipping her coffee, which was lovely and milky in the way her mother used to make, and realized she already felt a little better. The kindness of strangers. The phrase came into her mind. She wasn't sure where from, she'd heard it somewhere, but it was true. Rick and Leonie, they'd been so kind to her without knowing anything about her at all, and she was grateful.

'George inherited this house from an uncle. It had been in the family for years and years, but the uncle didn't have any children so George got it. And because George had no child either, and he'd run out of other family to leave it to, he left it to me. I was living here, you see.'

'What happened to your husband?' Stef wanted to know. 'Oops, that sounds a bit nosy.'

'I don't mind you asking at all,' Leonie said, 'but it's rather a long story for today and I ought to get on with drawing Arthur.'

Leonie was smiling at her, but Stef sensed that she had asked one question too many and was sorry. She thanked Leonie for the coffee, rose and gathered up the empty mugs.

She was about to leave when she saw that Leonie was standing before a painting Stef had no more than glanced at, because she'd been sitting side on to it. She couldn't see it clearly past Leonie, but it was of a little flying bird, painted in bright colours and in quite an unusual, flat style, like a poster. The bird had escaped a bell-shaped cage with an open door, and above the cage there floated the figure of a girl wearing what looked like a nightdress. There was something dreamlike about the whole thing and Leonie seemed quite lost in it. Stef tiptoed out. She would have to study the painting properly another time.

It was three in the afternoon when she went down to the kitchen after a nap and was surprised to find Rick there pressing a slice of brown bread onto a doorstep of a sandwich.

'Hi!' he said cheerfully, licking his finger. 'Do you want one? I didn't have any lunch today.'

'No, thanks,' Stef said, yawning. 'Don't you get a lunch hour then?'

'Yes, but I went to the library. How are you then? You look better.'

'I feel lots better,' she said, watching him bite into his giant sandwich. 'Just tired. What about you?'

'I'm still sore' – he pressed his ribcage tenderly – 'but at least I got off hefting boxes around.'

'That's good. We'll wait till you're better then.'

He stopped mid-chew and raised an enquiring eyebrow.

'Leonie said I can stay for the time being, and that you might help us clear the attic, but not until you're up to it.'

He swallowed. 'Good old Leonie! Doesn't hang around. Sure, but maybe tomorrow.'

Rachel Hore

'OK. Thank you, Rick. You've been lovely.'

He looked pleased. 'You're welcome.'

'Hey, I got my bag back.'

'Did you? That's great. I was going to offer to go for you.'

'I went this morning. And guess what, everything was still in it.'

'Terrific. Did you call your mum?'

'No, I'm going to in a minute.' She didn't know Rick well enough to explain that she was frightened to turn on the phone and find more messages from Oliver.

There was a silence, then Rick said, 'Well, you got your bag. That at least calls for a celebration. I've no fancy champagne, but I bought some elderflower that was on offer.'

She laughed and sat down at the table as he brought a litre bottle out of the fridge, selected two glasses from a cupboard, and checked they were clean. It was peaceful with him here. As she watched him pour the sparkling drink her mind slid away from him. What would Oliver be doing now? Was he looking for her? Maybe even now he was ringing her number, speaking to her mailbox. She ought to give him an update, it would only be kind. No, she told herself. She knew what would happen then. She'd end up telling him where she was and he'd fetch her back and then it would be the same as before, her sensation of being trapped in that beautiful apartment with its shiny, sterile surfaces.

'Biscuit?' She shook her head. Rick placed a glass before her, sat down opposite, and rather self-consciously continued to eat his sandwich. She smiled at him as she sipped the sweet drink and tried to relax, but her thoughts still tumbled in her mind, round and round.

When she marshalled her attention back to him, he was looking at her with concern.

'I'm sorry,' she said, 'just daydreaming.'

'No, that's fine. You've had a hard time, I can see that.'

'I suppose I have.' She wanted to tell him her worries. He was so kind, but she didn't know him, didn't know what he'd think of her, didn't know what she thought of herself even, so she kept quiet.

'How long have you lived here?' she asked instead.

He swallowed a mouthful and brushed crumbs from his fingers. 'A year now. I went back home to my mam's in Watford after uni, but then she moved back to her mam's in Ireland, but I didn't want to go. I'd done a couple of internships in London, but nothing that set me alight, you know? I came down here because I could sleep on a mate's floor for a bit. Anyway, I got this job then met Leonie in the local library. She needed help finding something on the internet and we got talking, and she offered me a room. She's terrific, Leonie, don't you think?'

'Oh, yes, she's been brilliant!'

'I can be myself here.'

Stef had not heard Rick give such a long speech before. There was something odd about what he said, as though he was missing some things out, but she was finding it difficult to focus on anyone else's problems.

'Are there other people who live here I haven't met? There was an Indian man I saw today.'

'That's Hari. He and Bela, his wife, have been here for years. That Eastern European girl Rosa's just come, so I don't know anything about her.'

'She's very striking-looking, isn't she?'

'Is she? Well, yes, I suppose.'

'Those lovely blue eyes. They're unusual.'

'And Peter, the older man . . .'

At that moment the door from the hall burst open and Peter himself came in. 'That's me. Someone want me?'

'Here, you can ask him yourself,' Rick said, grinning.

Peter scowled. 'Ask me what?'

'Stef was wondering who everyone was here.'

Peter's scowl switched to Stef. 'I'm the old bear who lives in the basement. Don't bother me and I won't bother you. I'm sure we'll get on very nicely. Now what did I come in for? Paint cleaner, that's it.' He opened several cupboards one after the other, before trying the one under the sink. 'Ah. Always hiding things, that woman,' he said, holding up a bottle of oily liquid in triumph. He left the kitchen with the cupboards still open, but shut the kitchen door behind him with a firm click.

'So that's Peter,' Rick said, his eyes alight with mischief. 'A model of charm and good humour, as you can see. Now he's been here for ever. He's an old friend of Leonie. He sits and paints all day. Quite why Leonie's so fond of him is one of life's great mysteries, but she is.'

Stef remembered something, the pictures in Leonie's drawing room. The one on the wall of the moody-looking youth. 'And who's Jamie?' she wondered.

'Ah, Jamie,' Rick said, his face darkening. 'Now there's another mystery. Jamie is Leonie's grandson.'

'Oh, I see. And he was living here?'

'I think his mum had thrown him out. The mystery is he's like the apple of Leonie's eye and I just don't get it. Don't let her know I'm saying this, but it's better when he's not here. Much more peaceful.'

'Where has he gone?'

'That's yet another mystery. Nobody knows. He had a row with Leonie, upped sticks and left. Leonie's in a real state about it.'

Stef remembered the expression of pain in Leonie's face when they were contemplating the picture. It sounded as though Rick didn't like Jamie much.

'He's on Facebook. A couple of times he sent me snide messages, which is how I know he's alive and kicking, but he never answered when I asked where he was living and now he's blocked me.'

Somehow after her conversation with Rick Stef felt a little stronger. Upstairs again, she switched on her phone and speed-dialled her mother's number.

'Stephanie? Wait a moment, I'm in the car.' Simply her mother's strong, warm voice was reassuring. 'OK, love, how are you?'

'I'm ... all right. But, Mum, I've left Oliver.' As she spoke, strangely, she did feel all right.

'Oh Stef, what a shame.'

'I – it's a bit complicated. And ... I was in an accident yesterday, but I'm OK.' She relayed how she'd been knocked down by a cyclist. She felt on much surer ground with that than with the reasons why she'd walked out on Oliver. Her mum had liked him on the two occasions they'd met, when she and Oliver had stayed the night at the old house in Derby, and when her mum had visited them in London. Oliver had behaved with just the right level of solicitous charm.

'Where are you now, love?'

'Staying with friends in north London.'

'Do you want to come home? There's not much room, but the boys could share and ... There's so much junk, you wouldn't believe it.'

She wasn't really wanted, that's how it felt. Stef knew underneath that this wasn't true, that her mother did want her, but she was feeling sorry for herself, and perhaps she didn't need to go home. She looked around her attic room. She liked it. It would be fine when it was sorted out a bit.

'It's OK, Mum, don't worry. How're the boys, and Smudge, does she like her new home?'

'Everybody's fine, love, and Smudge is, too. We're still keeping her inside till she's used to the place, but there's a lovely garden here for when she's ready. Now I'm just on my way to buy a fridge. The old one's too big for the space and is sitting in the middle of the kitchen.'

'Oh dear.'

'I'm sorry about Oliver. Are you sure you're all right, love? If you've banged your head you ought to—'

'Yes, Mum, the hospital said it all. I'm fine, really.'

When she'd finished the call she felt better for having

spoken to her mother, but, confusingly, also more alone. She could go to the new house, but it wasn't her home. Her mother was obviously preoccupied and nothing was simple or convenient. There were more text messages from Oliver, she saw, but she forced herself to switch off the phone without reading them and turned her attention to organizing her things. There was a built-in cupboard in the room where she freed a couple of shelves for clothes. She lined up her shoes by the end of the bed and placed her washbag and make-up on a chest-of-drawers. There was a dusty mirror there that reflected her face back, tired, pale and uninteresting. She turned away, and her gaze fell upon her portfolio case propped against some cardboard boxes. The sight of it troubled her. She was glad she'd brought it, but it wasn't time to look at it yet. Thinking about it was enough to make her reach into the bottom of her holdall and bring out an A4 sketchbook. She sat on her mattress and started slowly to turn the pages, examining the illustrations inside. When she reached a blank page, she searched her handbag for a pencil and, after a moment's thought, began to draw with long, firm strokes.

Over the following few days, with Rick and Leonie's help, Stef turned the dusty attic into a comfortable bedroom. Into the rickety cupboards on the landing outside went the old suitcases, an artificial Christmas tree, cardboard boxes of dusty books and ornaments, several plastic storage bags of linen and numerous other bits and pieces. After dark, Rick made several trips out to a builder's skip down the road with bits of broken furniture and came back triumphantly bearing an acoustic guitar he'd found there, its soundboard cracked, but remarkably still with all six strings. He sat in the kitchen for the rest of the evening, strumming away at an old Oasis hit, until Peter came in and asked him to 'cease forthwith', after which he looked hurt and retired with it to his bedroom below Stef's which meant she heard its faint sounds as she fell asleep.

The last thing left in the attic was a rail of clothes, individually bagged, the whole contraption covered by a polythene sheet. 'One day I suppose these ought to go,' Leonie muttered as Stef helped her wheel it out onto the landing, 'but for the moment we'll leave them out here. '

The clothes in their bags intrigued Stef, but Leonie, fetchingly dressed in a pink housecoat and rubber gloves, her hair tucked under a scarf, was already handing her the vacuum-cleaner plug, which she gingerly inserted into the ancient socket.

With the room clean and a set of flowery curtains hanging at the window, it began to look welcoming. And gradually, as she went up and down the stairs and ate her meals in the kitchen, Stef got to know the other members of the household a little.

Hari, the diminutive man she'd met her first morning, and his wife Bela kept very much to themselves, cooking and eating in their room, so that a fragrance of curry and incense often floated over the first-floor landing. 'Poor Bela', as Leonie sometimes referred to her, suffered from various complaints in addition to the bunions, though it wasn't clear what all these were. Stef was coming up the stairs when she first saw her, a dumpy woman with salt-and-pepper hair, making a slow, swaying progress back to her room from the bathroom. Bela wore a thick cardigan over a blue sari, and her round face with its caste-marked high forehead would have been beautiful if not so worn with suffering. She gave Stef a timid nod before opening her bedroom door and shuffling inside. The door closed again with a sigh and a waft of incense and there was silence.

'I don't think she's been outside the house for a year,' Leonie told her. 'Hari does everything for her, but she likes to clean, it gives her something to do.' The couple had come from Kashmir, originally, where Hari had been a civil servant. A terrible political feud had turned violent and Hari, who had accidentally got embroiled, had had to leave the country in a hurry. One of Leonie's neighbours had referred them to her, knowing she had a spare room at the time. They had a grown-up daughter who now lived in America, having married another refugee from Kashmir.

The old man, Peter, who occupied the basement and was an artist, had painted some of the swirly abstract pictures that hung on Leonie's drawing-room wall, but Stef hadn't yet seen inside the rooms where he worked and slept. Leonie made dinner for him and they ate in the kitchen most nights, hearty old-fashioned English food like steak and kidney pie and nourishing stews followed by fruit pies or sponge pudding and custard. Stef was invited to join them one evening and was astonished by the amount the wiry old man put away. He talked all the while about himself, the difficulty he was having with the particular painting he was working on, and she was admiring of the way Leonie managed him, asking him questions, making suggestions. He hardly appeared to notice Stef's existence except to comment, 'Don't eat much, girl, do you? I don't like skinny girls myself, nothing to hold on to,' to which Leonie, mortified, replied that Stef looked 'lovely'. After that, Stef made sure she ate before Peter came in for his dinner. She bought her own food, sugary cereal, cheese and pasta, eggs and fresh fruit and vegetables, and stir-fried favourite little meals for herself.

Leonie

Several days had passed and the bird was still trapped in the chimney. Leonie could hear it in the day sometimes when she visited the bedroom, fluttering about in the small space, making its staccato cheeping noises. She tried to imagine what sort it was. Not a pigeon, from the sounds, but about the size of one, she thought. She developed a visual sense of it from the amount of noise it made bashing against the sides of the chimney. It seemed to have given up trying to fly upwards. Once she heard it in conversation with another bird, whose cries echoed down. Perhaps the newcomer would advise it on how to escape, she fancied, or maybe drop bits of food down for it so it would remain strong. How long did it take a bird that size to die in a chimney? Not long if it had no water. She hoped it would give up quickly and let death take it. She couldn't bear its suffering. Once again she examined the fireplace, searching for a way to help it, but the bricks looked too solidly embedded. About the only thing in the building that was. It would require considerable strength and violence for someone to break a way through, and perhaps they'd accidentally kill the bird while doing it, or simply frighten it to death. She tried talking to the bird in gentle soothing tones, and she thought it must hear her because it fell silent.

At night, when the bird had settled, she went to sleep aware of it there in the darkness. What must it be like to be huddling in the cold, lonely and starving, waiting for death to claim you? She'd read somewhere that creatures were more accepting of illness and death than humans, but of course they still experienced pain and separation.

That made her think of Jamie, Jamie whom she missed so much whilst knowing that something had had to happen, he couldn't have stayed here in an unhappy sort of limbo between childhood and adult life. Leaving home at eighteen had been a sensible idea. He and Tara, his mother, flew into such rages, it was obvious they couldn't continue to live together. Poor Tara. She was never cut out to be a mother. In some ways she was still a child herself, living on hand-outs from her father and never properly settling down. Tara didn't see things in that light, though. To her, living for the moment was the important thing. She was in her late forties now, her prettiness faded, though she was still attractive. She lived in a flat overlooking the sea in Brighton. Leonie had only been invited to it once, to collect Jamie's things when he moved into Number 11. Trudi had driven her down and they'd both been alarmed by the barefoot man playing video games in Tara's living room, introduced only as Dogger, and the shelves of self-help books and the fish-and-chip papers in the overflowing kitchen bin. Dear Tara. How could one love one's daughter so much and at the same time dislike everything about the way she lived?

It had seemed feasible at the time for Jamie to live at Number 11, but perhaps he'd caught something from Tara because, in the end, after a long and eventful couple of years his presence had become intolerable for the household. She remembered regularly trying to get him out of bed in the early afternoon after he'd been out until all hours the night before, disturbing the other residents with the noise of his return. And the cannabis. She'd tried banning it, but sometimes she'd been aware of the sweet smell of it percolating through the house. He'd had work for a short while, delivering free newspapers, but he was bored and frustrated by it and allowed it to trickle to a halt. His unhappiness seemed to poison the house, and there seemed to be nothing she could do. Rick had tried befriending him, but Jamie didn't understand Rick, who, though also spending much time in his room, was after all pursuing projects that interested him, and after a while Rick, in the face of Jamie's rudeness, gave up.

She'd gone over and over the conversation she'd had

with Jamie, shortly into the new year, when she'd lost her temper with him.

'You haven't seen daylight for weeks. How can you live like this?' she'd complained. She'd entered his bedroom for the second time that afternoon to find the coffee she'd left him cold and untouched.

'Mmm.' He hardly stirred.

She bent to gather up yesterday's jeans and hoodie, strewn across the floor like a reptile's shed skin and still bearing the shape of Jamie's body. 'And this room,' she cried, laying them on a chair already piled with unwashed clothes. 'It stinks.'

He twisted up to sitting, a wave of animal heat coming off him. 'Leave my things alone! I'll deal with them.' His voice was hoarse and smoky.

'But you don't, Jamie. You never do.'

He fell back on the pillow. 'Why does everyone go on at me?' he grumbled at the ceiling.

'Because you don't go on at yourself. Jamie, you can't continue like this. You've got to take responsibility for your life.'

The beauty of him as he lay there, the vulnerability of him, his Adam's apple quivering in his throat. She reached and switched on the ceiling light and he laid his arm over his eyes.

'I want you up and downstairs in twenty minutes, Jamie.'

'It's worse here than ...' His words were lost in mumbling.

'What?'

'I said it's worse here than at Mum's.'

Something snapped then. 'Well, go back to your mum, then. You're welcome to live here, Jamie, but only if you pull yourself together. I'll help you as much as I can, but it's no good if you don't try to help yourself.'

With that, she picked up the undrunk coffee and withdrew, closing the door a little too sharply.

She busied herself in the kitchen while she waited. Hari was in and out, collecting an assortment of vegetables from the fridge and a bowl of whitish liquid with specks of some sort of spice in it. An hour later, Jamie had still not appeared and Leonie was furious. Hari nodded to her sympathetically. 'It's that boy, isn't it? He is disrespectful to his elders. You should put your foot in it.'

'I did put my foot down, Hari,' she said. 'That's what I'm worried about.'

They both froze as they heard footsteps stomping down the stairs. A silence, then a scuffling, the creak of the front door opening, then the shaking of the house as the door slammed.

'Jamie!' She reached the front door and wrenched it open, only to see a battered car lurch away, her grandson's pale face at the passenger window. As it sped off a thudding music beat started up.

'Jamie,' she cried again in desperation as she hurried down the steps into the street. 'Oh Jamie.' The car's brake lights came on and hope lifted in her only to plummet as the vehicle turned left out of Bellevue Gardens and out of sight.

Where was he? She had no idea, really. He'd left no message and when she eventually managed to speak to Tara, she found that he hadn't contacted her either. His room had been emptied, well, sort of. The mess of torn paper, broken gadgets and dried-out fruit peel was all he'd left behind along with a cigarette burn on the bedside table and an assortment of stains on the carpet. It took her a full day to clean up, soaking the stains and airing the room, and she could hardly see what she was doing for sadness.

Three

Rosa

Rosa had been unpacking the baker's delivery and thinking about Michal when Karina had to answer her phone and told her to take over at the till. 'What would you like?' Rosa asked a boy of about twelve with his arm in a sling and a tear-stained face. The man in a business suit with him, presumably his father, ordered him a hot chocolate with cream and marshmallows and sprinkles, and an espresso for himself.

'I'm at work now, Cathy,' she heard Karina say tiredly. 'Can't you ring the surgery yourself and say you got to have that appointment? Well, I can't do it for you at the moment, sorry, I've a line of customers to serve. Look, I'll phone you later.' With a grim expression, Karina stuffed the phone into her apron pocket and rescued a panini that had toasted in the grill. 'Anyone would think Jared's mum was completely helpless,' she said, rolling her eyes at Rosa who was squirting cream on the hot chocolate.

'There you are,' Rosa said to the boy, shaking on the

sprinkles, and watched a smile transform his face. Like Michal's smile, she thought, in its innocent pleasure.

'I'll have to phone her later or I'll never hear the last of it.' Karina was still grumbling.

On the whole, Rosa liked her boss, or at least understood her, which wasn't quite the same thing but meant they worked well together. Karina didn't waste energy on charm, but she had a sympathetic nature that the clientele appreciated, especially the older ones who liked a moan about life. She hadn't had an easy time, what with losing her own mum a few years back and working by herself to turn the family café into a success. Now she'd got her boyfriend's mother always phoning her about some difficulty or other. Rosa had asked why Jared didn't help, but Cathy, it appeared, didn't like to bother her son, whom she idolized.

It was all quite different from Rosa's own experience. In Poland, after her grandmother had been widowed, she had moved in with them. It had been a squash – Rosa and Michal had had to share a bedroom for several years – but it had seemed the right thing to Rosa's mother and everyone had got on with it. It was one of the many ways in which things seemed to be bewilderingly different in England.

She felt that she was living in a limbo. Yes, she had a job, and she was thankful for that. She was extremely grateful to Leonie for giving her a home, and Leonie had been as good as her word, the rent was really very modest. After all the government deductions her weekly wage seemed pitiful, but there was only herself to think about and she was managing, just. It meant that she could remain in the area and look for her brother, and that was enough.

In truth, Rosa did not know what to do next. She had been back to her father's address twice at different times of day and pressed the doorbell, despite knowing as she did so that there would be no answer. It was obvious each time that no one had entered the house since her previous visit. Obvious from the junk mail fluttering from the letterbox and from the blind that hung in the front window at exactly the same haphazard angle, obvious from the dead bluebottles still lying upside down on the windowsill next to the dead pot plant.

That afternoon after work she made more of the enquiries as to the whereabouts of Mr and Mrs Dexter as the man next door had suggested but they were met by denials and a certain amount of suspicion. One frightened young woman, her figure slight under a shapeless tracksuit, muttered, 'Sorry,' without meeting her eye and practically shut the door in Rosa's face. She'd seen women like that before, back in her home city, women who hardly left their apartments, and who when they did muffled themselves up and wouldn't look anyone in the face.

She had better luck at the house staggered opposite, which, so the two doorbells indicated, was divided into flats. There was no response when she pressed the one for upstairs, from where she'd seen the man watching her that first day, but the woman in her seventies living downstairs invited her in and proved very talkative.

Yes, she remembered the Dexters. He'd helped her start her car one winter when she'd been late to take her sister to the hospital. And his wife, very sweet, what was her name, Yvonne, but they'd moved away, oh, a year ago, was it? She'd seen the removal van and gone across to ask. They were going to the coast somewhere, where was it? Brighton, possibly, or somewhere like that. She was surprised that the house hadn't been sold. And that they hadn't had their mail forwarded. That seemed a bit strange, didn't Rosa think?

Rosa did think, but then she knew her father wasn't always reliable, and she had met his wife only once or twice. She supposed there to be other family somewhere, but she didn't know where. There were no more children. Yvonne either couldn't have or hadn't wanted children – she'd never shown much interest in the ones Harry Dexter already had.

She explained to this elderly neighbour how her parents had met in 1980 when her mother, Frieda, had come to work in north London as an au pair. The family she worked for didn't treat her kindly and her mother had cried every night, wanting to go home, but didn't dare to actually go because her relatives regarded it as an opportunity for her to learn English and make a mark in the world.

Harry Dexter had been managing a building project for the house next door to Frieda's employers. He used to arrive regularly in a stylish old black saloon car to check that everything was being done properly. Frieda, walking the two children to school, or coming back from the shops, would smile when he greeted her with obvious admiration. He had charmed her with an old-fashioned courtesy that surprised her, eventually insisting that he take her away from her servitude to install her in Number 28 Dartmouth Street.

'So you were born here?' the old lady asked, intrigued, pouring Rosa more tea.

Rosa nodded. 'I lived here until I was six years old,' she said, 'but I don't remember it well. Then my mother took me and my brother back to Poland, she argued with my father, and I did not see him very much after that.'

When her mother had died two years ago, Rosa had telephoned him to let him know. It was Yvonne who had answered the phone and promised to pass on the message, but it was several days before he rang back and too late for him to attend the funeral. 'You and Michal must come and visit,' he'd said, and that had been the last time she'd spoken to him.

A few months later Michal had decided to go and find his father. However, this time the phone number didn't work. Michal had gone just the same. Rosa had written to their father instead.

'I think I saw your brother,' the old lady said, offering her another biscuit. The biscuits had the word 'Nice' written on them, which seemed very English.

At the old lady's suggestion, Rosa went to the police station on the main street near the Underground station and reported her brother missing.

An athletic-looking constable who introduced himself

as PC Ben Sharp led her into a small office and sat her down opposite him and asked her questions, whilst he typed the answers with two fingers into a computer. Yes, Michal was only twenty-two. She had heard from him by text when he'd reached London six months before, no, he wouldn't have had much money and had only recently opened a bank account in Poland. The idea had been that she would supply funds if he needed them, but he'd never asked. No, she didn't know his passport number, but perhaps she could find it out. He took a note of their father's address, too, in case he could discover his whereabouts.

Then PC Sharp printed out a copy of the form for her, gave her a reference number and explained the procedure. There wasn't a great deal the police could do. Michal was, after all, over eighteen. They could discover if he was officially living in the UK, claiming benefits, for instance, or legally employed, but that would take time and there was only a limited amount they would be allowed to tell her. They would, however, call her on the mobile number she'd given him if they found anything. And they had the addresses of where she lived and where she worked.

She thanked him and left the police station, feeling as though she hadn't got anywhere, sensing, despite Ben Sharp's politeness, that her missing brother must be one of thousands, but at least she'd started the trail and other people were helping.

She returned home exhausted with emotion.

*

It was lighter in the evenings now and she took a can of lager into the garden and sat at a small round metal table. A few minutes later, the conservatory door opened and the fragile English girl, Stef, came out hauling a full black rubbish sack. There was an alley running along the backs of the gardens and the wheelie bins had to be dragged down the path and out onto it once a week, which was a chore the household bickered over.

'Hi. Aren't you cold out here?' Stef said as she manoeuvred the sack into one of the bins.

'A little, but ...' Rosa indicated her cigarette. Leonie would not have smoking in the house. It was well known that Peter disobeyed the injunction and smoked in his basement. If he tried to light up in the kitchen, though, Leonie always sent him outside, which was why the terrace was usually littered with stubs.

The English girl folded her arms, shivering. She was looking particularly slender in a long soft jumper of powder blue with sleeves that fell over her hands. So pretty, she was, Rosa thought, puffing at her cigarette, like a fluffy kitten in that jumper with her long hair newly washed, but the clothes she wore were impractical for housework.

'Sit down with me,' she said. 'Have one?' She offered the packet but Stef shook her head.

'I tried once, and it made me feel sick.'

'You are lucky then, save money. I try to give up.' She plunged the stub into the metal ashtray on the table. It hissed briefly in some rainwater and went out.

Stef smiled uneasily. 'My boyfriend hates them, too.

He made me take his suit to the cleaner's once because it smelled of smoke. It was after a party in someone's house.'

Rosa watched her face change. Was it mention of the boyfriend that had made her sad? She'd been out all day, every day, so had hardly spoken to Stef in the week they'd both lived here. In the evening Stef had spent a lot of time sorting out her room. Rosa had heard her shifting things around upstairs.

Rosa's phone bleeped briefly and she picked it up, hope leaping as ever, but it was a text from Karina asking her to come in a little early the next day. She sent an answer and sighed. When she looked up Stef was watching her. 'Just work,' she told the English girl.

'What do you do?'

'Waitress. The café near the tube station?'

'Not the one with the picture of the cat?'

'Yes.'

'It seems nice in there. Do they need anybody else?'

'I can ask, but I think not. You look for a job?'

Stef nodded. 'I need one pretty bad. I ... I left home. And now I don't have much money. Well, none, really. Oliver, my boyfriend, used to give me some because I lost my job. I was in catering. But now ...'

'You have broken with him?'

'We are ... taking some time apart. I need some space really.'

Stef looked so unhappy that Rosa felt concerned for her. Normally she kept herself to herself, she hadn't wanted to talk about all the things that had gone wrong in her own life, but there was something about Stef which touched her. She waited, but Stef didn't say anything more, instead twisted her hands inside the sleeves of her jumper, like a Chinese mandarin.

'I can ask my boss, Karina,' Rosa said finally.

'Oh could you? Thank you.' Stef gave her an appealing smile that for a moment set Rosa off-balance.

'Have you lived here long? In London, I mean,' the girl rushed on. 'I'm sorry, I don't know anything about you.'

'Don't worry. No, not long. Two weeks. I lived in London before. When I was a little girl. My father is English, you see. But ...' She hadn't even confided properly in Karina about this, but it came out in a rush. 'I don't know where he is. I have been to the house and there is no one there. It is a mystery because my brother—'

'Your brother?'

'I am telling it wrong. My brother Michal came here six months ago to find work, but I have not heard from him for a long time. I thought he would be living with our father, but the house is empty and ... I cannot find out where he has gone. I went to the police station this afternoon and told a policeman, but now I don't know what to do.'

'Oh, I see.' She glanced up to see Stef's eyes were full of pity. It was suddenly as though their positions had reversed. She was the weak one and Stef blazing with concern. Stef put out a woolly hand and touched Rosa's arm briefly. 'I can't imagine what that's like,' she whispered.

'It was soon after our mother died, you see,' Rosa

said, reaching for another cigarette. 'Michal has always been, well, restless. He did not like his work. It was in a petrol station, taking the money. His boss was not a good man, but Michal had not worked hard at school, so it was difficult for him to do something better. He got this thought that he must come to England, that our father would help him and he would make money and be successful then come back home and start his own business.

Michal had been so determined about the idea, had talked and talked about it. Their mother had left them a little money when she died, not much, but enough for him to pay the coach fare to London and to buy a few things he needed. Rosa had seen him off at the coach station early one morning. She frowned, remembering that last sight of him waving as the coach moved off. He sent her a text message to say they were waiting to leave Calais. He'd phoned from a call box to tell her he'd arrived in London, said that he was trying to make his mobile work, and that was all.

'He must have tried to let me know that he hadn't found my father, but I didn't hear anything, that's what's so strange. I don't know where he is.'

'I'm sure you would have heard if something bad had happened to him,' Stef said gently.

'I don't know. What if no one knew who he was or his address, they would not know to tell me.'

They were both quiet for a moment. There was a picture that lately would come into her mind. It was of a young man flailing about in slow motion in dirty water, fighting to swim to the surface, desperate for air. She'd try to think of something else, but this picture always reasserted itself. Suppose Michal was . . . no, she mustn't think like that. What would he have done when he'd realized their father was gone?

'Maybe like you he went to a hostel,' Stef suggested. 'Someone, the police, would have helped him.'

'Yes,' said Rosa, but she did not feel reassured. Surely she would have heard from him if this is what happened.

'The police will check their records and find him.'

'I hope so,' Rosa said. She stubbed out her cigarette half-smoked and rubbed her arms against the coolness of the evening. 'If not, I don't know what to do next.'

Rick

Rick lifted the pen from the page and in the light from the window considered what he had drawn. The girl's hair still wasn't quite right. He laid the pen across the inkpot on the narrow table he used as a desk and once more picked up the photograph and studied it. The young woman in it, sitting in profile, her chin resting in her hand, was actually a friend of his sister Claire, Julia. He'd liked her large, unusually shaped eyes and small mouth, the slightly disgruntled expression she wore, and knew she'd do for one of his characters. She'd shrugged her shoulders when he'd asked, then smiled, said, 'Sure, if you want,' and allowed herself to be photographed in various casual poses while she and Claire carried on their conversation as though he wasn't there. It was about getting a black-and-white sheepdog, he remembered, though why Claire would want to complicate her life even further by acquiring a dog, he didn't know. Perhaps it could be trained to fetch the boys from school.

He sighed, picked up the pen and looked from the photograph to the paper before continuing. An extra line or two. That was better. The girl's face challenged him from the page, shadowed by the bars of her prison window. He blew gently to dry the ink and carefully set the paper on top of the others. That made three panels this evening. Not much, but a step forward all the same. He screwed the top on the inkpot, wiped the pen and leaned sideways across the bed to collect his scanner from the shelf on the opposite wall.

Leonie often apologized for his narrow room, but he rather liked it. Everything was in reach and it was cosy. When it was cold outside he turned on the convector heater and the room warmed up nicely. He switched on his laptop. As he waited for it to boot up, he plugged in some earpieces and stroked the dial on his iPod. With atonal guitar jangling in his ears he was usually quickly lost in his own world. But not this time. There was an image that kept bothering him, the face of a different girl. She had longish blonde hair and a vulnerable expression on her face. He knew he wanted to draw her, but there wasn't a place for her in the story he was creating. As he scanned his latest drawings onto his laptop, he thought about her.

He was rather proud of himself, rescuing Stef. He'd never been in a hero role before. Not that he had been really, this time. But he'd made a point of seeing if she was all right after the collision and had found her somewhere to live. For the time being, anyway. She'd looked so grateful when he'd told her about the room. Poor thing.

He didn't feel he knew her much better since she'd moved in. He'd taken care to help her when he could. Clearing out the attic had been fun and had its reward – he glanced at the battered guitar leaning against the wall near the door.

His laptop gave a gentle ping and he saw the latest scan had loaded. He named it and filed it away with the others, then started uploading them onto his blog for his followers to see. He had over a hundred followers now, all eagerly waiting to see the next instalment of 'Dark Journey' and share it or make comments. Mostly these were words of encouragement, which were what he liked best, but occasionally people made suggestions about how to develop the work, and even less occasionally these were useful.

He clicked on the previous posting he'd made and saw there were two new comments. One said, *Awesome, mate, keep at it*, with an emoji of a smiley face. The other he read twice with a feeling of discomfort. *You need to get out more*, someone called 'darkstar494' sneered.

This was bad. Who was it? On the whole he didn't have trouble with internet trolls though there could be a little professional jealousy. He tapped out an ironic answer, *Cheers, will bear this in mind*, took a quick glance at one or two other blogs he followed, sharing a link to one, then logged out. He'd look again tomorrow when he got home from his shift and hope the unpleasant follower had given up. It was as he was closing the lid of the laptop that it occurred to him that 'darkstar494' might be Jamie. 494 was Jamie's birthdate: April 1994. Oh well, it wouldn't be the first time. He shrugged.

It was a funny life he lived at the moment, Claire said. For a long time she'd been like everyone else, always on at him to get a 'proper' job, but the supermarket suited him. It lacked challenge, no doubt about that, putting stuff through the till hour after hour, stacking shelves or, even worse, having to monitor the self-service tills, where people kept putting the wrong things in the bagging area or getting cross when they couldn't understand which button to press. At least he could forget about it afterwards, and it gave him time to do what he enjoyed doing, working on his various writing projects, none of which had yet made him any money. Thank goodness the rent he paid Leonie was so low or he might not manage.

'You're wasting your talents, Ricky,' Claire had said that day he'd taken the photographs of her friend. 'What was the point of paying to go to university if you're going to be on the minimum wage for the rest of your life?'

'There aren't any good jobs,' he'd muttered, reluctant to be caught up in this argument again. 'Not that I want to do, anyway.'

'That's the trouble. How do you know? You've hardly tried anything.'

'Shut up, Claire. Stop going on at me. You're worse than Mam.'

'That's what older sisters are for.'

'I s'pose.' He knew she was fond of him, but it wasn't fair. If he ever made any suggestions about her she'd be on him with her sarcasm. No one had ever been able to tell Claire anything, but she'd done well all the same. Made a mess of her A levels but had worked her way into a well-paid job as an events organizer. Rick could imagine her charming people, getting what she wanted, and supposed that she was much more organized at work than she was in her social life.

Rick had been quite happy for the first year or so after uni, or had thought he was, but lately things had begun slowly, imperceptibly, to change. There was always something happening at the supermarket, it wasn't that. Any job around people had its human interest, its dramas, and people-watching was important to his writing, he'd told himself. It was the mundanity of the tasks he hated, the lack of responsibility. He'd got into trouble once for piling some cheap umbrellas into a wire bin near one of the tills when it was raining. Obvious, he thought, but no, for some bureaucratic reason it was wrong and he was made to take them away. Individual initiative was not required.

The manager had been otherwise pleased with him, and suggested he apply to be a customer relations supervisor, whatever that was, though it seemed to mean wearing headphones and standing at a booth close to the main doorway so he'd be on the wrong end of any icy north wind. It also meant going on training courses and possibly even paying into a pension fund and he didn't want to be bothered with any of that. He was an artist, he wanted to be free. Yet somehow, if he said no, he'd feel dissatisfied, too. Why that should be he really didn't know. If only he could get somewhere with his writing. That's what he worked so hard for at university, all the reading and learning how to express himself. He'd be pouring his talent away doing what Claire called a 'proper job'.

He sighed as he closed down his laptop, then took up a spiral-bound notebook from the desk and swung himself onto the bed where he sat against the wall, the notebook folded open on his drawn-up thighs. He tapped the end of his pencil on his lower lip as he gathered his thoughts then began to write. After a couple of sentences he stopped, frowned as he read back what he'd written and struck out a spare adjective, then half the previous sentence. A few minutes later he tossed the notebook aside and, leaning over, reached for his guitar. Sometimes, he found, music helped the ideas flow.

Stef

Up in her attic room, Stef heard the distant sound of strumming and felt comforted. She'd been lying on her bed struck by inertia and thinking about Rosa, whether she'd asked her boss about the possibility of work. She liked Rosa, was intrigued by her. She seemed to be so sorted, self-possessed. However, there was a deep sadness about her, too. Perhaps it was worrying about her brother, what was his name? Michal. Stef had twin brothers of seventeen, much younger than her, Vince and Mark. Half-brothers from her mother's second marriage. She didn't see much of the boys, but she was fond enough of them. She knew she'd be distraught if one of them went missing. Michal, at twenty-two, was old enough to look after himself. Still, that made his disappearance odder.

Rosa usually kept the door to her room shut, but once Stef had seen it ajar while Rosa was in the bathroom, and couldn't stop herself peeping in. Everything was neatly put away, the duvet pulled straight. There was nothing in the room that expressed anything about Rosa's personality. She glanced round at her attic space, the clothes spilling out of the cupboard, the pile of paperbacks strewn across the floor. It was the sort of thing that drove Oliver mad.

Oliver. A conversation they'd had a few days before she left was bothering her. She remembered it as clearly as if it had just taken place. The sting of it was still fresh.

They'd been to dinner in a restaurant with a friend of Oliver's, Jago, whom he played squash with every week. Jago, an accountant with one of the big firms, Stef always forgot its name, had proudly introduced them to his new girlfriend, Nora. Nora was very beautiful, with dark velvety skin and a tiny jewel through her eyebrow that flashed in the candlelight as she talked with animation about her work, which was something to do with buying and selling things that didn't actually yet exist.

Stef had done her best, patiently asking questions about the fruit that wasn't yet grown, the houses that hadn't been built, but the whole thing sounded to her so unreal that she struggled. She preferred to deal with the material, the concrete, things she'd designed and made. Like the desserts for the catering firm, she'd been good at desserts. Her eyes widened at the one the waiter set in front of her now, dragon-fruit cheesecake as light as a soufflé, a lattice of crystallized coloured sugar cast over the top. So pretty she hardly liked to eat it. She'd only ordered it to annoy Oliver who'd said, 'Stef doesn't eat pudding, do you, Stef?'

She picked up the spoon and prodded at the sugar.

'Looks gorgeous,' Nora said, her intelligent eyes friendly. She bit a corner off the tiny square of chocolate brownie that had come with her espresso. 'So what is it you do, Stef?'

The sugar lattice snapped. Stef glanced up. 'I'm resting at the moment. Waiting for the right thing. You know.' She noticed Oliver's fingers tense on the stem of his wine glass. She didn't need to look at him to know the way his eyes would have narrowed.

'OK.' Nora inclined her head brightly. 'What are you interested in?'

As Stef opened her mouth to say, 'Fashion design,' Oliver leaned across his fruit crumble and cut in. 'You on for next Tuesday, J? I'm going early, get a bit of a warm-up in the gym. I'm viciously unfit.'

'Tell me about it,' Jago said, pushing his empty plate away. He did everything quickly. 'Won't be back from a client's before seven myself, so I'll see you there. Nora's got yoga, haven't you, Nora?'

'Do you do any sport?' Nora asked Stef, who shook her head.

The conversation moved on. Stef spooned up her cheesecake in silence, hardly able to swallow for the swell of sadness in her throat.

In the taxi home over Westminster Bridge, she said tentatively, 'Nora seems nice.'

'Yeah. A notch or two above Jago's usual standard, I must say. But God, Stef, what must she have thought? Are you really quite so pig-ignorant about hedge funds?'

'People like being asked about themselves.' That's what Mum had always taught her.

'I should think Nora was bored to death.'

'Don't say that.' She wished her voice didn't sound so small. He hated it when she cried.

'Good thing I rescued you, eh?' He put out his hand and squeezed hers, smiling at her lovingly. He'd be terrified of dating someone confident and glamorous like Nora, she thought. He liked gentle girls he could look after, he often said that.

She stared out of the taxi window at the lights moving past and felt numb. She told herself how lucky she was having Oliver, how well he looked after her. For a long time she'd thought this and believed it, too, but lately the gratitude wouldn't come. What was the matter with her? She wasn't anyone important. Sometimes she felt someone could come along and simply rub her out, like she did with the drawings she made of girls with no faces, their long slender figures clad in marvellous dresses. She liked Edwardian at the moment, the tiny waists and high-necked blouses. She'd been watching a period drama on the television and thought the women were so elegant back then.

She mostly bought what Oliver liked her to wear, since he paid for it, figure-hugging designer jeans with smock tops, or pretty dresses. He loved to see her in feminine things, he'd always say, and she didn't mind. Sometimes, though, she'd scour the charity shops for something more unusual, cobweb cardigans, little skirts. She liked the layered look. It was easy enough to alter clothes to fit. Her nan had taught her to do that when Stef had tea with her those afternoons after school before the boys were born, waiting for her mother to finish work. Nan had been a great knitter, too.

The room was settling into dusk now, the sharp lines of the sloping ceiling softening into darkness. She rolled over and switched on the lamp, blinking at its sudden brightness. Shadows leaped up the walls. Beyond the ring of light the solid shapes of the furniture reared up to protect her.

She had had to go. It was something the women were speaking about in the television studio that morning, she remembered now. They'd been talking about partners who had eradicated their self-esteem. 'Emotional bullying,' they'd called it. It was one particular phrase that had caught her attention.

'He made me feel I couldn't exist without him.' That. It was almost exactly what Oliver had told her the night before she left. When they'd had that row.

'I've given you everything, Stef. We're bound together. We wouldn't exist without each other, don't you feel that?'

The row had been about something Stef even then thought petty. These rows often were. An old school-friend of hers had been in touch. There was to be a weekend reunion in Derbyshire in July. A bunch of them were going to a spa hotel. Would she come? She couldn't afford it, of course, and Oliver wouldn't lend her the money. She was already in debt to him, he said, and she supposed she was. She really ought to try harder to get a job. 'I know, I know,' Stef had said, 'but I still don't know what I want to do.' She tried not to think of the fashion course. Oliver was right. It was a bit much for her at the moment. She'd got herself in a state about it.

They'd had a lovely evening up to that point. He'd got back from work in good time and she'd cooked them a delicious pan-fried chicken dish. They were sitting together at the table in the kitchen. He was so gorgeous, freshly showered in a soft blue sweater over his jeans, his dark hair glossy as a blackbird's wing, that she wanted to bury her face in the lime and basil scent of him, safe, not having to think of anything except him, but then, when she raised the matter, he denied her the opportunity to see her friends and she felt resentful.

Why shouldn't she go? 'I'll ask Mum for the money,' she said. 'An early birthday present.' Her birthday wasn't till August.

'I don't want you to go,' he said. 'Please don't.'

'But I haven't seen them for ages. I never see my friends at all now.'

'I'm not invited, am I?'

'It's not for partners, silly. Anyway, you wouldn't want to do a spa.'

'I thought we might go away by ourselves in July.'

'Ol, it's just a weekend.'

It was then he said the words that annoyed her, about them being bound together, and she gazed at him in dismay. That was how he saw their relationship; they mustn't do things without each other. The excuse was that he simply didn't want her to go away.

'You went on that work-bonding thing.'

'But I had to, that was part of my job.'

'And you play squash with Jago.'

'You can come and watch if you like.'

She shook her head. Of course she didn't want to spend an evening in a smelly old squash court. She felt a flutter of panic. When had she last been out with one of her friends? Weeks ago. Weeks and weeks. And then she'd been watching the clock half the time because she knew he'd hate it if she was back late. She saw all of a sudden how isolated she'd become.

'Well, I'm going to go,' she said in a petulant voice, and was alarmed to see Oliver's face darken with anger. He fetched a beer from the fridge, and without looking at her went into the living room and shut the door. There came the sound of shouting, then gunfire, which frightened her then ... the television, she realized. In the kitchen the clock ticked as she slowly wrapped the remains of the food and slotted plates and cutlery into their places in the dishwasher. She scrubbed and dried the pans and wiped the surfaces with extra effort. After everything was spotless she went to bed.

When Oliver came in later, he leaned over her with beery breath and whispered her name. She had pretended to be deeply asleep.

In her attic, the sound of the guitar strumming below stopped abruptly, pulling her out of her reverie. She was lying on her side, her gaze fixed on the wall opposite, against which the lamp cast the shadow of the chest-of-drawers. What funny legs it had, like a bow-legged dog's, its tummy almost reaching the floor. Her eyes narrowed. There should be a clean strip of light falling on the skirting board from between the chest's legs, but instead the shadow bulged, as though something was hanging down. She shifted on the mattress until she could see under the piece of furniture. She was right, something was hanging down. She stared at it with mild interest. Was it paper or cloth or the bottom of the drawer sagging?

Ordinarily, she wouldn't have noticed it or, if she had, cared, but tonight there was nothing much to amuse her. Her thoughts were stilled. Into the silence had come this distraction to rouse her curiosity.

She levered herself onto the floor, crawled over the

boards and knelt before the chest. Grasping the knobs on the bottom drawer, she pulled, gently at first, then harder. The drawer shifted a little then stuck. She tried again, edging out one side until it was level with the other, then shook it as she pulled. It shot out several inches before jamming again. As far as she could see the drawer was empty, but something prompted her to reach in. She could just fit her arm inside to feel around. The tips of her fingers met something hard and smooth lying on the bottom of the drawer. A book or magazine. She tried to grasp it but it slid beyond reach. That annoyed her. She withdrew her hand and tried to peep under the furniture, but the drawer was in the way now and the chest was deep. There was definitely paper hanging down, though. Two eyes, a woman's face, stared back at her from it, goading her.

She clambered to her feet and switched on the ceiling light, then shuffled the lamp closer to the chest. She could see into the drawer to the plain paper lining its bottom. The drawer still wouldn't move, so she grasped the handles of the one above and when she tugged it came out more easily. Soon she had manoeuvred it out altogether and brought it awkwardly to the floor beside her. Now she could see what had happened to the one beneath.

The back of it had come away and it was fixing the drawer in place. Several magazines were caught up and falling down the gap. With a little wiggling, she managed to free them without tearing any.

There were four, very old, their pages yellowing.

Women's fashion magazines, all of them. Three had titles she recognized. Her nan used to get one of them every week, she remembered. Sometimes she'd read a copy, liking its cosy old-fashioned nature, its world that wasn't hers but her grandmother's with its photographs of children and pets and articles about cruise wear or miraculous recovery from illness. She'd liked the short stories, too, though she thought them unrealistic. She didn't believe in Mr Right or love at first sight, surely none of her generation did. Her grandmother had, though. She'd met Grandad when their dodgem cars bumped together at a fairground in 1958 and that had been it.

Nan had died before Stef had met Oliver. She had wondered sometimes what Nan would have thought of him. Her mother had often been too bound up in her own problems to notice much about Stef's.

She bundled the magazines together and retreated to the bed with them, bringing the lamp with her. Pulling the pile onto her lap she began to turn the pages.

They were mainly from the early Sixties, she saw from the dates on the tops, and the covers weren't thick and glossy like those of today. The pages felt rough and many were printed in black-and-white. She smoothed a cover where it had been pinioned under the collapsing drawer. The girl on the front stared out at her, sweet-looking, with pencilled, heavy-lashed eyes, fair hair in a bob, the ends flicked up, a long fringe falling down her high forehead. *Easy knits for autumn* said a strapline, referring to the high-neck sweater the model was wearing. Stef flipped through, studying the pictures, thinking how simple and innocent the world once was, in the pages of women's magazines, at least.

She came to the article about the autumn knits and studied the pictures of the same young woman modelling a cardigan with a smart stripe up the front, then a beret and scarf with a matching zigzag pattern. She was pretty in that stylized way of the time. Did they touch up photographs like they did today, Stef wondered. Not with computers, of course, but surely skin couldn't naturally be that flawless. The coat the girl wore with the beret and scarf was really gorgeous, in cream, with flaring sleeves. She wanted to copy it down right away.

Instead she studied the girl's face with its heavy make-up and wondered whether she was one of those famous Sixties models, perhaps Jean Shrimpton or Sandra Paul, or who was the other one she was thinking of? Not Twiggy, she'd recognize Twiggy's face anywhere. From when the Sixties were starting to swing. She loved the clothes from then. She turned to the copy of *Vogue*. That was definitely Jean Shrimpton on the cover. She leafed her way through and stopped at a feature about summer dresses, liking the simple waistless shapes and bold patterns. Red and yellow vertical stripes fanned out from the neckline of one. They were like the rays of the sun, and made her feel happy. She turned the page to see a beach dress with a halter neck and a cutaway at the sides. She carefully studied the effect of this, and how the colourful pop-art pattern skilfully emphasized the model's figure, and frowned. It might work well now using a modern latex material.

She glanced through the magazine that was dated a little later than the others, 1966. It was full of miniskirts and minidresses. That wide-eyed waif was definitely Twiggy, sporty here in bright yellow vest top, shorts and baseball shoes. She was wearing a little badge with a flower design like the one Stef had pinned to her jacket. She turned to the Sunday newspaper supplement. There was a piece in it about Mary Quant. One of the models could have been the autumn-knits one, she thought, though the hair was a completely different style.

An idea occurred to her. Those clothes on the rail she'd seen. She set the magazines to one side, got up and went out onto the landing. She listened. The house was tranquil, a voice from a distant radio, the cheerful clinks and crashes of someone tidying up in the kitchen. There was the slightest whiff of curry spices in the air, masking the dampish old-house smell. It was as different as it could be from the chemical new-wood-and-carpet aroma of Oliver's apartment, and she knew which she preferred. There was a softness to the atmosphere here, a lived-in feel. It was as though all the people who'd inhabited this house had left a mark of their presence behind, a sigh, the swish of a long dress stirring the dust on the stairs and making it sparkle. It was impossible to believe that anyone had previously lived in Oliver's place. All evidence of the past had been torn out; he liked everything to be brand new. He hated it when she bought clothes in charity shops. 'How can you bear to wear other people's leavings?' he'd said when she'd shown him a little fur stole she'd found. 'It's probably got moth.'

She'd bravely worn it to a cocktail bar with Oliver's colleagues, but Oliver had made sarcastic comments about the smell of mothballs all evening so it stayed unworn in a drawer for a few weeks until she hated to see it there and gave it away.

Leonie's rack of clothes loomed in the shadows of the landing. She wheeled it round into the circle of light thrown from her attic lamp and pushed the plastic covering off one end. The clothes hanging in their individual bags were like secrets waiting to be uncovered and she felt guilty for prying. In the end she couldn't resist edging up the zip of just the first one.

It gaped open to reveal something red and crocheted. She felt it between her fingers, soft to the touch, then pulled the zip up a little more to reveal a black-and-white chevron design at the bodice. It was a sleeveless dress; you'd need a jacket with it. She zipped it back into its bag and, after a moment's guilty hesitation, investigated the next one. This was a pretty polka-dot dress with frills at the hem and cuffs, identical to one she'd seen while flipping through the magazines. From a third bag a wide-legged jumpsuit unfurled itself. These outfits were gorgeous, but what did they all mean, the clothes and the magazines? Her conscience finally won out and she replaced the plastic cover and pushed the rail back into the shadows. Had Leonie worn the clothes? She could ask her, though she'd have to do so in a way that didn't look as though she'd been snooping. Leonie herself, Stef had observed, was very respectful of people's private space and something told her she expected to be treated the same way. However, Stef couldn't help wanting to know more about her and longed for the chance to present itself.

Rosa

Rosa was emptying the dishwasher at the Black Cat Café the next morning when her phone rang.

'Is that Rosa Dexter? It's PC Sharp here.' She recognized the voice of the young police constable who'd interviewed her, what was his name? Ben. And at once she was alert.

'Yes, I'm Rosa.'

'No news of your brother yet, I'm afraid, but I have managed to find out where your father is.'

'Oh! Thank you. Where ... ?'

'I'm not sure how to put this ... it might come as something of a shock to you.' He paused to clear his throat. 'Miss Dexter, your father, his name is Harry John Dexter, is that right, born 1947?'

'Yes.'

'Miss Dexter, I am afraid to say that he is in prison.'

'*Prison?*' Her whole body tingled with shock.

'Look, I think you should come in again to talk about it. I can explain properly and help you arrange a visit if you like.'

'Thank you,' she whispered.

After the call ended she realized that Karina was staring at her curiously. 'What's happened?' the other girl asked. 'Your face has gone all blotchy.'

Rick

It was late on Saturday morning and Rick was sitting in the kitchen with his feet up on a chair, reading a book and sipping from a steaming mug of fruit tea. He glanced up as Stef came in, smiled and closed the book on his finger, remembering with embarrassment that he'd been using a sock as a bookmark.

'Don't let me disturb you,' she said, moving past to reach for the kettle. She had to raise her voice above the grind of the washing machine as it worked itself up into a spin.

'You're not. I'm waiting for that monster to finish.'

'Are you all right for green tea or whatever?'

'Yeah.' Rick nodded. 'Kettle's just boiled.' The shriek of the machine prevented further conversation for a couple of minutes. He watched Stef as she swirled a tea bag in a mug of hot water and thought she looked more lost than usual today. He longed to reassure her, but he couldn't think of the right words. That wasn't much use for a writer. When the noisy spinning subsided he decided he should try anyway.

'So how're things going?'

She curved her lips in that appealing way she had, an attempt at a smile.

'I can't really get myself going on anything.' She yawned. 'Sorry. See what I mean?'

'Perhaps you need the rest?'

'I shouldn't do. I've been resting for months.' She fed her tea bag to the swing bin, carried the mug over and sat down opposite him, one leg folded under her in the way he'd noticed she had. She brought with her the scent of fresh mint from the tea and something flowery and all her own. Rick thought how unusual her eyes were as she regarded him, the golden brown mixed with flecks of green, the lashes lustrous with mascara. A stray black crumb lay against her nose, like a beauty spot amidst the sprinkling of freckles. It bothered him that he didn't know whether to tell her about it.

'Is there anything I can help you with? You know, the job search.'

She took a sip of her tea, scooped back her hair and said, 'Do you know where I should look, websites, that kind of thing?'

'What sort of job would you want?'

She shrugged. 'Anything really. What about where you work, the supermarket?'

'I'm not sure. I can ask,' he said, though he didn't think they needed anyone. 'Hang on a moment, I'll get my laptop.'

When he was back with it he found information about the local jobcentre and some websites advertising vacancies. When he was about to close it down, she exclaimed at his desktop picture. It was one of his own making, the girl he'd modelled on his sister's friend.

'You did that? It's great.'

'It's for a story I'm writing, drawing, I mean. You know, a graphic novel.'

'Wow, really? Will you show me?'

He saw that she really was interested, so he opened a document and scrolled through some of the pictures for her and explained what he was doing.

'It's amazing,' she whispered. 'You're really good,' and he felt a swell of pride.

'It'll need to be. It's a very competitive area,' he remarked as he closed the file.

Her expression set and for a second he thought it was because of something he'd said, but then she wrested a vibrating phone from her jeans back pocket and tapped on the screen then stared at the result, dismay clouding her face.

'Are you all right, Stef?'

She sighed and lowered her head. In the background the washing machine stopped sloshing and began to make a sucking noise.

'Stupid of me. You're not, are you?'

'It's OK,' she muttered. 'It's Oliver. He keeps texting me. I shouldn't have turned the phone on.'

'Oliver. That's your boyfriend, right?'

A nod. 'I feel awful. He sounds really upset. Perhaps I shouldn't have left.' The horrid draining noise stopped abruptly.

'Why did you?' Rick said softly into the silence.

'It's difficult to explain.' Now the machine cranked once more into action, its spin rising to a deafening wailing sound that went on for several minutes. Rick shut down his laptop, painfully aware of Stef wiping her eyes as she tapped into her phone. When the machine quietened to a whine and thudded to a final halt she glanced up, unseeing. Rick saw that the crumb of mascara was now smeared across her cheek.

'Your make-up's run. Let me,' he said, unable not to, and reached with his little finger to wipe it away. Her cheek was wet and she sat blinking at him as she submitted to his touch.

'That's better.' He stood up, a little embarrassed by himself, and he was aware of her watching as he dragged the damp washing from the machine into a basket.

'I'll help you hang it out if you like.'

'Thanks,' he said. 'It's not a job I'm good at.'

It was sunny out in the garden and Stef's spirits seemed to lighten. She giggled at his cack-handed efforts with a bedsheet and showed him how to fold it and peg it up in scalloped pleats so that it didn't take up half the line.

'You're as bad as my sister. She always laughs at me trying to be domestic.'

'I'm not surprised. It's obvious you're not remotely interested. Here, grab the end of this.'

'I can't help it,' he said, taking the duvet cover, enjoying her instructing him. 'There are more important things in life to do than the washing.'

'You'll have to get rich then,' she said, reaching into the peg bag, 'and pay someone else to do it.'

'Yeah, well, not much chance of that at the moment.'

'Perhaps you will. Maybe one day your story will sell millions.'

'Hurry along, that day! I have to finish it first.'

He handed her pieces of clothing, and watched her pin them deftly on the line. She laughed at a shirt with a rip down one sleeve. 'You'd better finish that story quickly!'

'I'm trying to!' He grinned. She was a different creature out here from the miserable bundle that had huddled in the kitchen. The spring air, he supposed, and getting busy. He'd felt protective of her inside, but out here in the garden she was in charge, laughing at him, and he didn't mind. Perversely, it made him happy.

These past couple of years he'd hidden himself away, taken a mundane job, put everything into his writing. He'd been happy, was grateful to Leonie for helping him, but now he sensed there was something else, a world beyond the greyish blue of his bedroom wallpaper, the evenings spent alone in the glare of his computer screen. He had friends, for goodness' sake, he wasn't a freak, but he hadn't seen many of them for a while though they chatted on Facebook. Now he thought he might get together with Sam for a drink, maybe introduce him and Tanya to Stef. Just as friends, of course, he didn't dare imagine ... His thoughts were running too far ahead. Stef was holding the peg bag and was simply standing staring down the garden, a faraway look on her face that twisted his heart.

'Well, thanks. You were a great help,' he said, and she

sent him a smile so distracted he feared he'd lost her. 'I'll remember that trick with the sheets.' She allowed him to take the peg bag from her. He picked up the empty washing basket and walked slowly back to the house. As he opened the back door he turned and saw her take her phone out of her pocket once more and stare at it, a confused expression on her face.

Leonie

Her friend Trudi was right about some things and one of them was definitely Peter. Leonie was furious with him. Every now and then, out of the kindness of her heart, she would descend to his basement rooms and try her best to clean them.

This morning as she was washing up after breakfast she watched him lever open a tin of ham and make himself a stack of sandwiches and, hope leaping, asked casually if he was going out. 'Yep. Fishing with Jeff,' was his unusually cheerful reply as he stowed the sandwiches inside a rucksack. Jeff was an old friend of Peter who travelled round markets all over Europe selling antique silver, only surfacing every now and then when it suited him.

Sure enough, twenty minutes later, Peter returned to the kitchen with a bag of rods and went to the fridge. In the twinkling of an eye two tins of lager had joined the sandwiches in the rucksack. Glancing over at Leonie mischievously, wisps of white hair backlit by the fridge light forming a halo around his craggy face, he winked. She shook her head and frowned. Both of them knew the lager wasn't his to take.

After he'd gone, she pondered how to spend her day. Actually, she longed to get on with her work – the owner of Arthur the Weimaraner had been on the phone to enquire after the picture, which was to be a gift to her husband on his birthday – but Leonie hadn't cleaned in the basement for ever so long and today was an unexpected opportunity. It would have to be done.

She tied on an apron, collected the hoover, a roll of bin bags and various cloths and sprays and, with some trepidation, descended the stairs from the hall to Peter's lair. The door had no lock, but when she shoved it opened only reluctantly. Poking her head round, she saw why. A stack of finished canvases stored against the wall behind was toppling over. 'Blast,' she muttered and felt for the light switch, then pushed her way in with all her stuff and stared round the gloomy sitting room with a sinking sense of despair. The curtains were still drawn and the stink in the room was vile, rank, like a wild animal's den, though no animal except Peter could be responsible for the high note of turpentine.

The pile of canvases by the door and a canvas up on an easel in the window were the only signs of organization in the room, which was otherwise a mess of painting materials, old newspapers and general clutter. A small television of antique vintage brooded in a dark corner, and, balanced on the arms of a moribund armchair where he must sit to watch it, and on the coffee table near by, were stacked the remnants of a dozen meals. She crossed the room, pulled back the curtains and threw open the sash window, and the bright daylight from the street immediately reflected on a half-eaten tin of baked beans down on the floor by the easel. Picking it up, she tried not to gag at the spots of green mould on its crusted contents. Into the bin bag it went, to be followed swiftly by fruit peel and several apple cores as she worked back towards the coffee table.

The stained mugs there she set on an abandoned tray, leaving a pool of milky liquid spilled across the wood, which was scarred with notches as though he'd cut food straight onto it. Then it was the turn of the plates and cereal bowls with their glaze of hardened food. She clattered them together, all the while cursing Peter under her breath by every name she could think of, none of which she'd ever dare say to his face.

'You wretched, stinking, selfish, rude, charmless, ungrateful old ... old ... git ... oh!' Lifting a towel from the floor she'd uncovered a scattering of grey moths crawling round a hole in the carpet. 'Disgusting!' She reached for one of the cans and sprayed the moths furiously. Beyond the sitting room was the bedroom and she didn't like to imagine what that looked like. Or the tiny bathroom beyond. She scooped up the tray of crockery and stomped back upstairs with it. It would all need to soak in the sink before she tried to wash any of it. She ran a furious spray of water into the bowl and added a big squeeze of detergent.

Back downstairs again, she did her best to restore

order. There were dustsheets around the easel, and these were spotted with paint, but smudges on the carpet elsewhere betrayed that Peter had walked paint around the room. She rubbed at the smudges with a rag dipped in brush cleaner, but it made little difference. 'Pig!' she murmured under her breath. '*Cochon*, swine, *Schwein*,' she added for good measure. What was Spanish for pig? she wondered.

It wasn't only Trudi who was puzzled by her tolerance of Peter – if tolerance it was, for she didn't feel tolerant of him at all – all her friends were, to say nothing of the other inhabitants of the house. Only Leonie knew. Peter was her burden, the price she paid for living here.

'It's a promise I made,' she would explain patiently to anyone who ventured to ask. 'He's not a bad person, just a bit lost.' Peter had always been lost and that was the truth. When she'd inherited this house Peter had come with it, a sitting tenant. He was part of the deal. She simply had to put up with him.

Trudi had tried quite hard. 'You could sell the house,' she'd said. 'Then he'd have to go.'

'It's not as simple as that. Anyway, I would never sell the house. I love it too much.'

'If you sold the house you could buy two places for the price you'd get and give him one.'

'I can't, Trudi, I simply can't. Who'd look after him? At least this way he has his own place. Sort of. And I can keep an eye on him. He doesn't bother me that much really.'

'What about the rats? They bothered you all right.'

'Yes, that was bad.' Leonie shuddered. It had been five years ago. The neighbours had complained and she'd had to get the council pest controller in. It was all the food Peter left around, that was the trouble. She made him keep a dish of rat poison in his sitting room now, and tried to clean regularly, but it was hard work.

Peter was a burden, but he was not an unbearable one. Sometimes he could be quite sweet. He had been kind to her daughter all that time ago, and to Jamie, too – he liked children, was something of a child himself, and he'd never harm anyone. He didn't ever lose his temper, he was simply grumpy and selfish.

By the time she'd finished cleaning it was midday and she sank onto a chair at the kitchen table with a cup of sugary coffee and a sigh of relief, for the moment too exhausted to make herself lunch. She no longer had the energy for industrial cleans, she decided. Either she'd have to force herself to see to Peter's rooms more regularly or she would need to pay someone to do it for her. There was no hope now of making Peter do it himself. Old dogs wouldn't learn new tricks – that chance had long gone.

Yet how would she afford a cleaner? She could hardly commandeer one of the other residents, could she? The arrangements for the rest of the house worked quite well. Everyone was responsible for their own rooms and Bela, without being asked, cleaned the two upstairs bathrooms regularly, albeit very slowly, and swept the hall and stairs. It gave her something to do, she would

always tell Leonie. To show her gratitude Leonie liked
to give her small inexpensive presents: home-made
carrot cake, which Bela adored, and once Leonie painted
for her from a photograph a portrait of Hari and Bela's
beloved daughter, who lived in New Jersey. Bela was
so overcome with tears and wailing at this gift that
Leonie was worried that she'd upset her. But after that
it appeared that Bela would do anything for Leonie and
they became firm friends. It was above all Bela who in
small ways showed her concern for Leonie when Jamie
left, alone in recognizing the depths of Leonie's attach-
ment to the youngster and the pain she felt at separation.
Still, she didn't want to presume on Bela's friendship and
ask her to do further work in the house. Bela was getting
older, too, and her health was far from good. Sometimes
Leonie heard her coughing and wheezing from the dust
as she cleaned.

It was as she was examining some wilting salad in the
fridge for her lunch that Stef came into the kitchen.

Glancing up Leonie saw at once there was something
wrong. Or rather, more wrong than usual. Stef's eyes
were huge and anxious in her small face and her gaze
darted around the room without focusing on any one
thing. She clenched and unclenched her fists in a contin-
uous restless movement.

'Have you had any lunch?' Leonie said in as calm
a voice as she could muster. 'I can make you a cheese
sandwich if you like.'

'Oh, no thank you, I'm not hungry.'

'Some fruit juice, perhaps.'

'Yeah, I'd like that.'

She sat down at the table in her graceful cat-like way, one leg twisted under her, her elbows propped on the table and her chin resting in one hand, the finger of the other playing with a strand of her hair.

'What's the matter, dear?' Leonie asked, placing a glass of juice in front of her. She sprinkled a bowl of greenery with grated cheese for herself and brought it to the table before settling down opposite.

'I'm not sure what to do. Oh, I can't make up my mind.'

'About what?'

'It's Oliver . . .'

'Your boyfriend?' Leonie said.

Stef nodded. 'I keep getting texts from him. He's terribly upset that I've left and . . . I feel awful about it. I suppose . . . well, I still love him, you see.' She was struggling with herself, trying not to cry. Leonie felt a rush of tenderness for her.

'Why did you leave if you love him?'

'I . . . I had to. There was a discussion on a morning TV show, and I knew they were talking about me. No, that sounds wrong, but I realized it was my situation exactly. He . . . Oh, I'll sound a complete idiot, but it's like he controls me. But the worst of it is, like, I let him. I see that now. I let him!' At this she covered her face with her hands and made a snuffling sound.

Leonie put down her fork and pushed the bowl away. She'd been tired and hungry, but now her appetite had quite gone. Instead she felt a swell of sympathy for

Stef fill her throat and for a moment she could hardly breathe. A shadow fell across her mind and she licked her lips, which were suddenly dry. It'll pass, she told herself, and after a moment she could breathe again.

'Stef,' she said, almost sternly, and the girl dropped her hands. Her face was creased, exhausted.

'I'm sorry.'

'There's nothing to be sorry for.'

For a moment there was silence between them, then Stef fished a tissue out of her sleeve and wiped her nose.

'Why don't you tell me. It might help.'

Stef shrugged, still lost in her private misery.

Leonie hunted around for the right entrée. 'How did you meet him? Tell me that.'

'Oh, that was funny, well, no, it wasn't really.' And she told Leonie about the business lunch when she'd accidentally spilled food on one of the guests. 'I liked him right away. He sorted everything out so cleverly, and the next moment he was like a little boy, asking for pudding.'

'His surname isn't Twist, by any chance.'

'No, it's Redman.' Stef look bemused, then she saw the joke and laughed. 'It was wonderful at first. We became close really quickly. It was like he was a relative or something, except he wasn't, obviously. I had only been working in London for a year or two and nothing had been going right. I was living in this really gross place, where there were guys dealing drugs, and I was going to try to get a flat with some girls I knew, but it didn't work out.'

Leonie was amused by how Stef spoke less formally as she relaxed into her story.

'But then, it was a couple of months after we met, Oliver asked me to move in with him. He lives in this amazing place.' She described a modern apartment block near the river built around communal gardens. How Oliver, who was on a high salary, paid for everything.

'I left my job. I hated it and they were fed up with me. Then I did bits and pieces with a temp agency, you know, catering work, but they were always messing me about so Oliver said why didn't I stop for a bit and think about what I wanted to do, and that was it, really. But that's when it started to happen. I did think and, this might sound mad, but I wanted to do something with textiles. Fashion design or something. But whatever idea I came up with seemed silly.'

'Silly?'

'Oliver would point out that it would mean I'd have to go to college and I hadn't done well at school, my A levels were rubbish, and when I started looking up courses online and they all said I needed a portfolio he wasn't encouraging. He'd criticize my drawings, say they weren't professional enough, and in the end I lost confidence. That sounds pathetic, doesn't it? I mean I should just believe in myself and get on with it, but, actually, it really got to me.'

She looked imploringly at Leonie, who said quietly, 'I can see how it would.'

'So, after a while, I didn't exactly lose interest in it but

I stopped bothering so much. I told myself I'd do it after Christmas, and then Christmas went by and I didn't. Oliver started getting annoyed about all sorts of things. What I wore, if I didn't tidy up after myself properly, and he didn't like me going out in the evenings unless it was with him. It was ridiculous, I can see that now, but it was my fault too. I should have ignored him, but somehow it wasn't easy to do. I don't know, I thought it was best to do what he said because then there wouldn't be a row.'

Leonie nodded. She recognized that feeling.

'It was little things sometimes,' Stef said. She was playing with her hair again, twirling a lock round and round her finger and staring into the distance. Leonie wanted to put out a hand to stop her, as she had with her own daughter when she'd done that, but of course she resisted.

'He didn't want me to go to a school reunion. He said it would take up a whole weekend. Once, you won't believe this, he got upset because one of the remotes went missing. It turned out it was my fault. I'd acciden-tally taken it into the bathroom when I was in a hurry and I'd left it there. You know, it's easy to happen, but he said I'd hidden it deliberately and was really mean about it. I know I'm annoying. I can be quite scatty and forget stuff, but I don't do it on purpose.'

Again it was as though she appealed to Leonie, who said, 'Of course not. Most people are like you. I know I am.'

'But I still feel bad, like I haven't worked hard enough

at things. I tried to talk to him about it, but he doesn't see there's a problem.'

'Why do you think he's like this?'

Stef sighed. 'I suppose it's a control thing, that's what you're going to say. Those women on the television, they said it, too, that men who do it are really insecure.'

'And is he?'

'Yeah, I suppose he is. I don't know his mum and dad very well but I think they're like it too. I mean it's probably the way he was brought up. Their house is really, really tidy, like you can't even put a cup of coffee down unless there's a little mat and you have to take your shoes off when you go into the house. That's one of the things I like about living here.' She smiled at Leonie. 'Nobody cares about that stuff.'

'You wouldn't have said that if you saw me earlier,' Leonie said, with a low laugh. 'I've spent all morning cleaning Peter's lair.'

'Doesn't he do it himself?' Stef's eyes were pools of surprise.

'Peter? Clean? I don't think he notices the dirt. I know exactly what he'll say when he comes back – he's gone fishing for the day, by the way. He'll go downstairs, then he'll come back and say, "Who's moved my things?" Never so much as a thank-you.'

'I can't believe you do that.' Stef was looking increasingly horrified.

Leonie laughed. 'But never mind that. You were saying. About Oliver's parents.'

'Yes ... When I went last, after Christmas, his dad

got himself in a really bad mood because Oliver's mum said she'd invited another couple over on New Year's Eve. "I'm fed up with never doing anything," she told him. "We have to sit here by ourselves while everyone else is enjoying themselves, so I've asked the Sampsons over." I was simply sitting and quietly eating breakfast, I think they hardly noticed I was there. And he gave her such a look, I can hardly describe it. His face went white. He was furious. And she got up and started clearing the table, and I could see her hands were shaking ...'

'Stef,' Leonie said, trying to keep her voice even. 'I know it's none of my business, but does Oliver ever, you know, hurt you?'

'Oh, he'd never do that,' Stef said swiftly. But as they stared at one another it was as though some border had been crossed and Leonie saw evidence of hidden knowledge in the girl's face.

'Because if he does,' she said slowly, 'that's absolutely beyond the pale and you were right to do something about it.'

'He doesn't.' Stef was trembling. 'It's just ...' She stopped.

'You think he might?' Leonie whispered.

Stef tipped her glass, frowned at the dregs of her juice, then quickly nodded.

The sun moved away from the window and the kitchen fell into sudden shadow. Slowly, Leonie reached for Stef's other hand on the table and covered it with her own.

Stef

She knew. Stef understood that Leonie knew. She couldn't say exactly how, whether it was the compassionate look the older woman gave her, or the way Stef's own unhappiness was mirrored in her face, but she knew.

Stef hadn't liked to admit it to herself until now, now that Leonie had asked her the question directly. 'I suppose,' she said slowly, 'to be honest, I'm sometimes frightened of Oliver. There have been a couple of times – oh, stupid things, you'll probably laugh.'

'No, I won't.'

'OK, well that time when the telly remote went missing.'

It had been as though his sudden failure to be able to control the television represented a loss of control over his whole life, and certainly over his temper.

He'd stomped about the living room, throwing cushions on the floor and pushing his fingers down the sides of the sofa, then, like a wrestler, had flipped an armchair onto its back in his frantic search. 'You must have used it last,' he shouted. 'I left it last night right there.' He gave the table a sharp tap where the controls to the MP3, the DVD player and the games console still lay obediently side by side. 'If you put it back in its proper place each time, then we'd be OK.'

'I don't think it was me,' she'd said. 'I didn't watch anything today. And don't get so cross. It's only a thing.'

At that, rage leaped into his eyes. 'You know it annoys me, yet you're always doing it,' he shouted. 'Why do you do it when you know it annoys me?'

'I don't do it to annoy you, Oliver.'

'You must, or you wouldn't do it. I've told you so many times.' He took a step towards her and in an instinctive gesture she moved so that the sofa stood between them. Her obvious fear seemed to check him, because the rage in his face suddenly died and he sank down into the second armchair and remained hunched there in a sulk, leaving Stef to right the upset room and continue the search.

It was half an hour later that she found the remote on the bathroom cupboard. She bore it back to Oliver in both hands like a medieval page bearing a coronet on a cushion.

'I'm sorry,' she said as she presented it to him and watched his face light up. 'It must have been me. I did use it this morning, I remember now. Then I needed the nail scissors and couldn't have been thinking properly. I didn't do it on purpose, Oliver, I wasn't trying to make you cross.'

How whining she must have sounded, yet she was genuinely sorry that she'd upset him. And frightened, too. That moment when they'd faced one another across the sofa. She remembered even now how pinched his face was with anger, how his fists were balled. How, for a moment, she'd thought . . .

It wasn't the only time. There was the occasion he'd pushed her. Not hard, but he'd wanted to reach into a cupboard and he couldn't because she was unloading the dishwasher. 'Get out of my way,' he'd muttered. He hadn't hurt her, but she'd been shocked at his impatience. It had been one of those evenings when he'd hardly spoken. A deal had gone badly wrong at work, she'd gathered that much, and he'd sunk into one of his sullen moods. He apologized later in bed and explained about the deal. A colleague hadn't given him the right figures in time and he had gone into the meeting ill-prepared.

'I'm sorry if I took it out on you, I'm sorry, I'm sorry.' His voice almost cracked with grief and this touched her. She rolled over and put her arms round him.

'It's all right,' she soothed. It was as though she were cuddling her child. He clung to her in the gloom and it made her feel happy and important to be a source of strength and forgiveness to him. This was what relationships should be like, she imagined. She and Oliver should depend on one another, succour one another.

Some of this she tried to explain to Leonie now, encouraged by the fact that Leonie simply listened, nodding from time to time, or asking a question for clarification.

Then when Stef had finished, Leonie asked gently, 'What about your needs, Stef? Does he do the same for you?'

Stef sat up and pushed her chair back, surprised. 'Of course,' she said. She gathered up her hair as she thought. 'He gave me a home and he paid for everything. He's been so kind, when I've felt so lost.'

'So why did you leave?'

'I don't know ... I suppose ... I felt invisible. Like I'm not worth anything.'

'And now?'

'I feel that ... I've thrown it all away. I don't know what to do with my life.'

'I felt the same once,' Leonie said.

'I can't believe that. You seem such a strong person.'

A twitch of a smile. 'When I first moved here. There's something about this house, though, that made me feel secure.'

'There is, isn't there,' Stef said, glancing round the kitchen, feeling the comfort of it. It wasn't simply the kettle sitting on the old Aga, the solid wood table at which they sat, the view of the garden, spring flowers swaying in the breeze. It was almost as though she could catch the presence of the people who'd lived here in the past. Not in a scary way, simply as though she might walk into one of the rooms and see a parlour maid dusting the mantelpiece, or a boy lining up his lead soldiers on the polished floor. Would they see her? Would she be like a ghost to them?

'Do you think it's haunted?'

Leonie looked at her shrewdly. 'Not in the way people usually mean, spectral figures and cold patches, no. Least, I've never seen or heard anything, but you get a sense of people's lives, the healing effects of passing time. Do you know, the people in one of the flats next door, when I was on better terms with them, invited me in for drinks one Christmas, and in that flat it felt as though all the past had been scoured away. I hope no one ever does that here.' Stef liked the affectionate way Leonie surveyed the kitchen. It didn't matter that everything was a jumble, that the furniture was mismatched. From the odd selection of plates on the old Welsh dresser to the dried flowers hanging upside down by the Aga to the New York calendar pinned to a corkboard, the place felt comfortable, lived in.

In noticing these things Stef realized she felt calmer. 'Thank you,' she said suddenly. 'For listening, I mean.'

'Oh, that costs little,' Leonie laughed.

'What do you mean, though, that you felt like me?'

'It was all a long time ago. You don't want to hear an old woman's story.'

'I do. That is, if you want to tell me. I don't want to, like, be nosy.'

'Oh goodness, girl. It's not that, exactly, it's in knowing which bits to tell you. Making it make sense.'

'Tell me more about Peter, then. He must have lived here for ever.'

'Not for ever, no, but he was certainly here when I first came. That was 1972. I must have been twenty-eight. The man who owned this house was a friend of mine. His name was George. George Stuart. He was a television director, but not a very successful one. He made comedy series for ITV, but they weren't very funny and I don't think you'd have heard of any of them now. Still he was a lovely man and he'd inherited this house from a rather raffish great-uncle and since George didn't have any family himself or anything he let people come and stay. Many of them were friends and acquaintances. Some were in trouble of some sort. He charged them

ridiculously low rents and of course some couldn't pay –
or wouldn't, I should say.'

'And Peter?'

'When he was a young man Peter was much more ...
engaging. I think you need to know his background and
about things that happened to him before you judge him
too harshly. He was exceptionally good-looking, for a
start. Too good-looking really, combined with being
very vulnerable. I won't go into the sordid details, but it
meant that he often fell victim to people who used him.
Men on the make who had earned too much money too
quickly and believed that they had a right to take what
they wanted. George rescued him and we sorted out
the basement flat for him to do his painting. There was
plenty of light through the window once we cut down
the hedge. You've seen some of his paintings, haven't
you, in my drawing room?'

'The swirly ones, yes, but I like the picture of Jamie
best, your grandson.'

Stef regretted mentioning Jamie, because an expression of sadness passed over Leonie's face.

'Yes, of course. I'd forgotten you had seen that. Well,
that's not typical of his work. Nor are the swirly ones. I
suppose it's best if I show you. I don't think he'd mind.'
She rose from the table and Stef followed her out to the
hall.

'You'll have to believe me when I say that it's ten
times better in here than it was a few hours ago,'
Leonie said grimly as she pushed open the door to the
basement.

'Oh,' Stef said, blinking in the sudden light. The room smelled strongly of chemicals and she sneezed.

Leonie was already bent over the stack of canvases against the wall. Stef knelt beside her. It was difficult at first to work out what the images were on the ones Leonie held up to the light. They were vortexes of energy in thick impasto worked over and over with layer upon layer of paint. Only when Leonie held one or two up at a distance could she begin to work it out. There were pictures of dense forests, the trees dwarfing figures of people and animals, the stuff of dreams, tranquil ones mostly.

'They're ... good,' Stef ventured, wondering if this was the right answer.

'He's talented, isn't he?' Leonie said. 'The trouble is he doesn't paint anything that anyone wants to buy. Oh, sometimes he'll take on a commission, a portrait or something, but he doesn't put himself out for people so it's not that often. And there's a friend, an art dealer, who occasionally takes a picture off him, but I think out of sympathy rather than for any other reason.'

Stef paused before a painting of a hut in a forest. Through the window a shrivelled old man like a gnome could be seen peeping out. The scene had the aura of a dream and she found herself drawn in. 'This is weird,' she said.

'Mmm, isn't it?' Leonie took the painting and propped it on the sofa and they both stared at it for a minute or two. 'It casts a spell, though. You know, it was Peter who got me drawing and painting. I will always owe him for that. I did animals because I was good at them. And there was more work to be had painting animals than people.'

Stef nodded. 'So you met Peter when you came to live here?'

'Yes. George was very fond of him.' As she spoke Leonie started restacking the canvases. Stef helped her and they went back upstairs. 'Come in a moment,' Leonie said, opening the door to her drawing room. 'I'll show you something.'

She moved over to a bookcase, the lowest shelf of which housed a number of outsized volumes. From this she selected a large square plastic-covered album decorated with geometric shapes.

It was, Stef saw, as Leonie opened it, full of photographs, and some of the pages were coming away from the spine. Leonie found the place she wanted and came to sit on the sofa next to Stef, laying the album across both their laps.

'Here.' She pointed at one of several monochrome snaps in the middle of the album, a shot of two men in what Stef recognized as the kitchen of Number 11. They were standing in a pool of sunshine. The older man, burly, hands in pockets, smiled cheerfully at the camera, the light making his fleshy face and balding head shine. The other, laughing, one hand pushed through his curly hair, smoke coiling from a cigarette stub held in the other, was a man of a different order, lithe, saturnine, his eye caught by something beyond the frame of the photograph. It took Stef a moment or two to realize that it was Peter.

'This is George. You'd have liked him. Everybody liked George. It was taken soon after I arrived. He must have been forty-two or -three then.'

'But Peter, you're right, he was good-looking.'

'He was, he was.' Leonie sighed. 'You wouldn't think it now, would you? George was besotted with him, but Peter has only ever been interested in himself. That's why George left the house to me. He died of a brain tumour in 1980, never came round from an operation. It was the saddest time.'

'And he left you the house. Why didn't he ...?' Stef hesitated, wondering if she was prying.

'Why didn't he leave it to Peter? The truth is he thought I was more reliable. Goodness knows what Peter would have done with the place. Sold it, I imagine, and spent all the money on ... oh, frittered it away, anyway. And I suppose he saw that I needed it more. Because I had a child.'

There was a catch in Leonie's voice that made Stef look at her, but Leonie's face was shielded by a veil of hair. Then came a rustle as Leonie pushed back the tissue paper that hid the photographs on the opposite page of the album, and Stef's gaze fell upon the face of a beautiful young woman with a tiny rosy-faced girl in a blue button-up coat and wellingtons.

'That's Tara.' They were in the snowy back garden here at Number 11, standing by a snowman wearing what must have been the woman's red woolly hat, though the orangey tint of the old print distorted the original colours.

'She's so sweet.'

'She's my only child. Jamie's mother. She lives in Brighton and I don't see her very often.'

Now Stef was staring at the photo again, but this time at the young Leonie. She really had been striking, her light-coloured hair blowing around her face. There was something about the confidence with which she confronted the camera that prompted Stef's curiosity. Where had she seen that look before?

'It's odd to think I have a daughter in her forties. That makes me feel so old.' Leonie laughed, but it wasn't a happy laugh. 'I do wish I saw her more. You see . . .'

Out in the hall the telephone began to ring. 'Oh dear . . .' Leonie sighed and got up to answer it. Stef could hear her through the open door, conversing about cats and oil paints, and wondered what Leonie had been going to say about her daughter. She stared at the album lying open on the sofa where Leonie had left it, the tissue paper fluttering in a draught.

She reached out a hand and turned back a page, then another and another, all the while her astonishment growing. There were dozens of colour prints of Leonie, but a young Leonie transformed into one of the models she'd seen in the old magazines upstairs. Leonie dressed in a crocheted blue suit, her hair pinned up onto her head, her eyes fringed pools of intrigue, her skin flawless. In a long halter-neck evening dress, her neat head crowned with a tiara. Here she was with her hair resting on her shoulders, the ends flicked up, her arms held out like wings to show off a minidress with a short policeman-style cape. The effect was completely stunning, sophisticated and assured.

So caught up was Stef in the album that she didn't realize Leonie had finished her call until she sensed her cross the room.

'I'm sorry,' Stef mumbled, putting down the album. 'I shouldn't have looked.'

'It doesn't matter. Not really.'

'There were some magazines upstairs . . . I didn't realize that it was you in them until now.'

'I'd forgotten I'd kept them. It must all seem rather a long time ago to you.'

'The Swinging Sixties are really in. I can't believe you were part of it. It must have been so exciting.'

'It was, I suppose. Bits of it. I think back on it now and can hardly believe that person was me.'

'You looked so glamorous.'

Leonie laughed. 'If you could see your face. "Starry-eyed" doesn't do it justice.'

'It sounds fascinating though. Go on, you must have known everyone. Twiggy and people like that.'

'I did meet her, Twiggy, yes. She was nice.'

'So how did you get into it? Did you go to modelling school?'

'I did, but it really started way before then.' Was it Stef's imagination, or did Leonie's voice tremble. 'It was when I was eighteen and met Billy, or . . .' Leonie paused to reflect. 'Perhaps it was longer ago than that. I was brought up in Suffolk, in a little market town near the coast called Saxford.'

Suffolk, January 1958

Like most teenagers, Leonie thought her parents were embarrassing. Dad was Harold Brett of H.E. Brett, Draper, Saxford, and Mum, Dolly Brett, when she wasn't busy looking after Leonie and her younger brother Bobby, managed the haberdashery side for him, selling ribbons and artificial flowers for hats, bits of lace and reels of cotton. They were proud that their daughter had squeaked through the eleven-plus and attended the grammar school in Ipswich, but now that she was old enough they were glad of her help behind the counter during the holidays. It was this work and reading trade catalogues sent to the shop that fuelled her early interest in fashion. H. E. Brett's stocked some of the easy-care new fabrics, which were proving very popular, especially with the youth, and she used to enjoy making her own dresses with them or artfully adapting old ones. Her father would give her remnants from rolls of material, and her mother let her have bits and pieces from her trays, especially anything that was shop-worn or damaged and thus difficult to sell.

Later in life Leonie would appreciate what a courageous woman her mother was, but as a young teen she sometimes felt ashamed of her. She would have been delicately pretty with her fair hair and blue eyes except that she had a livid scar in the shape of a handprint along her jaw and down her neck. She would cover it as best she could with high-collared blouses and often wore a silk scarf around her neck, even in summer. The scar made her self-conscious and shy and sometimes standoffish with people she didn't know and trust, but her dad obviously didn't mind it and certainly never referred to it. It was the result of a childhood accident with a boiling kettle, but to her mother it was a disability, and Leonie noticed how she'd touch it or shield it with her hand while she was talking to customers and Leonie hated her doing this, though she wasn't able to explain to herself why. Perhaps it was for this reason, though, that she admired physical beauty so much and would pore over the flawless skin of the models in her mother's magazines.

It was while Leonie was helping in the shop one day early in the new year that something happened to make her look beyond Saxford and ordinary life. She was turning fourteen and growing up fast, but, like a baby giraffe, she wasn't used to her gawky new shape. She'd been chubby as a child, but now the puppy fat had gone and her dad teased her about being clumsy. It was true, she was always bumping into things and falling over her own feet. That very morning he'd scolded her for knocking over a revolving stand full of sewing patterns, and she was still collecting them all up and slotting them back into their places when the shop bell tinkled and she glanced up to see a smart mature lady she didn't recognize enter carrying a dress box under one arm. Leonie's father returned her brisk 'Good morning' and stared after her with curiosity as she walked over to the haberdashery counter, court shoes tapping on the wooden floor, before going back to his stocktaking.

'I want a replacement zip-fastener for this,' the new-comer said to Leonie's mother, and she opened her box and shook out a dress of a gorgeous shiny apricot material. 'The silly thing kept sticking,' she explained as Leonie's mother measured the broken zip, 'and I'm afraid I yanked it too hard. Such a nuisance. I'm staying at the Hall and I've left my other evening gowns in London. One of the maids says that she'll mend it if I can find the right zip.'

'The zip's not a regular length.' Her mother turned and started sorting through drawers for one the right size. Meanwhile, Leonie was aware of the customer watching as she scrabbled on the floor for the last of the patterns. The lady bent down gracefully and picked up one that had slid almost under the counter.

'You've missed this, dear,' she said, holding it out.

'Thank you,' Leonie said, nearly over-balancing as she took it. She felt her face pink up as she wiped the dust off the pattern. She knew she must appear a fright from crawling around in the dirt and was conscious that her hair was all over the place. She'd washed it the night before and slept on it and it had fluffed up like a halo around her face.

The lady was so beautifully turned out that it made sense she was from London. London seemed a far-off place to Leonie, though she'd been there on school trips to museums, and once to Madame Tussauds for a birth-day treat. She'd loved the grand parks and riding past Selfridge's on a red bus and spotting the fashionably dressed people in Regent Street, but if the weather was dull it could be a drab and noisy place, full of black umbrellas when it rained, which it often seemed to, and people didn't smile at you in the street or ask, 'Are you all right?' like they did in Saxford.

This lady had a glossy sheen about her that you didn't see in rural Suffolk. She must have been only a little younger than her mother, but to Leonie she was perfect, slim and poised, and she loved the way she wore her little hat tipped to one side. Her cherry-red coat was beautifully soft, Leonie knew, because the cuff had brushed against her hand as she'd taken the pattern from her.

'Is this young lady your daughter?' the lady asked, smiling, when her mother returned to the counter triumphantly bearing the right zip. 'She must be. She's got your good looks.'

'Oh nonsense,' her mum said with a surprised laugh, her hand flying to her jaw, but the woman was smiling at Leonie and didn't notice. Leonie thought her comment a bit personal, though at the same time she lapped up the compliment. No one had ever said she was good-looking before or called her a young lady except when they were chiding her. Both the Brett family and her mother's were suspicious of that sort of talk. They'd say 'Handsome is as handsome does' and 'Beauty is in the eye of the beholder'. Mrs Brett senior, Leonie's widowed grandma, was a devout church-goer and firmly set the tone. Whether you were pretty or not wasn't important, it was how you were inside that mattered.

At the same time Leonie knew from the odd comment that grown-ups made when they thought children were not listening that her eyes were her finest feature, so she always took care to wear blue if she could to match them. She was wearing a pale blue shirt and cardigan that day, though they were grimy from the pattern search. You could have knocked her down though after what the lady from London said next. 'Have you ever thought of her becoming a model?'

It was as much as Leonie could do to stare in amazement and when she glanced at her mother it was to see she was taken aback, too, but the lady said, 'I'm quite serious. She's a little young yet, but she has the right height and bone structure.' She was staring at Leonie quite critically now, as though she were a mare she was buying, and this made her feel uncomfortable. 'I write for *Vogue*,' the lady went on, 'and I assure you the magazines are always looking out for girls like yours, girls who have something about them.'

Leonie's joy knew no bounds, but her mother disappointed her by muttering that her daughter should be keeping to her schoolwork for the moment, and the lady said of course she understood and paid for her zip and left.

'What rubbish,' her mother murmured, glaring at the departing figure. They watched the woman ease herself into the driving seat of a shiny green car and desolation swept over Leonie.

'Why are you always so crushing,' she cried with all the passion a teenage girl can muster. She was sure that she'd missed some wonderful opportunity that would never come again.

'Say sorry to your mother,' her father snapped from a

stepladder at the back of the shop where he was counting boxes. 'And don't go getting silly ideas in your head.
You've plenty enough to be doing here, girl.'

But it was no good him saying that because the
elegant lady's words had slid into Leonie's head and
bedded down. Over the next year or two, they were to
grow and flourish.

Four

Rosa

'Wait here, will you? They'll bring him along in a minute.' The warder who'd escorted her to the visiting room sounded bored. He did not smile as he left. She held the worn Formica surface of the table for support as she sat down in the chair that was fixed to it and in a mind's flash was in a bare classroom again, copying down sums from the blackboard into an exercise book. Though screwed to the floor, the table and chair were rickety and wobbled. She cast her eyes around the room at the others there, couples sitting face to face, speaking earnestly or gazing past one another in strained silence. An exhausted-looking mother clutched the hands of her inmate son, a lumpy shaven-headed lad who stared sullenly down at the table. 'You should be so lucky!' An indignant voice rose above the general murmuring and everyone's eyes fastened upon a small worn woman, who'd half risen from her chair, the prisoner opposite her, a man of twice her size in every direction, grabbing at her hand and begging her to sit. The two warders watching from opposite sides of the room looked as bored as the one who'd shown Rosa in.

It seemed an age before another door to the room opened and a slightly built man in the regulation navy tracksuit came in. There was an air of dispiritedness about him and his cropped hair was dusted with grey. He glanced about and it was an instant before Rosa recognized him.

She stood up slowly in growing dismay. His eyes met hers in recognition then shifted away. He shuffled towards her and she saw with a shock that his slippers were too big for him. It was something that had always been very noticeable about her father, his small neat feet in polished leather shoes, and she could only guess at his humiliation now. He did not try to kiss her, instead eased himself onto the chair across from her. Finally his gaze lifted and she met the kind face she remembered.

'Hello, Rosie.' A ghost of a smile.

'Daddy,' she breathed, sitting down again, pitying how lined his forehead was, the eyes sunken. His old jaunty air was quite gone.

'What are you doing here?'

'I-I found out where you were.'

'I suppose it was Yvonne who told you, damn her. I said I didn't want you or Micky to hear anything about this.'

He spoke as though he knew nothing of her brother's whereabouts and her heart sank.

'Not Yvonne, no.' She explained quickly how Michal had come to England to find work and that she'd followed because she hadn't heard from him. About the policeman who'd traced her father and arranged for her to visit.

'He said you were here ... for fraud. That's stealing, right?' She felt again the blaze of anger that he'd done such a thing, her own father. She'd never put him on a pedestal, her mother had seen to that, but she'd still looked up to him as someone to help her. At some level she had loved and trusted him, thought him basically good.

'Yeah, well ... it all got a bit of a mess. The recession and everything.' His voice acquired an unpleasant whine.

'You took other people's money!' she hissed, unable to conceal her emotion. She remembered her horror when Ben the policeman told her what he'd found out. Building contracts that weren't honoured. Borrowing to the hilt from dodgy sources. Deposits unreturned, then the moonlight flit.

'I'm paying for it now, ain't I?' The whine grew more noticeable. 'The house is gone. Sounds like the bank haven't sold it yet then?'

'I don't know. What's happened to Yvonne?'

'Living with her sister in Eastbourne last time I heard. She wants a divorce, Rosie.'

'I can't blame her.' She was surprised at her own viciousness.

'I can see why you're angry. That's why I didn't want you to find out. I've let you down. Thank God your mother's dead and never knew.'

'That's a terrible thing to say! You've no right. You didn't even come to the funeral.'

'I didn't mean ... Well, I was in the middle of the police investigation. They probably wouldn't have let me go. But you're right, I should have tried to be there.'

'Hardly a word from you. Michal was upset, but he still believe in you. I still believe in you.' From across the room, one of the warders was staring at her with interest, so she lowered her voice. 'You let us down bad.'

Her father was the picture of misery. 'Where do you think he is then, your brother?'

'I don't know. I've been trying to tell you. I'm so worried and I don't know who to ask. What can I do?'

'Blimey. Don't ask me.' He ran his fingers along the table edge as he thought. His nails were neatly cut and this detail comforted her. At least he still took some pride in his appearance. What must it be like in here? Ben had explained that this was a low-category prison, not for the violent criminals, but still. Several years in here would diminish anybody.

'There are organizations to find missing people, in't there? And you can ask the council. Maybe if he was homeless he might have gone to them?'

'The police have enquired. They've tried hospitals and hostels. I must find other people from our country, the policeman says. See if someone has looked after him. That is what happened for me.' She told him about her job at the Black Cat Café, and how Leonie had given her a room. He was worried about Michal properly now, she could see, and this softened her. He loved them both still, but she saw that their positions had changed. He seemed overwhelmed by what had happened to him, the loss of Yvonne. Rosa felt stronger than him now. Still, she longed for him to solve this problem, to say something that would help her find her brother. But what could he do, really, from in here?

One of the warders was calling that time was nearly over, so she stood up, buttoning her coat.

'Will you come again, Rosie? Please?'

'Yes, but don't ask me when. I have to work.' It was bad of her, but she relished this moment of power.

'Don't leave it too long. I don't get many visitors.' He touched her shoulder in farewell. 'It's been good to see you. You look ...' He studied her face. 'Beautiful,' he decided. 'Still my beautiful daughter. I haven't asked you, but have you got over it?'

She stiffened.

'I mean Eryk. It was a terrible thing to happen. How are his parents coping, poor sods?'

'I don't want to talk about it,' she said in a colourless voice.

'Sorry, stupid to ask. My poor Rosie. There will be someone else for you.' He reached out and touched her cheek in a gesture of farewell. She tried not to flinch.

She stood holding the back of the chair, watching him shuffle out with the other prisoners and trying to steady herself. It was important that she stay calm and strong for Michal, but she felt so alone.

*

Karina glanced up from some paperwork as Rosa hung up her coat in the café early the next morning.

'I shall have to leave you to manage for a bit sometimes, Rosa,' she said. 'Can you do that? Jared's mum has to go to hospital. You wouldn't believe it but there might be something wrong with her after all.'

'Oh dear, what is it?' Rosa was tying on a pinafore prior to sorting out the bakery delivery.

'They don't know. She's got to have all these tests and someone's got to go with her and take her home later.' She gulped down some coffee.

'And I suppose Jared is too busy.'

'You got it in one.' Jared was a foreman for a large scaffolding company. 'Anyway, it's better that I do it. He'll be no good getting information out of the doctors.'

'Well, sure, I'll help, but what about Beth or Stu?' Beth and Stu were part-timers. There usually needed to be two people serving, and one working behind the scenes. Rosa remembered a conversation she'd had with Stef. The girl had asked her about a job. Hadn't she said she had been a caterer? She took a breath. 'I know a woman with experience of cooking who wants work. I could ask her.'

'Great!' Karina said, frowning at a delivery invoice. 'I'll talk to Beth and Stu, but we might want an extra pair of hands. Ask your friend to drop by and see me.'

Rosa felt pleased. She liked Stef and liked, too, the idea of doing someone a favour for a change. After all, so many people had helped her.

Leonie

Stef seemed much more cheerful now that she was occupied and no longer wandered aimlessly around the house worrying Leonie. At the same time, Leonie felt she needed to keep a special eye on her. Stef clearly appreciated this, and one morning when she wasn't working Leonie sat down with her at the kitchen table and Stef asked what happened next in her path to becoming a model. 'I'm interested particularly,' she said, 'because I'd still love to work in fashion. It must all have been very different back then.'

'Oh, it was, it was, but as ever, luck played a part. In my case the luck wasn't all good. The next step towards my future career didn't turn out very pleasantly.

London, Spring 1960

Just after Leonie turned sixteen, she took a trip to London with a schoolfriend, Jean. Jean was mad about the singer Adam Faith and had heard that he was appearing at a record shop in Oxford Street on a certain date in the Easter holidays. She talked Leonie into going with her. Leonie wasn't as keen on the pop idol as Jean, but the prospect was more exciting than working at H.E. Brett's or hanging around the town park watching the boys play football, so they raided their piggy banks and caught an early morning train.

When they arrived at His Master's Voice they joined a long queue of girls and after a wait everybody surged towards the road squealing as Adam's taxi drew up. They got a glimpse of gorgeous corn-coloured hair as his minders hurried him into the shop and then the girls all pushed in after him. Leonie thought that close up he was much less glossy than on the television, but Jean thought he was fabulous and they each bought a record and he signed the cover.

It was after they emerged onto the street that something strange happened. They must have been talking excitedly as they compared their precious signatures when a man stepped in front of them, gave a polite cough and tipped his hat. 'Excuse me a moment, girls. Can I have a word?'

Leonie had never seen anyone like him before and was amazed. He was quite old, forty at least, with a fringe of greying hair visible under his fedora, a moustache and a short neat beard, which were not at all the fashion at that time. In his long frock coat, a carnation in the buttonhole, he looked like a raffish Victorian gentleman. Leonie was later to realize that this distinctive style was part of him, his trademark, so to speak.

'I assure you that this is quite above board,' he said in a cultured voice, but the lilt of it and the softness of the way he said 'above' told them he wasn't English. 'My name is Rostov, Jerry Rostov – here is my card – and I wonder whether you might consider calling on me at my studio so that I may take a few photographs.' He wasn't looking at Jean when he said this, though Jean was petite and pretty, but at Leonie, who was puzzled. She felt as gawky as two years before when the lady from *Vogue* had asked about her becoming a model.

She took the card, though, and mumbled that she'd have to ask her parents and he bowed and said of course, he'd be delighted to meet them should they wish to accompany her. Then he tipped his hat again, which made her glance at Jean, trying not to giggle, and he said, 'You will come, won't you? I insist that you do,' very charmingly, before continuing on his way.

'Will you go?' Jean squeaked. Her eyes were as round as a goldfish's as she snatched the card from Leonie and examined it. 'He is a photographer, it says so here. Oh, Leonie, you must go. It's your chance, don't you see?'

'I don't know,' Leonie said coolly, though it was hard to hide her excitement. 'Mum and Dad wouldn't approve, I know they wouldn't.' But to her delight she was wrong.

Up until that point her mother had been desperately trying to keep Leonie at her schoolwork, even though all she really tried hard at was art. Her mother nursed an idea that Leonie would pass into the sixth form and eventually secure an administrative job in the Civil Service or a high-flying secretarial post, some kind of occupation that was a step up from working in a draper's shop. But she and Leonie's father were beginning to recognize that since meeting the *Vogue* lady her ambitions lay in other directions, and when she brought out the card to show them at teatime, they weren't as condemning as she'd feared. Her brother Bobby, who at fourteen was developing a world-weary brand of sarcasm, thought it all a terrific hoot, and said the man must be desperate.

'Shut up,' she told him. 'I really want to go,' she whined to her parents and found herself echoing Jean's words. 'It's my chance.' Her parents, used by now to her mulishness, exchanged looks full of meaning.

'You know nothing about this man,' her mother began, but her voice sounded weak, as though she knew already she was defeated.

'He's not a white-slave trader, Mum, if that's what you mean. It's a proper printed business card.' She felt triumphant when, later that evening, she managed to find his name credited for some photographs in one of the back copies of *Woman's Weekly* that her mother kept by the sewing machine for the fashion tips and recipes. The article concerned was for summer dresses and the shoot was set in a garden with a fine display of roses and really was impossible to object to. In the end her father agreed to take a day out of the shop on the pretext of visiting a wholesaler in north London, and so, with shaking fingers, she dialled Mr Rostov's number and arranged an appointment.

The studio in Kentish Town, a part of London she had never visited before, turned out to be the ground floor of a light-filled modern building with an air of whimsy about its design, for it was all open staircases and whitewashed walls decorated with modern abstract paintings and blown-up photographs of models, one or two of whom Leonie recognized from the glamour magazines her dentist kept in his waiting room, elegant debutante types whose hourglass figures were nipped into twinsets and ball gowns. She studied the photos with a sinking heart, believing that she would never look like those models, no, not in a million years, with her turned-up nose and flat chest. Later she was to realize that this was a good thing. The world of modelling was changing and the type of model that was fashionable was changing, too.

The design of the building seemed out of keeping with its traditionally attired inhabitant, but also curiously appropriate given the man's eccentric ways. He welcomed Leonie and her father with an old-world courtesy that clearly impressed him, and insisted on calling her Miss Brett. He showed them into a large photographic studio which had several smaller rooms opening off it. From one, with a sign that said *Darkroom*, emerged Rostov's assistant, who Leonie thought a sullen young man, despite his glossy brown hair and bright blue eyes. Rostov introduced him as Master Fletcher, a tag which she could see he hated. He nodded without speaking and set about pegging several freshly printed photographs on a line to dry. Leonie saw that these were of a large-eyed girl not much older than herself, wearing a rather frightened expression as though she'd been caught under a searchlight. Rostov sent Master Fletcher off to make some tea, then he helped her off with her coat and bade her sit on a divan to one side of the room whilst he threw the black cloth of an old-fashioned plate camera over his head and began to fiddle with the machinery, muttering to himself. The young man returned with brimming mugs of strong tea and set about adjusting the lighting.

'Mr Brett,' Rostov said, coming out from under the cloth, 'although you are more than welcome to stay and observe, I wonder whether your daughter might, er, feel more at ease if you were to go away and come back later. An hour or two should settle it.'

'Right you are,' Leonie's father said gratefully, for he'd looked out of his depth in these surroundings. 'I do have some business to attend to . . .' He finished his tea hurriedly, returned his mug to Master Fletcher and urging his daughter to do her very best for Mr Rostov he fitted his hat onto his head and left.

Rostov's manner towards Leonie altered. He became even more attentive, intimate even, his fingers readily brushing her arms and hair as he set her standing and sitting in various poses for the camera. She was aware of the assistant bustling about in the background, bringing his employer fresh photographic plates, and bearing away exposed ones, but eventually Rostov told him they'd done enough for the time being and ordered him to go home. Fletcher glanced at Leonie unhappily as he shrugged on his jacket and mumbled, 'I suppose I'll be off then,' as if he were reluctant to leave.

Once they were alone, Rostov said, 'Now then,' and rubbed his hands together. 'You may relax a little more. Sit down on the couch again.' She perched on its edge very tentatively. 'That's right, now undo those buttons, it's important we can glimpse your, ah, *embonpoint*.' Very reluctantly, she undid the topmost button of her blouse and then the next, revealing the lace trim of her training brassiere. 'No, that won't do, take that dreadful thing off altogether. You don't need it, I think, you're very small.' She felt her face flame for she was self-conscious about being only an A-cup, but she turned from him and did as he said, pushing her arms back hurriedly into the sleeves of the blouse and doing it up to above her breastbone. At his instruction she lay down, considerably nervous now, especially since he simply stood there looking at her, breathing heavily, his dark eyes glittering.

'Are you going to photograph me again?' She tried to sound confident, but heard her voice waver.

'Yes, yes, all in good time,' he muttered, picking up her bra from the floor with a ridiculous reverence and placing it on the chair with her coat and handbag. Then he spent a moment or two slotting plates into the camera and whisking the cloth over his head, checking the settings, before taking a few pictures. After he had finished, she sat up and hastily buttoned her blouse.

'We have yet to see the results, but I sense you have a certain something most other girls don't, girls like this one.' He gestured towards the now-dry prints of the stiff-postured waif, whose image peered unhappily back. 'You're untrained, of course, and need to allow yourself to relax more.' Here he leaned and squeezed Leonie's thigh with an encouraging hand. She tried to inch away, anxious to put him off whilst trying not to offend him and thus lose her 'chance'.

'When will the pictures be ready?' she asked. She was greedy to see them.

'I will print some tonight and you may come and view them sometime next week.'

'I won't be able to until Saturday,' she said, remembering she'd be back at school.

He considered this for a moment then said, 'Come next Saturday afternoon,' and, anticipating the return of his roaming hand, she rose to her feet and put on her coat, stuffing the bra into the bottom of her handbag.

'I'll wait for Dad outside,' she said. 'Thank you ever so much, Mr Rostov. You've been very kind. I look forward to seeing the photographs.' She left the studio as quickly as she could without actually appearing rude. Oh the relief to see her father trudging into view across the street, his briefcase bulging with samples for the shop. She ran to greet him, never so glad to see him in her life.

'Steady on, my girl,' he said in delighted surprise as she hugged him. 'Everything tickety-boo, I hope?'

'Yes,' she said in joyful relief. 'Yes, very tickety-boo. I'm just happy to see you, that's all.'

'That's good,' he said, looking pleased. 'He seemed a very nice gentleman and I hope you said thank you and that you were most obliged. It was kind of him to photograph you.'

'Yes, it was, wasn't it?' Her relief ebbed in the light of his complete ignorance of the Jerry Rostovs of this world. 'I have to come back next Saturday to see the results.'

'You'll have to come up on your own, love. It's all right

like today when I have business to conduct, but your mother and I can't keep taking time off from the shop.'

'He was a dirty old man,' she told Jean on the bus to school. 'I don't think I can bear to see him again, but I'll have to.' Leonie described what had happened and it seemed less horrifying in the telling. They both collapsed into such hysterical giggles that their schoolmates pestered them all morning to find out what their secret was. They didn't tell. Leonie didn't tell her parents either as she was desperate to see those photographs and couldn't have her mother and father making a fuss. Suppose they wouldn't let her try any further with a modelling career? Despite finding Mr Rostov so creepy, she was determined to go back to see the prints, and to find out more so she could take the next step towards her chosen career. Jean thought she was foolish and tried to dissuade her, but Leonie simply wouldn't listen to her.

That afternoon with Rostov would have put many young girls off modelling for good, but Leonie decided she must have some perverse streak in her because it galvanized her instead. Despite her struggle to keep him at bay, she had enjoyed the novelty of being photographed. She had liked the bright studio and seeing something of the mysterious processes of photography. It was all a huge adventure.

The prints, half a dozen fanned out on a table, made her appear more glamorous than she'd dared hope. She was stiff and self-conscious in them – Rostov was right – but she was also able to discern what he had seen in her, that the camera liked her. She met it in the eye, it challenged and flattered her. Later on, *Vogue* was to gush on about Leonie's 'gamine style' and this was already obvious in her small face and large eyes, her pointed chin, which Rostov told her was the new young look. And, she was startled to see, in a sideways shot, that she had a good profile. The turned-up nose that Bobby was always teasing her about wasn't at all like a pig's snout; it was endearing.

There was no sign, however, of the more lubricious pictures he'd taken the previous week after Master Fletcher had gone. She wondered if he kept those for his own private use.

'You should be pleased with these,' Rostov said, making her a present of two of the best prints, 'but sixteen is still a bit young and you need training up. Go to modelling school, do something about your hair and your posture. You walk like a goose, my dear. Come back and see me in a year and we'll see where we are.'

Leonie was hurt, and wondered if she had offended him by not letting him get his wicked way with her, but on reflection, and after discussing the matter with Jean, who could be shrewd, she understood he was merely being honest.

Her mother had banished decent-sized mirrors from the house, probably because she could not bear catching unexpected sights of her blemish, so Leonie took a tally of herself in the full-length cheval glass in Jean's parents' bedroom. She was tall, five foot nine, which was good, she realized, and slender, but she slouched to counter her height and mostly wore her long hair brushed back in an unflattering ponytail, because her mother said it was a girl's crowning glory and it would be a shame to cut it.

But cut it she had to if she wished to be a model, so she saved up her earnings from the shop and a couple of months later went to a good hairdresser near Oxford Circus. It turned out to be one of the best decisions she ever made.

Stef

Stef found the pace of work difficult to get used to at first, for although it involved serving food it was different from any other job she'd had, but she liked the people, Rosa, of course, and Karina, when she was there, and Beth and Stu, and also the assortment of customers.

She quickly began to see a pattern. First there were local workers from shops and offices near by, calling in for a quick breakfast or a takeaway cappuccino. Then there were mothers with small children taking a break from shopping, or meeting friends, a student or two from the local technical college typing on their laptops and making a coffee last an hour. If Leonie came in, she insisted on paying for her coffee, but Rosa would stubbornly add free biscuits to her saucer which Leonie was too embarrassed to make a fuss about. As lunchtime approached the café started to become really busy, with queues building towards the door. Rosa put Stef on sandwich making because she was quick and

nimble-fingered and never forgot the details of a complicated request. It was hard work, but it suited her because
there was never time to brood and she'd begun to feel
much happier.

'It might be only for a week,' Rosa had warned when
she'd first told her about the job, and Karina had underlined this when she interviewed her. But the news of
Cathy, Karina's 'mother-in-law', was not encouraging
and, by the onset of the second week, it was apparent
that she would have to be admitted to hospital for an
urgent operation to replace a valve in her heart. This
meant that Cathy's elderly mother, Jared's grandmother,
needed visiting, and Cathy's timid rescue greyhound
looking after.

'And all sorts of palaver after the op,' Karina explained
bitterly on one of the days she'd made it to work. 'Jared's
just going to have to take time off. I've told him he has
to ask for compassionate leave, or take it as holiday. His
boss can't sack him for that, believe me. The trouble is
he's about as much use as an ashtray on a bicycle when
it comes to nursing. He's brilliant when you want something mechanical mended, but it'll be embarrassing for
him to help his mum with getting dressed and stuff. I'll
still need to be around.'

So Stef, listening to all this, saw the job would continue for a while yet and was thankful, while of course
feeling sorry for Karina. To have money in her pocket
was wonderful and one of the first things she did was
to make a proper arrangement with Leonie. She knew
that £40 a week was a ridiculously small rent to pay

in London, so in addition she offered to clean Peter's rooms every week. Leonie accepted gratefully. It wasn't a pleasant job, and Peter complained the first time, after Stef threw away some paint tubes he said weren't empty, so Leonie had to broker an arrangement. 'Stef promises she won't move anything important,' she told him, 'but the rooms must be cleaned,' and with that they all had to be content.

The other advantage of working at the Black Cat was that Stef came to know Rosa much better. It was one Monday after the lunchtime rush that Karina came in unexpectedly and insisted they take an hour off for their own lunch.

'I bet you haven't had time for a break, have you?' she scolded. Beth had arrived, too, and was washing up at the tiny sink, so Karina cut them some sandwiches and sent them off together.

They went to a tiny park near by and sat on a bench to eat. It was a war memorial garden and the bench was in front of the memorial itself, a large stone cross, recently scrubbed clean, perhaps for the World War One centenary, with dozens of names of the dead from two world wars carved into its plinth. The sun fell through the budding branches of the trees, making patterns on the silver stone. It was a warmish day and Stef stretched out her legs as she took a sandwich from the bag, glad to be outside. Rosa simply sat smoking, gazing quietly at the memorial.

'Are you OK?' Stef wondered.

'Mmm, yes. Good to sit down. It was so busy today.'

Stef, her mouth full of tuna sandwich, nodded.

'I think Karina will need you for some time. The mother is not getting better quickly. It is very hard for Karina.'

Stef swallowed and wiped her mouth with a napkin. 'Well I need the work, so that's the good thing.'

'Yes. Though I need time off. To look for Michal.'

'What can you do next?' Rosa had told Stef about visiting her father in prison. Rosa had also explained about the background work that Ben, the police constable, was doing. From time to time he rang her to give her a report and Stef was surprised that he was giving the case so much attention. Once she'd joked that the man must fancy her or something, but Rosa simply frowned. She wasn't amused and Stef was made to feel that she'd crossed some unseen boundary.

'I don't know. He has not been seen at any of the hostels, or at a jobcentre. The police do not know about him. They say it is blank.'

'They've drawn a blank?'

'Yes, that is it.' Rosa's voice was dull. Stef glanced up at her. She was impressed again by how striking her friend was. She wore a dark red pinafore-style dress today, with leggings and short, low-heeled boots, a practical style. Her dark hair needed cutting, but the longer fringe suited her high forehead and emphasized her fine blue eyes. There was an air of capability about her. It was there in the sureness of her movements, the way she crushed her cigarette stub under her heel, tossed it into a bin and dusted her hands, then broke off pieces of her sandwich, which she ate without obvious enjoyment. All the while she did not smile, though in the café she was always professionally pleasant to the customers and spoke cheerfully to any children. Only Stef seemed to notice the sadness in her eyes.

'There must be some other people from your country,' Stef ventured. 'Who you could ask?'

'I've tried.' Rosa's voice was dull. 'There are the men at the garage. I have spoken to them, but they don't know anything. They told me about some other places to try. A restaurant near the library, the Catholic church up the road, so I will do that.'

'I'll come with you if you like,' Stef said, a little doubt-fully, for what use would she be. She certainly couldn't speak Rosa's language. 'I mean, to keep you company.'

'Thanks.' For the first time there was a trace of a smile. 'You are very kind, Stef. I think I'll be OK, but I'll ask if I need you.'

Heartened by this, Stef asked, 'What was it like for you at home? You lived in a city, didn't you?'

'The capital, Warsaw, yes.' Rosa shrugged. 'It's ... fine. Like any big city, you know. Expensive, noisy, but with many beautiful parts. Lots of buildings look old, like London, but they are not. It is illusion. So much was completely destroyed by the Nazis. It had to be built again.'

'Couldn't your brother get a job there?'

'Yes, but a well-paid one, no. He wanted more, not just money, a different kind of life. After our mother died he was always talking about finding his dad, working for

his dad. He was sure everything would be great here.'
She shuffled her feet and stared at the war memorial
without focusing on it. Stef felt her unhappiness.

'What do you think has happened to him?' No, that
sounded doomy. She corrected herself. 'I mean, what do
you think he would have done when he found your dad
wasn't there?'

'I always thought he would have called me before
doing anything. I can't think why he did not. Something
stopped him. That's the most worrying thing.'

'He had trouble using his phone, you said?'

'There are other phones. There are computers. He
should have got a message to me.' Her voice was scorn-
ful, angry.

'You're right. I'm sorry.'

'It's Mik who makes me angry, not you, Stef!' She laid
a hand on Stef's arm. 'Why didn't he phone me?'

'I don't know, but perhaps . . . he couldn't.'

'That's what I am frightened of. Stef, I read the papers
and sometimes there is a bad story, you know, somebody found dead, and I worry it'll be him.' She stood up
suddenly, throwing her sandwich paper into a bin, and
walked round the little garden, hugging herself.

When they returned to the café only two or three customers sat at the tables and Beth, a large and not particularly forthcoming girl, was being engaged in conversation at the counter by a youngish man in a dark jacket. He
looked up at their entrance, his shrewd gaze passing over
the girls before he said goodbye to Beth. In that moment

Stef had got a glimpse of a clever narrow face under short scanty hair.

Beth's expression was wary, and when he left she stood staring after him. 'Weird,' she murmured and started to wipe the counter. 'He was asking people's names and stuff. Who worked here and that.'

'What did you tell him?' Rosa's tone was sharp with alarm.

'Nothin',' Beth said defensively.

'Do you think it's about Michal?' Rosa asked Stef. She went back out to the street and looked about, but after a moment came back in, shaking her head. 'Gone,' she said. 'Where's Karina?' she asked Beth.

'Out getting milk.'

It was an odd incident, but the young man didn't turn up again and after a while they forgot about him.

Leonie

The morning was not going well. For a start Leonie had slept badly again. The bird in the chimney had been quiet for a day or two and she'd thought with a painful relief that it must have died, but then, in the very early morning, she'd been woken by the sound of it shuffling about and chirping gently as though consoling itself. She'd gone to crouch shivering in her pyjamas by the fireplace and whispered to it until it had quietened.

Now she was tired and anxious, and though she'd reported for duty at her easel as usual, she didn't seem able to concentrate on Mr Jenkins, the darling moggy of one Sibyl May Worth, an American lady living in Mayfair – could anyone actually afford to live in Mayfair these days? – who wished for a large oil painting of the animal to hang over her mantelpiece.

She was staring at a photograph of the fluffy white cat and making some preparatory drawings when she glimpsed the postwoman passing her window and shortly afterwards heard the snap of the letterbox. The cat really looked extraordinary. It was literally a great ball of fur with two round eyes staring back at her, and the tips of two ears. Quite how she was going to be able to give it any form on the canvas she didn't quite know. She'd try the eyes first. If she got the expression right, perhaps the rest would follow more easily. She sketched them in pencil and the dot of pink nose and wondered whether she had enough white paint for all the fur. Perhaps she'd see if there was anything of interest in the post then have another go at Mr Jenkins. Really, what an odd name for a cat. A change from Snowball, she supposed.

She went out into the hall and saw at once that someone, Hari or Bela probably, had already picked up the letters and laid them on the stand. She flicked through them. Something from the Inland Revenue for Rosa. The others were for her. A postcard – her heart missed a beat as she thought of Jamie – but it turned out to be from Trudi, who was on a cruise around the Dalmatian coast. *No one dines at the Captain's table any more*, she was complaining in her dashing scrawl. *No style, no allure, but I've met a lovely writer gentleman who gave such an interesting talk. Allure* was underlined. The vulgarization of everything was a constant theme with Trudi, who longed for an older, more elegant world. Leonie stuck the card into the frame of the mirror and saw that the only other item of post was a letter with the now familiar name of the solicitor's firm on it.

'Now what,' she muttered, but this time forced herself to open it. She scanned the sheet inside quickly, then, puzzled, read it again. *RE: 11 Bellevue Gardens*, it said. It referred to a previous letter, one she didn't recall. Something about an answer to it being urgently required.

There might have been another letter, now she thought about it. She pulled open the top drawer of the stand to find a whole heap of mail. She snatched it out in handfuls and started to go through it. Junk mail. Letters for past residents who'd not left addresses. Jamie's bank statements, which he'd never bothered with. Nothing. She hesitated, then shut the drawer and by a steady series of little tugs inched the groaning stand away from the wall. From one side tumbled an envelope, all covered in dust. She identified it at once as the one she was looking for and tore it open. After she'd read it she stood staring down at it for a long time, feeling the shock course through her veins.

Rick

Usually, during his coffee break, Rick made green tea from the stock of tea bags he kept in his locker in the supermarket's tiny staff room, and took the disposable cup out to the memorial garden, or ambled along the street with it to browse in the window of the Japanese manga shop.

More recently, though, if he knew Stef and Rosa were there, he would go into the Black Cat and blow two quid on a cappuccino in the hope they'd have time for a chat. If they didn't, he enjoyed sitting down with a newspaper and watching them bustle about, feeling that he was part of it all. If Karina wasn't there to object, Rosa would sometimes top up his cup for nothing. Stef, he realized, was too nervous of the sack to do anything like that.

He'd noticed, though, how much brighter she seemed these days. She liked working again, he could see that, even though she'd told him she didn't see it as a for ever kind of job. Not only was she more cheerful, but she was emerging from her state of fearful diffidence. She would meet his eye and smile at him across the counter and he saw with what natural good humour she helped a young mother whose oversized buggy was jammed between two tables. The job required her to wear her hair differently, tied up under a cap, and this made her look older and more sophisticated. He liked it, but it also made him feel less sure around her. Now, when he looked in the bathroom mirror to shave, he was more critical of what he saw. He must get himself a proper haircut sometime, he thought, and some of his T-shirts had really had it. These things cost money, though, and money was something he simply didn't have much of and had got out of the habit of spending.

Another thing he'd noticed was the growing

friendship between the two girls. Sometimes they even cooked together in the evenings. He'd come downstairs to make himself some noodles or fry up some vegetables, and he'd smell the delicious buttery aroma of frying chicken and find Rosa pushing the meat around the sizzling pan whilst Stef chopped onions and what might be beetroot. They'd glance up at his entrance and greet him, then return to their conversation. He would listen intently whilst trying to seem as though he wasn't. And it was in this way one weekday evening that he learned more about Rosa's missing brother. He knew the bare facts from Stef, but he'd never heard Rosa speak about the boy.

'I have always protected him, since he was a little child,' she was saying. 'He is very kind, always sees good things in people. He trusts them when maybe it is stupid. But everybody likes him, that is a good thing. I cannot think he would make anybody angry so that they would want to hurt him.'

Stef exclaimed as she accidentally caught her thumb with the knife. Rick leaped up and grabbed a tissue from a box and folded it into a pad for her to press against the wound.

'How old is your brother?' he asked Rosa quietly.

'Twenty-two. But people think he is younger.'

'It's awful for you. Our manager's Hungarian, I think. I'll ask her if you like. In case someone like Michal came asking for work or something.'

Rosa gave him a steady look and smiled. 'Thank you, Rick. I, too, have been asking in the shops.'

'Have you been to the church yet?' Stef said, examining her thumb, which had more or less stopped bleeding.

'No. Sunday, I think. It is a long time since I went to mass.'

Rick did ask his boss, but she said foreigners were always coming in asking for work and, no, she didn't remember anyone in particular. She'd have sent him away. Did Rick think it was worth her time interviewing someone who couldn't speak proper English?

Rosa

Rosa had stopped attending mass after her fiancé Eryk's death, but today it soothed her. The rite was, of course, in English, but the familiar rhythms of it were as comfortable to her as a lullaby. She knew without thinking when to stand or sit or to cross herself, which was just as well, for she was too busy studying the other members of the congregation to concentrate. Some small part of her hoped to see Michal, as it did everywhere she went, but she was so used now to being disappointed that his absence did not unduly upset her.

Instead, what did surprise her was how full the church was and how lovely inside, high-ceilinged with a beautiful stained-glass window above the altar of Christ in Majesty, his hand raised in a blessing. The whitewashed walls and the dark wood beams reminded her of the church where she'd worshipped in her own country, raised in recent years above the ruins of an old guard house.

There were some who might be her own countrymen and -women, she saw, looking about. She never thought of herself as English; her early childhood in London was like a distant dream. Her home city in Poland was where she'd been to school, where she'd worked, Polish the language that she'd mostly spoken. Warsaw was where, too, she'd met Eryk and where she would have married him, yes, and where they would have raised their children if they'd been born.

It was the thought of this that when the prayers began sent her sinking to her knees where she rubbed her hot dry eyelids with the heels of her hands and tried to pay attention to what the priest was saying, instead of to the thoughts that tumbled in her mind.

The priest was middle-aged, an Irishman, she knew by his accent, like Rick, who had been born in Dublin, she had learned, but had left there while still a child. After the service she watched the Father moving amongst the congregation, talking softly to some, laughing with the children, his restless pale eyes always alert, careful not to miss anything. And so he noticed her, standing apart with her cup of lukewarm coffee because she knew no one, and he came across and asked her if she was new.

She nodded and explained that she had recently moved to the area and was sorry that she hadn't been here before.

'It's important that you come each week, Rosa,' he said. 'Will you promise me you'll try? It's a good way to meet people, you'll find. There are some lovely families here from your part of the world. You'll find everyone very friendly.'

'Yes, thank you. I will try. But, Father ...' There was a pause as a woman with a tray came for their empty cups, which gave Rosa time to gather her courage. 'I am looking for my brother. His name is Michal, Michal Dexter. Did he ever come here, do you know?' And she quickly described the circumstances and showed him a photograph of Michal on her phone.

It was the first time since meeting the man who lived next door to her father in Dartmouth Street that she saw a twitch of recognition and it made her heart beat faster.

'I can't be sure,' the priest said. Father Matthews, he was called, she remembered from the notice sheet. 'Michael, did you say? Maybe, I can't be sure ... you'll not be surprised to hear we see quite a few young men like him. Lost, you know, can't speak much English. Most of them we send to the housing people, but ... wait a moment. Let me introduce you to Will. He works for the local council and I usually let him deal with such cases.'

He led Rosa over to where a tall, lean man of perhaps thirty stood in polite conversation with a trio of young people, students, from their identikit clothes and earnest expressions. The man, Will, allowed himself to be drawn away by the priest and introduced to Rosa. Velvet-brown eyes fastened on her face from under a mop of dark curls. He had to bend his head down a little to speak to her, then listened, a thoughtful expression on his face, as the priest explained that she was searching for her brother 'Michael', as he pronounced his name.

'Michal,' she insisted, showing Will the photo on her phone.

'Michal,' Will repeated. He angled the phone in his big sensitive hands and frowned. 'Yes, there was some-one who looked like him. He came here for a service once, do you remember, Father, oh, months ago. It must have been back in the summer.'

'I remember those eyes,' Father Matthews told Rosa. 'The blue is most unusual.'

'I'd have told him where to find a hostel,' Will con-tinued. 'But I wonder if he ever made it there. He didn't come here again, that's all I know, though I hope I was encouraging.'

'Which hostel, please?'

When Will told her, she was disappointed. She knew the police had asked there specifically. And it was the one where she'd stayed and they'd known nothing of him, or at least if they did they weren't telling her. Client confidentiality, they'd said, which had annoyed her. Mother of God, she was his sister.

'I'm so sorry for this trouble,' Will said to her. She liked him. His voice was soft and deep and she felt his concern. But she also felt angry. No one had tried hard enough at the time, it seemed, to help Michal, to keep him safe.

She nodded and said thank you, then turned to walk away, suddenly wanting to be alone. 'Hang on a moment,' Will said, coming alongside, his long strides slowing to match hers. 'Let me know how to get hold of you. In case.' He slipped a business card into her hand.

'This is me.' She glanced at it. *Will Turner*, it said. *Youth Worker.* He wrote down her phone number in the pocket notebook he opened for the purpose. She thanked him and walked out into the cold spring air, still troubled, but suddenly more optimistic. Another sighting of Michal, she told herself, however long ago, however fleeting, was a positive sign. If only she could see a way of finding out what had happened to him next. The feel of Will's card in her hand was reassuring. He seemed like someone who cared.

Five

Leonie

'Waiting room' was exactly the right name for this one, Leonie thought crossly, having been sitting in it for half an hour. She gave up trying to concentrate on a dull booklet entitled *Before you see your solicitor* and dropped it back onto the glass coffee table, then stared up at the oil painting of the original Mr Threlfall of Threlfall & Hicks Solicitors, presiding sternly over the shabby-genteel surroundings.

At last the door of the room opened and the petite receptionist peeped round and said in her small, high voice, 'Miss Brett, we're so sorry. Lizzie is ready for you now.' *Lizzie?* Mr Threlfall junior, whom Leonie had consulted on her previous visit, some thirty years ago, and who'd been a stickler for protocol, would have shuddered in his grave.

The woman who greeted her when she arrived at the top of the stairs was not some freshly qualified girl as the name had given her to imagine, but a harassed, plain-faced brunette of forty, in a short-skirted business suit, who showed her into a comfortably messy office.

'Do sit down. I'm ever so sorry to keep you. The wretched intern couldn't find the file and we had to have everything out. Not his fault though, I suppose. It's a long time ago since we last saw you, isn't it?' She fixed Leonie with a stern look.

'Oh dear,' Leonie said humbly, wondering if it was she who was in the wrong in not having needed to visit her solicitor for over thirty years. The booklet downstairs hadn't said anything about regular legal check-ups. It had, however, indicated that the fees had gone up substantially in the interim.

'So how can I help today?'

'It's this.' Leonie passed her the letter that she'd recently received plus the one she'd rescued from behind the hall stand and watched whilst the woman read them both.

'I see,' Lizzie murmured, setting them down on her desk. She pulled a manila folder towards her, opened it and consulted first a legal document printed on thick paper, then some flimsy typewritten pages pinned beneath. 'Ah, yes,' she murmured. 'It's all very clear.'

'What is? Can the letters possibly be right?'

'The letters are from the solicitors who represent the freeholder of 11 Bellevue Gardens. I think he must own the whole terrace, in fact.'

'That doesn't make sense. Surely I own the house, don't I? My friend George Stuart left it to me.'

'Actually, Miss Brett, no. Mr Stuart was merely the leaseholder, so the lease is all that he could leave you. It's something a lot of people get mixed up about.

Leaseholders only have the right to occupy the property for a contracted length of time and, in your case, it was a hundred years. This latest lease was drawn up in 1915, so I'm afraid that it expires at the end of this year.'

'No!' The room had felt warm, but Leonie found she was shivering.

Her elbows on the desk, Lizzie folded her hands under her square chin. 'Miss Brett.' She studied Leonie with a stern gleam in her eyes. 'Since it appears you have made no arrangements for the renewal of the lease, the freeholder is giving you appropriate notice for vacant possession.'

'*What?*'

'You must move out of 11 Bellevue Gardens by the 31st of December.'

Leonie's hands flew to her cheeks.

'Move out?' she wailed. 'My God, I can't. It's been my home for forty years, no, forty-three. And my friend left it to me in 1980.'

'You were only left the remnant of the lease by the aforementioned . . .' She glanced down at the open folder. 'George Stuart esquire. Don't you have a copy of his Last Will and Testament?'

'I might, I don't know. If I do, I haven't the faintest idea where it is. Mr Threlfall junior dealt with it all. He was so very reassuring. Oh dear, it's so long ago now.'

'This latest letter you were sent by the freeholding company indicates that earlier ones about renewing the lease were sent to you over the last few years. You've given me one of those, but weren't there others?'

'I ... don't remember any.' Leonie clutched the handbag in her lap and crossed her ankles tightly. A ghastly realization was beginning to creep over her.

'Are you sure?' Lizzie was sounding quite severe, making Leonie feel like a girl again, sent to the headmistress after some misdemeanour.

'Well,' she said with care. 'The thing is, I had been getting letters from next door every now and then. I mean, from their lawyer. About some building work they said needed doing. And since I couldn't afford it, after a bit I stopped opening anything I thought was from them.'

'What did you do with the letters?'

Leonie closed her eyes against the memory. 'I ... filed them. Behind the hall stand.'

'I don't understand. You keep your post *where*?'

'In my hall, there's a big hall stand with a mirror. People leave the post there. Sometimes I drop letters behind it.'

'How unusual.' Lizzie was looking disbelievingly at her and Leonie felt even more like a naughty schoolgirl. 'And what else have you put there?'

'Anything financial that's too big for me. I know this sounds silly, but I don't have much spare money, you see, and sometimes I can't face things.'

'I see,' Lizzie said, and now Leonie saw she was trying to keep a straight face.

'I don't mean I'm in financial trouble, exactly. I manage to pay the bills, just. The council tax can be a problem. We usually have a whip-round for that.'

'A whip-round.'

'Yes, amongst my tenants.'

'You have tenants?'

'Unofficial ones, yes. I don't have formal agreements or anything. They come and go a bit really. Is that a problem?'

Lizzie let out what sounded to Leonie like a giggle, but might have been a cough.

'I'd have to check that they don't have any rights in this case,' she said, making a note on a pad. 'The whole situation is very unfortunate. I can try to negotiate with the freeholder for you, if you like, but at this late stage it might be difficult to do anything. They talk here' – she waved one of Leonie's letters – 'about wanting to take the house back and turn it into flats.'

'Oh God, how awful. That's what's happened to most of the others.'

'And even if they agreed to renew, it is likely to be very expensive at this late stage. I expect you'll have been paying quite a small annual sum to the freeholder up to now.' She examined her papers. 'Yes, here we are. Thirty guineas. Now, if a guinea was 21s and a shilling was 5p ...' She tapped the buttons of her calculator. 'That's £31.50 a year.'

'Thirty-one pounds fifty? I recognize that amount, but I always thought it was a life assurance policy or something.'

'No, it's the rent to the freeholder. It's tiny, isn't it? What they used to call a peppercorn rent. I imagine that the freeholder made a hodgepodge of negotiations over the years with other properties in the street, which is why he's been able to convert them all before yours.'

'Oh Lizzie. I ought to have known about all this. I can't believe I've been so stupid. It's never interested me, the money side of things. I don't think I can't bear it.' Leonie took a deep breath to fight off a rising sense of panic.

'I'm sorry. We'll simply have to see what we can do, but I can't make any promises.'

It wasn't until Leonie emerged onto the street that she realized how shaken she felt. The world carried on as normal around her. A bus pulled up and deposited passengers. She passed a youth hunkering down to wipe chocolate from a toddler's face. Outside the tube station the *Big Issue* seller stood in her usual position with her hijab held across her face against the wind. Leonie bought a copy, fumbling for coins as though in limbo. Only something very important had changed. She couldn't go home. That would make the horrible lease thing seem real. Instead she entered a café – not the Black Cat, she couldn't cope with seeing anyone she knew – but a run-down place that smelt of fried onions. When her coffee came it was scalding and bitter, but she drank it feeling it was all she deserved. At least she could sit by herself and try to absorb what had happened, the fact that likely as not she would lose her home and, almost worse, cause others to lose theirs. If Lizzie couldn't persuade the freeholder to renew the lease, and for a reasonable sum, Leonie would be left with nothing. Nothing. She wouldn't be due any compensation, Lizzie had made that clear.

Leonie sat there a long time, sipping the coffee until it went cold. Then she took out her phone, selected a number and waited. The ringing went on and on until an automatic voice answered. 'Tara, it's your mother,' she said when the beep came. 'Please, darling, it's important. Would you ring me back?' For a while the phone lay on the table, blank-screened and silent. Eventually she gave up hoping for it to ring, slipped it into her pocket and set off slowly for home.

It was several days before she heard from her solicitor again, and in that time she said nothing to anybody about the terrible situation she found herself in. There was no point, was her reasoning. Until she knew for certain, why upset them? After all, if the lease could be renewed and the new arrangement wasn't too expensive, normality could resume.

What hurt her more was that Tara did not return her call, but to be honest, she had learned to live with that pain.

Stef

Stef sensed that something was wrong, but she didn't know Leonie well enough to ask what. She knew Leonie was worried about Jamie, and was bothered by a bird in the chimney. Indeed, it had upset her too, having been invited into Leonie's bedroom, to hear the poor creature. She'd liked the room very much. Leonie slept on a big day bed with high white wrought-iron bars on three sides and soft white linen topped by a patchwork quilt. Leonie had let her examine the quilt, which she said she'd bought at a local charity auction. It was made up of dozens of differently patterned materials from the past thirty or forty years, so far as Stef could guess. The mixture of markings and colours should have been discordant, but somehow it wasn't.

She'd liked the sheepskin rug by the bed, too, and the pictures on the walls, which were not, as she might have expected, like any of the ones downstairs, but prints of landscapes and animals, the sort of art that comforted rather than disturbed. The bedroom was at the back of the house overlooking the garden, so the cool air from the open sash brought in birdsong and the distant whirr of a hedge-cutter. Shining above the houses opposite was a pale misted disc of a sun.

This morning, Stef had taken the opportunity to run the hoover over Peter's floors while he'd gone out to buy some painting materials. She'd put her phone on charge and was now sitting at the kitchen table sketching on a piece of paper as she waited for some pasta to cook for her lunch. She glanced up as the door opened. It wasn't Peter coming back as she expected, but Leonie. The older woman smiled vaguely at Stef and the way she went about filling the kettle and then paused before remembering to put it on the hob indicated the extent of her distraction.

'You're not working today?' Leonie asked finally.

'Yes, I am,' Stef said, getting up to rescue the pasta. 'But not till two.'

Leonie opened the fridge door. 'How is Karina's boyfriend's mother?' she asked, bringing out skimmed milk. 'Lord, sometimes I think there are not enough words for all the different relationships you can have these days.'

Stef sprinkled herbs and grated cheese on her lunch. 'Cathy? I just call her Jared's mum. I think she's OK. Jared's started helping, too, finally, so Karina will be back at the café properly soon.' She paused then said gravely, 'I don't mean I want Cathy to go on being ill, but I kind of hope Karina doesn't come back too soon.'

'I know what you're getting at.' Leonie smiled. 'Can't you ask Karina if she'll keep you on?'

'I was going to do that, yes, but it's too early. Oh sugar.' She'd been drawing a girl in a close-fitting dress with a high collar, but as she sat down with her lunch and looked at the picture again, she saw she'd made a mess of it. As she picked up a pencil and crossed it through, she became aware of Leonie standing behind her.

'Why did you do that? It wasn't bad.' She sipped her tea and pointed to the ruined drawing. 'I had a dress like that once in the Seventies. Laura Ashley, I think, with leg o'mutton sleeves. I wore it to parties a lot.'

'The style is meant to be Edwardian. I like their necklines and the frills. I know they all had corsets then and you wouldn't want that now, but it's like lacy necklines frame the face, and the face is the most important part of a person.' She'd been thinking about this for a while. 'Some people are uptight about being too fat or the wrong shape, but, actually, everything you need to know about someone shows in their face.'

'I agree with you wholeheartedly about that.' Leonie had come to sit down and she gave Stef such a tender smile that Stef felt warmed.

'Tell me more,' Stef said impulsively as she swallowed a mouthful of pasta, 'about your modelling. How did you get into it in the end?'

'If you like. Where did I get to? Had I told you about Lucie Clayton's? No? Well, that's where it started properly.'

London, Summer 1960

Mr Rostov had said Lucie Clayton's was the best in London, and over the next few months until she left school Leonie badgered her parents about going. 'I need to see if I can be a model,' she insisted. 'If it doesn't work out then I'll try something else, I promise.'

The trouble was that one had to pay upfront to attend Lucie Clayton's, and she needed the princely sum of £30. Her parents were understandably reluctant to part with such a large sum of money, but in the end she argued it out of them. She would work in the shop as much as possible to earn some of it. Her father would have to cash in his National Savings account for the rest and she promised she would pay it back through future earnings. Suddenly she had more invested in her chosen career than simply desire.

Long afterwards she wondered what she'd learned at Lucie Clayton's that was the result of actual teaching. They had lessons in posture, of course, which involved walking around with books on their heads, lessons in applying make-up – models were expected to arrive made up and with their hair nicely done as there were no make-up artists to do it for them. The latest fashion was for lustrous eyelashes and Leonie simply hated gluing on those strips of falsies that lay coiled like malevolent millipedes on the dressing table.

More valuable were the things that one absorbed informally, and the contacts that one made. Lucie Clayton herself was also the best-known and most exclusive model's agent in London, and if at the end of the course one was lucky enough to be taken onto her books it was a real boost to one's career. Sadly, this didn't happen to Leonie.

The school itself would accept anybody, a girl simply had to be able to pay, but despite this there was a certain cachet to having been trained there. There were often photographers on the make hanging about looking for new talent, and this led to low-level work for Leonie, mostly for clothing catalogues, for which she was paid a pittance. It wasn't very interesting work either, the point being that she was simply a clothes horse. There could be a great deal of waiting around, then a rush of climbing in and out of garments and being photographed, and she was sometimes treated in quite a peremptory way by the client. Any money was very welcome, though. Since she was living on the little her parents could spare, in a girls' hostel near Marble Arch, anything extra went straight away. There were always things to pay for, accessories, make-up, hairdos, never mind food and other necessities.

And then there was going out. In Suffolk there had been nowhere really to go in the evenings except the cinema and the occasional hop at the British Legion Hall. London was the place though, but with so little money there was only so much she could partake in. If a girl had a well-heeled boyfriend, well, he would pay for a few things, but most of the boys she met didn't have much money either. A few of the more streetwise girls went about with rich older men and enjoyed being pampered, but Leonie would never have wanted to do that. She was sophisticated enough to know that there was usually a price to pay in the end.

By the spring of 1961 her time at Lucie Clayton's was almost over, but she was still waiting for luck to strike. It was eleven months since her little adventure with Mr Rostov and she mulled over his invitation to 'come back after a year'. She was seventeen and in terms of life experience still very young. Some things had changed. When she consulted a mirror now she saw reflected a more poised figure than the clumsy schoolgirl of a year ago. She hadn't quite turned into a swan. Her feet were too big. She'd always hated her feet. The rest of her didn't appear to be too bad. She wore her hair in the new bobbed style with a fringe, which everyone said suited her face. With careful make-up, her eyes could look enormous, as was becoming the fashion. She hated the heavy foundation they wanted her to slap on for shoots. Since her skin was generally good she preferred just a bit of powder, but the magazine editors said she was too pale, as if she hadn't slept properly, and were always crying, 'Pancake, more pancake,' if she started a shoot without any of the horrid stuff on.

'I don't like the feel of it,' she grumbled once to a crabby woman with a clipboard and red lipstick.

'Then you can always go home, dearie,' was the response. 'There are plenty queuing up to take your place.'

After that she made up and shut up. It was ghastly stuff to get off, too. The tubs of cold cream she got through; she'd joke that she should acquire shares in Pond's.

At Lucie Clayton's, the would-be models were all too aware of who were the real stars. The name on everyone's lips at that time was Jean Shrimpton. She'd graduated a while before Leonie, and Leonie had never met her, but Lucie Clayton herself said Shrimpton was the way of the future. Leonie followed Shrimpton's career with envy, admired the 'Young Idea' shoots she did for *Vogue* with David Bailey, and saw that it wasn't long before she made her name in America. With models like her about there was a marvellous sense of change in the air and Leonie longed to be part of it. The voice of youth was what everyone wanted to hear. Of course, some of the girls with classically elegant looks, like those whose photos were on the walls of Rostov's studio, were still in demand, but they weren't cutting edge any more, and Leonie had no desire to emulate them.

She understood that something else was changing, too. The new breed of photographers, like Bailey, rarely used those old plate cameras. They were all into 35mm film and an informal, almost impetuous snapshot style. It was an adventurous time to be setting out, but an uncertain world. There were a lot of people on the make and not all of them could succeed. New models, new magazines and new photographers. Would Leonie need to return to Jerry Rostov or could she make her way in the world of the young and the new?

It was a spring day in 1962 and she was exceptionally pleased because she'd been sent to be photographed by a very well-known and respected traditional photographer, John French. One of the models who'd been selected for a shoot by him for *Vanity Fair* had had to back out at the last moment, because her mother was dangerously ill, and apparently someone had suggested Leonie because she had similar colouring. The shoot took place at his studio in out-of-the-way Clerkenwell and after being the subject of lovely Mr French's old-fashioned courtesy for an hour Leonie felt simply on top of the world.

It was after she was finally dressed in her own clothes again and coming out down the steps singing to herself, that a vigorous voice said, 'Miss Brett?' and she glanced down to the street to see a young man leaning against the railing, smoking.

'Hello,' she said tentatively as she reached the pavement. He threw away the cigarette, shrugged his heavy camera bag onto his shoulder and put out his hand to shake hers. 'Billy Fletcher,' he said. 'You won't remember, but we met when I was working for Jerry Rostov.' His clasp was warm and firm and she liked his voice, which was slightly hoarse. He spoke with an East End accent that he didn't try to disguise.

Her mind cleared. 'Why, yes, I do remember you.' It was the way he pushed back his dark hair as he looked her up and down in a way she found pleasurable. He'd been Rostov's assistant, the sullen youth whom Rostov had sent away. Seeing him now brought it back. Her nervousness in Rostov's studio, the strangeness of it all.

'I hope the old goat didn't put the frighteners on you. I used to try to hang about when he had the really young girls in, to put him off.'

'He was a creep,' she agreed, while determined to be cool, 'but nothing I couldn't manage, thank you.' She didn't want to describe what had happened, it would be too embarrassing.

'I'd have done something, reported him, if I thought he'd gone too far, but I don't think he ever did. All bark and no trousers. If you know what I mean.'

'I wouldn't quite say that,' she said, remembering Rostov's hand on her thigh and how intimidated she had felt. Her face grew hot at the memory. She recognized

Billy properly now, though he'd changed quite a bit in two years. There was a hungry look in his eyes. She knew that expression, she had seen it in the faces of many of the young blades who worked in the studios of the established photographers. They felt their time had come and they were impatient.

'Well, he didn't seem to put you off, anyway. I mean, here you are, all grown-up.' He glanced up at the portico of the building. 'You must be doing well to be here.'

'It would have taken more than Mr Rostov to have put me off,' she said, trying to be superior. Billy was cockier than when she'd seen him last, and she wasn't going to let him know how fragile her success was, that this was her first time at John French's studio.

'What about you?' she asked him.

'What does it look like?' he said, grinning. 'I've been working for French since last July, but I'm trying to set up on my own. There's plenty of work for me.' Yes, she thought, here was another young man on the make. She thought he was probably exaggerating. There were lots of opportunities opening up; and there was plenty of competition.

'Good luck then,' she said, but as she made to move away he stopped her.

'Wait, what's your telephone number? We should hook up, you and me.'

'Listen, I'm already late.' She spoke in that dismissive way she'd heard the smarmier models use. There was something about him that baited her, his air of arrogance perhaps, but beneath it there was a challenge, too, and she couldn't help but rise to meet it.

'Who are you with? I'll look you up.'

There was no harm in telling him the name of her agent. After all, business was business. 'Heather Ford,' she told him. Heather had started small and selective, but was well liked and increasingly successful.

'I know her,' he said. 'Not a bad sort. Don't mess you about like some of 'em do us younger ones.'

Leonie smiled and moved away, but as she ate a lonely sandwich at the corner café she couldn't help thinking about the latent energy in those piercing blue eyes and wondering what he'd be like to work with. Not polite and gentlemanly like Mr French, that was for sure.

She kicked her heels for a few days after that, but when she got fed up with waiting and rang the agency to ask if there was any work Heather Ford told her that a new photographer had been looking at her portfolio and there might be a booking. Leonie guessed at once that the young man was Billy. She didn't hear any more until on the Tuesday Heather's plummy receptionist called to say that if, as hoped, the weather was fine on Thursday, a Mr Fletcher requested her presence for a shoot in Kensington Gardens. Leonie was given the address of an office near by where she was to turn up to change.

It was for a new monthly magazine that targeted smart young women, and she adored the clothes as soon as she saw them. There was a fitted shirt dress that she particularly coveted. It was tied down the front with small bows, and had a white shawl collar. It was worn with white gloves and a pretty beret and she simply loved it. It was with reluctance that she yielded it up at the end of the shoot.

Billy was very good; she could tell that even before she saw the pictures in the magazine. He could be commanding or coaxing by turns. There was a way about him that made her want to please him, but she also sensed that if she didn't try he'd become impatient.

'Walk this way,' he'd say. 'No, relax, more. Stop now, and turn. Hook your thumb in the pocket. No, like this. Twist towards me.' And all the time the camera would be flashing, or he'd be adjusting the lighting umbrellas, then be back giving orders. There was no let-up. It was exhausting. And yet she could tell how involved he was. He made her want to do her best for him. Like when she was modelling a knee-length coat with a belted waist. He wanted her to walk away then half-turn to emphasize its flattering shape, and he made her do this over and over again until he was happy. What worked finally was when he wolf-whistled, so that she glanced back over her shoulder in surprise. She knew never to smile, of course; models were meant to appear aloof, expressionless, like dolls, to draw all the attention to the clothes. The magazine loved the sense of movement in the shot, and Leonie could appreciate why. She looked like a shy forest creature caught mid-flight, trapped in the eye of the camera.

When she leafed through the copy of the magazine a few weeks later she could hardly believe that the gorgeous creature in the fashion feature was her, yes, Leonie Brett. She took the magazine home with her that weekend, only to discover that half the town had bought it already and had passed it round their relations. At H.E. Brett's, business had been booming as women suddenly found they urgently needed cotton thread or hair ribbon as an excuse to come in and talk to Mrs Brett about her daughter. Leonie's mother was terribly proud, but a little anxious, too. Most of the customers were admiring, she said, but one or two had been disapproving and this upset her rather. The vicar's wife had suggested that she shouldn't allow Leonie to become 'too full of herself'. That really incensed Leonie. Why, she raged, were some people always out to take one down a peg or two? This was one of the reasons she admired Billy. Billy wasn't bothered by the idea of 'knowing your place', and couldn't care less about people who were.

It wasn't long before Billy asked for her again. This time it was a shoot for a knitting pattern feature for *Honey*, hardly onerous, there being only two jumpers, very pretty both of them, but it was a matter of teaming them with the right garments and accessories and finding a pleasant background, someone's terraced garden in Hampstead in the end. The woman from the magazine was awfully fussy, but Billy played along with good humour. He had to, of course, or she wouldn't book him again.

'That skirt bulges at the back,' Madam barked. 'Try the other one again.' Leonie hurried indoors to change for the fifth time.

It was a very intimate relationship between photographer and model, but Leonie had not considered this much before she met Billy. She was aware of his gaze upon her, assessing her, remarking her good points or clocking that she'd had a late night. That was his job, she reminded herself. She could still be graceless and self-conscious sometimes, but he taught her to move more instinctively, to present her left side where possible, which was better than her right.

'Swing round a bit, no, the other way. Chin down, more, now look up at me. Try doing this with your hair.' Snap snap snap. 'Raise your head, darling, look at me. Widen your eyes. That's good, good.' Snap snap snap.

The *Honey* woman was finally satisfied. Leonie changed back into her own clothes and Madam left. In the garden, Billy was packing up his equipment when Leonie stepped out to say goodbye.

'That went all right in the end,' he said, taking out a pack of cigarettes and offering her one. She took it to be friendly, though she didn't smoke much. She felt her skin prickle deliciously when he leaned in close to light it. The flame leaped between them and he drew back. 'Perfect, in fact,' he said, regarding her thoughtfully, and she felt herself flush. 'Are you free on Monday?' he added. 'It's only a catalogue, but I said I knew a good model.'

'I might be,' Leonie said, picking a shred of tobacco

from between her lips. Of course she was free, but she wasn't going to let him know that. 'You'd better ask Heather.'

He shrugged. 'I already have,' he said and she laughed.

Billy was handsome, with an intense electric energy. His heavy brown hair was floppy in front, but short at the back and sides as was the fashion. She would watch him covertly, fascinated by his blue eyes, which could be sharp, his gaze darting hither and thither as he thought about props and light settings, or intense when they focused on hers, diamond-brilliant against the soft planes of his face. He had an habitual bruised look, the shadows under his eyes the price, she imagined, of long hours in the darkroom, late nights in smoky bars and early risings for shoots. He never ate properly and, funnily enough, considering his job, he had no interest in what he wore. It was always a variation of the same uniform, trousers, shirts, a roll-neck sweater in black or charcoal. At work he'd shrug off his jacket like an old skin and away he'd go, an unlit cigarette between his moulded lips, his deft fingers with their cropped nails busy fitting film into the camera. There was a restlessness about him, and yet sometimes, too, he would be still, gazing inwards as if at some memory. Even then, some part of him would always be moving, his fingers tapping the arm of his chair or a foot twitching to some unheard beat.

She didn't realize then how important he was to become in her life, filling her whole horizon ...

Stef

Leonie had drifted to a halt. She looked miles away. So sad, Stef thought with concern.

She glanced down at her paper. All the time that Leonie had been talking she'd been drawing. She hadn't realized. Again, it was a girl, but this time with a fringed bob like Leonie's and a shift dress with a single, bold V design at the neck, like a chevron, her waist shaded to give her more shape. She put down her pencil, fearing that the fact that she'd been drawing would appear rude, though actually she'd been listening intently all along. 'Do you have any pictures of Billy?' she said softly. 'I'd love to see what he was like.'

'Mmm? Yes, yes, I do. I'll show you if you like.' Leonie bade Stef follow her into her drawing room. She went to the shelf where the photograph album was and selected a large book called *Faces of the Sixties*. She turned the pages, then passed it to Stef saying, 'Here, this is him.'

Stef took the book from her and turned it towards the light. The young man who scowled back at her had been interrupted in his own darkroom, his face framed by drying prints on a line, shadows emphasizing the sharp angles of his clean-shaven face. The hair was dark, rumpled, and there were bags under his eyes, as though he'd been up half the night, but there was no mistaking his brooding good looks, his energy. 'Wow.' She passed the book back, and couldn't help noticing Leonie's face as she stared at the picture before shutting the book and replacing it. Her expression was immeasurably sad.

Stef had opened her mouth to ask a question when the telephone rang outside in the hall. Leonie went at once to answer it, leaving the door to the drawing room open. Stef wandered over to the window to see what was on the easel, but couldn't help hearing Leonie's voice, dull, sometimes questioning, though the conversation didn't make much sense. It was the person at the other end who seemed to be doing most of the talking.

She studied the canvas on the easel. The form of a large white cat was emerging – at least she assumed it was a cat, it was sketchy still – its round eyes staring out at her with an astonished expression, which made her smile. She felt a sudden, unexpected bolt of happiness, a freedom, being in this strange house, trading secrets with a woman she hardly knew and yet feeling so much at home.

Some tiny movement outside made her glance through the window. In the road stood a man with short dark hair holding something up towards the house, then a light flashed, dazzling her. She blinked and looked again to see him walking quickly away. He wore smart jeans with ankle boots and there were leather patches on the elbows of his jacket. Had he been photographing her? Or the house? Indignant at what felt like a personal assault, she ran into the hall, was briefly aware of Leonie's astonished face as she wrenched open the front door. She was down the steps in an instant, but already the man was far off. Very slowly, she went to stand where he'd stood and gazed up at the house trying to see what might have interested him. Leonie's sitting room was above street level but she could see clearly the easel and the form of the fluffy white cat on it.

'What happened?' Leonie called down from the top of the steps.

Stef shook her head. 'I'm not sure,' she said as she watched the man disappear from view. She told Leonie what she'd seen.

'He might have been foreign,' she explained to Leonie weakly, and stared uselessly towards the main road. 'I mean a tourist?'

Leonie said, 'Do you think so?' She didn't sound quite there. They both trudged up the steps again. Inside Leonie picked up the phone again, but did not speak into it. She simply stood there. Stef, aware that it was time to go to work, nipped upstairs to fetch her bag.

Leonie

She'd half been expecting the news, but now it had come it still felt as if something heavy had fallen on her chest and she was dizzy, disoriented. For a while she stood with the receiver in her hand, then she came to herself and replaced it in its cradle where it gave a little self-satisfied bleep. She stared at it, then very slowly, like an aged version of herself, she stumbled towards the kitchen. The doorknob wobbled in its usual fashion under her hand and the damp, buttery aroma of the room smelled familiar when she entered. The kitchen was usually the place she felt safest of all. Except now she saw it with new eyes, and it didn't seem safe any more. It wasn't even hers, not really. She stood amidst its bright muddle and stared around. Everything she'd put into the house – the odd bits of furniture, the paint on the walls, the patterned cushions for chairs in the conservatory, the frail eucalyptus tree in the garden beyond – and belonged here, was now for nothing. A phrase came into her head. Breaking up a happy home. It was a line from a once popular song. If she concentrated she might remember the tune. But instead of music, it was her solicitor's voice that came back to her from the phone call just now. *'£250,000. That's the sum the freeholder mentioned, Miss Brett, to renew the lease at this late stage.'* Money like that was out of the question. He might have asked half that and it would still be impossible. No, they would all have to leave.

And where would everyone go, exiled from their refuge? She'd let them down, badly. The young ones, Rick, Stef, Rosa, they would probably be all right, they had their lives before them, but what about Bela and Hari; they had no money that she knew of, no work. They lived on the minimum pension and, Bela had indicated, small disbursements their daughter managed to spare from the family budget in America. She imagined the pair sharing a bedsit in some rundown house, or rooms in a residential home, which they would hate. And Peter, worst of all, what about Peter?

She had to tell them, somehow she had to tell them, but she didn't know how. Eviction was still months away, but it wasn't fair to dither. They would all need time to get used to the idea and to search for somewhere else to live. Never mind the others, a voice spoke in her mind, where would she go?

Oh, it was no good simply hanging about and being gloomy. She was tempted to go and lie on her bed and give herself up to misery, but what use would that be? She had to be strong. She remembered the people who had helped her, and what had happened to them. Her mother's dogged care for her father after he'd become ill and sold the shop, how they'd carried on although their world dwindled to a circle of light in the bedroom of their small cottage, when each dawn brought an agony of tasks to be got through before they could settle once more for the night, another day numbered against the approaching end. Her brother, retired now from the fire service, living quietly in Suffolk with his materialistic second wife, with whom Leonie had little in common. And George, and what had he said: 'Hope is a form of defiance.' George had been the most hopeful person she'd ever known, but even his spark had gone out.

How can I tell them? she whispered to herself. In the end she changed into her gardening shoes and went outside to dig the vegetable bed. If she was quick about it she could get the courgette seedlings in before the light failed.

*

Leonie couldn't remember ever calling a residents' meeting before. It wasn't her sort of thing. They had all arranged themselves in her drawing room after supper that evening looking distinctly uncomfortable, although the artificial flames of the electric fire and a couple of bottles of wine did their best to impart a convivial air. Hari and Bela sat side by side on the very edge of the sofa, upright, hands on knees, like statues of themselves. Bela had accepted a glass of fruit juice which stood undrunk on the table before her. Hari had wanted nothing.

'Well, this is nice,' Peter said with a sardonic grin, lifting his brimming wine glass to the generality. 'What's it in aid of then, Leo?' He'd taken the best armchair by the fire, without asking. Leonie, who'd made Stef sit in the other one, finished handing out drinks and stood with one hand on the carved mantelpiece, trying not to meet Rosa's calm eyes upon her from the arm of the sofa where she sat. Only Rick was turned away from the group, wandering the room to examine the pictures on the walls.

'Can't we simply be social sometimes?' she scolded Peter, and his mouth crooked into a sneer. He knew her too well, that was the trouble, with the long familiarity of sharing a house for many years. People had often thought they must be an item, she and Peter, but there had never been that between them, though he had tried once, long ago, when he was drunk. She'd never been drawn to him that way. Sometimes she thought the only person Peter truly loved was himself, and that had proved to be a lifelong affair.

Studying them, she saw that they'd all caught her mood for they waited quietly, expectantly. Even Rick ambled over to stand behind the sofa where he drank his wine in nervous gulps, as though it were cordial.

'Well, Peter, you're right,' she said with a sigh. 'It's lovely to meet like this, but I'm afraid I've something important to say.' The room fell silent. Outside a vehicle drove by, causing the windows to rattle.

She'd thought all afternoon about how to tell them, but had hit on no easy way. 'At the end of this year,' she said simply, 'this house won't be mine any more. We're going to have to move, all of us.'

There was a gasp from Bela, her plump little hand with its chipped red nail varnish clapped to her face. Hari put his arm round his wife's shoulder. 'But where, Leonie? I don't understand.'

The young ones appeared worried, Leonie thought, but the end of the year must seem like a long way off. She dared not look at Peter, but she heard his soft expletive.

'What do you mean? The house is yours. What rubbish is this?' he growled and finally she turned to face him. 'Are you telling me—?'

'Apparently it's not.' She raised a hand to stall his questions. 'Mine, I mean. That is, it is now, but it won't be. The lease on it runs out at the end of December. We are going to have to find ourselves somewhere else to live. Including me.'

There was a wail from Bela and, 'They can't do this,' from Hari. 'We have rights,' he said, 'We must have rights.'

Leonie felt the hot prickle of tears, but forced them back. 'I'm sorry, but I don't think we do. I've discussed it with my solicitor and it seems we have to go. The people who own the freehold – it's a property firm now – say it's too late for me to renew the lease in the normal way. They're planning to gut the house and make it into flats. There's a possibility that they would reconsider, but the sum of money they've mentioned is far more than I could ever raise. I ... it's my fault, I think. I should have done something about it years ago, but I didn't realize. I'm sorry.' As she turned to fumble her wine glass from the mantelpiece she caught a glimpse of her face in the mirror. She looked old, she saw with horror. She sipped the wine, but found it sour and set down the glass again.

Peter was growling in anger about it being outrageous, he'd have somebody for it, but the flow of curses passed over her. Still Rosa, Rick and Stef sat quietly. Stef hadn't touched her wine, but twirled her hair unhappily. Rosa was staring down at her boots as though thinking of something else far away.

'I'm sorry, Leonie,' Rick managed to get in when Peter finally stopped to draw breath. She threw him a brief smile.

Bela started to speak, but Peter cut in. 'Be quiet a moment, Peter,' Leonie said and was surprised when he obeyed.

'Where will we go?' Bela quavered, wringing her hands. 'We have so little money and at our age we cannot work.'

'I don't know, Bela. But there will be somewhere for you. People don't starve to death in this country.' Even as she said this Leonie wondered if it was true. There were many ways to die, especially when you were poor and vulnerable.

'The council, the council will help us, surely.' Hari sounded as upset as his wife.

'We'll end up in some dump or other,' Peter said gloomily and poured himself the rest of the red wine, 'where they won't let me have all my stuff, I'll be bound.'

'I'm sure it won't be that bad,' Rick said, trying to soothe him, and Leonie sent him waves of warmth with her smile.

Peter's eyes narrowed with cunning. 'What did you mean, Leo, when you said you could have done something?'

Leonie clutched the mantelpiece tighter, as though to assert a grip on the house. It was as if Peter could see through her to the heart of her guilt. 'There were letters,' she explained, 'a chance to renew the lease, but I didn't do anything. I expect it would have been too expensive, anyway. Thousands. Where would I have got that kind of money?' She didn't actually know what it would have cost, but couldn't resist the white lie.

'I don't know. Borrowed it? Stolen it?' His shoulders slumped. Grumpy Peter might often be, but rarely did she see him so morose. Again, that dreadful realization that she'd failed him, and in so doing failed George, George for whom she'd have done anything.

'I will do what I can to help you all,' she said. She spoke humbly, knowing there was little she could do when it came down to it. She wasn't even sure how to help herself.

Rick

Back in his room, Rick felt terribly sorry for Leonie. For Bela and Hari, too, even for Peter, whom he disliked, but who'd seemed angry and bewildered. But most of all for Leonie. She'd appeared so lost and anxious standing there before them, gripping the mantelpiece or picking up the photographs and putting them down without really seeing them. She was so different from the calm, capable Leonie he'd come to like so much, the woman who'd given him a home and shown interest in what he was doing, simply listened to his mumbled account of his ambitions without passing judgement.

Everyone else who belonged to him saw him as open season. His sister Claire, who teased him constantly about wasting his time drawing comics, and he only took it from her because she was his sister and fond of him; his mother who was always irritable with him as though his failure to follow her advice somehow cast a poor reflection on her parenting. Leonie, though, had given him what he'd needed, an inexpensive room of his own, peace and freedom to be himself, to order his life. It would be months before he had to leave, it was too soon to worry about where he'd go, but he could see that

Leonie feared losing everything and he wished he could help her. But how?

He thought about it as he worked in the pool of light from his lamp, the night closing around him and music playing softly through his headphones.

His work was going well. The girl was alive for him now; he felt her longing and her pain as he drew her. The story had changed slightly, grown darker. She'd met a man who adored her, but who kept her in a cage, not a real one with metal bars, but a metaphorical one. A cage, all the same. This man, with his cruel comments, his lies and his selfish desires, sent away all her friends and kept her for himself. He dimmed her bright spirit and dulled the lustre of her eyes. Now she was his, it really was as though he possessed her, an object to be kept and lusted over. How he loved her, yes, but his love was really for himself and she was his mirror. Rick's pen inked in the final strands of her lank dark hair as she sat hunched up on a kitchen chair, her arms folded around her waist, her face fallen with misery. When he'd finished he studied her expression before adding a tiny tender line to the downturn of her mouth. There, it was perfect. He tore the page carefully from his sketchbook and laid it to one side, then instantly began drawing the next. He sketched quickly, knowing now exactly how the narrative should go. She would peer down a dark tunnel and far away at the end of it would see the tiniest dot of light. His mind eager, he reached into a drawer, withdrew a small bottle from a paper bag and unscrewed the lid. The not unpleasant smell of ink filled the air. He'd need a lot of black for the tunnel.

Stef

Meanwhile, in the kitchen, Stef heard the front door close and glanced up from her drawing to see Leonie, who'd been pretending to read at the table, visibly relax.

'Thank goodness he's gone,' Leonie said, pushing the book away and raking her fingers through her hair. 'I don't think I could have taken much more of him this evening.'

Stef laid down her pen and leaned back in her chair. 'Peter only worries about himself, doesn't he? I think he's the most selfish person I ever met.'

Immediately she wished she could unsay her words, for Leonie looked so taken aback.

'I suppose I'm used to him. And understand a little more, but yes, he is selfish.'

'I'm sorry, that was rude of me, but why do you let him be so unkind?'

'I don't, do I? Oh, I suppose I do. I've always been a bit sorry for him because he had a damaged upbringing, and now it's difficult to regain the lost ground. As I've said before, he was nicer when he was younger.' She tucked her bookmark into place and closed the book. 'I used to find him terrific fun. I think it's disappointment that has made him worse. He was dreadfully fond of George, and he's got this strange explanation that George dying was the reason he never got anywhere with his paintings. The real reason, I suppose, is that they are simply not fashionable.'

'They're not bad,' Stef said, 'but I can't imagine anyone paying a lot for them.'

'Exactly. Whereas I scrape a living by what I do. Even though I know Peter thinks I'm not a proper artist. Which of course I'm not, but I'm all right at what I do.'

'We're a house of artists, aren't we? I mean Peter, you, Rick and now me. I think your pictures are lovely,' Stef said with sincerity.

'You're a kind girl.' Leonie laughed and they smiled at one another.

She likes me, Stef realized, she really does. They were friends. The thought delighted her. 'I'm so sorry about, you know, this place.'

'Thank you.' Leonie's expression grew serious again. 'I keep trying to tell myself that in the long run it's not important. Really, it's only a roof and walls. I'll find somewhere else to live. I'm sorriest for Peter and Hari and Bela. Don't think I'm not concerned for you, too, but—'

'Don't be worried,' Stef rushed in. 'I haven't been here very long and I expect it will only be a short while before I move on. I mean, I don't feel I belong anywhere at the moment, to be honest. Here's like a lovely resting place until I work myself out.'

'That's a good way to look at it. That attic isn't the most marvellous of bedrooms.'

'Oh, it's wonderful, it's not that. It's simply ... I'm drifting, aren't I? Even I know that.'

'You'll work everything out, I know you will. It takes time for things to settle, that's all. Your generation, oh, listen to me, I must sound like an old granny, but every-body these days expects things to happen at once. You know, at the push of a button.'

'Or a touchscreen!' Stef prodded her phone, resting on the table.

'You know exactly what I mean. Anyway, life's really not like that, not when it comes to the really important things. Those you have to wait for. You've had a hard time, haven't you?'

Stef felt very tired suddenly. 'Yes, but I think it must be my fault. I don't try hard enough.'

'What do you mean?'

'I give up on things, don't leave them time to work.' She thought of all the different jobs she'd had, how nothing had really engaged her. Except the drawing. She picked up her sketchpad and studied what she'd done. The usual female figure. This one she'd dressed in a short skirt slashed with generous pleats that somehow conveyed the look of a Tudor prince. It would only suit someone very skinny, it occurred to her. She wondered how it could be made more flattering for larger women. With less gathering at the waist perhaps. She upended the pencil to erase the offending lines.

'That's nice,' through her thoughts she heard Leonie remark. 'A smock top could work with that.'

Stef considered this and rather agreed. If it was made from a light material, something gauzy perhaps. She drew one in with faint, quick lines.

'Were you ever involved in the designs themselves?' she asked Leonie, who shook her head.

'Most of the clothes one had to give back. The ones upstairs I bought. Or were bought for me. You might think it strange for a model, but I wasn't actually that interested in clothes. Not in an obsessed kind of way, anyway. There was so much hassle involved in dressing up for the camera. It must have put me off rather.'

'You were telling me about that photographer, Billy,' Stef remembered. 'How it was like you were his favourite model. What happened? Did you go on working with him?'

'I did,' Leonie said softly and she watched Stef draw.

London, 1962

Before she met Billy, but after she'd left Lucie Clayton's, Leonie had acquired her first boyfriend and for a while she walked around in a happy romantic haze. His name was David and he was from a well-to-do background, but his parents were lovely people, remarkably laissez-faire, and didn't seem to mind where their younger son's girlfriends came from. David had attended a small private school on the outskirts of north London, then one of the newer universities, but he'd been chucked out for not doing any work and had returned home to try to set himself up in the music business. He was doing rather well, managing a couple of rhythm-and-blues bands, one of whom, The Melodymakers, became very successful for a time.

Leonie met him when they both tried to climb into the same cab late one night in the West End outside the 100 Club. When it became clear that the addresses they wanted were only a few streets apart they agreed to share the ride and by the time they reached Leonie's they were the greatest of friends. He asked for her telephone number and rang her early the following evening. Did she want to meet at the Club, where The Melodymakers were due to play later? She said yes without hesitation.

She was thrilled by the experience of going backstage and meeting the musicians, and, later, going on to a nightclub with them. She liked David immensely, he was so good-natured, adept at soothing people and sorting out the band's disagreements. After they'd been out together like this two or three times they settled into a sort of pattern. Leonie was David's girl. It felt comfortable, he was lovely and easy-going and although a lot of their 'dates' were at venues where he had business, it was fun to be in on it all. She didn't know much about music, which made her shy, and sometimes she felt like a spare part, but everyone was friendly and she always managed to relax and enjoy herself.

David had one of those open, boyish faces people trusted and warm brown eyes and he always treated Leonie very politely, nipping round on the pavement to protect her from puddles and helping her on with her coat. He had lovely manners.

Leonie's parents were impressed, too – he gave her mother flowers when they arrived on his scooter to lunch with them one Sunday. 'You can tell he's been very well brought up,' her father said later, though they were also a bit stiff with him. David's background and posh accent marked him out as the sort of man her father would have called 'sir' if he'd come into the shop, which of course he wouldn't have done because he bought his clothes in John Stephen's in Carnaby Street. Narrow trousers, short suede jacket and vivid yellow scarf: sleepy Saxford had seen nothing like it, and the couple received some curious looks when they walked down the high street to the park that afternoon.

Leonie thought she was in love with David, but it took Billy to show her that there was more than one kind of loving. There was a kind that was all-consuming, that could drive you almost crazy with longing and cause everything else to seem monochrome.

There was a hint of that between her and Billy when they met outside John French's studio in Clerkenwell. It was as though they struck sparks off each other. At the time she didn't think anything of it. After all, she had David, and she was fond of him. They'd been going out together about four months and she'd recently slept with him for the first time, at the stylish flat near Marble Arch where he lived with an old schoolfriend and a friendly basset hound named Keeper. She had felt very wicked doing so. The general belief was still that nice girls didn't, and certainly her parents would have been horrified if they'd known. They would have started asking when she was going to get married and there would have been all sorts of pressure. It was therefore a big step for her, though she knew some of the other models did it regularly, even if they didn't talk about it. It was kept much more private in those days, and it was such a worry if a girl missed her time of the month. Leonie arrived home early one evening to find Alison curled up in bed, whey-faced and weeping. She and Trudi guessed what had happened, though Alison wouldn't actually spill the beans that she'd had an abortion. It wasn't simply the shame and the upset. What she'd done was illegal then, though all the models knew it went on.

Billy knew about David almost from the start, and Leonie knew, too, that he had someone, a girl who another model took great delight in telling her was his fiancée.

Leonie and Billy's partnership was initially strictly professional and the spark between them was one of the things that made them so successful as a working duo. Leonie knew she was naturally photogenic, though she still sometimes felt as shy and awkward as any teenage girl. She tried to concentrate on her strengths. She had the kind of figure that made clothes look good. She was tall and had learned not to disguise her height. She no longer hated being horribly flat-chested. With the younger-look clothes this was proving an advantage. She was as skinny as anything and never had to watch her weight. She could eat and eat then and it made no difference.

She could genuinely never understand, though, when someone described her as beautiful. She had regular features, high cheekbones and a high forehead and most hairstyles suited her. She would always laugh at any such comment and say that she 'scrubbed up all right'. Importantly, she learned to use make-up in ways that enhanced her lovely eyes. Lucie Clayton's might not have taught her all that much, but it had given her that all-important confident presentation. They had never suggested that she was good enough to become a catwalk model, but that was all to the good, because the camera was one thing, but she would have hated performing in front of crowds.

Everything was to change in January 1963, just before her nineteenth birthday. It had been a very cold winter, and she and Billy travelled by camper van down to Sussex for a shoot on the Downs. It was cold, absolutely perishing, up in those hills, and the snow was a foot deep in places. Leonie was modelling winter dresses and coats with fur collars for one of the weeklies, but was instructed to wear fashion footwear, not proper snow boots, and after the first few minutes outside she couldn't feel her feet any more. They had to keep stopping so that she could rub some life back into them. Despite the cold the sun was shining and a blue light reflected off the snow. It was beautiful, so beautiful, but she had never felt so uncomfortable in her life.

The shoot seemed to take hours and hours, and afterwards the team, wrapped in blankets, a paraffin heater going full blast, sat in the back of the camper van drinking hot soup made on the tiny stove. Some of the garments had got wet and the woman in charge of them was moaning and tutting to herself as she hung them up and inspected them for damage. Despite the soup, Leonie couldn't get warm. Billy wrapped her up in more blankets to stop her shuddering with cold. Finally he looked at her closely and gave a broad smile that set his eyes twinkling.

'And what exactly do you find funny?' she said crossly.

'Your nose is actually purple with cold,' he said, touching the tip of it in a sort of wonderment. 'It really is.'

'Thank you,' she retorted, rubbing it with a blanketed hand. 'That makes my day perfect. And to think I believed modelling would be glamorous.'

He chuckled and stared at her strangely for what seemed like a long time, his dark hair wild from the wind and his eyes almost navy in the dimness of the van. This attention made her uncomfortable, but she liked it all the same.

'That was the moment,' he told her, months later. 'The moment I started to see you differently. What a mess you were wrapped in those old army blankets, your hair standing up like a street brat's, mascara running down your cheeks. You were beautiful. You could have been a film starlet – you know, playing a heroine rescued from a war zone.'

For Leonie the 'moment' came about two weeks later. They were in a bar in Soho after a long day in a studio photographing a catalogue's summer collection. It had been strange to be stepping into bathing costumes and cruise-wear when the sleet was coming down outside. At least they hadn't asked for beach shots, Billy had joked.

Instead there was a painted background of palm trees and a sea of brilliant blue, and golden lighting to give the illusion that Leonie had a tan.

They were in the pub with some other photographers swapping stories about their day: a model had had a temper tantrum; a fashion editor had rejected the results of an entire shoot. Leonie was sitting there quietly next to Billy, nursing a tonic water because alcohol was giving her spots, when she noticed that he had a single white hair glistening amid the luxurious mop of dark brown. It fascinated her, and after a minute or two she couldn't resist laying a hand on his arm and saying, 'Stay still,' then reaching up and plucking the hair out.

'Getting like your old man already,' one wit sneered as Billy stared at the hair in horror, but then he smiled, pulled her to him and kissed her briefly on the temple. 'Least it's not going at the sides like yours, Gaz,' he shot back at his tormentor, while his arm rested on Leonie's shoulder a while longer, his fingers caressing her hair.

So simple a gesture, his kiss, but so intimate, and for the rest of the evening she rejoiced in the warmth of him next to her on the bench, their thighs touching. More rounds were bought and the talk grew rowdier, but that night instead of bridling at these mostly East End boys' casual chauvinism, the risqué jokes, Leonie let it drift over her, content just to be with Billy. It was a wrench when she had to leave to go and meet David.

It was after that evening that she began to lose interest in David. At first she tried her best to pretend that everything was all right, it was simply a funny mood she was in. David wasn't stupid, though. He could tell Leonie wasn't thinking about him when he kissed her, and she began to make excuses as to why she couldn't go back to his. She even came up with the excuse that she was allergic to dogs, Keeper was making her sneeze. That's how unsure of everything she was then, reluctant to hurt David, who was after all a really nice person, and simply say that she didn't want to be his girlfriend any more.

Finally, though, he confronted her. 'It's obvious you've gone off me, Leonie. I can't stand you pretending.'

'I'm sorry.' She started to sob. 'I tried, I really tried.'

'You shouldn't need to try,' he said, scratching his light-brown hair with that puzzled, good-natured expression he had. 'That's the point.'

Billy's fiancée was another matter entirely. Leonie had met her once, and in the most curious of circumstances.

It had been shortly before that wintry shoot when her nose had turned purple that Leonie and Billy had gone to a drinks party given by one of the magazines for a special anniversary edition that contained photographs Billy had taken of her in that season's cocktail dresses. Billy arrived unusually late.

'Where've you been?' she hissed, going up to him immediately. She hardly knew anyone at the party and had been finding it a bit of a strain.

'With Shelagh,' he said. 'We're going to see her mum and dad later so I picked her up from work.'

'Where is she now?' Leonie scanned the crowd, though she didn't even know what Shelagh looked like.

'Outside, of course, in the car.'

'In the *car*? Why don't you bring her in?'

'Don't fuss. She's quite happy. I can't stay long, though.'

She glared daggers at him, but he didn't seem in the least embarrassed. Handing him her cocktail, which she shouldn't have been drinking anyhow, but which was probably responsible for this rush of courage, she marched outside. She glanced about until she saw his battered car, an elderly Ford that he'd recently bought from a friend, parked on the opposite side of the May-fair street. She went across and peered in through the driver's window.

In the passenger seat sat a neat, fine-boned girl with perfectly coiffed blonde hair. She was knitting some-thing white and frothy, a baby's jacket perhaps. Leonie went round and tapped on the window, and she wound it down so Leonie could introduce herself. Shelagh was surprised to be invited in to the party, but put aside her knitting readily enough, checked her appearance in the vanity mirror and got out of the car, her high heels clack-ing on the paving.

'Is it really posh?' she whispered anxiously as they walked. Her accent was broad East End.

'You'll be fine,' Leonie told her. 'Just stay with me.' The truth was Leonie was grateful to have her there. Events like this were rare and always an ordeal. The men treated her like a dolly bird and the magazine women could be brusque. She was only a model, after all. A paid mannequin, and not well paid at that.

Shelagh was simply a nice, ordinary, attractive girl, smartly dressed – she worked in women's fashion at C & A – and there was no side to her. She was clearly out of her depth. Billy was at first solicitous and fetched her a Martini, which she didn't like, but seeing she was all right with Leonie he set off on his habitual trawl of the room, talking to the people he needed to, and the two girls were left alone together. Leonie learned a great deal from her that evening. She and Billy had met at school in Bethnal Green when they were fourteen, so were childhood sweethearts. They'd decided two years ago to get married and had been saving up since. She shared a room with another girl in Clerkenwell because it was too crowded at home with her three sisters, and seemed to think it quite normal behaviour for Billy to have left her out in the car.

Alarm bells should have rung for Leonie then, but somehow she thought Billy would never treat her like he did Shelagh. She belonged to his old life, Leonie could see that as she spoke about her plans to 'settle down' with him. Shelagh seemed to have no clue as to how the worlds of magazines and models and big money intertwined; she didn't seem to understand that Billy was operating in the vanguard of new ideas about art and taste and society. She said wistfully that she wished they could see each other more often and that he'd find a job that meant he needn't be away from home so much. Leonie felt sorry for her, but also wanted to shake her, to say couldn't she see that this wasn't going to happen, didn't she realize that he was no longer the callow working-class lad who'd flirted with her in the playground, but a shrewd and talented young man with his eye on money and fame? The odds were that he'd get bored and better sooner rather than later. Of course, Leonie couldn't interfere, and so merely listened to Shelagh chatter on artlessly, though she felt increasingly guilty at the thought that she was gradually taking her place in Billy's vision.

In the following weeks the times she and Billy spent together became more intense. Leonie was all too painfully aware of Shelagh, waiting patiently for Billy to be ready to set their wedding date, knitting her baby clothes. (Thankfully these turned out to be for a newborn cousin, not in anticipation of any child she and Billy might have.)

Now that Leonie had broken it off with David she knew it was inevitable that she and Billy would get together, although she resisted like mad because of her guilt about Shelagh. Billy should have done the decent thing right away and explained the truth to her, which was that, although he loved her, their lives were turning in different directions; but he was young and without that long-term perspective and excited by living in the moment.

Another of their problems was lack of privacy – they both shared flats that were always full of people sleeping on sofas and knowing too much about each other's business. As winter melted into a beautiful cool spring, they would drive out into the countryside in Billy's awful old car and sit inside with the engine on and the heater blowing in a car park on Epsom Downs or Box Hill, watching the rain fall outside, just talking and feeling cosy together, and sometimes she would let him kiss her, though then they would find it difficult to stop at the kiss and she would end up protesting and crying and he would be cross.

Finally, he talked himself out of excuses and saw he'd get nowhere unless he did the right thing with Shelagh. 'I'll tell her,' he said, on several occasions, but then he didn't. The moment hadn't been right, was his reason, or Shelagh had been upset and he couldn't bear to hurt her. It was incredibly frustrating, but then she felt so guilty about being the cause of all this pain that she wasn't as firm with him as she ought to have been.

All this while they were working together as photographer and model, and she used to study the magazines, expecting the printed results to be somehow charged with their pent-up passion. She fancied she wore a special dreamy expression in those pictures, or was she imagining it, deluding herself with self-importance? Nobody else seemed to notice it. Their clients simply wanted the clothes to look good, which they did, which is why they kept asking them back.

There came a Saturday in May 1963 when she woke up with a temperature and a mild headache, brought on, she'd thought, by a long and difficult job the day before, an outdoor shoot when they had to keep stopping for heavy showers to pass. Feeling incredibly sorry for herself she huddled on the sofa in her dressing gown and Trudi brought her aspirin and weak tea before her glamorous actor boyfriend arrived – he was to become her first husband – and they went off together on a quest for some tailor's shop Leonie hadn't heard of in Soho. The other girl, Alison, was out who knew where and Leonie was relieved to lie down in solitude and drowse.

She was woken sometime later by the telephone ringing and dragged herself up to answer it. It was Billy.

'Oh, you *are* there,' he said.

'I'm ill, you woke me,' she managed to mutter.

'Sorry. What's wrong? Can I come round?'

'No, I look dreadful. Don't.'

'I'll be twenty minutes.' And she was left holding a dead receiver.

Head throbbing, groggy, she stumbled crossly into the bathroom to splash water over herself and grab clean underwear from the towel-rail. By the time the doorbell sounded she'd turned herself into a faint imitation of presentable.

'I told you—' she started to say as she opened the door. There was Billy with the biggest bunch of red roses she'd ever seen and a smile she could only describe as sheepish. She simply stared at him in incomprehension.

'What's that for?'

'Can't I come in?'

She sighed and opened the door wider and he stepped in, holding the bouquet out to her for all the world like a child presenting flowers to the Queen.

She took them from him somewhat suspiciously and went to the galley kitchen where she dumped them in the washing-up bowl and leaned against the sink for support as she ran the water, glad of the cool drops spraying her face and the breeze from the open window.

She felt Billy's arms come around her, and his warm lips nuzzle her neck, and she closed her eyes and shivered, despite the waves of heat coming over her, which might have been fever or desire. 'Billy—' she started, twisting round in his arms. He looked at her gravely, then reached past her and turned off the tap.

'I told her,' he said. 'It's finished. Over.'

'Shelagh, you mean?' She struggled to understand. He nodded.

And at last relief flooded through her. Relief, but still guilt. 'Oh, poor Shelagh.'

'Well,' he said, again that sheepish grin. 'I suppose she told me. We both agreed it was right. She cried, though. Said her parents would be disappointed.'

'Yes, I suppose they will be,' Leonie said. Billy would have been something of a catch in their eyes, and of course they'd known him for a long time, had seen his ambition, his progress, and would probably have been proud of him for their Shelagh. Surely, though, they would come to see as their daughter had eventually done, that what had happened was for the best.

But here she was in Billy's arms, and they could only stare at each other in delight. She felt light-headed, airy as the net curtain blowing in the wind.

'You do look a mess,' he said, laughing, and she patted his cheek in a mock slap. He did the same to her and then he lunged forward and kissed her on the mouth,

Rachel Hore

deeply, then broke away for a second to add, 'But beautiful. Madly beautiful.' And then they kissed again and she relaxed against him, the relief and happiness at the release of all that pent-up desire bubbling to the surface. Her headache, miraculously, was gone. Then he took her by the hand and drew her into the living room and down onto the sofa which recently had been her bed of pain, but was now to be a bed of delight, where their hands explored one another's bodies and he moved over her in such a way that her fever was heightened by the heat of their passion.

She felt a wreck by the time they finished their frenzied lovemaking, her head thudding again, her body juddering with illness. He picked her up and carried her into the bedroom she shared with Trudi and laid her more or less tenderly on her narrow bed and helped her put on a fresh pair of pyjamas. The rest of the day she would surface from sleep occasionally to find he was with her, mopping her forehead with a dripping flannel, bringing her tinned beans, which she couldn't eat, and sitting on Trudi's bed watching her while she sank back into sleep.

When she woke at dusk he'd gone, and Trudi was sitting there in her underwear instead, about to try on a new dress she'd bought and wanting to know what had been going on in her absence.

The period that followed was an extremely happy one. Leonie was wildly in love for the first time in her life. Her fondness for David was a pastel affection compared to the fiery colours of the passion she found with Billy. If she wasn't actually with him, her senses filled with him, she would be thinking about him. They would be together most of the days and soon many nights, too. For it wasn't long after this that he found his own place to rent, a small but smartly furnished flat that belonged to a friend who was working in New York. It wasn't far from Leonie's flat on the Edgware Road, and Billy used a studio near by, too, so it suited both of them down to the ground. She began to spend a great deal of time at his, but as her parents would have been horrified if they'd known their daughter was 'shacked up' with a man, she kept up the old place. It was nice to stay there occasionally, too, and share the friendly reassurance of the other girls. They looked out for each other. Apart from the usual squabbles about housework and bills they got along well.

She was so wrapped up in Billy. Most days she'd be aware of his attention on her at work. With his camera he possessed her, urging and cajoling so that she'd bend this way and that at his will. But often, too, as others fussed over the hang of a dress or the length of a sleeve, she'd be aware of him watching her with those piercing blue eyes, a sort of brooding expression on his face, then she'd smile and he'd smile back and he'd be his normal self again. It disturbed her, that moodiness, even then, as though somewhere deep down lurked a Billy she didn't know. That was to be expected, she soothed myself, they were still learning about one another. At the time she was too happy to dwell on it much. She

knew he loved her and cared about her and that was
more than enough.

Their work together was going well. They were a
team and editors usually asked for them both. They
liked Billy's photographs. He had a way of teasing the
best out of a model, she felt him do it with her, but his
pictures caught something everyone wanted. It was difficult to say exactly what it was, a feeling of the times, a
sense of fun, and the possibility of youth, exactly right
for the all-important thing, the fashions. For a long time
she loved seeing herself in the magazines, enjoying the
attention, even though it was hard work.

She got to understand Billy a lot more when he took
her to visit his family in Bethnal Green. His childhood
home was a Victorian worker's cottage, the door of
which opened straight onto the street. The area had been
badly damaged during the Blitz and here and there were
piles of rubble still, but new buildings were starting to
fill the gaps with varying attempts to harmonize with
the existing style. The Fletchers' house had escaped the
bombs, though the parlour window was warped and the
front door stuck as though to deny the visitor a welcome.
Mrs Fletcher's face peered round it suspiciously and she
said, 'What's wrong with the back door, for lawk's sake,'
but Billy bade her stand back, gave the door a good
shove and it opened.

Hilda Fletcher was a small, stringy woman and lost
none of her suspicion as she stared at Leonie in that
mean front room where a bicycle had been left against
the wall. 'Nice to meet you, Mrs Fletcher,' she said and

held out her hand, but it was a moment before Mrs Fletcher took it. There seemed no strength in her grip and her arm quickly dropped to her side. She seemed tired, very tired, as though something was gnawing away at her inside, and, though her eyes warmed briefly as they fell upon Billy, the light in them died when her husband entered the room.

To meet Ned Fletcher was to glimpse how Billy might look in thirty years' time, the sturdy muscular body slackening, deep-set eyes hooded, only that cobalt-blue gaze undimmed. After he'd shaken Leonie's hand he put his arm round his wife, but she stood tense at his touch, unyielding. Billy and his father were doing all the talking. She and Billy had come in passing because Billy needed to borrow a particular-sized spanner for a leaking tap – Ned Fletcher was a plumber – and as soon as the business was transacted they left, Billy shrugging off his mother's tentative offer of a cup of tea.

'Couldn't we have stayed?' Leonie asked Billy as the car pulled away. 'They'll think me rude.'

'We'd have been late,' was all he said and sounded the horn at a gaggle of boys who were kicking a football in the street. They scattered obediently, but Leonie looked back when a pebble struck the rear window and saw their sullen expressions. 'Bloody hooligans,' Billy cursed, but did not slow. He had grown beyond his home and was on his way somewhere more glamorous. He was no longer welcome here. What did it matter to him, he told her later when they discussed the incident. Those boys were stuck in their grimy streets but he'd escaped.

She couldn't share this resentment of upbringing. She loved her parents dearly, and tolerated her brother, who was doing well at the grammar, and often went to see them, sometimes with Billy. She watched them warm to him. He liked them and turned on the charm.

'That's a classy dress,' he complimented her mother, and she blushed, actually blushed, as she put her hand to her face.

'Do you think so? It was very simple to make. I know it's not fancy like the clothes my daughter wears, but we can't all afford those.'

Billy helped Leonie choose a very pretty blouse from Selfridge's for her mother's fiftieth birthday. It was much more expensive than anything Leonie would normally have bought but he persuaded her. He liked her parents and he liked the draper's shop, too. He helped them put on a little fashion show in the village hall and took photographs of Leonie and her friend Jean in clothes made at her mother's dressmaking class. It was only a bit of fun, but they got a good crowd and it made the local paper.

They'd been going out together a couple of years and Leonie's parents were beginning to drop those embarrassing hints that parents do about whether they were going to make a go of it. Not in front of Billy, thank heavens, but Leonie definitely felt under pressure. 'He's a nice young chap,' her father said, 'and there seems to be a call for his line of work. You could do a lot worse than him, your mum and me think.'

'Thanks, Dad,' she said, squeezing his arm and grinning at him. 'I'll bear that in mind.' To tell you the truth she was pleased they liked him, but she wasn't yet ready to decide.

Leonie

Leonie sighed as she lay awake in the depths of the night. How clear her memories were of things that had happened fifty years ago. The salty scent of Billy's skin, the sheen of his hair, the way it sprang back from his face. There was a little nick in one of his earlobes where once a dog had bitten him, or so he'd said.

Her mind drifted to her current worries. What was going to happen to the house? Oh, if only she could sleep. She turned over and the bone-coloured strip of moonlight that lay across the bedside table showed the face of her travel alarm. Three o'clock. She sank back on her pillow and tried to remember the sound of Billy's voice, but all she could hear was the click of the clock and the murmur of distant traffic. Like sea rushing over shingle. The freezing sea and skimming pebbles, then the warm sand between her toes. Holidays from her childhood long ago. Her eyes fluttered closed and pictures of the past began to play in her mind. There was one delicious day, one summer with Billy when it seemed that their youth and happiness would last for ever; life was good and the world was made for them. Gently, slowly, she slipped down into the memory, which became a dream ...

*

It had been a gorgeous August Sunday, the sky a cornflower blue, the heat wafting in great enervating waves. They'd driven out west into Oxfordshire in two cars, a whole group of them, laughing and singing all the way, plus a lively Afghan hound. They'd stopped at a pub on the Thames and thrown the crusts of their lunchtime sandwiches to the ducks. The river was wide and slow-moving, and soon somebody, Trudi probably, it was usually Trudi, pushed one of the boys into the water and he splashed about gasping before scrambling out to try and catch her, more of a job than it sounded as he was hampered by his sodden clothes. Catch her he did and into the river she went, screeching. And soon the others had stripped down to their underwear and were jumping in too, the girls yelping at the cold and the boys hollering or spouting geysers of water at one another. Only Billy remained on the bank, fully clothed, watching, and as Leonie plunged about laughing, ducking and being ducked, she saw him pick up his camera and start to take shots of them all. That was Billy all over, a part of the group and yet not. When she yelled at him to join them he narrowed his eyes and shook his head. When Trudi splashed him and called him a spoilsport he laughed and backed away. As they ran about to dry themselves and pulled on their clothes he stood alone smoking and looking out over the water. Leonie went and slipped her arm through his and he smiled down at her as though she'd brought him back from somewhere far away.

After they'd returned to London that evening and dropped the others, he drove straight to the studio and she made tea on the tiny stove whilst he developed the negatives in the dark-room and made prints of some. She studied them where they hung to dry and drew breath, seeing the ones he'd chosen were all of her. Here she was in the water stretching her arms out as though to dive with an expression of deep seriousness. Or flailing, mouth open. 'That's when somebody grabbed my legs,' she laughed. And splashing Si who was bearing down on her. And here, with Trudi, their arms wrapped round each other, Leonie pointing, astonished, at the camera. 'They're good,' she said, 'but weren't there some of the others?' and felt him step up behind her and put his hands on her waist then run them up to cup her small breasts. He nuzzled her neck and blew softly in her ear. 'There's only you, darling,' he whispered. 'You, and you're mine.'

'Don't, Billy. That sounds creepy,' she laughed, thinking he must be hamming it, but when she turned in his arms she saw he was completely serious.

'Oh, thanks.' He appeared hurt and a little angry and she was immediately sorry.

She reached up and stroked his rough cheek and smiled an apology. He hugged her to him then as though he'd never let her go.

The next thing Leonie knew it was morning and from downstairs came the sound of the front door closing. Stef or Rosa, she supposed. Then the house was quiet once more. For a while she lay in a doze, trying to remember the dream she'd had. Something about Billy, that's all she knew. She recalled a fleeting sense of sunlight, happiness and laughter, before the shadows closed in. The dream lay across her consciousness like a cobweb. Billy. She hadn't felt his presence like this for many years, the passion she'd felt for him, the way he'd coloured her whole existence, left her breathless. It must be talking to Stef about him that had brought him back to her in her dreams, leaving her tender so that, oh no, the sadness filled her eyes.

Silly, sentimental old woman, she told herself, brushing away the tears. Why are you crying over the past when your life is full and there are so many things to do?

Spring 1964

It was a wild March day when Billy and Leonie were married in Saxford with Jean as bridesmaid and Billy's mate Si as best man. Leonie's mother had made the girls' dresses to Leonie's specifications, a knee-length froth of satin and lace for the bride and a pale blue A-line for Jean. Leonie's perky net veil billowed like the flag on the tower as they walked up the path to the church, and she cried out in dismay when the blossom from her bouquet scattered in the wind like confetti. Her father clasped her arm tightly on the way down the aisle towards Billy, who was clad in the sharpest royal-blue suit the gathered townspeople had ever seen. He was grinning self-consciously as though he really hadn't argued that they could have got the whole thing over in a twinkle with no fuss at the Chelsea Register Office and a couple of pints at the World's End pub.

After the service the two families exchanged covert glances from opposite sides of the church hall, then made nervous forays into conversation as they loaded their plates with ham salad and tinned-salmon sandwiches, whilst buxom Aunt Maud topped up their lemonade glasses. Leonie's brother Bobby came up, bright-eyed, slurring because Billy's bull-headed Uncle Reg had given him something alcoholic from a flask. Even Granny Brett didn't object, though, when Si produced champagne for the toast. It was to pass into family legend that Si, Trudi and their other London friends were later found playing strip poker in the vestry, surrounded by empty bottles.

On the Monday the happy couple flew to Paris, where Billy photographed Leonie for *Honey* under the budding chestnut trees by the Seine. Billy, she'd long ago learned, lived and breathed his work.

At first they were very happy. Isn't that how so many of these stories begin? It's the newness, the hope, the expectation that all will be wonderful. And of course they were very young. Leonie was often to remember Billy talking about how they could go on working together, how getting married would make it easier, but it didn't turn out that way at all.

She had moved in with Billy before the wedding, since his friend Oswald, the owner of the flat, was spending more and more time in New York and there was an extra bedroom to accommodate him if ever he was staying in London. It was a lovely apartment with lots of rugs and minimalist furniture and framed black-and-white film posters of Marilyn Monroe and Audrey Hepburn, which gave the place a glamorous feel. They bought a new sofa from Heal's on the never-never, a television and a better car.

On the wall above the television Oswald had hung a solitary oil painting, a greenish nude, which made Leonie feel uncomfortable because she knew her parents wouldn't like it. She liked it though and felt that if they were ever to see it they should accept that this was how she was. Later she discovered it was by Lucian Freud, whom of course no one had heard of then, and she was often to wonder whether Oswald had eventually sold it and for how much.

She and Billy were both very busy; there was plenty of work. People loved Billy's pictures and Leonie's face looked out of many of the magazines. The pair were professional, too, Billy saw to that, managing Leonie's scattiness, but sometimes he annoyed her agent by stepping in to argue terms if he thought she was being hard done by.

On occasion he'd be invited to work with other models, which was entirely to be expected and which Leonie didn't mind at all, but he didn't like it if she was asked for by another photographer. He would never say anything out loud, but she could tell by his surly mood. He was jealous, she saw. He wanted to be the only one to photograph her. Unfortunately, she couldn't resist taunting him by taking these jobs. Then she'd feel annoyed if he didn't ask her how it went or when he refused to admire the photographs in the magazine. They didn't actually row about it, but she hated the sullen way he would treat her, which left her feeling rejected.

Everything darkened when they'd been married a couple of years. It was 1966 when the Heather Ford Agency began to take bookings for television commercials and Leonie was asked to appear in one. It was only a non-speaking part, but it was something different and it made her ridiculously excited. There were two important consequences. It changed things with Billy and because of it she met George Stuart.

Life in fact was already quite exciting professionally. The buzz was that London really was the place to be. In the new magazines that were springing up, on advertising billboards, the line being sold was that life was bright and anything was possible, especially if you were young and had money, which, of course, a lot of people didn't. Every business wanted to be in on it. Billy found himself in demand to photograph the beautiful and the famous for feature pieces. There was an article about The Who for the *Sunday Times* for which they needed a freelance at short notice, and once he and Leonie were sent to New York for *Vogue*. She adored that trip because everything was so new to her, and because they were Londoners they were treated like kings. They were made to work hard, but they enjoyed giving the photographs an air of youthful rebellion, which the magazine loved.

The truth was, though, that behind this glamorous façade they were both changing and too much of the time life wasn't fun at all. She was twenty-two, he twenty-six, but by the time she was asked to do the TV commercial it was she who had started to flag. She'd been modelling for five years by then and would have been the envy of her sixteen-year-old self. Her face had appeared under the masthead of a host of magazines, she could have worked every day of the week if she had wanted. She had modelled in Paris and New York, Sweden, and once in Southern Spain where she had wilted in the scorching summer heat. She didn't want to admit to herself that she was bored. Not of the places themselves, but bored of turning up unspeakably early to travel to locations in far-flung parts with the right hair and the right make-up, of waiting about for editors or other models, of being treated as an object, pulled and pinned into clothes, of being rudely criticized for shadows under her eyes or a spot on her face, and twisting herself into uncomfortable positions, of shivering or baking in all sorts of weather. It was with less and less enthusiasm that she crawled out of bed in the mornings.

Billy, on the other hand, was a driven hard-worker. He was doing what he'd always wanted to and loved it. But he couldn't forget that part of his success was to do with the fact of their partnership and he became impatient with Leonie's moaning. 'We need the money,' he'd tell her, if she begged him to turn something down. They had plenty of money, she knew that, but she supposed his attitude was to do with how far he'd come. He couldn't throw off the fear that it would all suddenly stop and he'd be back where he started in that nondescript back street in Bethnal Green which he hardly visited any more.

Leonie approved of the fact that he sent his mother money so that she needn't do cleaning jobs, and she knew that his father resented this. She thought it was because it made Ned Fletcher feel less of a man, but when she ventured this view Billy disagreed. 'The old bastard's never forgiven me for standing up to him. And getting hit instead of her.'

This was the first Leonie had heard of her father-in-law's violence and she was horrified. Nothing like that had happened in her family; her father was the mildest of men. She thought of poor, shadowy Hilda Fletcher in that prison of a house and asked, 'Why doesn't she leave? I wouldn't put up with anything like that.'

Billy laughed without mirth. 'She wouldn't want to. It's all she knows. At least he doesn't raise his hand to her much now. Or as far as I know. I told him what I'd do if I ever heard about it.'

Leonie imagined them confronting one another, those two stocky men, father and son, so alike, yet so different, the anger blazing between them, and she shuddered.

There are so many ways for a marriage to turn bad, but as Trudi pronounced once, it's often about power.

The struggle began in small ways, so small she didn't at first notice them, or else confused them with professional attentiveness. 'That lipstick takes the colour out of your face.' Or, 'You shouldn't have eaten that cream thing. There's a great fat spot on your nose.' Of course she needed to look fabulous. It was her job. He said it with good humour, so there was no mistaking it for unkindness. Sometimes it was wrapped up as a bit of larking around. He'd pat her on the bottom or prod her with his elbow to take the edge off the comment.

She noticed that, when they argued, it was always she who had to say sorry and make it up. Then, instead of saying sorry himself, he'd simply restate his case, as though he'd won. Once, before they were married, when his friend Si had publicly given his girlfriend a dressing down, Leonie had intervened and told Si he was a bully. Si ignored her. Instead he told Billy to keep his bird under control.

'Yeah, you shouldn't have said that,' Billy told her later. 'It's really mucked things up with me and Si.'

'But she was really frightened.'

'Stay out of it, Leonie. You weren't wanted.' His face was pinched with anger and she was confused. It wasn't her in the wrong. Billy had not only failed to defend her in front of Si, but was now blaming her for the whole thing. Then he'd got over it and was back to his affectionate self. He liked everyone to know she was his girl. In public he was attentive, liked to sit next to her in a group, his arm round her, or across the table so he could look at her. If she was talking to someone else he'd often listen in and brood. Sometimes, she was faintly irritated by this, but it seemed to upset him even if she went to sit with a girlfriend.

When they were first married it didn't matter very much, everyone expected them to be together, but as time passed and she wanted to see her friends by herself, he'd sulk.

'Why don't you go out with Si and the boys?' she'd ask.

'I don't feel like it tonight,' he might reply and instead spend the evening in the studio doing work that could have waited. But if she came back late after seeing Trudi and climbed into bed he would reach for her and their differences would dissolve in their lovemaking. She loved him, it was as simple as that, and his possessiveness made her feel safe and wanted. But as time went on it began to feel suffocating.

She still did the work he wanted, but often she had to force herself, felt wooden inside. Sometimes she'd complain to him about certain clients, the over-controlling fashion editor who never seemed satisfied, the man from the catalogue who called her 'Miss', because he couldn't remember her name. 'It's all part of the package,' he'd say. 'Grin and bear it, there's a good girl.'

The advertising company picked her out of the book at the agency for the TV commercial. They wanted someone fresh, a certain indefinable style that their client had seen in a fashion shoot with a Morris Mini car. She would be required to hurry down the steps of the television studio building and ease herself into an open- topped sports car driven by an actor who, it turned out, was an Adam Faith lookalike. She smiled at their first meeting, remembering bumping into the real Faith with her friend Jean. The car they were advertising was pillar-box red, matching the court shoes that shone as she swung her feet into the passenger well, the neat handbag she held on her lap and – she had to wave for the camera as the car sped off – her polka-dot headscarf blowing in the wind.

On the fourth take, she became aware of a man coming out of the building behind her, and standing at the top of the steps, waiting for her to descend. From the car, she waved obediently and registered with surprise that he waved back.

On the fifth take he was still there watching, a puzzled expression on his face. He was well-built and dressed in a very proper dark grey suit and tie, and had a spruce yellow handkerchief tucked into his breast pocket.

'I wasn't waving at you, I'm afraid,' she called to him as she mounted the steps. 'It's part of the commercial.'

'Oh I see. I'm sorry. I knew it had to be too good to be true.' He sighed and she pitied his embarrassment. She liked his round, good-humoured face, the honest brown eyes and the shy quirk to his small mouth. His sparse brown hair rose in a question mark at the front in a way that reminded her of Tintin. She smiled.

'I liked it though. That you waved back!'

'Miss Brett, are you ready for us, darling?' The bored tones of the snub-nosed young producer floated up from the street.

This time when the car pulled away from the kerb she turned in her seat and waved directly at the man on the top of the steps, to be rewarded by a wide grin and a mock salute. She laughed.

Whatever she'd done it must have looked right because the producer wrapped up the shoot.

'George Stuart,' the brown-eyed man said by way of introduction, and she shook his outstretched hand. His beaming face was without lust or guile, just kind and friendly. 'And you're Miss Brett, obviously.'

'Leonie Brett, or Fletcher. Fletcher's my married name.' She'd been advised not to wear her wedding ring for work in case a client had qualms about employing a married woman. For the same reason, she and Billy had agreed she'd remain Brett. Anyway, it would confuse long-term clients too much if she changed it.

If she had feared that the discovery she was married would make him back away, she was pleasantly surprised. The unwavering warmth of friendliness that emanated from him she'd not often sensed in a man.

'I didn't mean to interfere with your shoot,' he said. 'I merely came out for a breath of air and found myself in a film set. A bit surreal, isn't it?'

'Aren't you used to it if you work here?'

'Alas, it's domestic comedies I make. No glamour at all. People don't realize.'

'Oh, this isn't glamorous either, I can assure you. Except possibly for Mr Faith over there.' Her screen partner was leaning against the car like a film star, smoking and watching runners dismantle lighting towers and wind up cable around him.

'Faith? Ah, yes, dear Adam, I see the likeness. Maybe he'll give us a rendition of "You'll wanta my love, bay-beh!"'

'Don't get him started. He already gives himself airs. We met the real Adam once, you know. My friend Jean and I. It was my lucky day. The day I started as a model. Well, that's how I remember it.' She told him how she was spotted in the street by Jerry Rostov. How through Rostov she went to Lucie Clayton's, and also met Billy.

She was aware of George Stuart's interested gaze on her as she spoke. He was easy to talk to. She was disappointed when a girl with a tape measure round her neck came across and told her to go and change out of her dress.

'Wait.' He reached into his pocket for a silver case and gave Leonie a card he selected from it. 'That's my work number,' he said. 'Ring me and you can come and see me when you're free. I might have a part for you. Only a little one, but I need a tall blonde.'

She studied him disbelievingly, but he seemed sincere enough. He nodded, touched his forehead to her and set off down the steps. She watched him go, then followed the girl with the tape measure down to the van.

She did go back and see George in the crowded office he shared with several others, in which phones were constantly ringing and the most extraordinary-looking people came in and out with odd requests. The part he had referred to was extremely small, a walk-on, and in the end that bit got cut so Leonie's television career never took off at all. In the process, though, she and George became fast friends. She was never sure what initially drew them together. They came from completely different backgrounds. George was what Shelagh had once called posh, but he wasn't Sir somebody or anything. It was merely that his family were faintly genteel. His father, who was dead, had been a well-known barrister and had sent George to a good school. Quite what his mother had thought about him going into television, Leonie didn't know. He didn't exactly shine at it. It's just that commercial television had recently got going properly and there was a demand for programmes and George's job was to come up with ideas and see if they'd fly. Some of them did, there was a comedy about a private eye that Leonie used to watch, but none of them made it into the annals of television history. George's talents lay in a completely different sphere, but not one that made him any money. They lay in the ability to be a true friend.

Six

Stef

It was very early on the following Friday morning and in the café Stef was filling the coffee machine with fresh grounds. Rosa unlocked the door and turned the sign to *Open*. 'Raining again,' she called behind her as the bell tinkled and she stepped outside. The door closed and Stef was alone in the café. She loved moments like this, when she could enjoy the warmth, the fragrance of the coffee and the smell of fresh pastries and believe she was safe and happy. Although she was getting used to the busy times, this was when she liked the café best.

The bell over the door rang again, breaking the peace, and a tall lean young man with a mop of dark hair and wearing cycling gear came in. She watched him glance about uncertainly with his calm dark-eyed gaze and smiled at him as he came up to the counter.

'Is Rosa here?' he asked. His voice was dark too, deep and soft.

'Rosa?' For a moment her heart raced. This couldn't be Michal, could it? But no, he looked older and more mature than the boy in the photograph Rosa had shown her. 'She's gone to buy some newspapers for the rack. She'll only be a moment.'

'Right, I'll wait,' he said, swinging his small rucksack off his shoulder and extracting a wallet from his jacket pocket. 'May I have a coffee, please, if the machine's ready. Just black.'

As she finished serving him Rosa returned, her arms full of papers. 'Oh,' she said, when she saw him. 'Will.' Her face was grave with apprehension.

The man from the church, then. Rosa had told Stef about him, how he'd been pleasant and helpful.

'Here, let me do those.' Stef slipped out from behind the counter and took the papers from Rosa and quickly folded each one into its slot on the rack. Then started clattering about with cups and saucers to give the pair privacy as they settled at a table in the window and began to talk earnestly.

She was glad when a customer came in, even though it was the rude, crop-headed estate agent who chatted on his phone as usual as she prepared his cappuccino and twisted a bag around his croissant.

From the corner of her eye she noticed Will stand and touch Rosa's shoulder briefly, then hefting his rucksack onto his shoulder he left. Rosa, still as a tableau, stared out of the window after him, before coming to herself. The café filled up with a bevy of customers escaping the rain, some sleepy-eyed and taciturn, others bright and talkative, and both girls worked quickly. There was no time for conversation, no time at all.

The morning wore on. More deliveries, the electrician to repair a faulty socket, then finally Karina, distracted and out of breath, to help with the lunchtime rush as the rain came down remorselessly outside. And all the time Stef worried about Rosa, what news this man Will might have brought. It grew quieter for a while mid-afternoon and she heard Rosa ask Karina could she leave at half past four and Karina agree.

'Is everything OK?' she managed to ask as Rosa pulled on her coat and tied her scarf, but Rosa only nodded and whispered, 'I will tell you later,' as she left. Stef saw her walk quickly up the hill. Not going home then, she realized, as she set to wiping the tables, but where then?

At a quarter to five, Karina turned the card on the door to *Closed* and Stef helped her to clear up as they waited for an old gent to finish the quick crossword in the paper.

'Rosa seemed in a strange mood,' Karina commented as they worked. 'Is something up?'

'I don't know. A friend of hers came in first thing, a man she knows from the church. She wasn't right after that, but she didn't tell me anything.' Stef didn't think there could be anything badly wrong. Surely Rosa would have said. 'How was Cathy today?' she asked hesitantly, for sometimes Stef got an earful of complaints for her trouble.

'Quite cheerful today,' came the surprising answer. 'She's talking about going to stay with Jared's auntie in Hastings. That would give us all a break.'

'It sounds like she's getting better then?' Stef hoped she wasn't about to lose her job in the café.

'Touch wood,' Karina muttered. There was a pause in the conversation as she said goodbye to the old man and locked the door behind him. She went straight to the till and started counting out money.

'I think,' she said, as she slid a roll of £10 notes into a plastic cash bag, 'it would be great if you could stay on another week or two. Cathy won't need me so much but I'm really behind with the paperwork and stuff.'

'Of course. I'd love to, thanks,' Stef said gratefully.

'You're quick to learn, I'll say that. I don't need to tell you things twice.'

'I like it here.' She was surprised and delighted by this praise. When it was time for her to step out into the twilight her heart was light. And the rain had finally eased off.

As she set off in the direction of Bellevue Gardens, she heard Rick's voice call her name. She turned to see him crossing the road towards her.

'Oh hi,' she said, pleased, as he fell in step beside her. 'Where've you come from?'

'Work. Someone went home sick, so they made me stay on today. It was really busy, there wasn't time for a break.'

'Us, too. The rain brought people in. But look, it's lovely now.'

The clouds were thinning rags, drifting away. The sky they left behind was a gorgeous swirl of orange and purple and navy blue.

Rick

He didn't know what gave him the courage to ask. The words had simply popped into his head.

'What are you doing this evening?'

'Nothing, really.'

'Nor am I. I wondered, shall we go and get a pizza or something?'

She shrugged. 'OK.'

Rick felt his heart swell. She'd said yes. Or at least OK. OK was yes, even though it wasn't enthusiastic. It was a long while since he'd asked a girl out, if that was what he'd just done. Now there were things to worry about, where to go exactly, what to wear. As they walked he cast his mind over his wardrobe. Jeans, mostly. At least there was a clean pair. And a shirt he quite liked his sister had given him at Christmas. Midnight blue in a soft cotton fabric. That would do. 'Should we go into the West End?' he ventured. It would be more expensive, but what the heck.

'Somewhere round here would do fine,' Stef said and Rick was secretly relieved. He knew a good place. One day he'd like to take her somewhere properly glamorous, but first things first. She'd been hurt and he was humbly pleased simply to be her friend. He felt very content ambling along beside her, slower than his usual dogged pace. She was so delicate and graceful and her fine, honey-coloured hair flew out in the breeze, so pretty he wanted to touch it, to feel its silkiness.

'Would seven be all right?' he asked, when she let them into the house. 'The place I'm thinking of gets busy later on.'

'That's fine,' she said, and gave him a smile before she ran upstairs to her room.

An hour and a half. Time to do a little drawing before getting ready.

When they met again in the hall it was five past seven and he was relieved to see that she was dressed casually like he was, but she'd washed her hair and pinned it up on either side with sparkling grips. Her face was a pale mask and her eyes smudged with kohl, enhancing her waif-like looks. Her gaze was steady, though, as she smiled at him in amusement.

'Is there something wrong?'

'No. I've never seen you so smart before. It's a lovely shirt.'

'Thank you.' He grinned, suddenly very happy. It was as he was doing up his jacket that his phone rang in his pocket. He scooped it out and studied the screen.

'My sister,' he said with a roll of his eyes. 'Hi, Claire.'

'*Ricky, how are you?*' Then, without waiting for an answer, '*Listen, can you come over tonight? I have to get to this work thing at half eight. Hey, stop it, both of you. Rick, sorry. Liam was supposed to have the boys, but he's just phoned from Oxford. His train's been delayed.*'

'Claire, I'm going out myself. Walking out of the door now, in fact.'

'*Oh Ricky, I'm desperate. What are you doing that's so important?*'

No, he simply wasn't going to give in tonight. 'Going out for a meal.'

'Is it a girl, Rick? No, don't tell me, it's a girl.'

'Yes.' He was all too aware of Stef listening, though she was pretending not to, poking about in the tiny shoulder bag she wore.

'Well, bring her, too. I'll feed you both.'

'Can't one of the boys' friends have them? Or one of yours – what about Julia?' The woman he'd photographed.

'Julia lives the other side of Clapham, Rick. And I can't dump two small boys on someone at no notice. Pretty please. I'll pay for a taxi. Or rather the client will.'

'We can go if you want,' Stef said, looking up. He gazed at her in astonishment.

'Hang on, Claire.' He lowered the phone.

'I don't mind babysitting.' She shrugged. 'Just saying.'

'But we were going out for a meal.'

'We can do that another time. Really, it's OK. If she's not coming back too late, that is. I've work in the morning.'

He sighed, knowing he was beaten by two women. On the other hand he'd feel bad all through his pizza if he stood his ground with Claire. He spoke into the phone.

'All right, if you can pay for the cab. And we need to be home by twelve.'

'Brilliant! I've got some bubbly someone gave me. I'll pop it in the fridge now.'

'How did that happen?' he said to Stef as he pocketed his phone. His life was not his own. 'It's a bit late to warn you, but the boys can be a bit lively.'

Stef looked at him with her closed-mouthed smile as she brushed a strand of hair from her face. 'Like my brothers were, then. They sound fun,' she said. And, no, he hadn't imagined it, her eyes were twinkling. She meant it.

Rosa

The daylight was failing as Rosa trudged up the hill in the misty rain, careful to keep away from the kerb and the spray thrown up by the traffic. Her feet dragged from tiredness after the long day, and she trembled with anticipation.

When she came to the church Will was there as promised, locking the door of the small community hall. Despite the cycle helmet and the fluorescent waistcoat there was no mistaking his tall slender figure. He noticed her and waved, then seized the handlebar of his racing bike which was propped against the wall and wheeled it alongside as he walked towards her.

'I'll drop this home on the way, if you don't mind,' he said, as she fell in step beside him. They passed the turning to her father's house and went on another half-mile to a great roundabout where the road was choked with vehicles from every direction. Down steps into a subway, Will carrying the bike as though it weighed nothing, then along a grey concrete tunnel daubed with garish graffiti. A young man sat cuddling a bullet-headed dog at the bottom of the steps at the other side. The dog looked in better condition than its owner. Will spoke to the lad briefly, laying some coins in his paper cup and handing him some kind of card.

'It gives him information about where to get help,' Will said when Rosa enquired. What he said made her warm to him. They reached ground level again, at the other side of the roundabout. A little further on Will led them left along a street of terraced workers' cottages edging the narrow pavement, quite attractive in the rays of the setting sun passing through the thinning cloud. Halfway along he stopped at a crimson front door, which he unlocked and pushed open, lifting the bike across the threshold. 'Come in a moment,' he said, flicking a light switch, and she followed, to find herself in a pleasant book-lined living room. A pair of squashy armchairs hunkered down by a low coffee table spread with paperwork and an empty mug. The back window gave a glimpse of a tiny shrub-filled garden. Will leant the bike against a bookcase, divested himself of helmet and waistcoat, then, 'Won't be long,' opened the door to a tiny kitchen and rummaged in a cupboard, emerging after a minute with an open packet of chocolate digestives and a full carrier bag. 'Tins?' Rosa said in puzzlement.

'Soup, mostly,' Will said cheerfully, holding out the biscuit packet. 'And meatballs. Booze and fags strictly not allowed.'

Rosa shrugged, but took a biscuit, then followed Will out to the street.

'We'll get a bus if one comes, but it's not far to walk,'

he said, glancing at her. His face was kind. She brushed crumbs from her lips and pushed her hands into the pockets of her coat for comfort as much as warmth.

'Are you all right?' he asked, touching her shoulder briefly, and she nodded, though in truth her apprehension was building. She daren't let her hopes rise too high in case they were dashed again.

He'd told her all he knew in the café that morning. He'd got word via a contact at work about an encampment of homeless people, many of them Eastern Europeans. It was worth a look, anyway, and Rosa of course had wanted to come, as he'd suggested. And he only spoke English anyway so her presence would be useful.

Along the way he asked her gentle, probing questions about Michal and their life growing up, and she told him about her mother's death and Michal's restlessness, but she couldn't tell him about what had happened to Eryk, her own personal tragedy. She could trust him, she sensed that, and maybe she would tell him at some point, but not now. She might cry and she needed to be strong at the moment, strong for Michal. Instead she told him about their father, and the visit to the prison. 'It doesn't sound too bad a place,' he said. 'I mean I've seen much worse, where they keep the violent offenders, and you wouldn't want him to be in there.'

The sun was gone now and darkness fell all round. Streetlamps marked their progress up the main road past lines of shabby lock-up shops, some of them shuttered and silent, but some still open. Every now and then a shaft of light fell on the street and tinny music, or laughter, came from an open door and a glimpse of bright produce within, the aroma of spices or frying meat. It was a view of a London she hadn't seen before, foreign yet homely at the same time. The only bus passed when they were between stops, but they noticed the office of a minicab company. 'We can take a cab back later,' Will said. The shops gave way to warehouses. The road narrowed and became a bridge with only a thin strip of pavement so they had to walk one behind the other. She glanced through the latticed metal fence down into a deep chasm criss-crossed by railway tracks at the bottom and heard the mournful cry of a train hooter in the distance. Above the road half a mile in front, headlights moved along the great concrete ribbon of a flyover. The susurration of the traffic on the wet streets and the stink of petrol fumes filled her senses.

At the far side of the bridge the road widened suddenly and sloped up towards the flyover. Will stopped under a streetlamp to consult a scrap of paper he took from his wallet. His forehead crinkled in a frown. 'Down here, I think,' he said, and he led her through a gap in the crash barrier she hadn't noticed, and down a steep footpath that clung to the side of the hill, the view from it obscured by a series of corrugated metal panels.

'Are you sure this is right?' Rosa asked, slipping on loose stones. 'I don't really like it.'

'I'm sorry. It's a short cut the guy I know recommended. Otherwise we need to go all round the houses.' He chuckled. 'Literally.'

She concentrated on his broad shoulders, which filled her vision as he moved lithely ahead of her, his boots scraping the crumbling cement that flashed white in the flickering headlights from the flyover.

Then suddenly the path widened and they were at the bottom, and entered a different world. The railway embankment reared up to their left, its black silhouette topped by the dagger blades of a protective fence soon left behind. Ahead were acres of a muddy tundra, scoured by tyre tracks, which separated them from the vast pillars of the flyover itself in the distance. On the ground beneath the flyover, the red eyes of several fires glared out of the darkness. As they set off across this alien landscape, slipping in mud and scratched by thistles, she began to make out the flames of the fires and the shapes of figures sitting or standing around them and the silhouettes of tents. There might be twenty or thirty people there, it struck her with astonishment. As they drew near the encampment she was uncomfortably aware that these figures were watching them. Will waved in a friendly manner. No one waved back. Finally the figure of a man separated from the crowd and strode out to meet them, his hands deep in the pockets of his cagoule. He and Will stopped with several metres still between them. The man's face was fleshy, but his expression hard, unwelcoming. Thinning black hair fluffed up from his scalp. He said something in a language Rosa didn't understand. Will asked if he spoke English and he said, 'Yes. What is it you want here?'

'My friend here has lost her brother,' Will explained. 'We are searching for him.'

The man looked Rosa up and down slowly. 'My brother's name is Michal,' she said. 'Michal Dexter. He is twenty-two years old. Is he here?'

A shrug. 'There is no one of that name here now.' Her hopes slumped.

'But has there been?' Will asked eagerly.

'We'll ask the others, yes?' He cocked his head and they followed him towards one of the fires. A man's voice there called out a question and the fluffy-haired man replied in the same language. Rosa heard him say her brother's name. Several voices chimed in then. Some people came forward from the other fires. They were almost entirely men, she saw, of varying ages but mostly the same indeterminate age of the first man, thirties, maybe. It was difficult to tell in the flickering light which hollowed their faces. Of the ones on the ground two or three sat in sleeping bags or with blankets round their shoulders. A young woman with a tumble of dirty fair hair stared up with such a desperate expression that Rosa had to look away.

Beside her, Will was handing out tins from his bag. They were received without comment but with evident pleasure. The girl ripped the top off a can of soup and started to drink greedily. How hungry she must be to do that, Rosa thought, horrified. And had Michal really ended up here like this girl, homeless, starving? The screech of a passing express train reached her ears and, as if in response, a great gust of wind swept up, lifting dust and rubbish and causing the fires to leap then falter. Here, under the flyover, there might be shelter from the rain, but the camp was otherwise open to the elements.

From the furthest fireside a slight man with a weathered face stood up and came forward. When he spoke, it was in her language. 'You are Polish?'

'From Warsaw, yes.'

'Ah, so am I. Tomasz,' he said.

'Rosa,' she said, shaking his hand, which was rough and calloused. 'And this is Will.'

Tomasz gave his hand to Will, too, then addressed Rosa. 'You are looking for your brother, eh? I don't think he has been here. I am sorry, this will not be the news you are hoping for.'

Rosa turned her face to hide her disappointment.

'Where else have you searched for him?'

'The hostels, the church and I've been to the police, of course. People have been asking in all the usual places.' And she told him more of the circumstances.

'Ah, well. I hope you find him. It is not easy if you have no qualifications and nowhere to go.'

She stared over at the people by the fires, then felt Will's hand on her arm. 'He's not been here?' he asked.

'Tomasz says no.'

'A wasted trip then. I'm sorry.' He addressed Tomasz. 'Someone my colleague spoke to at one of the hostels thought he might have come here. It would have been some time ago now, November maybe.'

'I was not here then. Come, I will ask the others.'

It was their quietness, the air of resignation that struck Rosa as Tomasz took her across to one of the fires, where the half-dozen people gathered surveyed her and Will with the faintest of interest.

'This girl is searching for her brother. His name is—' Tomasz said in English. He turned to Rosa. 'Michal. Michal Dexter.'

They murmured it between themselves. There were shrugs, then one man, stocky with cropped greying hair and a bulbous nose, called behind him several times. After a short while the slight figure of a youth climbed out from the folds of a tent, rubbing his eyes and yawning.

The stocky man barked a question at the youth in a language Rosa didn't understand, though Michal's name was mentioned. The sleepy newcomer blinked in the firelight then spoke to her in broken Polish.

'I remember your brother,' he said. His voice was hoarse, perhaps from the smoke. 'He was here maybe four, five days. He had no money. His money had been taken. We gave him food, he slept right there, in my tent. One night he did not come back.'

'Where did he go?' Rosa was struck by a mixture of relief and alarm. Michal had lost his money. How? Did he not ask for help? She would have helped him.

'I don't know. He said he was going to meet someone. That maybe there would be work, I forget. Then ...' Again that shrug, that resignation. 'He did not return. People come and go all the time.'

'What does he say?' Will murmured and Rosa explained.

'Ask him who he was going to meet. What kind of work,' and Rosa translated.

'I do not remember. Maybe I didn't ask. It is many months ago now. How do I remember?' His eyes were obsidian, shining in the firelight.

'Here!' From the other fire the young woman was approaching, her blanket like a cloak, in each hand a grimy teacup brimming with something steaming. 'Tea,' she said. 'I hope you find your brother.'

Rosa and Will each took a cup and thanked her. The tea was black and tasted bitter, but Rosa sipped it politely, grateful for the warmth of the cup in her hands. Then they gave their thanks and set off back across the wasteland once more.

For a while they walked silently, as the sound of voices faded behind them, then, 'I am so sorry,' Will murmured.

'At least we know he was there, Will,' Rosa said, unable to stop her voice catching, and again she felt sympathy in the touch of his arm.

'That's true.'

'If he found work, though, maybe the police can trace him.'

'Not if it was casual labour, I mean if they paid him cash,' he explained, seeing her puzzled face.

'Of course, but where do we look now? Round here.' She turned and stared back across the desolate scene to the distant fires. Everything was as it had been. Above, the cars continued to pass, their lights strafing the landscape as they passed on unseeing, uncaring. How could they live like that, those people under the flyover? What would become of them? And, as they walked back up the narrow path towards the road and the minicab office, she pondered the question that consumed her most of all. What had become of Michal?

Stef

The taxi dropped them outside a modern apartment block some way south of the river. Although it was only half a mile from where she'd lived before Stef had had no cause to know the street, which was wide and busy with cars and cheerful-looking people on their way out for the evening. The buildings themselves were five- or six-storeyed, fronted with flowerbeds, the walkways between softly lit and edged with grass.

Rick's sister buzzed them into a rather functional lobby and they walked up several echoey flights of linoleum-covered stairs that smelled cleanly of pine. At the fourth floor, the front door of a flat shot open, but no one could be seen. Childish shrieks emanated from within, the door shuddered on its hinges, then two small boys tumbled out and fell into a hot heap of limbs and flying dressing-gown belts at their feet.

'Whoa,' Rick cried, bending to push the boys apart.

'He started it,' panted the bigger one, who had a cap of ink-dark hair, and launched himself again on the furious younger one who kicked out with the ferocity of a buck rabbit. 'Stop it,' Rick ordered, stepping between them. 'Be polite and say hello to Stef.'

At her name both boys sat up and stared at Stef

round-eyed. 'Hi,' the older said, and put out his hand. Amazed at the sudden transformation, Stef shook it.

'This is Henry, who's six, and that's Terry.'

'No, he's called the Terror,' Henry said, which led to him being kicked again.

'Hey, hey,' Stef said, squatting down to separate them once again. The Terror stepped back beyond her reach and crouched looking up at her, thumb in mouth, his huge angry brown eyes and scruff of gingery hair giving him the appearance of a fluffy owlet.

'How old are you, Terry?'

The thumb was removed only long enough for him to say, 'Four 'n' half.'

'Boys, come out of the way and let them in, for goodness' sake. Hello, Rick. And this is—'

'Claire, this is Stef.'

Stef found herself being kissed on both cheeks by a lively brunette in a tight black sheath dress and fashionably high-heeled shoes. 'Very glad to meet you, Stef, and great of you to come. Don't let the boys put you off liking Ricky. They can be quite cute sometimes. Chocolate helps. There are some KitKats in the fridge. They can have one each before they clean their teeth.' Her voice had the same faint Irish lilt as Rick's and her pale skin and greenish-blue eyes underlined her origins. There wasn't much of a likeness between her and Rick, though little Terry was more like his uncle, in looks anyway. She couldn't imagine gentle Rick ever having had the little boy's temper.

'I'm sure they'll be fine,' Stef said, smiling. 'I'm used to boys. I've got twin brothers.'

Claire, chatting all the while, led them through an untidy living room where Terry was curled up on the sofa whilst his brother sat cross-legged on the floor flicking through TV channels, and into an even messier kitchen.

'Now, the leaflet to order the pizza's in that pile somewhere. The drink's in the fridge and there's a cheesecake, I think.' She was fiddling some earrings into her lobes, then seized a handbag and started counting out banknotes from her purse. Rick, Stef noticed, looked embarrassed, so she tactfully withdrew and went to sit next to Terry to watch a cartoon about a family of squirrels wearing T-shirts. Or at least she thought they were squirrels. Then Claire was calling goodnight and rushing out of the door.

After a while, Terry shuffled nearer to Stef and leaned his head against her arm. He seemed sleepy, she thought.

'Peace and quiet,' said Rick, coming through with the KitKats. Mesmerized by the television and comforted by chocolate, the boys were indeed quieter and when the squirrel episode ended and Rick proposed that it was bedtime, only Henry put up a mild resistance.

'I'll read to you if you like,' Stef suggested and Henry nodded to close the deal. They really were very biddable, these two, she thought, and they seemed completely at ease with Rick, who seemed to know all about teeth-cleaning and the unwiseness of drinks before bed.

'Henry, give Terry back his bear,' he ordered in a no-nonsense tone, when they were all in the boys' bedroom with its small single beds.

She was touched that though she hadn't met them

before this evening the boys came to her readily once Henry had selected a book, and Rick tidied the room whilst she read aloud to them about a boy and his dog who travelled into space in pursuit of an intergalactic criminal who'd stolen the family cat. She did all the voices, too, but the story was so ridiculous that when she caught Rick's eye – by this time he was sitting, arms round drawn-up knees, on the opposite bed – he made such a clownish face at her she started to giggle.

'Go *on*,' Henry ordered, so she choked down her laughter and continued. The cat had been stolen to order to rule over a planet of cats and chose to stay there. When the book was finished Henry tried to stave off lights-out with a discussion of how the cats breathed on the planet since in the accompanying illustration there wasn't any atmosphere.

'Is that the only thing you didn't believe about the story?' Rick teased, as he arranged bears, penguins and plastic dinosaurs around little Terry. 'The talking cats were OK then? And the boy building a rocket that actually flew?'

'Don't spoil it,' Stef said, appalled, but Henry reckoned anyone could build a rocket.

'If they had a big enough battery,' he said, but already he was yawning and snuggling under his duvet.

When Terry's nightlight was glowing and the boys were settled, Stef followed Rick into the kitchen, where he popped the champagne.

'They are sweet,' she sighed, thinking of her own brothers when they were that small. Vince and Mark were seventeen now and not sweet at all, smelling of sweat overlaid by Lynx rather than bubble bath. She hadn't seen them since Christmas and suddenly yearned to. 'You're very good with them, Rick.'

'They're great little boys,' Rick said, pouring the champagne and making a mess of it.

'Let me.' She did it expertly. 'I had to learn for my catering work,' she explained, seeing his shamed face.

'I don't often get champagne. Claire said it's from a client. She has to organize these conferences and business events. She's always being given this free stuff.'

They ordered pizzas, and when they came, laid everything out on the coffee table and sat on the sofa eating hungrily, a comedy series on the TV as background.

'What will you do,' Rick said, 'when we have to move out?'

'I haven't thought about it. Or where I'll live in the autumn if I go to college. There's a lot of ifs. And December's ages away.'

'Yeah, I suppose it is. I feel sorry for Leonie.'

'So do I. Really sorry. That house means so much to her. She's been telling me about it.'

'What did she say?'

Stef considered. She sensed that a great deal of the story that Leonie had told had been in confidence, for her ears alone. Much as she liked and trusted Rick, she couldn't betray that confidence.

'She was married and I think it didn't work out well,' she said carefully. 'The house was owned by her friend

George. That's who she inherited it from. He died, you see.'

'She said she'd inherited it, but I didn't know who from.'

'I don't know all the story yet. It's taking quite a long time to tell. She used to be a model, I've seen the photos. She looked amazing. You know, like Jean Shrimpton.'

Rick hadn't heard of Jean Shrimpton so she had patiently to explain, and found some pictures of Shrimpton's pretty, pointed face on her phone. Then she entered Leonie's name and was delighted to see several images come up, one that she'd seen before in the book Leonie had shown her.

'This is Leonie.' She passed him the phone and Rick ran his finger over the screen in astonishment.

'She looks like . . . a film star!'

'She was beautiful, wasn't she?' she said, stuffing the phone back in her handbag. Stef thought she was still beautiful, so elegant and graceful. If she really had been gawky in her youth then she had grown out of it long ago.

'What will you do? When we leave Number 11, I mean.'

He sighed. 'I don't know. Maybe it's like a wake-up call. Time I did something different.'

'Different? Aren't you going to finish your story?'

'I want to, yes, but . . . I can't go on like this for ever, can I?'

'What's stopping you if you really care about it, your writing and stuff? It's good, Rick, what you showed me, it's really good.'

He smiled at her, pleased, then his face clouded. 'It's not getting me anywhere though, is it? Claire says I'm dreaming my life away, and maybe that's true.' He played with a coaster on the table, the words *My best Mum* turning over and over in his fingers.

He was a dreamer, Stef saw that. He cared about deeper ideas, but was useless when it came to all the things Oliver was good at, ambition, gambling and winning, pouring champagne, sharp dressing. Rick did look nice this evening in his jeans and blue shirt, but his hair was untidy and his snub nose and gentle gaze, the nervous way he turned the little mat made her heart go out to him. He'd become her friend and she badly needed friends. This house on Bellevue Gardens had been wonderful for her, a sanctuary, and she'd found there the people she needed, Leonie, Rick and Rosa.

'Anyway, I'm thinking about it all. It won't be long before I finish the story and then I'll see. Maybe I'll have to do as Claire says and find a proper job. Not that I can think of anything I'd be good at.'

'There must be loads of things,' Stef insisted, though she couldn't name one immediately. 'You could train for something. Teach, maybe. You'd be good at that.'

'That's what Claire says,' Rick sighed. 'I did some work experience in a school once, but maybe it was too soon after being a pupil in one. It felt claustrophobic.'

'I see what you mean.'

They drank the last of the champagne, then opened the cheesecake they found in the fridge. It tasted synthetic. Rick didn't mind, but Stef ate only the mandarins from the top of hers. They took turns answering a quiz that Stef found in a glossy magazine from a pile under the coffee table. It revealed that Stef was more assertive than Rick, which amazed her, but sent Rick into an even gloomier mood.

'Does that mean I'm a doormat?'

'The thing is,' she told him, 'I could see what the right answers were. Like this one about talking to your line manager about a difficult colleague. Obviously you need to sound reasonable and not diss anybody. It's just in real life I might not have the courage to complain at all.'

'So basically you cheated?' He laughed with relief.

'And you were too honest,' she said, pointing the biro at him. 'Sometimes we have to put on an act in life.' It was her turn to feel sad.

He was studying her now, concern in his expression. 'Is that what you've had to do?'

'Yes. A lot of the time I have to pretend.'

Rick

It was the way Stef pushed back her hair that he liked. It was the drawing back of a curtain to reveal her face, her gaze honest and direct, and a little sad. The way, too, she sat cross-legged on the sofa. It suited her, made her seem more relaxed and confident than he'd ever seen her. There was still that shyness. Her smiles were hesitant, as though she needed permission first, but with the boys just now she'd forgotten that and when he'd seen her throw back her head in laughter at one of Henry's comments about the cats on the planet, exposing her long white neck, the sight had made him feel tender. When she'd spoken of her twin brothers a softness had come into her face.

He mustn't delude himself, there was a wariness about her still. When she'd taken the bottle from him to pour the champagne she'd avoided touching his hand, and he hadn't been sure about sitting himself on the sofa next to her, so he'd chosen the armchair instead, not wishing to intimidate her in anyway. He sensed that her personal space was important to her, and he should wait for an invitation to move closer. Though perhaps that might never come. Talking to her now, he felt a kind of ache in his throat that made him want to swallow.

The quiz about assertiveness and the resulting discussion upset him more than he could say. It had struck at the roots of some deep anxiety inside himself. He didn't mind not being a pushy type of person, but he realized that he minded very much the sense that he was simply marking time. Was he ever going to emerge from his cocoon, to find the courage to take his place in the world?

It was well after midnight when his sister returned, almost falling through the door, her make-up streaked with tiredness, not drunk exactly, but not sober either, hyper with talk of a glittering restaurant at the top of a glass tower, of exotic cocktails and vapid small talk.

'I got away as soon as I could,' she assured them. 'I'm sorry it's later than I said.'

Going home in the taxi, Stef was subdued, her face turned to the window, shaded by her hand. He wondered if she was crying and with great daring reached out and touched her shoulder. 'Are you OK?' he asked, but when she turned and smiled at him he saw no tears.

'I was just thinking about something,' she said. 'I used to live round here. We passed the flat a moment ago.'

Bellevue Gardens lay quiet and clear in the moonlight. Rick slotted the key into the lock of Number 11 and they crept inside and closed the door quietly. In the thick, lavender-scented dimness of the hall he whispered, 'Cup of tea or anything?' and her pale hair glimmered as she shook her head.

'No, I'll go straight to bed, I'm shattered.' She stepped closer, like a shy deer, and he felt the warmth of her breath on his face. 'Thank you, Rick, it was a lovely evening, your family are great.' And she leant and kissed his cheek with a butterfly touch. 'Night.' Her hand briefly on his shoulder and she was gone, stepping lightly up the stairs into the darkness.

Stef

On the Saturday she worked in the morning and spent the afternoon studying the college website and filling in an application form. She didn't see Rosa at all to talk to until the evening, when she heard the story of Michal's sighting, and how they didn't know where the boy had subsequently gone. It was heartbreaking and she hugged Rosa, thinking how terrible it would be if one of her own brothers went missing.

On Sunday she woke early out of habit and after she'd dressed went out into the fresh morning to eat her breakfast. She liked the tiny café round the corner, which was smaller than the Black Cat. Rather than tables and chairs it had a breakfast bar against the window, and stools, but they sold the most delicious almond croissants she'd ever tasted. She ordered one with a large frothy coffee and sat turning the pages of a fashion magazine as she ate, watching the joggers and the early dog-walkers and listening to Ana and María behind the counter who were chattering away in Spanish, a language she didn't understand but found very musical.

She jiggled her feet and thought about what she would do today. Ring her mum later, was one thing. She'd arrange to go and stay for a few days after the job in the Black Cat was finished. Then there was more to do for her portfolio, and the application form to finish and submit to the college. The deadline was approaching. She hoped Leonie would agree to be a referee; that would be impressive. Who else was there? Maybe a teacher from school. Her mother was friendly with her old art teacher. She'd contact her.

Stef enjoyed doing her drawings, but it was curious. Whilst she was doing them she believed in them utterly, put herself into them, executed them with confidence and care. It was only when she took the pages out and studied them afterwards that she worried. Suppose they weren't good enough, that Leonie was merely being kind when she said she liked them. There was a bridal dress she was working on, which she imagined as a sheath of lace, long-sleeved with a flattering waist and a large bow at the back. Her fingers itched to draw it from several viewpoints, to design the pattern. She could almost feel the sensation of the scissors cutting through the lace and the shiny satin lining. When she had time she'd search for samples.

As she returned her crockery to the counter she smiled at the Spanish women, who thanked her in their soft musical accents, and stepped outside to find that the mist had lifted and a lemon sun was peeping between puffs of cloud. She shivered in the cool breeze as she set off home. As she drew near, light danced off the row of silver cars outside. Why did everyone choose silver so their cars all looked the same when there were so many beautiful colours in the world?

She was aware as soon as she opened the front door that something was different. A jacket that she knew hanging on the post at the bottom of the stairs, a familiar lime and basil scent. The door to the kitchen was closed, but, heart bumping against her chest, she followed a faint sound of voices and pushed it open. A dazzle of sunlight from which, when she blinked, two figures emerged. One was Rick, standing at the stove, turning to face her, the kettle in his hand. The other, coming forward, his hands held out to her as though in supplication was . . .

'Oliver!' she whispered.

Rick

He'd glanced out from his bedroom window and known at once who this man was on the doorstep asking for Stef, but when he rushed down he was too late to answer the doorbell. Oliver had already talked his way past Hari, who was holding a bowl of what looked like fruit salad, and staring at the newcomer in the hall.

'This is Rick,' Hari said to Oliver. 'Rick, this young man has come to see Stef.'

'I think she's out,' Rick said, sizing Oliver up. Expensive smart-casual jeans, shirt and jacket, an air of ease and entitlement that came with the state-of-the-art car key he held and the polished leather boots. Glossy, that was his impression of Oliver, and impatient. Did he imagine condescension in the way he shook Rick's hand and allowed Hari to take his jacket? In the way he slid his palm over his hair as he explained that he was passing and had arranged to call on Stef. Rick suppressed his surprise and a feeling of betrayal. It only gradually dawned on him that Oliver might be bluffing.

Hari excused himself with obvious relief and scurried upstairs, still cradling his fruit salad.

In the kitchen Rick felt obliged to offer Oliver coffee. Oliver frowned at the jar of instant in Rick's hand and seemed about to say no, then changed his mind. 'Why not? Cheers.' Whilst Rick filled the kettle he was aware of Oliver gazing around the kitchen, turning his car key in his hand and whistling very softly under his breath.

The bright morning sunshine searched out the worn patches in the décor and the cracks in the lino.

'So,' Oliver said in a friendly voice. 'Interesting place. What's the set-up here?'

'Set-up?'

'Whose is it, who lives here?'

'Well,' Rick said with a frown, 'the place belongs to Leonie. Stef's told you about Leonie?' And seeing Oliver's puzzlement, 'It's Leonie's house, but she lets out the rooms and we share the bills. We all seem to get on all right, I like it.'

The kettle seemed to take for ever to boil. Oliver paced up and down consulting the expensive watch on his wrist, or peering through the window at the garden with an air of impatience, occasionally shooting Rick a question about the other people in the house – 'which must be worth a few bob now' – wanting to know who they were and what they did, and whether Leonie had help with the garden. Rick received the uncomfortable feeling that Oliver was pumping him about Stef's situation and made his answers as evasive as possible without seeming actually rude.

'I've no idea where Stef's got to,' he said as he spooned coffee powder into mugs. 'She lives her own life, you know.'

'Sure. I'm happy to wait,' Oliver was saying when there came the sound of the front door closing, then Stef herself entered the kitchen.

It was the expression on Stef's face that upset Rick most. Surprise, shock even, at the sight of Oliver, but

then something else, too. A strange sense of accept-
ance, as though it was Oliver she'd been waiting for
all along.

Stef

In her surprise Stef stepped backwards, but her heel
encountered the step and she almost fell.

'Whoa.' Oliver's hand caught her arm and pulled her
upright. 'Didn't mean to frighten you.'

'What are you doing here?' she managed to say, her
voice tight in her throat. Oliver. His presence filled her.
That once beloved face, the gorgeousness of him. His
eyes full of longing as they raked her body. Part of her
wanted to fall into his arms, but she stopped herself. She
didn't want him here in her new life.

'Come to see you, of course. To see if you're all right.
Stef, we need to talk. All I want to do is talk. It was so
sudden, you see.'

The clunk of the kettle on the stove. They looked at
Rick who said, 'Um, I'll leave you to make the coffee,
shall I? I mean, I've something to do upstairs. Work, you
know.'

'Rick ...' Stef said, but he'd stepped past them with
eyes averted. The door shut behind him with a fretful
click.

She turned back to Oliver.

'How did you know where I was?' But her mind was
turning, the clues all clicking into place.

'There was the piece in the newspaper. I told you I'd seen that.'

'Oh, the accident.'

'It said which hospital you'd been taken to. After that, well, let's say there are ways of finding things out. If you know who to ask.'

'That man ... the one who took my picture ...' She gasped, appalled.

'Stef, I needed to find you.'

'But to have me followed?'

The sun must have disappeared behind a cloud, for the room was cast into shadow. Oliver swung the nearest chair round towards him and sat down on it, legs apart, arms crossed. It was an aggressive pose, as though he was waiting for her explanation and she suddenly felt afraid.

She slowly pulled out the chair opposite and lowered herself into it. Below the edge of the table her hands clenched tightly together. The nails would leave marks, but the pain helped.

'I'm very sorry,' she began. 'I shouldn't have left like that. Without any warning.'

'No,' he said softly, leaning towards her, his forearms resting on his thighs. 'It hurt, Stef, it really hurt.'

'I tried to explain in my texts—'

'Texts. After everything that we had together, just a couple of texts that said ... nothing that made any sense. You said you couldn't be yourself with me. What had I done wrong? I'd always looked after you, given you money, for goodness' sake.'

'I'll pay you back. I always intended to do that and I'm earning a bit now.'

'Forget it. It's not the money.'

He stared up at her and his eyes were full of sorrow. It struck her that she hadn't really thought before how he might feel. His face was tired, she thought, thinner, too, and there were pouches under his eyes as though he hadn't slept. Had she done that? His hair needed cutting, too, not badly, but he'd always been very religious about going to the Italian barber's by the bus station. His aggression was quite gone and he seemed only vulnerable to her for a moment. Vulnerable and lost.

'I . . . didn't mean to hurt you, Oli, only I wasn't strong enough to tell you face to face. I was a coward, I know, but it was the only way I could do it.'

'I miss you, Stef. I miss you every day. I wish you'd explain properly because it still doesn't make any sense. We were so good together.'

'Oli.' She closed her eyes briefly as she searched for the right words. 'We were good together. I loved you so much and that's part of the problem.' She saw at once she'd said the wrong thing because hope leaped into his eyes. She forged on quickly. 'I felt I was . . . disappearing. I'd lost myself, any sense of what I was for.'

'And now, here—' He gestured. 'Are you magically yourself again in this place?' She saw it through his eyes suddenly, the shabby house, the chipped butler's sink, the cheap lino on the floor. 'You're working in some pathetic, run-down café, no doubt for peanuts, and living in this . . . commune.'

'Commune? It's not a commune. I like it here. Everyone's been really nice to me.'

Oliver gave a contemptuous snort, then seemed to realize that he'd overstepped some mark. 'I'm sorry. It's just not my sort of place, that's all. There was this old guy that walked in, looked like an old hippie. And Rick, he says he works for Tesco or Asda or somewhere.'

'He's a writer, Oli.'

'Oh, a *writer*.' Again, that sneer. He was drumming his fingers on the table now, playing out some tune that only he could hear. It was a habit of his. 'Listen,' he said suddenly. 'Why don't you come back with me, have a proper talk? It doesn't feel right here. I've got the car, we can easily pack your stuff. I don't like to see you here, slumming it.'

'Oli, I'm not slumming it, that's insulting, don't you get it? I'm happy here for the moment. I don't want to go back with you.' She took a deep breath. 'That's what I didn't like, that you tried to run my life. It's not that I don't love you – didn't, I mean – it's that you took me over. You were so generous, don't get me wrong, giving me a home and money and stuff, but I couldn't be me. I want to try and do something with my life, be a success at something. I've never given myself the chance and somehow living with you I lost the will to do that. I felt lost, invisible.'

It was the best way she could explain it, but he didn't seem to grasp what she was saying. 'That's nonsense,' he said. 'You could have got a job of some sort if you'd wanted, but I thought you were happy as you were.

And we had some great times together. I didn't think we needed anyone else. That's what couples do, they do things together.'

'Of course they do. But it's important to have friends as well, to see other people. And I felt you never wanted that for me, you seemed really pissed off if I went out with friends. Remember Mandy's birthday? You were so angry, Oli, when I came back late.'

'I was worried sick. You could have texted me back.'

'You were so rude, I didn't see why I should.'

'Rude? When I was frantic? That's all you can say?'

'Yes, Oli, that's all I can say. I'm not coming back with you, I'm staying here. With people who aren't rude to me and don't think I'm useless.'

'I never said you were useless.'

'No, but you didn't need to say it, I could see that you thought it all the same. You said applying for that fashion design course would be too much for me, that I shouldn't get my hopes up. You were always implying that I was stupid, telling me I'd said the wrong things to people, so I'd keep quiet and then you'd go off on one because I hadn't said anything at all.'

'Stef, I . . .' His eyes were flashing now, dangerous.

'And then,' she continued, 'there were all those other things I did wrong all the time. I didn't clean the kitchen properly, I hadn't picked the bathmat off the floor or put a CD away after I'd played it.'

'You've got to admit, Stef, you are one mucky puppy.'

'I'm not that bad, but you went on and on and on about it as if it was the only thing.' It was the tone of voice he'd used that hurt so much. A constant barrage of moaning, and once he'd tossed her clothes at her when she'd left them strewn on the bed. Balled them up and thrown them viciously.

'Have you finished now?'

'Yes,' she sighed. She felt she hadn't, but she was exhausted. She was amazed at herself for having had the courage to say all these things, but it had taken until now for them all to come out. They'd been stored up inside her and now they'd all burst out.

They glared at each other across the table, then Oliver said in a deep, ugly voice, 'You little bitch. To think of everything I did for you,' and before she could do or say anything he'd lunged across the table and punched her in the face. She cried out in pain and shock.

Rick

For a while he'd simply knelt on the unmade bed with his forehead against a bookshelf. It was an uncomfortable position, but the discomfort made him feel alive when actually he was aware of something dying inside. Oliver had come and Rick's writer's mind was running ahead, already constructing the story of what would happen next. Downstairs, Oliver would apologize to Stef and then in a minute Stef would come upstairs and knock on his door, her face full of what? Relief? Joy? She would tell him that she was leaving, going back to Oliver, and needed only to collect her things.

He sat back on his heels, nearly falling off the bed in the process, then manoeuvred himself around to sit more conventionally with his feet on the floor, his forehead throbbing from the pressure of the bookshelf, watching his hands clenching and unclenching as they rested on his thighs. He listened, waiting for whatever was to happen to happen, but nothing did. All he could hear was distant canned laughter from Hari and Bela's television, which was annoying because it stopped him hearing anything else.

He stood up and opened the door and was immediately aware of the sound of raised voices from downstairs. They weren't loud enough for him to hear what was being said, and it was the deeper vibration of Oliver's he could hear most. He crept to the top of the stairs and stood anxiously, wondering if everything was all right. It probably was, he thought, and felt self-conscious being there, apparently eavesdropping. He didn't like interfering in other people's affairs, but this was Stef and Stef was important to him. If Oliver was being unkind to her he ought to stay in case she needed him. He felt his heart thud faster. If someone came out and saw him, what would he say? The voices grew louder, Oliver's hectoring, and Rick could not stop himself from creeping down the stairs to hear better. And when there came an awful crash of a falling chair and Stef's shriek of pain nothing could hold him back. He charged down the final few stairs and into the kitchen.

Stef was clutching her cheek with a look of such agony on her face he wanted to take her into his arms and comfort her. But it was as though she didn't see him. Instead she was staring at Oliver, who ignored them both, then pushed his way past Rick as if Rick was nothing.

After the front door slammed there came the sound of a car roaring off down the road.

Rick glimpsed the tears in Stef's eyes before she, too, rushed past him, and up the stairs. He followed, calling her name, but she fled from him like a wounded animal wanting only the dark safety of her lair. When he reached her room the door was closed against him. 'Stef?' He tried a timid knock.

'I'm all right,' her muffled voice replied. 'Go away, leave me alone.'

He hovered outside her closed attic door for a moment or two, before retiring to his own room, hurt and in turmoil. He wished Leonie were here, she would have dealt with it better than he had, but no, he had to cope on his own. He lay on his bed, projecting what he hoped were messages of comfort up to Stef in the room roughly above his. Pictures of her on Friday night rose to his mind, her white throat as she'd laughed at the ridiculous story she read the boys, the way she curled up on the sofa, cat-like, as she smiled at him. How could someone treat her as Oliver had done? And how could she have looked at Oliver like, as if, as though she *belonged* to him. Was that really how she felt about Oliver, even now, after what he'd done to her?

He sighed, and in a desultory fashion switched on his laptop. Opening his blog account helped him push that last ugly scene from his mind. Here he was in control. He stared at his latest post. The story was nearly finished now, and this was one of the very last scenes. Three pictures of his heroine in deep despair. Soon she would be released. He already knew how he'd draw those shots, her determination as she turned the key in her prison door and opened it, then the light falling on her joyful face . . .

There were several comments by followers, he was pleased to see. One was particularly complimentary; he read it through twice. He scrolled down and sighed as the tag 'darkstar494' came into view, then stared more closely, surprised. *Know how that feels*, 'darkstar494' had written. Jamie, sympathetic! How very un-Jamie-like. The other comments were encouraging, though their missives hardly original. He thanked them all, but paused at Jamie's, his fingers hovering over the keys. He shouldn't get involved. That was the second time he'd thought that today, and yet he had got involved. If he hadn't rushed into the kitchen after Oliver had hit Stef, what else might he have done to her? What would happen if he ignored Jamie's vulnerable-sounding comment or made a facetious reply or a bland one like, *Sorry about this, mate*, which was usually as far as he would go.

Instead he found himself typing, *Why don't you come back and visit us? Your room's still here waiting*. He sent the message and tried not to regret it. With any luck Jamie was actually OK, or would realize it would be disastrous to come back and would simply send another, possibly sneering, message. Whatever, Rick had done his best and Leonie would be pleased if she knew. He wondered if he should tell her, or whether she'd merely be alarmed at the possibility of Jamie being in a dark place.

To calm his troubled mind, he switched on the desk lamp, pulled his sketchpad towards him and taking up a pencil began to draw.

Stef

Upstairs, Stef lay in trauma, sobbing. Oliver had struck her. That had been awful enough. Her face still smarted from the blow, which had caught the side of her nose and her cheekbone, but it was the shock of it that distressed her more than any physical injury. She couldn't block out the vision of his face before he did it, his expression grim, cold, the mouth twisted with contempt rather than anger, the eyes opaque, glittering. She shivered and sobbed again. Still crying, she rolled off the bed and went across to examine her face in the mirror. And gave a little gasp. Oliver's fist had left a livid mark across her cheek as though she'd been scalded. The cheek looked swollen and her make-up was streaked with her tears. She touched the mark with her fingertips and thought about going to bathe it, but she didn't want to run into anyone, even Rick. She wanted to be alone. So she dabbed moisturizer on it and sank back down on the bed.

It was a while before her heartbeat stilled, she could

breathe more calmly and her mind became clearer. But the memory of that face and the words he said persisted, and gradually some hard truths fell into place. He had come, she'd thought initially, to persuade her to come back to him, because he loved her and missed her, but the whole time he'd been here he'd never spoken of love, nor had he listened to her complaints, but instead denied their validity.

It was as though she were some prized pet that had escaped him, she thought with bitterness, yes, that's how it had felt. It wasn't love, but the fact he'd lost control of her that angered him. He could only accept her independence if she became an object of contempt, not worthy, yes, that had been the look on his face as he'd struck her. Contempt. He'd said something as he left, what was it, she'd hardly registered. 'Nothing.' No. 'You're nothing,' that was it. In his job he was used to assessing the amount of profit a fund would yield. Staff were rewarded in accordance with their value to the firm. In his private life he chose carefully and he chose the best – his car, his apartment, his designer fridge. He'd paid someone to find out where she'd gone. It was the worst insult that he could give anything – that it had no worth. And worthless is what he'd just labelled her. She had been judged by his high standards and found wanting. Or had it been a deeper reaction in him, more complicated than that? Because she wouldn't come back to him it was his way of coping. To tell himself she wasn't worth having. It would enable him to cut her off and forget her.

Forget her. How did she feel about that? Mourning all over again. When she'd come in from her breakfast and seen him she'd been alarmed, but also her heart had been traitorous and remembered its yearning for him. She'd left him, after all, because she had to, not because she hadn't loved him. It was love that had made it so hard. And there was another facet of the truth. He'd called her worthless because that was how she'd come to see herself, as having no value apart from the one he placed on her.

She lay exhausted now, the thoughts whirling in her head. And finally, she slept. She didn't hear Leonie arriving home or her cry of surprise as she entered the kitchen to see the chairs in disarray and Stef's handbag lying spilt on the floor.

Leonie

It wasn't until later that Leonie managed to piece together what had happened. She'd collected up the coins, the lipstick and a foil packet of pills from the lino, replaced them in the handbag then, after a moment's hesitation, carried it upstairs to Stef's attic to be confronted by the closed door. More hesitation, then she'd knocked softly, and on hearing no answer, turned the doorknob and peeped inside. Seeing that Stef was asleep, and definitely breathing, she closed the door, hung the bag on the handle and retreated. Perhaps there was nothing wrong at all, but all the same, she felt a worm of worry wriggling away inside.

Rick's door also was closed, and Bela and Hari had the telly on, so she descended to the basement to tell Peter, who was at his easel painting, that lunch would be at two. Then she tried to banish her worry by activity, tidied the kitchen and set about cooking a chicken. On the whole she liked Sundays, the old routines of her childhood, morning service at the Anglican church, where there was a popular lady vicar and there were lots of young families to smile at, and roast lunch, which Peter always appreciated. There was a recipe for a raspberry syllabub from a supermarket magazine she wanted to try out today. If it worked she'd do the low-calorie version for Trudi when she came to lunch in a fortnight's time. Trudi loved desserts, but usually denied herself them.

She stuffed the chicken, laid it in a dish with root vegetables round it and slid it into the oven. If anyone else was around they could have some, otherwise it would do for supper, too.

It was while she and Peter were eating that Rick came into the kitchen. 'There is plenty if you'd like some,' she told him.

'Thanks, but I'm fine,' he said, but something about his tone didn't convince. She watched him as he stood waiting for the kettle to boil and thought he seemed down, but Peter was talking about some dead painter she hadn't heard of whose exhibition had been previewed on the television and there wasn't the chance to ask Rick what had been going on.

As Leonie was washing up, Stef drifted through like a

ghost to fetch a yoghurt from the fridge, her hair pulled across her face like a blind, and Leonie was alarmed. It was as though Stef had gone back to being the withdrawn figure she'd been when she'd first arrived over a month ago. 'Are you all right?' she asked her, but Stef merely nodded and murmured, 'Fine, thanks,' before disappearing once more.

'It's odd,' Leonie remarked to Peter, who'd been outside smoking. 'Do you know if something happened here this morning?'

'Dunno. There was a bit of a row while you were out, doors slamming and whatnot, but I didn't interfere. The kids are old enough to look after themselves.'

'I don't know about that,' Leonie said. 'After all, you don't,' she wanted to add, but bit her tongue. 'Now, I'll make us some tea and then I think I'll do a bit of weeding.' Gardens were so much easier than people.

The following morning, Leonie came downstairs just before eight to find an envelope on the table addressed to her in Stef's beautiful flowing hand. Inside were several banknotes and a short letter, which read:

Dear Leonie

I'm sorry that I've gone without telling you, but I need a break from everything so I've gone to stay with Mum. I expect Rick will tell you, but basically Oliver found out I was here and came over yesterday. It ended really badly and I need to get away. I hope that the enclosed covers the rent till the end of the week. You've

been really kind and I've loved living here, but I quite
understand if you decide to rent out my room given
that I'm not sure when I'm coming back.
  Yours truly and thank you again
  Stef xxx

'Damn,' Leonie said to herself. 'Damn, damn, damn.'
Why hadn't she interfered after all and asked Stef yes-
terday what was wrong? Maybe she could have helped.
It was too late now.

She trudged up the stairs to the attic. The door had
been left open and she stood in the doorway, her heart
sinking. Stef had packed all her things and taken them
with her. The bed had been stripped and the linen left
folded neatly. The message was clear. Stef thought she
might not be coming back. Leonie went and picked up
the linen, smoothed it against her. It smelt pleasantly of
Stef's flowery scent and she felt terribly sad. She tucked
the little bundle under her arm and turned to go. But
wait, something caught her eye, half hidden behind the
chest-of-drawers, something she recognized with further
dismay. Stef's portfolio. She slid it out, put down the linen
and looked inside. All Stef's drawings and idea boards
were there. Had she forgotten it, or not been able to carry
it, or – the worst thought came to her – abandoned it?
Had Stef really given up on all her hopes and dreams?

She returned the portfolio to its hiding place, picked
up the bedlinen again and took a last glance round. Stef
had made this haven pretty, with a vase of daffodils
on the chest-of-drawers and a string of fairy lights left

draped round the mirror, but now there was an absence, which Leonie felt most keenly. Stef had become important to her, she saw now; she missed her as she had her own daughter when Tara left to live with Billy.

The pain of this memory led her to close her eyes for a moment. It had perhaps been the most heartbreaking moment of her life.

London, 1982

Tara was fourteen. Growing up fast, yet in all the ways that matter still a child. 'It's not fair,' was the constant cry upon her strawberry-glossed lips, so perfect apart from their turned-down sulkiness.

How pretty Tara was already, a fragile willowy figure in a minidress, leggings and little boots, her short spiky hair completing the pixie appearance. A very angry pixie much of the time.

'Why can't I go to the party?' Tara all but stamped her foot.

'Because they're all older than you,' Leonie sighed. 'Goodness knows what they get up to.'

'But they're fun, and they'll look after me. I won't drink, I promise.'

'I can't run the risk.'

'Mum, it's not fair. You're so boring. Everything's so boring here. Boring, boring, boring. I can't stand it.' She screwed up her lovely heart-shaped face, burst into tears and ran out of the kitchen, slamming the door. When Leonie, distraught, tried her bedroom door a moment later it was locked and no amount of knocking or cajoling would get her to open it.

Not for the first time, Leonie wondered if she'd handled Tara badly, but the last few years had been so sad, so difficult. George had been ill, then had died, leaving them all bereft.

During one of his periods of treatment for the brain tumour, Leonie had been sitting with him in the garden one warm day, trying not to think with dismay how emaciated and ill he seemed. His skin had a loose look because he didn't fill it properly any more and he had lost the few strands of hair he had left. They'd been talking about the future.

'You know what it means, Leo, if it doesn't work? That very risky operation.'

She studied his face and hated what she read in his grave expression. 'But it will work, won't it? Surely there's every chance.'

He reached out and squeezed her hand. It seemed wrong that he was having to comfort her when it was he who was dangerously ill.

'Of course there is,' he said gently. 'But all the same, there's something I need to talk to you about. It's Peter.'

She frowned. 'Peter?'

'If anything does happen to me, Leonie, I'm worried about how he'll manage. Where he'll live. His family are no good. They kicked him out, you know. He was literally on the street when I found him. Not much more than a boy and trying to sell his paintings to passers-by. It was pouring with rain, for heaven's sake.'

'Oh George,' Leonie said fondly, shaking her head. 'Most people would have simply given him some money and walked on by.'

'I couldn't just leave him there. The way he gazed up at me, Leo. With eyes like a stray dog's. No, I told him I had somewhere he could stay for a night or two, then we gathered up his pictures and took a taxi. And that was fourteen years ago.'

'Just before you met me.'

'Yes.' George glanced up, distracted by a blackbird flying down from a tree, then said conversationally, 'Leo, if it comes to it, would you look after Peter for me? I'd make it worth your while.'

Leonie was filled with dismay. 'George, don't talk like that, please.'

'Would you, Leo? I'm serious.'

'You care for him, don't you?'

'Strange though it may seem, I really do, yes.'

'Then yes, George, I will look after him. But it's not going to come to that.'

'Thank you, my dear girl, thank you. That's a weight off my mind.' He closed his eyes and again Leonie was struck by how exhausted he was.

It was only two short months later that George was dead.

Wonderfully, he'd bequeathed Leonie the house, but somewhat less wonderfully, a clause added to the will on which the ink had hardly time to dry arranged that Peter should continue to live in it, rent free.

*

During the time of George's illness and death, she hadn't kept a proper eye on Tara. In her grief and the general chaos after he'd gone she had been too self-absorbed to reassure Tara after her best friend at school dumped her. She should have intervened when Tara got off with an older boy at a school disco and started to hang out with a crowd from his class two years above hers.

It was after the boy in turn dropped Tara that her daughter's self-esteem plummeted further, and just at this wrong moment that Billy turned up again in their lives.

Having hardly seen Leonie and Tara for a year, one sunny Sunday in May he stepped out of a taxi, clutching a bunch of roses – yellow, this time – for Leonie and a bottle of duty-free Giorgio perfume for Tara, which caused her eyes to widen, for no one else at school had something so expensive and exotic. That was the moment that Tara fell in love with her father.

He was living in New York now, his second marriage having collapsed, but being alone had obviously made him nostalgic for family life for he'd been determined to see Leonie and his daughter.

Billy looked different, his hair, still plenty of it, brushed neatly up from his forehead, defying gravity. He'd developed an interest in fashion, for he wore a stylish suit and from one of the many pockets of its jacket he withdrew a pair of gold-framed specs to examine his daughter's terrible school reports. He'd become vain, Leonie saw, suppressing a smile, but at least he still had something to be vain about. His tanned skin might be weathered from holidays in the California sun, but his blue eyes were as bright as ever and his figure trim.

He merely laughed at the school reports, which made Tara, perched on the arm of his chair, look at him more adoringly than ever. 'Tell you what, girl,' he beamed at her. 'Why don't you come and stay with me over the summer? We'll have some fun, eh? Forget all this lark.' He threw the reports contemptuously on the coffee table.

'Billy ...' Leonie said weakly. 'I don't think that's possible. She's supposed to go to my parents' ...' But she already knew, the way the two of them were smiling at one another, that she was defeated.

What she didn't expect, as she waved them both off at the airport the following week, was that the sense of loss at seeing her elfin child disappearing into the departures lounge was to last for ever. For Tara made her home in America and did not return for several years. And by then she was a beautiful, rather hard-edged young woman who seemed to think the world owed her a living. She set out on a haphazard trail through a whole series of jobs, from running a restaurant to being a travel courier with much in between, any financial low points subsidized by handouts from her father. There was a series of men, too. Jamie had been the result of a short affair with Alastair, her business partner in the restaurant. When the affair ended tempestuously and Billy refused to bail out the restaurant any further, it was the last anyone saw of Alastair.

Apparently he'd never wanted to become a father in the first place. Leonie sometimes saw Tara over the years, but it was too late to help her much. The closeness they'd once shared had gone to be replaced by suspicion on both sides. Billy had done that, though to be fair he hadn't meant to.

Leonie sighed as she left the attic room, closing the door gently behind her. She hoped that Stef didn't lose her way like Tara.

As she returned downstairs, Rick came out of his room on his way to the bathroom. Briefly, she explained to him about Stef and watched with alarm as his face became suffused with unhappiness.

'I expect she'll be back soon,' she said, trying to comfort him. 'Do you have her number? Send her a text or something to ask if she's all right.'

'No, I don't have it,' he said. 'I never needed to ask her for it.'

'Oh well, maybe Rosa will.' She decided not to tell Rick yet about the abandoned portfolio and to wonder what it might or might not mean. She'd done all she could for Stef at the moment. Now they would simply have to wait and see.

Rosa

Sorry not to say bye. Things not gr8 ... Gone to my mum's. C U soon maybe. Tell Karina sorry. X was the message Rosa received at work from Stef. She had to ask Karina to make sure she'd understood it correctly, before replying. *Hope you OK. Yes, C U soon. Karina says hi don't worry. X.* Actually, Karina had been a little annoyed, but it wouldn't help Stef to tell her that.

She missed Stef already, though it was good that Karina was back at work properly. Some things Rosa hadn't known how to do, like fixing the freezer, which kept icing up, and complaining when the latest delivery from the wholesaler hadn't been right. It was Stef's friendship she missed most. They'd worked well together as a team, and Stef had been very sympathetic about Michal and disappointed for Rosa when she had described to her the visit to the flyover camp and how the trail had once again gone cold.

It was four days after Stef's departure, on the afternoon of Good Friday, when Rosa was serving a customer, that a police car drew up outside the café and Ben, her police contact, stepped into the café, a woman police officer close behind. They hovered politely in the background while she'd finished her task then Ben came forward to the front of the queue.

'I'm sorry, but have you got a moment?'

'Karina? Karina, can you help, please?' she called out in a faint voice. Her boss heard, and came in from the back of the shop, and diagnosing the situation took over immediately. Rosa squeezed round the edge of the counter and Ben introduced her to his colleague, Cheryl, a round-faced young woman with a neat figure and a friendly manner.

'Perhaps we ought to go out to the car?' Ben's face was

sombre and Rosa knew instantly that he didn't have good news. Her limbs prickled with fear and she felt slightly faint, but forced herself to rally.

'No, we can talk here.' She led them both across to a table in a quiet corner.

Ben glanced around at the other customers with not a little anxiety, then sighed and gave her his full attention. 'There has been a development. I'm sorry, but early this morning, the body of a young man was found in the canal up by Camden Market.'

'No!' Rosa's hands flew to her face.

'Please try to be calm,' Cheryl said. She had a voice as golden as honey. 'We don't yet have reason to believe that it's Michal.'

'But it might be?' she whispered.

'The thing is,' Ben said, hurrying on, 'that this lad is the right age and build so we have to explore all possibilities. Having said that, it might not be him and normally we wouldn't have told you anything at this point, but we need to ask you for some information. The name of your brother's dentist, anything you can tell us about his medical history, things like that.'

All she could see was whirling darkness. All she could feel was the weight of black water, blood beating in her head. Then the warmth of the policewoman's hand on her arm. 'Steady, Rosa,' she said.

'You don't need me to . . . see him?'

'We . . . no. The body . . . the lad had been in the water for some time, you see. Even his clothes . . .'

'His face is not—' Cheryl whispered, breaking off as

Karina came across with mugs of coffee on a tray. 'Can we have a glass of water, too, please. The girl's had a bit of a shock.'

Rosa was aware of Karina's touch on her shoulder. She opened her eyes and managed to say, 'They've maybe found him. Oh Karina, he may be . . .' She could not say the word.

'Rosa, I'm so sorry. Look, you must go home.'

'No.'

'We can take you,' Cheryl said.

Rosa shook her head. She didn't know where she wanted to be, but not at home doing nothing, not alone to let the thoughts pour in.

'I'll manage better if I'm here,' she said and Karina sighed.

Rosa checked her phone for numbers and gave the police officers the information they needed and they promised that they'd be in touch as soon as they knew anything at all, and then they left, the car pulling away from the kerb as quietly and slowly as a hearse. For the next hour she worked away mechanically, wiping tables, restoring dropped toys to toddlers, setting cakes on plates and filling cups, watching the whirling froth of milk and coffee and trying not to think.

When it was quieter Karina insisted that she take a break and Rosa pulled on her coat and slipped out to sit in the garden where the war memorial was. There she lit a cigarette with shaking fingers and sat for a long time trying to calm her racing thoughts. It couldn't be Michal, could it? She prayed that it wouldn't be, told herself there was no real reason for it to be him, though would the police have taken the trouble to tell her if there wasn't a serious possibility? If only she could do something to find out more, but she couldn't think what. Her job was simply to wait.

She'd been staring at the war memorial, her eyes unseeing, when her attention was caught by the sight of her own name etched on it. *Dexter.* The soldier's first name had been John and it wasn't likely that he had had any connection to her family at all. She knew Dexter was not an unusual name in England. Still, she allowed herself to wonder about him and the circumstances in which he'd died. In November 1918, the inscription noted. Right at the end of the war, then, how particularly sad. In her mind John assumed the face of Michal, innocent, boyish and eager. She could imagine how his loss would have devastated his family. There were memorials like this all over her home city. Sometimes she was amazed by the amount of sorrow in the world and how lives could turn into a long accommodation to loss and grief. She thought of her mother, of her dead fiancé Eryk, of how her whole young life had seemed to be about losing people. Even her father ... *God!* Her father. She threw down her cigarette and trod on it. She'd have to tell him about this latest development, have to, now, this afternoon. Who else should she speak to? She thought about texting Stef, but she didn't want to upset her when she was troubled enough. And Leonie she'd tell at home later. Then she knew who she wanted to speak to most. She felt in her bag for her phone, rubbed a greasy fingerprint from the screen with her sleeve and selected Will's number.

It was a largely silent meal eaten at the table in the kitchen that evening. Rick had cooked it, a big saucepan of spaghetti bolognese. Rosa glanced about at the house-mates who had gathered to support her, amazed and grateful that she had these friends. Leonie, concerned and tactful, sat at the head of the table, exerting an air of calmness and order to proceedings. Peter, next to Leonie, had produced a couple of dusty bottles of claret from somewhere and kept refilling Rosa's glass, which was his way of helping. Rosa was aware of drinking more than she should, and she was struggling to eat anything, which of course made the effects of the alcohol worse. Every time she thought of Michal she felt the tears well up.

'Rosa.' She looked up to see that Will, making his way through a great pile of spaghetti opposite, had set down his fork and was studying her with compassion.

'Sorry,' she sniffed, blinking and taking another mouthful of wine. Next to her Rick poured a glass of water from a jug and pushed the glass pointedly towards her.

The interview with her father, arranged for her at prison-rule-breaking short notice by Ben, had been excruciatingly painful, though she'd felt she needed to keep him abreast of developments.

She'd been struck all over again by how much he'd aged, but after today's conversation he'd looked worse, stooped and old, his head bowed with sadness. Ben said the police had not informed him about the grisly discovery in the canal, since nothing was sure. They'd only spoken to Rosa about it because they'd required further information from her. When Rosa had relayed in broken stumbling words the conversation she'd had with the police officer, her father had given a low cry.

'No,' she'd told him when he asked whether there had been any identification on the body. 'They don't think so.'

'There is hope? Rosa, tell me, is there hope?'

And she found herself comforting him, though it was comfort she needed herself. 'There is hope, Pappy, yes.' Was it wrong to hope? She felt so weary keeping going, but it was the only thing to do.

'I keep thinking, girl, since you came last, I'm sorry, I've been a useless dad to you, haven't I? I've let you both down, and your mum. And then all this that got me put in here. It was a muddle. I don't know why, but I made some bad choices.'

She nodded wearily. She didn't want to know about any of that at the moment. All she wanted was for Michal to be alive.

'Me and Yvonne, we'd have been quite happy if I hadn't gone and messed things up. It was that bloke lives opposite did it. Lenny. It was he set me up. Said it was a good scheme. The returns looked so good, I should have known better. Well, it's all water under the bridge now and . . .'

He stopped, seeing her wince at the unfortunate

phrase. She didn't remember him being like this, moaning, full of self-pity. He'd always seemed cheerful, robust.

'I must go,' she told him, reaching forward to touch his fingers where he clutched the table. He clasped her hand and gazed at her, his eyes sad and imploring.

'You will let me know what happens, love, won't you? They'll pass on a message. They do that for you here. Compassionate and that.'

'Of course, Pappy, I'll make sure you know everything. I'll come to see you again. I ... I don't know when, but I will come.'

After the washing up, they each quietly made excuses and left Rosa with Will. The two of them put on coats and went out into the back garden so she could smoke. She was surprised when Will asked her for a cigarette, but readily gave him one.

'I used to,' he told her. 'I'm supposed to have given up, but sometimes I can't help myself. '

'That's not good,' she said with a sad laugh. 'I am bad for you, no?'

'When it comes to cigarettes, yes,' he said, as he took the lighter from her. His eyes, meeting hers, were steady, unreadable.

She realized she knew very little about him, only that he was thirty and worked with young people, for the council. That he was kind and respectful and she trusted him.

The chill of the evening was sobering her up. There was a full moon rising over the garden, and cold stars pricking an indigo sky. Beautiful. Too beautiful. They sat on either side of the wrought-iron table, smoking and watching the trees moving in the breeze. She found that her mind kept wandering down the abyss of her fears.

'Tell me about the work you do,' she said to steady herself.

She sensed Will's keen eye upon her. 'Do you really want to know?'

'I do.'

'We have a centre on the High Street. Any young person can come to us for advice or a chat, just to hang out. And we try to get help for them if they need it, rehab or housing, things like that, though there's no money for anything. We work with a lot of charities, too, they're brilliant, great people. There's so much deprivation round here, not only poverty and unemployment, but emotional, spiritual, too. Anything we do feels like emptying a lake with a bloody teaspoon, but at least it's something.'

'Oh yes, it sounds good, Will. I wish . . .' She stopped. 'Did Michal go to your centre? Did you see him there?'

'I did tell him about it. He came to the church and I directed him to the hostel. I was expecting to see him at the centre, but he didn't turn up. Oh Rosa, I'm so sorry. I wish now that I had done more. It's . . . but you can't force people.'

'No.' Rosa's voice was dull.

'If there was some help I could give . . . but I can't think of anything. Rosa, I hope so much that this boy isn't your brother, but what a tragedy for—'

'I know what you are going to say. He is brother of somebody. I know, I know, but I don't want him to be Michal. Let someone else suffer this time, not me, not again.' She almost whispered the last part to herself. Some things were still too painful to speak about, but he heard.

'What do you mean, not again? Rosa?'

She ignored him, instead staring at the screen of her phone, longing for it to ring. Ben had said she could call him any time, but she didn't like to. She imagined disturbing him during a meal with his girlfriend, or when he was putting his children to bed, or when he was in a noisy pub and trying to hear her. She trusted that he'd be in touch when he had something to say.

Beside her, Will stubbed out his cigarette and stood up. 'It's probably time I went now.' He appeared subdued and she saw that she'd upset him.

'Please, don't.' She laid the phone back down on the table. 'I know I am not good company tonight, I'm sorry.'

'You're fine,' he said gently, sitting down again. 'But wouldn't you prefer to be alone? I don't like to intrude.'

'No, you don't intrude. Please stay, Will. Just for a bit more.' She gave him a wan little smile, all she could manage, and he nodded.

By now it was getting chilly, so they returned to the kitchen where Rosa put the kettle on and they were soon sitting at the kitchen table nursing hot drinks. Will brushed his hand through his dark curls. 'There was something you said a moment ago, Rosa. Can I ask you?'

'What?' She glanced up at his kind face, knowing exactly what he was getting at. She hadn't wanted to talk about it since it happened, even to her father, but maybe now was the time. To have another human being share her buried sorrow would be a relief.

'I'm sorry,' he was saying. 'Perhaps you didn't mean to say it. Something about someone else suffering *this time*. Rosa, I know very little about you. Maybe I can help. You know, I'm used to listening.'

For a moment she was silent as she circled the rim of the cup with her forefinger.

'It is not so bad,' she said eventually with a shrug.

'What isn't, Rosa?' he prompted. 'I think your life must have been very hard. You lost your mother quite recently, and your brother ... well.' Rosa saw his face grow anguished. 'I can't think what that must be like. I still have both my parents, and my brother, Max, he's making a fortune in financial services. We get on well enough, but we don't understand each other's choices.'

Rosa took a deep breath. 'I've always been very close to Michal. He needs me to protect him. He trusts people too much. He thinks everyone will be nice, then is surprised when he gets hurt. Often I have to say no, Michal, don't be friends with this person or that person, they only want your money.' She felt she wasn't explaining it well. It was why she had half expected to have found Michal amongst the campers under the flyover, homeless. He was the sort of boy who would agree to look after a stranger's rucksack, then be surprised when Customs officials found illegal drugs in it. He'd open his wallet to a bleary-eyed beggar when anyone sensible would recognize that the money would be spent on vodka. His friendliness was why she loved him so very much and worried about him, but it also exasperated her.

She glanced away, trying to fight the thought that it might indeed be Michal whose body now lay in the morgue. Maybe she would after all have to go there to see him. She would have to be brave. It would be her duty. *As it had been once before.*

She fought the prickling tears as she turned to Will who was watching her anxiously.

'Three years ago,' she said, her voice cracking, 'I was going to be married.' She saw his eyes widen. 'His name was Eryk.'

She placed her hands briefly over her face and then wiped her eyes and continued. 'He was a policeman. He sometimes used to come into the café where I worked when he'd finished his shift and we started to go out together. He was a special person because he enjoyed life so much. He liked his job and he was like you, Will, he always wanted to make things better for people. He would talk to the kids like he was on their side, you know? Trying to stop them getting into trouble.'

She stopped and, raising her eyes, saw that Will was listening, so continued. The story tumbled out.

They had known one another for a year when Eryk suggested they get married, and she'd readily agreed. She loved him, he was fun, and she felt comfortable with him. Her mother had initially been suspicious about a policeman. She remembered a time when a visit from the police usually meant trouble, but even she was won over eventually. His jokes made her chuckle, and he often arrived with a paper bag of the almond cakes she loved. His prospects were good. He'd be able to look after her Rosa so that maybe she wouldn't have to work as hard. The family started to make plans for the marriage.

Rosa first saw the grainy footage on the evening news. There had been a tip-off about a break-in in a warehouse, but when the police arrived they walked into an ambush. A policeman had been killed. When she saw it she shivered. What if one day this happened to Eryk? Only when Eryk's father arrived soon after, distraught, hardly holding himself together, did she realize the worst had already happened. She had accompanied Eryk's parents to the hospital to see his body and found herself trying to comfort his mother, whose only child he'd been. Even up to the time she'd left Poland she visited them when she could in their gloomy apartment where photographs of their son stood all around and time had not moved on.

'"You are young," everybody told me. "You will get over it and find someone else." But I didn't want anyone else. I wanted Eryk to come back, to walk into our flat with a bag of my mother's favourite little cakes and tell us stories about his day. Michal wanted to be a policeman because of him, but after Eryk's death we begged him not to try. Perhaps we were wrong to do that, I wonder now.'

All the while that she was talking, Rosa was aware of Will listening quietly, sipping his coffee. When she trailed to a halt, he asked tentatively, 'Did they ever find out why the criminals opened fire on the police? Did they know it was Eryk? I mean, was it personal?'

She shook her head. 'They didn't mind who they killed, policemen were all evil to them. It was revenge after the police had broken up a gang. Eryk had a gun, but he had no chance even to draw it. The whole thing was completely unexpected.'

'I'm sorry, Rosa. You must feel very much alone. You're not close to your father, are you?'

She shook her head. 'We've not seen him much through the years, no. And now, well, it is difficult to help him, though I will try. I am lucky, though, to have friends. Good friends here.'

'I hope you count me as one of them.' He smiled.

'Will, of course. I can't thank you enough for all you've done.'

He was standing up now, moving their cups to the sink, then she went with him into the hall, watching him wrap his scarf warmly round his neck, handing him his coat and his cycle helmet.

'Goodbye,' he said, placing his arm round her briefly in a farewell hug. 'I'll phone tomorrow, find out how things are. You'll let me know if anything ... happens, eh?'

'Yes, I will do that.'

She held the door open whilst he carried his bike down the steps, then watched him glide away on it down the silent street, his reflective clothing shining in the lamplight, giving him the appearance of some contemporary angel.

Back in the kitchen her phone lay black and silent on the table. She picked it up for the umpteenth time, feeling the familiar rush of apprehension as she checked to see if anyone had called. Nobody had. It was, she saw, just after midnight.

She locked the back door and as she went upstairs to try at least to sleep, she wondered whether to turn her phone off. After all, the police had the landline number of the house if they wanted to speak to her during the night. But she was used to keeping it on always. It would be a betrayal of Michal not to. Suppose he needed her help and could not reach her because she'd set her own well-being above his? She'd never done that, she'd looked after him.

As she lay sleepless on her bed, going over the events of the day, she remembered that it had been Good Friday, the day of Christ's torment on the cross, his death. Will had come straight from a church service to see her when she'd called him. It had indeed been a day of darkness and mourning, a day of vigil. Tomorrow ... no, she must not think about tomorrow. She was exhausted. Despite everything she drifted into a troubled sleep from which the phone did not ring to wake her.

Seven

Rick

The electric hammering of the school bell ripped him from the exam dream. Not the school bell, his alarm. He fumbled his phone to silence it then pulled a pillow over his head to shut out the merciless daylight. He'd forgotten to close the curtains the night before. Seven o'clock on Easter Saturday. He groaned. All hands on deck at work. The shop would be a nightmare with trolleys blocking the aisles, long queues at the tills, customers fighting for the last chocolate eggs, and overhanging it all the scent of hot cross buns wafting from the instore bakery. Rick used to like them until he had to smell them all day. He hadn't bought any eggs for the boys yet. The thought caused him to come out from under his pillow. He'd have to pick out a couple before the rush began. And a posh one for Claire, who liked presents to be beautifully wrapped. His nephews only cared about size and how long it took to tear the packaging off.

If Stef were here he might have bought her an egg, he thought as he trailed out to the bathroom. There was a particularly pretty one he'd had his eye on a week ago, drizzled with gold like a child's painting and with flowers painted over the cellophane box. He glanced in the mirror as he washed his hands and hated his miserable reflection. Shaving was an effort like everything else at the moment, but he forced himself to do it. His manager would be on him if he looked too scruffy. The uniform would cover a shabby T-shirt, but not a stubbly chin.

He'd dragged himself through the previous week in a haze of misery. With Oliver's appearance at Number 11 the seriousness of Stef's situation had finally made itself known. He understood her reserve now, the way she retreated inside herself, her fragility, her fear of the world.

She'd changed over the weeks that she had lived here, there was no doubt about that. He'd seen her gradually, cautiously emerge, as shy as a young fox, eager to explore her new freedom, but definitely still wary. He'd caught glimpses of the person she was underneath. It was there in the increasing confidence of her fashion designs, her encouraging comments about his story, and, oh, in the way she'd laughed that evening with Henry and Terry.

As he wiped the soap from his chin, instead of his face in the mirror it was Stef's terrified one he imagined before him, her eyes bright with unshed tears as she'd rushed past him up the stairs.

For days he'd replayed that moment, trying to establish what he should have done, what he should have said to Oliver. He remembered staring at Oliver then Oliver sort of side-stepping him to sweep out of the room. He should have punched him. A real man would have done that, but Rick had never punched anyone. Not since primary school, anyway, when he'd had to because a bigger boy was sitting on him, squeezing all the air out of his lungs. He went into the shower, gasping at its initial icy blast, but glad of the way it banished the memories.

Downstairs in the kitchen, there was evidence that Leonie was up and about. The garden door was open. As he dreamily ate some muesli he turned the pages of the plant catalogue she'd left on the table. Garish flowers with impossible names. It was a foreign world to him, horticulture.

The door to the hall opened and Peter bludgeoned his way in. 'Hello. Up early, aren't we?' His voice was heavy with irony. He carried across the kitchen a gilded picture frame the size of the screen of a portable television, which he proceeded to scrub under a running tap, while whistling under his breath.

'Easter Saturday,' Rick explained between mouthfuls of cereal. 'It'll be murder in the shop.'

Peter, busy examining the frame, grunted in reply. He nodded with satisfaction, and dried it with a tea towel, which he then threw down on the table. It was covered in greasy stripes. He returned the way he'd come only to reappear a moment later with the frame and a piece of hardboard, both of which he set down against a wall while he started to rootle around in a tall wall cupboard. A scree of small hard objects inside could be heard gravitating to the floor, accompanied by Peter's muttered curse.

Seeing Leonie's shadow pass to and fro across the grass, Rick glanced at his watch and decided to beat it before the inevitable row. Whatever work of genius Peter was framing, Leonie wouldn't be happy about the mess.

The morning was every bit as busy as Rick expected. He was on till three, the one with the dodgy conveyor belt that lurched forward rather than glided, toppling bottles onto their sides and sometimes to the floor if he wasn't quick. People were constantly handing him unwanted items that their kids had secretly added to the shopping and more teenagers than usual were trying to buy alcohol on obviously borrowed ID.

'You can go on your lunch now,' his manager said at 11.15. Who wanted lunch at 11.15? Still, he slid out of his seat gratefully and set off down the chocolates aisle to replace some abandoned creme eggs on his way to fetch his things from his locker.

There was a woman standing just where he needed to get, her trolley skewed at an angle. She was arguing with two tiny girls in Disney princess dresses, one of whom dumped herself down on her tummy and started beating the floor with her fists and wailing. As he stood to one side with the creme eggs, politely waiting for the woman to move away from the shelf, he noticed that the handbag hanging from her trolley was open and her plump wallet was poking out of the top.

People were pushing past them now, and he became aware of a tallish young man among them. As this character passed the trolley, Rick saw him reach out his hand and cup it over the wallet.

'No!' he managed to croak and stepped out in front of the youth, who dropped his arm. Rick glanced up at his face in astonishment and the youth stared back.

'I came in to find you,' the boy mumbled. 'Thought you might be on this morning.'

'Jamie!' Rick said, setting the creme eggs on top of some nougat.

'Your handbag's open, madam,' he said to the woman as he grabbed Jamie's leather-coated sleeve. He pulled him out of the aisle and along to pet food, which was quieter.

'I should report you. What the hell did you think you were doing?' He stood four-square, arms crossed, glaring at Jamie, who swivelled on his heel with a groan and made a helpless gesture with his hands. 'If it had been anyone else—'

'I know, I know,' Jamie said. 'I hadn't been intending to. I was looking for you, honest, and it was just there, asking for someone to take it. I mean, how stupid can you get?'

'Theft is theft, Jamie. You don't need me to explain that. Listen, wait here, I'll get my jacket and we'll go and have a chat. Now, promise me you'll stay here.'

'Yeah.'

Rick felt something like panic as he scooted to the back of the shop, waved his electronic card to get through the staff-only door and, once inside, snatched his jacket out of his locker, checking the pockets for wallet and phone. That Jamie should have picked this moment and this particular way to come waltzing back into their lives was typical. It was as though the boy could sniff out trouble and be drawn to it like an unwound paperclip towards a dodgy lock. Well, at least Leonie would be pleased and that was most important of all. Let's hope he could persuade Jamie to go home and see her at least.

He sped back to find, remarkably, that Jamie was where he'd left him, frowning at a display of cat food. 'Is this like real?' Jamie pointed to a tin that claimed to be a gourmet dinner. 'Some people don't get as good as that.'

'Too right,' Rick agreed hastily. He'd spotted the woman with the two little Disney girls, faces blotchy, mouths downturned, up by the guinea pig food and was anxious to get Jamie out of the shop in case she'd realized Jamie had been about to steal from her.

'Come on. No, this way.'

He led Jamie across the road to the Black Cat Café, thinking he'd kill two birds with one stone and see if Rosa was there and if she was all right, but she wasn't there, the other girl was, the gormless one, Beth. As he ordered cappuccinos and toasted sandwiches, Karina joined her at the counter and when he asked confirmed what he feared.

'She texted me first thing, said she hadn't slept well, so I told her to come in later. Poor thing. Won't pretend it's not a pain for me, though. It's been manic here. I could have done with Stef.'

'Yes, I'm sure you could,' Rick said, looking away to hide the sudden stab of tenderness. He handed Jamie a coffee and they negotiated a way to a table for two in the window that had just become free. They sat down opposite one another and Karina brought the sandwiches over. When she'd gone, Rick decided direct attack was the best way with Jamie given he only had twenty minutes.

'You can't go on like that you know, nicking things. You'll get caught quick as quick and then where will you be.'

Jamie, wolfing down his sandwich, swallowed and wiped his mouth with his napkin. 'Trust me, it was the first time I was even tempted. And I wasn't going to do it, honest. It was my hand, trying it out.'

Rick decided to pass over that muddled line of thinking.

'Anyway, where've you been? Your gran's been so worried. You just walked out without even saying goodbye.'

'Yeah, well, I've been feeling bad about that. I've been dossing at a mate's. Well, first at my mate's, then at a mate's of his. It's been OK, but this second mate's got a girlfriend now and she's not too keen on me being there.'

I can't blame her, Rick thought. What he said was, 'Leonie's kept your room free, I told you. It's like a shrine to your beloved memory.'

'Yeah, that's brilliant, isn't it?' Jamie's eyes filled with joy. 'I mean, I didn't expect her to.'

'I wouldn't have done, but you're her grandson. For some reason she loves you to bits.'

Jamie finished the final inch of sandwich and grinned bashfully.

Rick put up a warning hand. 'But,' he said, 'if you're thinking of coming back like you were, then don't bother. And before you get antsy with me, let me explain things. Your grandma's having a hard time.' Rick told him about the threat to the house and filled him in briefly about the new inhabitants and their various problems.

'Wow,' Jamie said on hearing about Rosa and Michal. 'That's not cool.'

Rick forged on. 'I know you didn't like it when I told you last time, but I think Leonie's right, you wouldn't be doing yourself or anyone else any favours coming back and being your usual old self. The same thing would happen again, you know, and you must be running out of mates.'

'Do you think I haven't thought about that?' The note of sincerity in Jamie's voice surprised Rick. 'Cos I have, you know. I'm getting a job.'

'Well, good,' Rick said, surprised. 'What sort of thing are you looking for?'

'No, I really am getting one. I mean I've got one. It's with this guy who's kind of a journalist. I drive him around and get things for him, organize things sort of. I've been doing it a bit for him on and off and then he asked me if I could help him full-time like. The money's not much, but it's a start.'

Rick could hardly believe what he was hearing. 'What do you mean he's a kind of journalist?' The whole thing sounded dodgy if you asked him.

'No, he's a great guy, no kidding. You know when they knocked down that tower block up by the flyover a few weeks back? It was on the news?'

Rick did vaguely remember.

'I was there and so was he, filming it. We got chatting. He said he'd been researching a piece about the people who'd lived there and what happened to them. Lots of 'em hadn't wanted to leave, they liked it there even though it was falling down. That's the sort of thing Blake does. I'm going to help him!'

Rick blinked at Jamie, not without a touch of envy. The boy was astonishing. He had this sort of presence. The good looks, yes, but there was an energy about him. This Blake must have seen something in Jamie that made him want to give him a chance. Yes, he was envious. Here he was, plodding away with his writing and his humble little job on the tills, making no impression on anyone really, and there was Jamie blazing away. OK, so the job itself might not be much, driving and gofering, but it had a seedy glamour about it, or so Jamie made it sound.

'So you see,' Jamie went on, 'if I came back to Belle-vue Gardens it might only be for a little while. Till I get established.' He said 'established' as if it didn't belong in his mouth, but then smiled as though he liked the sound of it, for he said it again. 'Till I get established. And it would be different. I might not be there all the time, for a start. Blake has to go on research trips, of course.' The way he said this conveyed an air of mystery.

'Well, that's all great, then!' Rick said, trying not to

sound mournful. 'I'm really pleased for you.' And now he'd said it he really felt it. He'd first seen Jamie today through the same dirty old filter, but now he'd been forced to look at him differently. Jamie had changed.

'I'll get you another coffee if you like,' Jamie said. 'My treat.'

Rick glanced across the road at the supermarket, where two elderly women were doing battle for the last trolley in the rack outside. He sighed. 'Thanks, but no time. I need to be getting back to work in a minute.'

He was getting up to put on his jacket and preparing to ask Jamie whether he'd see him later at home, when a familiar figure caught his eye hurrying past the window, then the door opened and Rosa flew in and dodged to the front of the short queue. He started to push his way between the tables towards her and heard her cry out something to Karina but not what she said. Karina came round from behind the counter to meet her, then in front of the astonished queue Rosa burst into tears.

For a second Rick stood there nonplussed. He had never seen Rosa cry properly before, never, never. She'd always seemed so resilient, though he could sense the strength of deep emotion swirling beneath her stoic exterior. Then he pulled himself together, told Karina he'd look after the girl, then managed to steer Rosa away to sit in the chair he'd just vacated. In front of Jamie, who was of course a stranger to her, she calmed down quite quickly. Jamie muttered that he needed to go outside to call someone, and liberated his chair, which Rick sat down on.

'Tell me,' he said to Rosa, though he could see from her shining eyes that it was good news.

'It's not him, oh, it's not him,' she whispered up at Rick, who understood at once.

'Ah, fantastic. The police called you?'

'Yes, about half an hour ago. Leonie was there so I tell her.' Her English was falling apart under the strain. 'It's so sad, I mean sad for the family of the poor boy, I keep thinking about that, but I can't help being happy, do you think I'm bad? It's not my Michal. Oh my God, I hope they tell my dad, I leave message.'

'Can you do that, just ring the prison?'

'I did.' Rosa sounded doubtful, then said, 'Well, I made arrangement to visit him tomorrow, so either way, he will know. Hey, here comes your friend.'

'I was talking to Blake,' Jamie said, in a studied off-hand way. 'You know, my new boss.'

Rick introduced him to Rosa. 'Jamie is Leonie's grandson, Rosa. He's got good news, too.'

They took to one another straight away and Jamie asked all sorts of questions about Michal and looked thoughtful. He seemed particularly interested to hear about the vagrants' camp under the flyover and that it appeared Michal had stayed there for a bit. He muttered something about migration being one of Blake's 'areas of enquiry'. Blake was doing 'some programme about immigrants' and knew about that camp. He, Jamie, might introduce Blake to Rosa, if that was all right.

Rosa nodded. Rick saw she wasn't really concentrating, that she was weary with emotion.

When her queue of customers had gone, Karina brought three coffees and three huge slices of chocolate cake across on a tray. 'Oh no, no,' Rosa cried, getting up. 'I've come to work.'

'I bet you didn't have breakfast, did you?'

'No,' Rosa admitted. 'I've been too worried to eat.'

'Eat up then. I'm not having you fainting on the job.'

Rick thanked Karina, but asked if he could wrap his cake up in a napkin. His fifteen-minute break had already turned into half an hour.

Leonie

It was a morning for digging. Leonie had woken soon after it became light and finding herself unable to get back to sleep and visited by all manner of troublesome thoughts she'd given up trying. Breakfast eaten, she had donned her gardening shoes and gloves and ventured outside. Last year's pots needed weeding, then she set about in a determined fashion turning over the second vegetable bed, which she'd cleared in preparation for runner beans. The weather was fine, but breezy, and the ground soft from recent rain, so it wasn't an unpleasant job. She had to stop every now and then to remove stones or errant roots, but it was quite meditative, she found.

It was while she was busy with this that Rosa rushed outside to tell her the good news that the poor dead boy was not Michal. She'd not seen the girl so emotional before, she was literally shaking with relief, and it came home to Leonie just how much stress Rosa kept suppressed, even over the last day or so whilst she was waiting in limbo, fearing the worst news possible about her brother.

'There is still hope, isn't there, Leonie? That I will find Michal.'

'Of course there is. Every hope. And it sounds as though the police are searching.'

'I think so, yes, but I am sure there is more I can do. There must be.'

Leonie thought of the vastness of London and didn't know what to say.

'I was thinking last night of what my dad said when I saw him. There is a man called Lenny who lives in a house opposite my father's. Pappy said it was Lenny who got him into this trouble, why he went to prison. Maybe Lenny saw Michal. Maybe he knows something.' Rosa was looking so impassioned, so intense that Leonie was worried.

'Rosa, I think you should be careful ...'

'Yes, yes.' Leonie didn't think she was listening. Rosa's mind was working away on this new line of enquiry.

'Rosa, if this man is a criminal you shouldn't try anything yourself. Tell the police instead, leave it to them.'

Rosa sighed. 'I suppose so.' She stood deep in thought for a moment then said, a little shakily, 'What's the time? I must go to work.'

Leonie leaned on her spade watching her go, a determined, upright figure. She shook her head. It was indeed a relief, the news of this morning, but it hadn't taken Rosa anywhere nearer to finding her brother. It was awful for her. She'd liked the young man who'd come for supper the previous night, Will. Perhaps he'd back up Leonie on her advice to leave her father's associate alone.

She returned to her digging with less vigour than before, every thud of the spade like a blow to her peace of mind. So much was wrong in her world and she couldn't see the answers. There was Stef, sweet Stef, on the run once more, and poor Rick bereft. He was poor Rick. She was beginning to worry about the boy. He'd been living in a bubble of his own making, shut himself away in a monastic kind of life, when actually he had so many gifts he ought to be out there using. Instead, he spent too much time in his room with that wretched computer. What with him and Stef, shut in her fearful little world, there wasn't much difference between them. Perhaps they'd have been the saving of one another if Stef had stayed. She sighed and bent to rip up a long white ground elder root. It snapped off, which meant she had to dig deeper for the rest of it and when she did she felt a hot ripping sensation in her back. Damn. She straightened slowly, rubbing the painful patch, and stretched. The daylight was dimming, a chilly wind blew, and she looked up to see a cloud passing over the sun. The scent of rain was in the air. She knocked earth off the spade and limped over to the shed to put it away. As she walked stiffly towards the house the first drops of rain dashed upon her face.

She listened to it hammer on the sun-room roof as she prised off her shoes and gloves, but above the rain a sawing sound started up. The very floor beneath her feet vibrated. She turned and walked into the kitchen. And gasped in horror. The place was a tip, with things falling out of open cupboards and picture canvases leaning against the fridge. In the midst of the chaos was Peter, stooped over the kitchen table, sawing at a strip of wood. He glanced up, flinched to see her, and an offcut broke away suddenly, clattering across the floor.

'What on earth are you up to?'

'Framing some pictures.' He followed the direction of her gaze and it was as though he saw for the first time the mess he'd made for he put down the hacksaw, wiped his nose on the back of his hand and grinned at her.

'Yes, I can see that. But why in here?'

'Run out of room downstairs, haven't I?'

Leonie could feel hot anger build inside her. 'This is the kitchen, Peter, not a workshop.' She stepped across nails and chips of wood to the stove and picked up the kettle from the hob.

'I'll have some if you're making it.'

She turned and gave him a murderous look.

'All right, all right. Keep your hair on. I'll clear it up in a moment.'

'Every bit of it, Peter.' From where she stood now she could see several more canvases propped up against the wall behind him, and curiosity momentarily got the better part of her anger. 'What are you up to, anyway?'

'Nothing.'

She narrowed her eyes at him, but his face took on a mutinous expression. 'Peter? Tell me.'

'Not yet. You'll have to wait. You and the rest of them.' Then, more softly, 'I'm just doing my bit for the cause, that's all.'

'The cause? Peter, what are you talking about?'

'I've been a burden on you all these years. I know that's how you think of me.' He stood straighter now, like an old soldier having an attack of nostalgia, but there was a hint of his younger self in the purposeful way he addressed her. It was the Peter before he'd been blighted by his sense of failure as an artist, before he'd shut out hope and ambition. 'Well, I'm trying to help now, that's all. And, if you'd let me get on, the quicker I'll be finished and out of your way.'

His air of dignity astonished her, quenching her anger. She shrugged, made them both coffee and stepped outside with hers once more. The rain was quickly passing, and she welcomed the brightness of the garden, the birdsong and the scent of fresh earth. She couldn't get over the difference in Peter and wondered what he was up to. He hadn't sold any paintings for ages. Surely he wasn't hoping to now. So many years she and Peter had shared this house and how little of himself he'd ever let her see. He hadn't always been a burden, she thought fondly, remembering how gentle he'd been with Tara. There was something of the child about him for he'd been endlessly patient with Leonie's little girl, whether teaching her to play cat's cradle, or racing snails with her in the garden.

He'd helped Leonie so much, too, showing her how to turn her schoolgirl artistic talent into a way of making a living, and despite his shyness, had been a friend during times of trouble – after George's death, when Tara left and, much later, at another sad time. When she was in her early forties, love had flowered again for Leonie, this time with Guillaume, a distinguished Parisian pianist who frequently performed in London, and whom she met at one of the famous parties Trudi used to hold when she was married to her third husband (the one who later complained that Trudi liked to be 'the star of her own show').

Guillaume was separated from his wife Véronique, who came from a very old and very litigious French Catholic family, and although he and Leonie saw a great deal of one another for a wonderful five years, in the end the relationship foundered on Leonie's unhappiness about his reluctance to press Véronique for what admittedly would have been an expensive and unpleasant divorce.

Leonie remembered now that Peter had liked Guillaume, and been pleasant to him when he came to visit. Peter had accepted, too, the everlasting turnover of waifs and strays who'd shared Number 11 over the years, had put up with their crises, their eccentricities, their hostility even, without complaint – or not much anyway.

Sitting in the rain-washed garden now, her thoughts running along so many tracks, she tried not to worry about what they would do, she and Peter, when the time came for them to leave the house. She'd have to broach the subject with him sometime. Trudi had asked Leonie to come and stay with her in that marvellous apartment at Chelsea Reach, to see 'how they got along'. It might be fun, Leonie thought, remembering the good times they'd had all those years ago sharing that bedroom in the flat above the clothes wholesaler on the Edgware Road, but, 'We aren't girls of nineteen any more,' she'd told Trudi, 'we'd annoy the pants off each other. Or, at least, I'd annoy you,' she'd added hastily, fearing she'd sounded rude. No, they were ageing women now, with their own complex histories, their own habits, their own obstinacies. Trudi had protested at this, but Leonie stood firm. 'I want to be your friend for ever,' she'd insisted, 'and living together isn't the way.'

She and Peter at least understood each other, got along with the way each other lived, even though he infuriated her sometimes, simply infuriated her. Yet with this arrangement, they each occupied their own space. After she'd broken up with Guillaume she'd not wanted anything more to do with men or marriage. She found these days she preferred to go to bed when she pleased, to be awake reading half the night if she felt like it, to come and go as whim took her. Up to a point – there were always responsibilities – but being single suited her now. She had plenty of company if she wanted it after all.

She set down her empty cup on the metal table and walked a little haltingly, because of her back, across the lawn to resume her digging. She'd finish turning the vegetable bed before lunch, she decided, and if the weather held do the planting in the afternoon. The morning was warming up nicely now, and the fragrance of lilac and damp earth greeted her as she walked. The drone of a solitary bumblebee wove a myth of summer. Her garden was always a solace. Her spade clanged on a stone. She was going to lose the garden! The thought struck her like a blow upon a bruise. Next spring the flowers might be trampled into the mud by workmen's feet. Great stacks of bricks, heaps of builder's sand would smother the grass; ladders, planks of wood, ripped-out baths and cupboards would crush the hedges. There would be no room for birds to make their nests and the foxes would wander away bewildered from this alien world. For a while she stood motionless with shock, constructing this nightmare in her mind. Then slowly she brought herself back to the present and began to dig again, this time as though every plunge of the spade into the soil took extra effort. The grumbling ache in her back underlined her mood.

She'd almost finished when she became dimly aware of the sound of a door opening and then sharp footsteps on paving. Peter, she supposed. She hoped he was clearing up now or he'd be hearing from her.

Her arms were painful from the effort of digging but she kept on grimly until the twinge in her back forced her to stop. As she leant on her spade and rubbed her spine, a flicker of movement caused her to direct her gaze between the hedges towards the house. Someone was coming down the garden towards her, not Peter, not Hari, but a younger man. It was his walk she recognized, that jaunty, bow-legged roll. His hair was shorter than when she'd last seen him, neater, and he held himself with confidence.

She was so surprised she couldn't move or speak, simply watched him approach.

'Hi, Grans,' Jamie said, and his grin was the old Jamie's, and when he reached the place where she stood he did something he hadn't for years, he opened his arms, leant in and hugged her awkwardly.

'My darling boy,' she whispered. She clung to him, her chin on his shoulder, her eyes squeezed tight shut, hardly able to believe that it was him, but he was warm and alive with that familiar Jamie smell, sort of leather and Lynx aftershave. Where had he been? Would he stay? Had he let Tara know where he was? She bit her tongue, sensing that such questions must wait. It was enough for the moment that Jamie had come home. Home for Easter, she remembered suddenly. It was Easter Sunday tomorrow and they were celebrating with a special lunch. She had worried that the occasion would be subdued because of the uncertainty over Number 11, but now she could properly rejoice because Jamie had come home.

Eight

Stef

Stef opened her eyes to see a man with bared black teeth glaring at her with hate. If she turned over there was another one, this time with his face slashed with red marks as though by some monstrous beast, and cradling a skull-shaped guitar. The safest place to look was the ceiling where a fat bluebottle rested, cleaning its wings, so she lay rigid on her back watching it and trying to ignore a persistent sweaty pong of teenage boy.

Downstairs could be heard the sounds of pottering, her stepfather's voice, a deep bass growl that made the very walls vibrate, and her mother's bright responding laughter. In Vince's room next door to this one, which was Mark's, the boys presumably were still sleeping. It was rare to see them much before midday during school holidays, but then she hadn't been much better. Since arriving home in deep distress six days ago, all she'd wanted to do was sleep and, in the last day or two, take short walks, exploring the neighbourhood. It was all right, this suburb of Derby, but she didn't feel at home here.

She sat up and rubbed her eyes and squinted at a bulging carrier bag on the floor by her open holdall. Of course, it was Easter today. She'd bought everybody eggs. She'd always loved Easter as a young child living in the Derbyshire market town, though her family weren't religious or anything and didn't much see the point of it. To them it was simply a day when the shops were all shut and people ate too much chocolate, but Stef had always found it a happy day when the birds seemed to sing louder and the blossom bloomed brighter and life seemed very full of hope. Not today, though.

Where had it all gone wrong for her? Where did it come from, this feeling of displacement, of never really belonging anywhere? Her family had had to move once or twice to follow her father's surveying jobs and she'd had to start over in new schools. And there had been a long period when she was seven when he and her mother had been perpetually quarrelling, which had frightened her. After her father finally left, he moved away and she rarely saw him. She'd missed him terribly. He was living in Scotland now, settled with a much younger girlfriend, and she saw him once a year if she was lucky. Her stepfather was OK, well, very nice really, but for a long time she resented him and when the boys had been born she was already nine and felt left outside the baby bubble.

She sighed, pushed back the Manchester United duvet and swung her legs to the floor. If she didn't get into the tiny bathroom first the boys would be up and in there, using all the hot water and leaving the place in a mess.

She made a moue as she found her own towel where she'd left it scrunched up, still damp, on the floor, grabbed her sponge bag and crept out onto the small landing. At that precise moment her stepfather's voice boomed up from one of the rooms downstairs.

'How long d'you reckon she'll be here?' The tone was casual, not complaining, but guarded all the same and her heart plummeted in her chest. She heard her mother replying but not what she said. Stef nipped quickly into the bathroom and shut the door very quietly so they wouldn't know that they'd been overheard.

The day proceeded pleasantly enough. She helped her mother by making a giant banoffee pie. The boys came downstairs one by one wanting chocolate breakfast cereal, which they ate while playing a computer game that involved a lot of noisy shooting. Enormous Easter eggs were given and received, the wrapping left strewn across the crowded living room for the cat to play with.

Back in the kitchen Stef's mother basted an outsized chicken whilst her stepfather peeled vegetables. He opened a bottle of pink fizz and they sat down for lunch around three. They talked about normal things that families do: table manners, football fixtures, the improbability of alien life, plans for the bank holiday. Stef moved her food about on her plate and tried to contribute to the conversation, but she found she had nothing to say about herself.

'What about you, Stef?' her mother asked at one point, and she felt everyone's eyes upon her and a silence fall.

'I . . . I'm not sure,' she stammered, and pushed away

the banoffee pie, having picked out the banana. 'I might see if Mel can meet up.' One or two of her schoolfriends worked in Derby, but they had busy lives and their own new friends. Stef felt like a fish out of water.

When she'd arrived the Monday before, the family had all been delighted to see her. Mark had moved into Vince's room to give her somewhere to sleep, her stepfather had been welcoming, and her mother had spent the first evening sitting on the end of Mark's bed talking to her and trying to find out what was wrong. At the same time she got the impression that they saw this, all of them, as a short visit. She would recover, say goodbye and return to London. Mark would get his bedroom back and life would proceed as before. But nearly a week had passed and she was still here and as far as anyone could tell she had no plans. Mark always knocked if he needed access to his bedroom, but if she was in there she noticed that he spoke to her less and less and if she peeped round into Vince's room where Mark slept on a mattress on the floor it was to see the most terrible tip. She was increasingly aware that she was a nuisance.

'I'm going for a walk if that's OK,' she told her mother after the dishwasher had been loaded and the boys had disappeared into the living room. 'No, no, I'm fine by myself.'

She'd discovered that her family lived near a big public park, previously the grounds of some grand house, now a museum and art gallery owned by the council. There was a boating lake and a children's playground and acres and acres of rolling grassland, which she walked across now, pausing to join other spectators at the lake to watch the mainly middle-aged men race noisy model boats across the water. Something about it, the obsessive expressions of the men, the lawnmower buzz of their machines, the smell of petrol, depressed her so she turned away and ambled up the hill towards the house.

It was rather fine, built probably at the same time as 11 Bellevue Gardens, for the sash windows and the white stucco reminded her of it, and she liked it immensely for that reason. Today it was open and she followed the trail of visitors into the entrance hall thinking she'd buy a cup of tea in the café on the right-hand side, but a poster pinned to a sandwich board on the left of the hall distracted her. It advertised an exhibition of photographs of nature for a local competition, and as much to see what the rooms of the house looked like as to view the photographs she passed inside.

It must once have been a huge reception room. She could tell that immediately from the unified design of the ceiling, from which hung a line of chandeliers and whose plaster decorations were painted light blue. The wooden flooring was darkly varnished, but scuffed and worn, and the room was divided up by tempo-rary cloth-covered partitions so it was possible only to imagine the original sense of space.

The photographs were mounted on the partitions at eye level and she noticed the different categories as she drifted round the room: landscapes, animals, birds, one called mysteriously 'Adventures with Light'. It was as she turned a corner that it caught her eye, a photograph of a greyish landscape of rocks and gnarled trees and up and away from it a bird flying, glossy chestnut and blue gleaming on its wings. She stared at the jay, seeing the creature's delight and relief at its freedom, the sense of possibility about the sky shot through with light. And as she looked, she felt something inside her shift and expand, as if the thing that bound her was suddenly loosened. She hardly noticed the other photographs after that, but kept returning to this one. It had, she saw, been awarded the prize in the 'Adventures with Light' category and was called simply *Ecstasy*. It reminded her of the flying bird painting in Leonie's drawing room.

Easter Day, she thought that evening as she sat on her bed, which was really Mark's bed, munching the white chocolate bunny the twins had given her. It did feel like the start of something new. She couldn't stay at her mother's for much longer, she knew that, not because they didn't want her exactly, but because they simply didn't have room. Moreover, they all had their own lives to lead here and she didn't. She'd always be able to visit, but she had other things to do. When she reviewed her stepfather's question to her mother this morning she now interpreted it differently. He probably hadn't meant it to sound as though he wanted her to go – it was merely an expression of concern. They must be anxious about her – how could they not be when she'd turned up last week in such an unhappy state, battered and bruised?

Her newfound sense of freedom was in the recognition of this, but it was also to do with Oliver. The long shadow that he had cast over her had finally passed. She'd been strong enough to tell him everything was over, and had paid for it by his anger – her fingers lightly explored her cheek, feeling still a slight tenderness where he'd hit her – but she didn't think it likely that he'd come back for her again. She'd loved him once and he'd loved her, but his love had turned into something possessive and suffocating, and in the end it had killed her love for him. She was free of him now.

She thought of the house on Bellevue Gardens with sudden longing. She'd been happy there, she saw that. She loved her little attic room, though it did need sorting out more, and she remembered with a prickle of anxiety that she'd left her portfolio in it. She tried to think back. The case was getting heavy now and she hadn't been able to carry it easily in addition to her bags, but she understood now that there was another reason why she'd abandoned it. It represented her ambitions, her future, and these also had been too heavy for her. Suddenly, though, she was glad she'd left it. It was something to go back to.

She took another bite of the sweet chocolate and closed her eyes, feeling suddenly joyful. She was looking forward to returning to London and Bellevue Gardens and her new friends. Leonie had been so kind and had explained so much to her. She knew that Leonie had been through something similar to her own experience and thus she understood, didn't make her feel stupid.

She had a job there – if Karina at the café would take her back – and she felt she'd abandoned Rosa by running away. But most of all there had been someone else who'd shown her kindness, a young man as unlike Oliver as it was possible to be. The image of Rick's dear, kind face rose before her. She took out her phone and texted Rosa to ask for his number.

Rick

That morning, Rick rolled upright in bed at nine and sniffed the air, which was spicy, and remembered that it was Easter Sunday and Bela and Hari were cooking a special lunch. All the inhabitants of Number 11 were invited, plus Will, who had let slip on Friday that he was free and as Rosa's friend had immediately been included. He also remembered that in the kerfuffle of Jamie's return yesterday he had completely forgotten to buy any Easter eggs for Claire and the boys and since he was due at theirs for late-afternoon tea he decided he'd better find a corner shop that was open and put matters right. With luck it would also sell a decent bottle of wine, his designated contribution to the lunch. He pushed back the duvet and stood up, yawning, finding he didn't feel all that bad considering his misery over Stef. Leonie was so happy at Jamie's return that it was impossible not to share in her pleasure, and Jamie did seem to have turned over a new leaf, so perhaps it wouldn't be too bad having him around again for a bit.

There were other reasons why Rick felt more positive that morning. He'd stayed up late the night before, finishing his story, and had laid down his pen with a sigh of satisfaction, though when he'd uploaded the final images and posted them online there was also a sense of loss as though the project had moved on and left him behind. He'd need to review it, of course, to check that its structure was sound, but the hard graft was over and he felt proud of the result. Now, pulling on his dressing gown, he sat down at his laptop and waited for it to boot up. Finding his account he was delighted to see there were already a dozen comments, some of them quite lengthy. The words *Brilliant* and *Awesome, mate*, filled him with joy, but more worryingly *You've changed my life* rose to his eye. That felt a bit burdensome. He didn't want to be responsible for anybody else's life, just to draw and write stories. He closed down the laptop, thrust his hands in his pockets, then lay down on the bed to think for a while.

Stef was always at the back of his mind and he was hoping to receive some message from her, but he was trying to get on with his life as best he could until she did. Finishing the story was evidence of that. He also knew that it marked the end of this phase of his life. So many things indicated that. At some point, though not until several months in the future, he would, like all of them, have to leave this house. Maybe this was a good thing, because it tied in with his general feelings of dissatisfaction with his situation. The story had absorbed him, but it was finished now and had to go out to find its place in the world – if it had one beyond his followers on his blog. He was fed up with the supermarket, and he was fed up with himself. He looked down at his scruffy dressing gown, then around his room with new eyes. He wasn't a man who cared about material things and never would be, but surely he could do better than this, a few clothes hung in a cupboard, a damaged guitar, piles of books and papers on his shelves and a couple of posters on the wall.

His sister's voice echoed in his mind. He should find a better job, get out more, mix with like-minded people and stop biting his nails. He sighed and sat up to reach for his towel, hanging on the bedpost. A haircut and some new jeans were about all he could manage at the moment. Still, it would be a start.

As he walked out onto the landing and down to the bathroom there was a commotion on the stairs below, the thudding of boots, Leonie's scream from the kitchen, and, suddenly, the solid figure of Jamie rounded the top of the stairs. 'Hey!' His earring glittered in the gloom of the landing, his teeth flashed in a savage grin. He was carrying a huge, rusty hammer.

His ghastly form swung away into Leonie's room. 'Jamie!' More commotion from the hall below, and Leonie came trotting up the stairs and almost fell into the bedroom after her grandson. Rick took a tentative step forward, then stalled as he heard a blow, a crash of metal on brick that made the very walls shiver. Horror spread through him like boiling butter, but then came the relief of Leonie's voice: 'Stop it, you stupid boy, you'll frighten the poor thing to death.' The sound of the hammer came again. Rick leaped forward and pushed open the door of Leonie's bedroom.

What a sight met his eyes. There was no need to ask what was happening, he could work it out at once. Jamie was poised sideways on to the fireplace, swinging the hammer at the top of the brick arch surround, whilst Leonie crouched near by, her hands clasped in a parody of despair. The hammer struck and flakes of brick rattled into the grate.

'What on earth . . . ?' Rick said mildly. Behind him he became aware that his other housemates were arriving.

Peter pushed his way past. 'Bloody hell.'

'I heard the bird again,' Leonie almost sobbed, 'and now Jamie's gone crazy.'

Jamie grinned up at them and struck again. Half a brick had gone now. Then they all heard it, a desperate scrabbling sound in the chimney. 'Oh my God,' Leonie moaned.

'Here.' Peter extracted a paint-spattered penknife from his jacket pocket and nipped open the blade. Jamie stood back and Peter knelt stiffly and began to jab at the mortar around the brick, working it away until the brick was fully exposed. 'One more should do it,' he said, moving so Jamie had room to swing the hammer.

Another thud followed by the crack of breaking bricks and after that a small landslide of crumbled masonry, a cloud of soot. Then an impression of something huge and black and angry flapping and squawking and flopping down into the fireplace before righting itself and rising into the air in a shrieking whirl of dust and feathers, furious and evil-smelling. Half-blind from its weeks in the darkness, the creature ricocheted off the walls and the furniture, leaving ghostly impressions of itself on everything it fell against. Above, the ceiling light swung crazily.

Jamie stood open-mouthed in delight, but Leonie was screaming. Peter lunged round the room after the bird, cursing, but missing, and almost lost his balance. Rick slipped between them all and scrabbled at the catch of the window, pushing up the sash with the heels of his hands. Eventually, between them all, they managed to corner the hysterical bird and bundle it outside.

Rick watched the crow – he saw now that this was what it was – veer off in a haphazard course over the gardens like a stricken plane, but then it crashed through the branches of a budding beech tree, managed to recover itself and balanced itself tipsily on a bough, where it set about cleaning its feathers.

He turned back to the crowd in the room. Bela, Hari and Rosa stood in a line by the door, looking distraught, Bela fanning her face with her hand. Rosa, he noticed, was fetchingly tousled, in a short pink dressing gown with a satiny sheen. Everyone was quiet, stunned by what had happened, the power of what had been released. Leonie sat down on a clean patch of the bed and stared at the heap of rubble in her fireplace with an expression of complete disbelief.

'I thought it would be something much smaller, a blackbird or a blue tit. It made those kinds of noises. And after that it was quiet so long, I was sure it was gone or dead.'

'Maybe it was little to start with, but it grew in the dark,' Jamie suggested in a ghoulish voice.

Rick gave a snorting laugh, having a sudden artist's vision of how this might be. Darkness and rainwater dripping down sooty brickwork, the bird's prison might have bred a monster. His fingers itched to draw it.

Peter returned to the fireplace and began trying to fit bits of brick like a damaged jigsaw back into place. It was hopeless.

'There's a skip up the road full of old bricks,' Jamie suggested. 'I'll take a look.'

'I will fetch the dustpan,' Bela said. The show was over and people started to drift off.

Soon only Peter and Rick were left, with Leonie still sitting on the bed, her hands clenched into fists of despair.

'Are you all right?' Rick said unhappily, shifting from foot to foot. Bela returned with cleaning tools and lots of newspaper.

Leonie shook her head, but said nothing. They watched Bela and Peter clear up, then Jamie reappeared weighing a brick in each hand and with a dirty plastic carrier hanging off his arm. 'There was a bag of cement,' he said. 'Didn't think they'd miss a bit.'

'Oh Jamie, you are wicked,' Leonie said weakly, but she smiled fondly at her grandson.

Peter grinned his approval and took the bricks. Rick, feeling like a spare part, left them all to it and went to get dressed. A new story was already forming in his mind. It was about a young man lost in a cave system. There was something out there in the darkness that frightened him, but he had to overcome that fear in order to survive. He'd just scribble down a few sketches lest the muse escape him.

Leonie

When the crow had burst hot, angry and destructive out of its chimney prison, it had destroyed more than the pretty serenity of her bedroom. The bird that had possessed her imagination for so long had been little and darling so that she'd come to identify with it and share its fear and suffering. That was how she felt inside, she'd believed, afraid of what lay ahead for her and Peter, trying to accommodate the prospect of the loss of the house. Now she knew that the fear she'd been harbouring was actually much bigger than this. It was hard to explain even to herself. With the crow's breaking forth she'd finally acknowledged the true size of her fear: losing the house would be devastating. As she sat on the bed watching Peter and Jamie making a reasonable job of repairing her fireplace – Bela went off downstairs to help Hari with lunch – she struggled not to give in to tears.

At the same time she was cross with herself. She and Peter would be all right, they wouldn't be homeless, there would be somewhere. Why did it matter quite so much to her? She was old, she told herself, getting old, that was it. She didn't like change.

She rose and went across to the window. In the beech tree of the garden next door sat a crow cleaning its feathers. Her crow, she thought. It seemed astonishingly perky given its ordeal. She watched it hop down to a lower branch before spreading its wings and swooping low, out of sight. She dropped the curtain, which she'd unwittingly been clutching, and turned back to the room. The bedding would have to be washed. And the soot wiped off the walls. She peeled back the patchwork quilt and began to strip the duvet of its cover, then became aware of Peter watching her with an expression of concern.

He got up from the fireplace and came over.

'Leo, don't worry,' he said, touching her shoulder. 'We'll sort something out. This place, I mean.'

'How did you know that was what I was thinking—?'

'It's obvious, isn't it? I promise, I'm working on an idea.'

'Oh Peter. It's not as easy as that. Where are we going to get such a huge amount of money? A quarter of a million pounds!'

'I'm working on it, I tell you.'

'If you mean you're going to try to sell your paintings I don't think that is going to work,' is what she wanted to say, but she bit back the words. It would be no good offending him, especially when he was trying to be kind. She sighed.

'What's the matter?' Jamie asked from his position by

the fireplace. Leonie, who'd forgotten that she hadn't told him, quickly explained.

'Oh yeah, Rick said. We can ask Grandpop,' Jamie said brightly. 'He's rolling in it.'

'You can try, but I don't think you'd have any luck.' The likelihood of Billy giving her anything more after the hard-won divorce settlement long, long ago was practically nil. 'He might help you buy a flat of your own, though.'

'One day,' Jamie said with a shrug. 'I want to work for Blake and do things by myself for a bit.' He laughed. 'Why are you frowning like that? Don't you believe me?'

She opened her mouth, but nothing came out. Jamie had just rendered her speechless. Could this be the same Jamie who wouldn't lift a finger to help himself, who'd stayed in bed half the day, earned nothing and paid for nothing? She felt proud of him suddenly, standing there, arms folded, with that mass of glossy dark hair. So like Billy, he looked, the thought stabbed her, Billy when she first met him, when they were starting out in life and the future seemed to be theirs for the taking. Before ennui and disappointment and anger ruined everything. She sighed.

'I'm sure you're capable of achieving anything you want to, Jamie, but it's no good giving up when things get difficult.'

'Bring 'em on,' Jamie said with a laugh, and the determination in his eyes was something she hadn't seen for a long, long time. It made her happy.

Nine

Rosa

It was too hot in the back of the car, and there was a sickly smell of vanilla. Rosa rested her face against the cool of the window and stared out at the passing scenery. It had been the same for many miles now. The straight, single-lane road passed field after field of purple-green cabbages, set out in military rows, or potato plants thrusting up like miniature bushes. Sometimes there was simply bare earth, with fresh furrows scored into the rich dark soil. The landscape was so low and flat, the early evening sky so vast and pregnant with raincloud, that the sight weighed down on her. Every now and then the fields would end and the road rise to cross a narrow river, which by its straightness and lack of features suggested manmade functionality. There was no heart-lifting beauty in this landscape that one might take pleasure in, no line of hills, no sparkling sea, the only sense of hope was suggested by the occasional church spire reaching above trees on the horizon.

Blake, Jamie's boss, was driving, with Jamie sitting next

to him, fiddling with the buttons on the radio, working his way through the stations. They were currently being subjected to a man's voice speaking urgently from what sounded like a battle zone, but in the back Rosa couldn't make out the words. She leaned forward and asked, 'How much further is it, can you tell me?' but they didn't seem to hear her either, and feeling the brief touch of Will's hand on hers, she turned to see his smile urge patience. She leaned back with a sigh and closed her eyes, trying to empty her mind of worry, but failing.

It was because of Blake that they were here at all. As Jamie had suggested, she and his new boss had met for a chat. Blake had come to the Black Cat near closing time one afternoon and he'd sat over a coffee in the empty café until she was ready to talk to him. She liked him, she had decided. He was fortyish, short and solid with sparse fair hair, a bit of a twinkle in his eye and a sympathetic way of listening. There was the sense that he squirrelled away in his mind anything he judged important, without revealing exactly what or why. She told him all about Michal and what she knew of his movements after he had reached London. Blake had been especially interested in the flyover camp, and also in the conman her father had mentioned, Lenny, who lived opposite her childhood home in Dartmouth Street. A few days after this conversation, Blake had phoned her and said mysteriously that he'd been 'making enquiries' and that he 'might be on to something' and needed her help. It was because of this request that the four of them were now driving north-east from London through this endless flat landscape. She still had frustratingly little idea of why.

Despite her anxious mind, she must have slept, for when she opened her eyes next she was lying with her cheek against Will's shoulder and his arm was round her. The car had slowed and there was a heavy vibrating sound and pieces of what appeared to be grass or straw were tapping lightly on the window before falling away. She sat up to see the car was stuck behind a huge farm truck loaded with straw bales. From the other direction on the narrow road streamed vehicle after vehicle, forbidding the prospect of overtaking. Will withdrew his arm enabling her to twist to look through the back window, only to be dazzled by the westering sun.

Finally, Blake seized the opportunity of a gap in the oncoming traffic and they passed the truck with the car engine straining. Ahead, their way was empty and they were driving towards a darkening sky. Before long, drops of rain instead of straw dashed against the glass.

Over another river, past a county sign, a long row of glasshouses, flashing orange in the low rays of the sun. The road passed through a strange collection of desolate roadside buildings too weird to be called a village, a garden centre complete with gnomes and tiny model tractors, a motel, a dusty café, its frontage half obscured by a pantechnicon parked across it. 'It's like a scene from the American Midwest, like a movie,' Will murmured near her ear and she nodded, seeing exactly what he meant. Soon, it too was left behind.

The rain swept in with real seriousness now and for a while it felt as though the car was surging through a waterfall. Then, just as suddenly, the downpour eased off and the sharp chiaroscuro of light through cloud set a dramatic atmosphere and the wet fields and the running surface water sparkled finally with beauty.

'Not long now,' Blake called back cheerily, his shrewd eyes meeting Rosa's in the rear-view mirror, and she nodded. Not long before what? Till something happened. She shuddered at the rush of adrenalin, and again felt Will's hand on hers. This time she held it firmly, glad of its comfort.

Was Michal really out here in these vast fields, or at least some clue to him? She'd seen no people in all this landscape, she realized now. Only the smoke from a roadside cottage and, once, in the distance, a tractor ploughing a great arc in a field. The only human-like figures were scarecrows, arms outstretched, pinned into a parody of the condemned. Her grip on Will's hand tightened.

The car was slowing again now, and Rosa's attention was caught by an impression of glaring light from the roadside ahead. Like a tiny football stadium, no, she saw, an old petrol station. A yellow sandwich board flashed past, then the car braked heavily and Blake swung off the road, bumping it over a potholed forecourt. They were bathed suddenly in a fierce golden glare that made Rosa blink. Blake edged the car forward, brought it to a halt, then he turned and said to Rosa in low, urgent tones, 'Not a sound. Whatever you see, you must not react. Do you understand?'

She nodded without speaking, then gazed out of the window at the frenetic activity outside.

Michal

That morning, the one named Marek had roused the men as usual as the sky was lightening beyond the scanty curtains. For a precious last moment Michal lay still, drifting in and out of sleep as the others shifted from their mattresses, groaning and scratching, taking turns to step over each other to visit the single grubby bathroom across the landing.

There were four of them sharing the room, which had been heated in the depths of the winter by a small electric radiator that had been taken away now spring had returned. Michal rubbed at a patch of red bites on his abdomen and tried to ignore the prickling of his scalp, then pushed back the lumpy duvet and reached to rummage in his rucksack for something cleanish to wear. What came out first was a T-shirt with *I love London* printed on it, which he'd bought in a moment of delirious excitement the morning of his arrival in the city. He no longer noticed the words on the front and his roommates had long since ceased to point out their irony. It was simply a garment to wear under his overall. Jeans were too heavy if the water got to them and since it could get hot beneath the waterproofs now that the weather was warmer, he usually chose shorts. More problematic were his deck shoes, which were worn through to holes in places, so the chemicals they used to clean the cars burned his feet. Marek had promised him a little extra money for replacements, but that was days ago.

Marek hadn't seemed so bad when Michal first met him. It was Lenny Block, the man living opposite Michal's father's house, who had introduced the boy to a Croatian named Igor, who had passed him on to Marek. When Michal had realized a few days after his arrival in London that his father didn't live in the house in Dartmouth Street any more he simply hadn't known what to do. He'd spent a few nights sleeping rough, once in a park where he woke up to find his wallet and his phone missing, then on a building site under a flyover before a woman cleaning the church where he went to sit introduced him to a young man who had told him about the hostel. He'd have been all right if he'd done as he suggested. Instead, Michal had gone back one final time to Dartmouth Street and had the bad luck to meet Lenny.

Lenny Block was an imposing figure, built like a bull and smartly dressed. He spoke Michal's language, albeit with a heavy accent. After spotting Michal sitting on Harry Dexter's doorstep he'd invited him into his flat, made a phone call to someone named Igor, and written down Igor's address for him. Igor would fix him up with work, no problem, Lenny said, and somewhere to live into the bargain. When Michal stammered his thanks Lenny's big face softened. He took out a fat roll of banknotes, peeled a twenty off the top and presented Michal with it, waving away the boy's gratitude.

It was Igor who drove him out here in the middle of the countryside and left him with Marek and Paula, the woman Michal thought wasn't actually his wife for she had a different surname, he'd seen it on an envelope she'd left lying about. The house he'd been brought to stood alone in a wooded area at the far edge of a small country town. Marek and the woman inhabited a comfortable flat over a large garage that had been built at a right angle to the house, a sort of barn opposite forming the third side to a muddy yard. Marek had invited Michal into the flat, explained about the work, and had taken his passport 'to keep it safe'. Then Paula had led him across to the house and shown him where he was to sleep. He was dismayed by the stained mattresses on the floor, the squalor of the small room, but before he could open his mouth to protest she'd closed the door and was gone.

The house had three bedrooms. Marek's brother, a scruffy, boorish individual named Boris, lived in one. Into the other two and a room downstairs were crammed eleven men. Michal knew only the ones in his room, who appeared to be Croatians, brought to Britain with the promise of money and work. There was no one in the house who spoke his language and few had much English. Still, they all managed to communicate somehow. The jokes about his nationality and his skinniness were a bit wearing, but he quickly discerned that they weren't meant to be cruel. Indeed, his roommates could be kind in a rough, joshing sort of way, because he was the youngest, alone, and the most homesick. Even so, he made sure that they didn't hear him when he cried at night.

Hunger was always with him, a muttering beast gnawing away at his innards, but this morning as he dressed it rampaged. He hurried downstairs in a panic, hoping desperately that the others had left him some breakfast. But there was Marek already standing in the front doorway, his bulk blocking the light, roaring that it was time to go and rattling the keys on his belt like a jailer. Michal ducked away into the kitchen, seized the rough-hewn sandwich the eldest and kindest of his roommates thrust at him and bit down a hunk as he followed the others out shivering into the cold dawn towards the waiting van. He hated this journey. Eleven men packed into the back with no windows, an hour's nausea-inducing round trip dropping several off at each of three destinations. His was usually the last, and it was almost with relief that he would step out onto the wind-blown forecourt and join the queue at the hut to collect his overalls under the eagle-eyed glare of the foreman.

Rosa

The artificial light was so bright it hurt. She heard the grinding roar of a machine, the hiss of water, men's harsh voices calling to each other, barks of loud laughter. Blake lowered his window to meet a rush of cold air and a man's looming face.

'Yes, sir, what can I do for you today?'

'Just the £4 job.'

'Of course. Park over here, please.'

The face withdrew and Rosa heard the man shout orders in a language like hers yet not her own. Blake edged the car forward into the space indicated then killed the engine.

'You all stay here, right. I'm going to have a look round.' He released his seat belt and stepped out of the car, slamming the door behind him.

'Where is he going?' Rosa addressed Will.

'I'm not sure. Let's just do as he says.'

Suddenly the car was set upon by a trio of men in overalls. Soapy water wept down the windows. The car rocked as it was rubbed by brushes and cloths. Rosa grew more and more alarmed. She couldn't see out. She felt she couldn't breathe. More water descended, there was more rubbing, the car roof appeared to ripple above her. Then dry cloths wiped the windows, polished the paintwork, and suddenly she could see out again. An overalled midriff passed close to her face, a hand gave the window a final wipe, then, as she watched the operative retreat, beyond him, seven or eight yards away, she caught sight of a thin young man, drawing a hosepipe through his hands, looping it around his elbow. The red rawness of his bare fingers drew her pity at the same moment as she thought, he reminds me of—

Somebody gave a shout and the boy raised his face. Seeing his eyes was like looking into her own . . .

'Michal!' She knocked on the window, pressed the electric button, but it was dead. He didn't hear her, returned to his work coiling the hose. She scrabbled for the door handle, yanked at it, shouldered the door open.

'No, stop her!' Jamie cried and she felt Will pulling her back, jerking the door shut again. 'Let me go,' she shouted in her own language, then, in English, 'It's him, my brother.'

'Rosa ...' Will held her firmly, though she thrashed and kicked at him. She was dimly aware of Jamie getting out, then in again with Blake the other side, doors closing, Blake starting up the engine and the car moving away slowly, calmly, as though nothing was wrong, as though they weren't really leaving the most important person in Rosa's life behind, in danger.

'No, no, it's Michal. We can't go without him.' She was practically hysterical now, but Blake didn't respond, rather, kept on driving. The car slid into a gap in the traffic and accelerated away.

Will, gripping her, spoke in her ear. 'We'll save him, don't worry. Just hang on. It's like Blake explained back in London. It would have ruined everything if he'd seen you.'

The fight went out of her then and she slumped exhausted against him, sobbing. He held her, rubbing her shoulders and whispering, 'It'll be OK, OK.' Her sobs and the shuddering of her body gradually subsided.

After a mile or two on the darkening road, Blake pulled the car into a layby, switched off the engine and turned to her, his face sombre, urgent. 'The blue-eyed boy ... ?'

'It was him.' Rosa's voice came out croaky.

Blake nodded, then picked up his phone from a cubbyhole in the dashboard and examined it. 'No bloody signal,' he said, laying it down again.

'Me neither,' Jamie said, trying his.

'Rosa, listen,' Blake said to her. 'There's a procedure for this. No, listen to me. Think of what might have happened if we'd simply taken him. The men in charge might have attacked us. They're criminals, Rosa. They can be violent.'

She nodded unhappily, seeing the sense in what he said, but also remembering the sight of her brother and his reddened hands and sodden shoes, his exhausted face.

'And what would have happened to all the others working there? They'd have been whisked away maybe, beyond rescue. No, we have to go to the police. I know how to get this done. Trust me.'

She shrugged, sitting quietly now, staring at her own hands lying twisted in her lap.

Blake fired up the engine and the car moved forward, then halted before moving off again into the procession of traffic.

'It isn't far,' he threw over his shoulder and, as they sped along a dual carriageway, she closed her eyes, feeling finally the sense of tightness easing inside her. All the months of worry, the weeks in London searching, the pain and disappointment of dashed hopes. And now, she'd finally found Michal. She knew what had happened to him. He was alive. And despite the fact that she'd been torn from him again, and he probably hadn't even seen her just now, something significant had been achieved. She'd know no peace until she held him safe, but at last she dared imagine that this moment would come.

Will had withdrawn his arm from her shoulders, but instead he reached across and covered her hands with one of his. The warmth and steadiness of his presence soothed her as they turned off the road and came to floodlit retail outlets, then the outskirts of a large town, where they inched their way through the evening traffic.

Michal

'Michal, hey, get up, boy.'

Someone was shaking him awake. Vlad, one of his roommates, was hunkered down beside him, and the urgency of his tone frightened Michal.

'What is it?'

There was an odd light from outside playing on the curtains, car headlights, and the vibration of heavy engines, a murmur of voices. Such odd goings on were not unknown and in the morning there might be a new face at breakfast, sometimes quiet and wary, sometimes closed and traumatized, but tonight he sensed something different. There was an excitement in the air.

Vlad peeped through the curtains. 'Police!' he hissed. The other two were stumbling around the room like bears, throwing clothes on, packing their bags in the darkness, then came a knock on the door, which opened, and a blinding light shone in. Michal put up his hand to shield his eyes.

'Police.' The holder of the torch, whom he couldn't see, gave an order Michal didn't understand, but he did as the others and stood up, raising his hands. Suddenly the ceiling light snapped on and the room was full of strangers checking the men and the room for weapons. Their leader gave another command.

'They say pack and go with them,' Vlad murmured to Michal. 'Jeans, T-shirt, go.'

As he dressed a shred of a dream he had had last night came back to him, about seeing his sister in a car, no, maybe it hadn't been a dream after all. He'd stared after the car, wondering if it had been a trick of the light, a girl, yes, who'd looked like Rosa. In the dream the car had stopped and she'd stepped out and come towards him with arms stretched but, that hadn't been what happened, had it?

His fingers slipped on the zip of his bag as he tried to do it up. His clothes felt as though he'd put them on wrong, and he was so tired he felt dizzy. The zip was well and truly stuck, so he slung the gaping bag on his shoulder and followed the others to the narrow stairway, its bare boards trembling under their weight as they filed downstairs. By the front door another policeman directed them outside.

Out in the yard, the cold air struck him, but he was more affected by the sight before him. The muddy yard was full of vehicles. Marek and Paula, their wrists bound before them, heads bowed, were being ushered into the back of a police van. Behind them, officers wearing gloves carried boxes full of paper from the flat, a bulging black bin bag, a computer tower.

The policeman who'd first appeared in Michal's room drew the group of workers together and spoke to them in their language. Michal didn't understand the words, but he grasped that they weren't in any kind of trouble. They were to leave the house, go with the police. There was a minibus waiting. It had windows, Michal saw with pleasure. They were to get in it now.

As they climbed into the bus, Michal looked behind him and caught sight of a bulky figure separating itself from the shadows of the house and moving off into the darkness of the trees. 'Hey, it's Boris,' he cried, gesturing, and the men behind him turned to see where he pointed. Police flashlights swept the scene and fixed on the back view of Marek's brother shambling away, trousers slipping down his fleshy flanks. From his seat in the bus, Michal watched the man's capture with a sense of relish. Boris was an oaf with a personal hygiene problem, who had ruled by intimidation and penned in his charges at night like dumb beasts.

On the journey he could at last see the countryside around the house where he'd been kept. What his sister had thought flat and dull seemed to him dazzlingly beautiful in the early dawn of a spring day. He thought about his captors, how they'd not been cruel in the sense of violence or torture, but nor had they treated him with humanity or kindness. They'd given him the status of a prisoner or slave. They'd kept the bulk of his wages, fed him insufficient food, herded them all together and watched over their every movement.

He glanced about at his fellow workers, seeing a curious range of expressions on their faces, fear on some, exhaustion, bewilderment on others, but on none any sense of hope. The policeman had said something about them going to a safe place, but these men had endured so much that they were not capable yet of understanding what such a place might be. Only Michal, the youngest, the least crushed, drank greedily the view from his window, thought of Rosa, back home in Warsaw, who must be so worried about him, and felt his world fill up with light and hope.

Rick

At the coach station that afternoon it was like being in a great goldfish bowl, staring out through the glass of the arrivals hall as he searched the forecourt for the coach from Derby. When it came, more or less on time, his heart lifted to see Stef's sylph-like figure step down, the familiar patterned holdall swinging at her side. He watched with tenderness as she swept her hair over her shoulder in that characteristic arm-behind-the-neck gesture, and stared vaguely about as she followed the other passengers towards the arrivals hall. The realization that she was searching for him made him hurry towards the door and the surprised smile that broke over her face when she saw him filled him with happiness. 'Wow, your hair is great!' she said laughing, and he put a self-conscious hand to his new, short style. 'You look smart, sort of ... different.'

'I'm still the same,' he said firmly. They hugged awkwardly and he breathed in her familiar flowery scent.

'It's great that you came,' she said, letting him take her holdall. Rick forged a way for them through the crowds, but when they were outside, it was as though she was trying to reassert herself. 'I can manage, you know,' she said, trying to grab back the bag. In the end they took a handle each.

'D'you want a coffee?' he asked.

'No. Let's go home, shall we?'

Home. She placed a little emphasis on the word and he caught her meaning. Number 11 Bellevue Gardens was her bolthole.

They decided another bus would be nicer than the tube and were lucky enough to find empty seats at the front. Sitting side by side, watching the passing scenery, it was easy to talk.

'How is everyone?' Stef was eager to know. She'd heard from Rosa, by the briefest of excited texts, that she'd found Michal. Rick said that Rosa was still waiting to see him. She and Jamie had arrived back late the evening before and, this morning, Rosa had been a bundle of nerves.

'And Leonie's so relieved Jamie's home,' Rick explained. Everybody else was fine, though Peter was behaving oddly. 'Not bad odd, exactly, just odd. He's up to something.'

Stef nodded. She was quiet for a moment.

'How are your family then?' Rick ventured. There was so much he wanted to ask her, about Oliver and why she went back to Derby.

'They're great,' she said. 'The boys spent most of the time on their games, though.' She mimed thumbs moving over a controller. 'And Mum and my stepdad, well, they tried their best, but . . . I don't belong there.'

Rick glanced at her, but her face was veiled by a strand of honey hair. He'd caught the catch in her voice, though, and wanted to touch her hand to reassure her, but wasn't sure whether he should. He feared doing anything that might frighten her away. After all, she must still be so caught up with Oliver. In his mind's eye he saw again Oliver's arrogant face, pinched with rage and frustration.

'This belonging thing's tricky, isn't it?' he ventured. 'I wonder when in life we start working it out.'

She shook her head. 'I don't know. It's deciding where you want to be, isn't it, and what you want to be doing. And who with – people, your friends and family. All these things mixed up.'

'Yeah.' Was now the time to tell her? It probably was. 'I've finished my story,' he said. 'That is, I've still got to fix a few bits but it's all there.'

'Rick, that's fantastic!' She pushed back the strand of hair and he could see she was smiling.

'There's something else.' He had seen it that morning, when he'd checked his laptop. There had been a message from a publisher. A very small publisher, who could offer him only a tiny sum upfront, but still. 'Someone wants to turn it into a book!' And then joy spread across her face and she reached over and squeezed his hand, just like that. She made it seem so easy. 'Rick, how brilliant!' He squeezed her hand back, pride and contentment spreading through him.

Later he'd tell her what he'd been thinking, that his sister was right and he ought to come out of himself more. Find a job with more responsibility. He wasn't sure what yet, but simply making the decision was a start, as though he were a boat testing its moorings, feeling the excitement of the swell. There must be things out there he could do that would interest him. It was time to work out where he belonged.

Stef

She saw the difference in him straight away. Of course there was the haircut. The new style suited him, short at the back and sides, but long at the front with a side parting, but it was simply the fact that he'd had it cut at all, instead of absent-mindedly tucking it into an elastic band as he usually did. As she'd followed him out of the coach station she'd noticed that his shirt was new, too, a slim-cut style in soft green cotton which he wore with the top button undone to reveal his collarbone. His whole look was different, more grown-up, more confident. Could all this have happened in only a fortnight? It didn't seem such a short time ago since she'd faced down Oliver. It felt much longer. Sometimes that could happen with a complete break, you healed quickly.

It felt different, too, stepping into the hall of Number 11. For a start, lots of paintings were propped against the walls; well, she assumed they were paintings, wrapped in brown paper and tied up in string, waiting to go somewhere, she supposed, but where? She was about to ask Rick when Peter bustled up the stairs from the basement with yet another.

'You're back, are you?' he said on seeing her, then, surprisingly, if a little grudgingly, 'Nice to see you.'

'Nice to see you,' Stef said, astonished, as he put down his burden and returned to his basement. Peter, friendly? What on earth had been going on while she'd been away?

Bela hailed her, making her way stiffly down the stairs bumping the vacuum cleaner in front, the long gauzy scarf round her neck billowing out behind. 'Welcome back,' she said. 'To this mess.' She nodded to the paintings. 'How can I clean, hey? Selfish, that's what he is. Selfish man.' She reached the hall and opened the door of the cupboard under the stairs with an indignant sweep of the hand.

'Come on,' Rick said to Stef. 'Let's find Leonie.'

'She's gone out somewhere,' Bela said, wheeling the vacuum cleaner into the cupboard. 'All in a hurry, she was. You go on up, girl, your room's ready and waiting. I gave it a good clean for you just now.'

'Thank you, Bela.'

Rick carried her bag up to her attic where she thanked him and he left her.

Stef found herself standing once more in the doorway

of her attic room. The bed was freshly made, the floor swept and a vase of tulips stood on the chest-of-drawers. Dear Bela. Significantly, her portfolio had been brought out from behind the furniture and laid on a table under the window, as though awaiting her attention. That must have been Leonie. She put down her holdall and went over to it at once, opened it up and shuffled quickly through the drawings.

She was astonished to see that they were better than she remembered. She had talked them down to herself on the journey to Derby, told herself they couldn't possibly be good enough. This had made her feel justified in withdrawing from them, but now she lifted out a sketch of a dress with panels that would be cut on the cross. It had a flattering, close-fitting bodice and elbow-length sleeves and she'd clipped to the picture a snippet of material that she'd found in a charity shop near the Black Cat Café, a sort of jersey material in a warm orangey brown. A belt, she thought, a very narrow belt, would finish the look. She'd have to draw one in. And tomorrow, she told herself, tomorrow she'd complete her application form for college, and send it off. She'd had an email from her old art teacher agreeing to be a referee.

But now she'd unpack, then, if Leonie still wasn't back, she'd see if Rosa was around. She wanted to hear the whole story about Michal.

Later she found Leonie in the kitchen cutting open a packet of digestives, a task which she immediately abandoned as her eyes lit up.

'Stef!' Leonie held out her arms. Stef flew to her and they hugged. 'I'm so glad you're back, dear.' They broke apart and smiled at each other.

'It's so lovely of you to have me back,' Stef said. 'I'm sorry I ran out on you. You must have thought me very rude.'

'That was the last thing I thought. You poor girl. I hope you don't mind, but I made Rick tell me the bones of the story.'

'No, I don't mind,' Stef said quickly. 'It was awful. Oliver had had me followed. I worked it out. First he found the piece in the paper about my accident, then he employed a private detective. I'd been so careful not telling him where I was, not posting on Facebook or anything, but maybe the detective tricked the hospital into telling him . . . He must have been the man who took the photo outside the house, do you remember?'

'So he wasn't a tourist?'

'Can't have been. And I went to the Black Cat just now. Karina reminded me about a guy a couple of weeks ago who'd come in and questioned Beth. Rosa had thought it was to do with Michal, but maybe it wasn't. Maybe it was me he wanted to know about.'

Leonie looked confused. Stef, who hadn't quite worked out that bit either, said, 'Anyway, never mind exactly how he found me, he just did.'

'I wish I'd been here when he'd come. I'd have seen him off.'

'I wish you had been, but funnily enough I'm sort of glad I saw him. Not glad that he hit me, of course, but, well, I'd still been muddled about Oliver. Wondering if I should have left, whether the things that had been wrong about us were my fault. I mean, I expect some of them were, I know I'm irritating sometimes.'

'We can all be.'

'But it made me see how overbearing he was. And very importantly that I was free of him. All the time I'd been here I thought I still loved him, but seeing him here and how appallingly he behaved, well, it made me see that these thoughts were an illusion. It was like a lovely, comfortable bubble popping. Suddenly it was gone.'

Leonie nodded.

'Hey, it's really helped me telling you. It's like I can see it clearly now.'

'That's often the case. I'm very glad you're back, Stef.'

Touched by Leonie's warmth, Stef regarded her thoughtfully and berated herself for her own selfishness. Over the previous few weeks, before the Oliver thing, Leonie had been telling her a story, a story which had enthralled Stef, not least because of its glamour, a story of beautiful models and famous photographers, of an exciting time in history which Leonie had lived through, been part of. But the story had started to turn dark and then, because of everything that had happened, she'd not had time to ask. Well, perhaps it wasn't that she hadn't had time exactly, rather she'd pushed it away, hadn't in her heart of hearts wanted to know. She'd sensed that it was getting too close to her own experiences and she'd been frightened of it ending badly. Yet that was illogical in a way, for here, before her, was Leonie, strong and smiling. Whatever had happened in her past she'd come through it.

I ought to have more faith, she told herself, but aloud she said, 'Leonie, can I ask you something? I need a bit of help with my portfolio for college. Would you mind looking at it with me?'

'I'd be glad to,' Leonie said. 'I was just having a tea break so we can do it now if you like?'

'That would be fantastic. I'll go and fetch it.' She found herself taking the stairs two at a time, almost falling over Bela who was rummaging in the linen cupboard as she turned the corner of the landing.

Leonie

The difference in the girl was remarkable, she thought as she took a tray of tea and biscuits through to her drawing room and set it on the table before the sofa. There was a new light in her eyes as though she was coming fully alive. The portfolio, when Stef brought it in, was as satisfyingly full as she'd suspected when she'd cursorily inspected it in the attic after Stef had taken flight.

Stef opened it up for her and she turned the pages. Some of the drawings in the sketchbooks she'd glimpsed before, for Stef had worked on them at the kitchen table and occasionally passed them to her, but many she hadn't. She admired the growing confidence, the way she'd drawn each clothed figure in a variety of different poses. There was a larger book, too, full of sketches,

pictures torn from magazines, pieces of material, photographs of accessories, people in the street, in a park.
There were designs, too, that she must have created on a
computer and printed out.

'Oh, I did those before I came here,' she explained
when Leonie asked. 'A lot of it involves computer soft-
ware now. I've still got so much to learn though.'

'That's why you're going to college,' Leonie said firmly
and Stef laughed.

'I'm so nervous about it all!' she confessed.

'Everybody is, from what I hear. Listen, Stef, I'm no
expert on how they do things today, but these look really
good to me. I mean it. You have flair. I keep telling you.
I can suggest some ways in which you could organize
the work better for the interviewer, and some gaps, like
here . . .' She turned to a double-page spread where Stef
had drawn a set of outfits with tabs to be fitted onto a
paper doll she'd sketched. 'You could indicate some of
the colours here, just by shading.'

'That's a good idea. Thanks.'

'And here,' she said, turning a page. 'This girl. Her
neck's awfully thick.'

'Oh-oh, I wondered why she looked weird. That can
be dealt with.'

They talked for a while longer, Leonie turning the
pages of the large sketchbook and admiring the range of
outfits and the sense of Stef's imagination at work, and
making the occasional comment.

Eventually, though, Stef parcelled everything up again
in the big portfolio case and leant it against a chair, then

sat down again on the sofa in her characteristic pose, one leg tucked under. 'You've been amazing. Thank you.'

'Not at all. It's simply that I was the person who had to wear the clothes, so I was considering your work from that viewpoint.'

'That makes sense.' Stef took a biscuit and Leonie watched her lick the chocolate from it thoughtfully. 'When did you stop modelling?' Stef asked, leaning back.

Leonie considered the question. 'I was finally given the excuse when I became pregnant with Tara. I was, goodness, in my mid-twenties then. But I'd wanted to give up before. I became exhausted by it, I'm afraid.'

Stef looked surprised. 'Seriously?'

'I know, everyone thinks it must be marvellous, but being a photographic model is extremely hard work. It definitely has its moments, I'll allow that. It's wonderful seeing your picture in the magazines, for instance, but there came a point when that wasn't enough. There's so much travelling involved, but you don't always get to see the places properly and it's tiring, then there's the hanging around waiting for other people, and the business of being photographed is not that exciting. Some people loved the whole thing and went on longer, or else they turned the job into something else like Twiggy did, but that didn't happen for me. I know it's easy to blame other people for one's own laziness, but I truly think my lack of ambition was partly down to Billy.'

She saw Stef's eyes widen with interest, and wondered how to go on. These memories were painful. Eventually, she bit her lip and continued.

'What I really wanted to do once we'd been married a year or two was have a baby, but Billy was against that idea for the moment. He was enjoying life too much and said a child would get in the way of that. He thought we should wait.'

She closed her eyes. It was hard remembering all this and telling it to this young woman, and she'd reached a part she couldn't easily share. Never mind, she would skip over some of those bits. Even though, as she started to speak, she could remember it all with bitter-sweet freshness.

1966

It was a secret joy that turned to sadness. For a very short while in the spring of 1966 Leonie had known that a small person had started to grow inside her. Billy had been furious when she told him she was pregnant. The tiredness and the nausea meant she had to struggle through her assignments with extra make-up caked on to disguise her paleness.

Then, one night she'd awoken with a sudden sense that something had gone, been lost. It wasn't for a day or two that the blood came, and with it pain, and Billy had to drive her to the hospital in a panic. He had been kind to her then, though afterwards, in the depths of her grief, she accused him of not caring, of being glad that the baby had gone. She was almost relieved to see the hurt leap into his eyes, to know that he really did feel sadness.

It wasn't long, though, before his usual pattern of behaviour resumed.

What Billy wouldn't accept was that she didn't want to perform for his camera 'like some circus animal', as she put it, any more, that she was tired of it all. He took her reluctance as a personal rejection, but he also felt professionally exposed without her.

They began to quarrel constantly.

'You shouldn't stuff your face, fatso. You'll spoil the line of the clothes.' He accused her of all sorts of things, from 'letting herself go', to 'becoming a frump' to actively setting out to destroy his career.

For her part she was depressed, partly because of the miscarriage, partly because she wasn't keen on working so hard any more, and his snide comments only made things worse. She started mixing with people outside their usual sphere.

George was one of them. He was generous and hospitable and she loved visiting Bellevue Gardens. The atmosphere in the house was so relaxed, too relaxed sometimes. She used to count the empty wine bottles from the latest party lined up against the back of the house. George was someone who collected people, he had so many friends. Everyone liked him back, but he had no one special of his own. Leonie sensed that he was someone who was intrinsically lonely.

He loved women, but she quickly realized that it was only friendship he wanted from them. The ones he idolized were always out of his reach, such as Petula Clark and Dusty Springfield. He'd adored Vanessa Redgrave in *Blow-Up*, and, like Billy, who'd enjoyed it for its satire of his rival David Bailey, went to see the film four times. His widowed mother George treated with reverence, going faithfully to see her in Hertfordshire every week, but no one had ever known him to have a girlfriend.

He sometimes developed close friendships with other men, but these never led to anything. There was a line he simply wouldn't step over. Maybe it was his upbringing, very strict and moral, but it was also something in him. He had a deep shyness of the physical. Leonie never knew him speak of this aspect of himself, nor would she have embarrassed him by asking.

She and Billy limped on together. The truth was that, despite the difficulties, they loved one another and neither of them wanted to be with anyone else. But the struggle couldn't go on in the same way indefinitely. Slowly but surely things between them began to come apart. They both began to feel trapped. Billy was increasingly away with his work, occasionally abroad. Sometimes she went with him as his model, but as time went by she chose more and more to stay at home. Then, if his work didn't go well or there were dry spells when the phone didn't ring, he'd take it out on her, say that she didn't support him or that she was poisoning things. This wasn't true, but she came to see that it was his way of dealing with his terror of failure.

Gradually she was becoming the scapegoat for anything that went wrong in his life. There was one occasion when she yelled at him, 'You should have married bloody Shelagh, then, if you wanted someone to lick your boots.'

'I wish I had. At least she'd have put a proper dinner on the table,' he'd replied, which was hardly a fair charge given that he kept such irregular hours. This level of bickering was ridiculously petty, but such was their battleground.

Everything changed irreparably after Leonie became pregnant with Tara late in 1967. Billy had finally given in on the question of having a baby after a long war of attrition. Even then, they were both astonished when she conceived so quickly.

Having a child can sometimes bring a couple closer together, but sometimes it can drive them apart. In their case it finally broke up their professional partnership and set their lives on different courses. None of this was Tara's fault, of course, though as a baby she brought with her no end of problems.

In those days fathers were not encouraged to attend the birth, and in this case it was just as well because Billy arrived home from a trip to the French Riviera four hours too late. He arrived at the hospital straight off the plane with a bunch of red roses and a teddy bear that was larger than the baby, to find Leonie anxious and exhausted, trying and failing to get the hungry mewling newborn to breastfeed under the strict eye of a nurse. Ill at ease, and denied use of his camera by the horrified nurse, he didn't stay long.

After Leonie came out of hospital, her mother arrived to stay for a fortnight. Billy kept away as much as possible or else skulked about in the background, wondering why no one had time to pay him any attention.

Tara was a colicky baby. For the first couple of months she would scream all evening before dropping off to sleep exhausted, only to wake every few hours so that Leonie got exhausted too. Tara was always ill. Bronchitis, croup – when Leonie feared for Tara's life because the poor mite could hardly breathe – chicken pox, which she caught from the little boy downstairs, it was endless.

Leonie had little time for Billy and everything got in a state. The laundry piled up, there was always a bucket of dirty nappies in the second bedroom which they now used as a nursery and Leonie couldn't deal with them because she was nursing a sick baby. Hilda Fletcher, Billy's mother, came over sometimes to help, and she worked so quietly and efficiently you'd hardly know she was there. Eventually they found a girl to help with the housework, and somehow they lurched from crisis to crisis until the end of the first year. With Tara sleeping through the night it was like coming out of a tunnel for Leonie. But by then she realized that something fundamental between her and Billy had changed.

Billy was out a lot of the time. Of course, he had to work to pay for everything, there could be no argument there. As well as the rent on the flat, and the bills, there were the payments for all the things they had bought on credit. Sometimes he would be away for a few days, in Rome, Lapland, once, or simply at the other end of the British Isles, at a shoot in a Scottish castle.

If he was home he wanted to go out every evening with his old friends. And he resented it that Leonie wouldn't always come too, refusing to leave Tara in the hands of a babysitter. Basically, Billy wanted to live the same life they'd always lived and she couldn't and didn't want to any more. Here was a new line of argument. He'd tell her that she'd become boring, and didn't make any time for him. 'It's not that,' she would say crossly, 'I'm just tired and what's more I don't like leaving Tara.'

Some of the best times were when she saw Trudi. Trudi was on her second marriage already, having ditched the actor who, she said, was in love with himself. This time around, it was to a rich magazine publisher ten years older than her. She need not have gone on working, but did because she enjoyed it and the publisher didn't object. Trudi adored Tara and when she was in town she'd visit them both with presents, especially the sweetest little-girl dresses. Then they might not see her again for weeks, but a postcard might arrive from Los Angeles or Paris, saying she'd met Paul Newman at a party, or Cathérine Deneuve. Sometimes Leonie would confide in her friend about Billy, and Trudi would listen and make sympathetic noises, but she would never offer advice. Probably sensibly, Trudi said that they had to sort it out themselves and that, anyway, she was the last person to take counsel from.

Between Trudi's visits, if Billy was away and Leonie was feeling lonely, she might telephone George. If it was a weekend he might take them both out in his car. He had an old schoolfriend, Charles, who lived with his wife, Bud, short for Rosemary, in an ancient manor house on the border of Surrey and Sussex, and they visited them on several occasions. It was a gorgeous place, Elizabethan, built of lovely old faded brick, with roses rambling all over the front, but it was crumbling away because Charles didn't have the capital to look after it. There was usually something going on there – all kinds of peculiar people stayed. Charles and Bud weren't modern or fashionable, a lovely change from the people she and Billy met in the London clubs and pubs. They were true old bohemians, in a polite upper-class kind of way. Charles wore sweaters with holes at the elbows and talked radical politics, which Leonie didn't think quite squared with the inherited house and the proper manners, but he was not at all snobbish and didn't care about money. But then, George once whispered to her, he had never really had to.

'Mrs Charles,' as George privately referred to her, was charming, too, but vague in the extreme. The two sons of the house were usually away at boarding school, the fees presumably paid for by somebody or other, but there was a little girl still at home who played with Tara, and a pair of long-suffering elderly retrievers who put up with being poked and rolled on by the children whilst the grown-ups sat around talking about art and politics and having drinks and meals at the oddest times.

Stef

It was at this point that Leonie broke off. She gazed up at a painting on the wall. It was, Stef saw, the distinctive one of the escaping bird and the floating figure of a girl. Confusion darkened Leonie's face, making Stef feel concerned. Finally she returned to herself and smiled at Stef.

'I'm sorry, you must wonder where all this rambling is leading to. I was simply remembering it all. I haven't seen Charles and Bud for years and years. It was soon after I came to live here that we visited them again in Haslemere and George bought me this painting. I spotted it in the window of a junk shop and couldn't tear myself away. The girl looks as though she's flying like the bird, doesn't she? Don't you think it's all about freedom?'

'Yes, I do.' Stef stared at it again, feeling its mood of exhilaration. She thought it sort of surreal, disturbing like a fairy tale. She remembered how she'd connected it in her mind to the photograph of the jay at the exhibition in the big house in Derby.

'It didn't cost very much, so I let him buy it for me. Dear George.' Leonie's focus seemed to be drifting again and Stef thought perhaps she was working up to the key part of her story that she didn't want to tell. She waited, quietly, to see what might happen. She was nervous, but she really wanted to know and hoped that Leonie didn't simply turn back into her normal busy self, pile everything up on the tray and become all practical again. Leonie's attention was still on the bird painting, however, and her eyes were sad.

'Billy was jealous,' Leonie said finally. 'He equated his possessiveness with love, but jealousy kills love, and trust, and freedom.'

1972

He'd always shown jealousy of other men, from early on in their relationship, but at first Leonie had been foolish enough to find it flattering. She came to be annoyed by it. She was never interested in other men; she had him and he was all she wanted. She thought he felt the same about her once he'd extricated himself from Shelagh. They were together, a complete little world, and she thought he trusted her.

At first she used to think he was teasing, but came to realize he was truly anxious. He'd complain if some man or other tried to chat her up, and cross-question her about whether she thought the individual was attractive. If she tried to be honest and say whoever was nice or good-looking yet that didn't mean that she was attracted, Billy didn't recognize such a distinction. He would insist in a small, cold sarcastic voice that if she found the man good-looking why didn't she go with him? It was hurtful and such a stupid thing to argue about.

As time went by this anxiety in him became more intense. He seemed genuinely afraid that someone else would come and take her away from him. She found this insulting and refused to engage with his barbs.

Together with the undermining little comments he would make about her looks and abilities, it quite bemused her and made her increasingly unhappy. She never did flirt with other men. Why would she? It would have been cruel of her and she was not like that. But something in her was stubborn, too. Why should he close down her life, tell her whom she could and couldn't talk to? Sometimes it made her blood boil.

And so it was with George. 'The thing about George,' she often explained to Billy, 'is that he likes women as friends and that's how I feel about him, too, that he's a friend.' George amused her, she said, and he knew such interesting, funny people who weren't bothered about superficial things such as your looks or how much you'd paid for a dress.

Having Tara had narrowed her social life. Her old friends from school didn't come up to town much, especially now they had children themselves, and she hadn't kept in touch with them properly, not even with Jean. Of her London acquaintances there were a few with babies; most were too busy having careers and making the most of being young, so George in his odd way really was a lifeline.

At first Billy accepted what she said. It helped that poor George was never going to feature on any list of the world's best-looking men. He was already going bald and carried a little too much weight on him. There was nothing about his appearance or demeanour that was at all threatening to a red-blooded male like Billy.

In the end what Billy couldn't stand was that she spent

so much time with George. Billy liked it best when he knew where she was and what she was doing. It was all about control. If she wasn't going to be working with him then she should be at home caring for his baby and keeping his flat looking nice.

'I'm not like your poor old mother,' she would cry. She was outraged by the way he expected her to stay under his thumb. Every time she saw his parents – which wasn't often – she shivered inwardly and told herself that she and Billy must never become like them, with Billy's father in charge and ruling Billy's mother by fear and threat.

'You're just like your dad,' she screeched at Billy once, and he was furious with her. He hated the way his father treated his mother, and yet he couldn't see that he was starting to behave the same way himself.

By the time Tara was three Leonie's relationship with Billy had become very fraught. If he was there in the flat she felt all the time that he was watching her, waiting for some mistake to pick her up on. It made her so tense to be constantly questioned about what she did and said. Billy would sigh heavily and she would ask him what was wrong and he'd say, 'Nothing.' Or she'd tell him of some harmless plan, to meet Trudi for lunch, perhaps – he tolerated Trudi because she made him laugh – and he'd say something like, 'It's up to you, isn't it? It's your life,' but in a sneering tone, which made her feel wretched. It sounded as though he was judging her every move and finding her wanting.

If Billy was away, on the other hand, he seemed to feel

no obligation to let Leonie know what he was doing. If he rang home from abroad it was not to reassure her or to send his love, but to check up on her. That's what it felt like, anyway.

Finally, there came an evening when he phoned from New York and she wasn't at home. She was actually at George's with Tara, having a pot-luck supper with some of his friends, and came back at midnight, Tara asleep in her arms. She went to bed without even knowing he had called.

The sound of the telephone dragged her to consciousness at 5 a.m. and his voice was furious as he questioned her about where she had been and who with, as though she'd betrayed him. Her judgement shot by the rude awakening, she shouted back at him that it was 'her business' where she had been, and it would 'serve him right' if she did sleep with someone else, then she slammed down the receiver. It was no good rolling over and trying to get back to sleep after that. She was too upset. Anyway, soon after, lusty cries started up in the nursery.

The following afternoon, as they had arranged, Leonie met him at Heathrow airport with Tara. It still gave her heart a tug to glimpse his darkly good-looking face and lazy smile as he strode through the crowd to the barrier. He kissed them both and was amiable enough, though tired beyond much conversation. They returned home and ate the supper she had cooked, then she went off to bathe Tara and put her to bed as normal, while he caught up with the television news.

Later, she was to remember these mundane details so clearly because what happened next was so shocking. There was simply no warning that anything was wrong. She tried to read a picture book to Tara, but the little girl was tired, so Leonie settled her in her diminutive bed, then wound up the musical bear she loved and set it on a shelf to tinkle away. 'Teddy Bears' Picnic', it played, and it started quite fast then gradually slowed, and by the time it ground to a halt with a final plink, Tara was asleep. Leonie stood in the shadows listening, heard Tara breathe deeply and sigh, and tiptoed out, drawing the door to behind her. She turned round. And he was there waiting.

The punch landed in her stomach, a blow so hard it winded her. She doubled over, gasping for breath. She felt him seize her by the throat, then he threw her to the floor. There she lay curled in a defensive ball, stunned by pain and disbelief. All she could think of was his face before he'd hit her, cold, hard, ugly. There had been no anger, no sign of the Billy she knew and loved. It had been the face of a brutal stranger.

Stef

Stef stared at Leonie in horror, the blood thudding in her head. The tone in which the older woman had described the event had been quiet and reasonable, and yet she sensed the fathoms of emotion underneath.

There was quiet for a moment, when Stef must have

gone inside herself, because she jumped when Leonie touched her arm, 'Are you all right?' she said, and once more Stef saw her concerned face, and noticed the tick of the clock on the mantelpiece. She nodded. 'Sorry. What did you do?' she murmured.

'Nothing,' Leonie said. 'I was in too much pain and my animal instincts told me to stay still. I feared he would come at me again, but he didn't. It was over.'

1972

She sensed him retreat, as waves of hot and cold pulsed through her. The pain in her belly was shocking, unbearable, but finally she could breathe again properly and she started to cry in great ugly hiccuping sobs. She couldn't have stopped if she'd tried.

Then, astonishingly, he was there again beside her, bending over her, weeping and begging her forgiveness, the old Billy, the Billy she loved. He was so sorry, so sorry, he couldn't think what had come over him, he loved her so much, but she had made him do it, made him. She drove him mad, he told her. She was bemused. What had she done wrong, exactly? He'd been upset and jealous on the phone that she'd been at George's, but she had given him no grounds to believe she'd been unfaithful.

After that he was as sweet as anything to her. He gathered her up in his arms and staggered to the bedroom where he laid her gently on the bed, then caressed her face and felt her body to find out if she had broken anything, which luckily she hadn't, murmuring all the time how sorry he was. When they'd both recovered a little they began to talk. He said he felt so mad at her sometimes, that she drove him to despair. He sounded as though he believed this, and it was a reasonable point of view, so she began to think, why, yes, possibly she had brought his anger upon herself by disappearing off with George. It must have been a result of her injuries that she couldn't think straight.

Eventually, because she hadn't the strength to resist, she let him make love to her, which he did very carefully, aware of her bruises, then afterwards he fell asleep in her arms. Exhausted as she was she couldn't sleep, not least because she was still in considerable pain. Instead she lay with her thoughts whirling as she wondered how he could have done what he'd done and yet be here sleeping like an innocent pressed against her as if everything was forgiven and forgotten and they could start over again. And even then she wished fervently they could. She stroked his hair and in his dreams he sighed.

Still, she could not sleep. The shock of what had happened was wearing off, but she could not get out of her mind the sight of his face as he'd punched her, the coldness, as though she had become something inhuman, contemptible, a creature he owned that needed teaching a lesson. After a long while she found the energy to slide out of his embrace, slipped her dressing gown on, and went to the bathroom to search for some aspirin.

In the merciless glare of the strip light she examined her injuries. A bruise had swollen across her diaphragm. Her upper arms bore the marks of his clenching fingers.

He hadn't hurt her face, she thought thankfully, then wondered whether that was deliberate. The world would have seen a black eye. And her face was her fortune. That was another reason.

The next morning Billy was cheerful and conciliatory, as though the clock had indeed been turned back and their world made new. She for her part played along, getting properly dressed for once and cooking him the breakfast that he liked best, bacon, eggs and crisp fried bread, while Tara chatted away to him about the Sindy doll he'd brought her from New York. He went off to his morning appointment in better spirits than she'd seen for a long time. Was that all it took?, she thought bitterly as she closed the front door behind him and untied her apron. A docile, pretty wife and a nicely cooked breakfast?

With his absence it was as though a dark presence had lifted. Her thoughts flowed freely again, though she felt such a lump in her throat from trying not to cry. She wiped Tara's face and hands and helped her from the table, though lifting her hurt, and set her down to play with Sindy whilst she cleared away breakfast and took time to think. Whichever way her thoughts spiralled she returned to the same conclusion. She could no longer live with Billy. She did not even want to be here when he came back that evening. But where should she go? Saxford seemed a long way away, and she could not imagine what her parents would say if she turned up on the doorstep with Tara and told them she had left her husband. This thing that had happened to her was beyond their experience as until now it had been beyond hers. A marital squabble was the sort of thing people believed was private, not anyone else's business. She felt dirty, guilty, that perhaps it was she who had driven Billy to violence.

In the end she found herself dialling George's work number. A receptionist answered and some time passed before he could be tracked down, but then suddenly his warm, reassuring voice was there on the other end of the phone.

'It's me,' Leonie said in a wobbly voice, then dissolved into tears.

'Wait there,' he said when he'd got out of her what was wrong. 'I'll come as soon as this job's over.'

'I can't stay here a minute longer,' she sobbed, and by now, Tara had caught her distress and came to clutch her legs with her sharp-nailed fingers, bleating and whining for Mamma to stop crying.

She heard George speak to someone else in the studio, something about cancelling appointments, then he came onto the line again. 'I'm calling a taxi for you,' he said. 'Go to my place. Peter will let you in, I'll phone him, and be there myself as soon as possible.'

Stef

Leonie shifted in her chair, making herself more comfortable before continuing. 'So I did as he told me. I packed a bag for Tara and a couple of suitcases for

myself and left Billy a note to say I was going away for
a few days and he wasn't to come looking for me. Then
the taxi driver arrived and helped with the luggage and
we left. I came straight here, as George had instructed,
and, well, I've lived here ever since.'

'Didn't Billy come after you?' Stef broke in.

Leonie's face hardened. 'He guessed where I'd gone,
so yes, he turned up on the doorstep the following day,
and was exasperated when I didn't let him in. After that,
things were extremely difficult for a few weeks with him
apologizing and begging me to come back and me sorely
tempted to give in, but too frightened actually to do so.
We'd meet, he and I, in public places, restaurants, parks,
and of course he had to see Tara.

'I visited my parents, but realized quickly that my
intuition had been right. They didn't fully appreciate
why I'd left Billy and tried to persuade me to patch
things up with him. I also saw that they would have
been uncomfortable with the idea of me living with
them. Tara and I would have been an embarrassment,
not that they'd have seen it that way, but I knew how
conventional their neighbours could be and it wasn't fair
on Mum and Dad to have a daughter with a failed marriage parked on them, and then Tara would have been
teased at school when she was old enough to go. No, it
was easier to be in London where people didn't know
so much about you, and our friends were less ready to
judge.

'After a year or so Billy got fed up with trying to make
me come back and then, on one of his trips to New York,

he fell in love. She was a catwalk model named Nancy, very young, very needy. I never met her, but Trudi did and told me all about her. He married Nancy eventually, but eventually she left him. Trudi heard one or two stories that suggested Billy hadn't changed his spots.'

'Didn't you worry about Tara going to stay with him?' Stef asked.

'Oh no, Billy would never have hurt Tara.' Leonie sounded very definite about this, but Stef wondered how she could ever have been sure. Their daughter sounded as though she was a troubled type.

'Billy's attitude to parenting was a sort of benign neglect,' Leonie said, as though reading Stef's thoughts. 'I've often wished I'd never let her go to the States with him that summer, or at least that I'd tried harder to make her come back. Fourteen is such a difficult age and she had no one there to guide her.' She sighed and added, as though to herself, 'But who's to say how she'd have turned out if she'd stayed with me? It's impossible to tell.'

'I knew you understood,' Stef whispered, looking up at Leonie with gratitude and sympathy. 'You guessed how I felt about leaving Oliver because the same thing had happened to you.'

Leonie smiled back. 'Not the same thing, exactly, but yes, there are similarities. I had an inkling of how you must have felt.'

'Thank you for telling me your story. It's helped me feel less ... alone.'

'I'm glad,' Leonie said. 'It's a long time since I've

spoken to anyone about what happened and, you know, it's been good for me too. I'm sure I've forgotten some parts and maybe embellished others, those are the tricks that memory plays. But it's useful to try to make sense of one's life, I find. We're survivors, you and I. Rosa is another. What doesn't kill you makes you stronger, eh? We must live life bravely, Stef.'

Rosa

It was a peaceful part of King's Lynn through which Blake was driving, where the streets met at odd angles and old brick houses rubbed shoulders with modern apartment blocks and lock-up shops as though a mad town planner had thrown the whole lot in the air and allowed them to put down foundations where they fell.

'There, past the pub,' Jamie said, pointing to a driveway, and they found themselves in a yard where they parked in one of several spaces before a white cube of a house with double-glass doors. It was a pleasant place, surrounded by lawns and bushes, though Rosa hardly took this in. She glanced at Will who, seeing her uncertainty, smiled reassurance.

'You will come in with me?' she asked him.

He shook his head. 'It's best if you go on your own. We won't be far away. Call me when you're ready.' She was aware of the three of them watching as she walked uncertainly to the entrance, protecting her, supporting her. In her heart of hearts she knew that they were right.

This was something she had to do alone. They would be close by. Blake said he knew an excellent café on the quay. She pressed the bell and waited. The morning sun reflected off the glass so she could not see inside, then was aware of a shadow, and fingers turning the lock.

The short, burly man, like a uniformed bouncer, who admitted her, requested her name then led her across yards of synthetic carpet to a small, bright office like a consulting room where a graceful woman of indeterminate age, oval-faced, dark hair neatly pinned up behind, sat at a desk writing reports. She introduced herself as Bridget, shook Rosa's hand and gestured that she should sit down opposite.

'You have my brother here,' Rosa said. 'May I see him, please?'

'Of course, in a moment, but we need to talk first.' Bridget sank back into her chair and seemed to size Rosa up before speaking again.

'Your brother was brought here very early yesterday,' she said, 'along with the other men he was found with. He immediately asked if we could contact you as next-of-kin, which is why you're here. He was relieved to hear that you were in London and had been searching for him. A doctor has examined him, but it's recommended that he stay here a little while longer. He has been through quite an ordeal, Miss Dexter. The people who have done this to him are under arrest. If he's well enough the police will be visiting to take his statement soon. Then there is counselling available and his situation will need to be assessed . . .'

'You will make him stay here?' Rosa broke in, puzzled.

Bridget shook her head. 'No, no, not make. He is free to come and go, but this place is meant to be a sanctuary and I think you'll find ... well, come, let me take you to him.'

She followed Bridget through a door at the other side of the hall and found herself in a tranquil living room where two men sat on a sofa watching football on an outsized television screen. The French windows were open and beyond there was a small sheltered garden. On a bench by the house Rosa could see the back of a slight young man. At the sound of their footsteps on the patio, he looked round, then stood up and came towards them, and seeing Rosa his eyes lit up with happiness. Those eyes, blue, clear, like a piece of the sky, like her own.

'Mik.' She ran forward and hugged him, felt the trembling reality of him in her arms. There seemed to be less of him than she remembered. She could feel the bones under his skin and there was little strength in his grasp, and then his stamina gave way altogether and he was shaking and whispering into her hair, 'Rosa, Rosa, oh, Rosa, I missed you.' Then he began to cry in dry, uncontrollable sobs. She drew him to her more tightly and murmured reassurances as their mother used to, and now she was crying too, but with joy, and stroking his lank shaggy hair. 'It's all right now, Mik, my little one, you're safe.'

They sat together for a long time after that with their arms round each other, crying and laughing by turn, telling each other everything that had happened since they had last been together. Finally, he said to her, 'They are kind to me here. Mrs Brigid thinks I must stay for a while and get better, then maybe I can come to London to be with you.'

'If that's what you think is best, Mik. It seems a lovely place.'

'I'm free to come and go, she says. Maybe this afternoon we can go to the town and I can meet your friends. I'd like to see Will again. He tried to help me.'

'Lots of people have been helping, Mik. So many care. When you come to London you will meet them all.'

Ten

Leonie

It was a sunny morning on the last Saturday in May when the inhabitants of 11 Bellevue Gardens arrived together at the church hall to be met at the door by a sheepish-looking Peter.

'Don't you think it feels like a wedding?' Leonie greeted him cheerfully. She meant there was that particular mixture of solemnity and jollity about the event that was just like one.

'We're all dressed up like dogs' breakfasts anyway,' was Peter's response. Even he wore a suit, and his shirt had been carefully ironed by Stef.

'I assume you mean that to be a compliment,' Leonie said, managing to swallow her irritation. Like the others she'd made an effort, having selected a pretty pale blue dress that she'd bought for the marriage of one of Trudi's daughters a couple of years ago. 'It is a great event, Peter.' She placed her hand on his arm. 'It really is a wonderful thing that you're doing.'

Peter gave an embarrassed harrumphing sound, but he

appeared pleased nevertheless. 'Are the lot of you going
to stand outside chattering all day?'

They followed him into the hall, Stef, cool and elegant in a linen shift dress she'd found during one of
her charity shop trawls, Rick in his new shirt and jeans.
Jamie was handsome in his usual black boots and biking
jacket. Rosa, neat in one of her pinafores, said she'd wait
outside for Michal, who was late getting up again, Will
had texted her to say.

Will himself, Leonie glimpsed inside the hall, was
helping Bela and Hari with refreshments behind the
kitchen hatch. It had been an early start for all of them.

Leonie had only been here once before, three weeks
ago, when Peter had announced the nature of the project that had kept everyone guessing for weeks and
she'd agreed to go with him for moral support while he
looked round the hall that the church was hiring out to
him.

That last time everything had been arranged very
differently. There had been stacks of chairs and folded
tables against the walls, cork boards festooned with
notices about yoga classes and Sunday school, a box of
toys in a corner. Now the space had been divided up
by felt-covered partitions on which Peter had hung his
paintings. Most of them she had seen before, but this
time they had titles and short descriptions on labels,
which interested her.

She collected a booklet from a pile on a small green-
baize table, examined it closely and was surprised to
see for the first time the prices Peter was asking. For a

moment she felt overwhelmed, touched by the knowledge that he would do this for her, make such a sacrifice
of his work. She closed her eyes then opened them again
as Stef's voice, close, anxious, said, 'Leonie, are you all
right?'

'Yes, of course, my mind was on something else.' She
replaced the booklet on the table. 'Will you come round
with me?' she asked. 'There's a sequence to everything,
I suppose?'

'Yes,' said Stef, who'd helped Peter hang the pictures.
'Sort of by theme, but also by when he painted them. We
start over here by the door.'

The first paintings, three still lifes of found objects,
brought back to Leonie the time after she and Tara had
moved into the house. She remembered how isolated
a figure Peter had been, how he used the conservatory
to paint because he liked the sunshine coming through
the leaves. It was only later that he started to use the
basement, after George had arranged for the thick
hedge to be dug up from in front of the window to let
the light in.

'Tara bought that shell for him in Cornwall,' she murmured, pointing to one of the paintings. 'And this cloth
was an old velvet curtain from one of the bedrooms,
such a beautiful blue.'

They moved on. Here were what she thought of as
the fantasy paintings. 'The one I really love,' Stef said,
ruefully standing before the picture of the house in the
wood. 'It makes me feel safe.'

Leonie didn't like to say that she found it creepy, but

then she knew that Peter had been going through a moody phase when he'd painted these and supposed the memory of that period affected her feelings.

She passed two canvases that were basically dark swirls of thick impasto without looking at them properly. Those Peter had painted after George's death and she couldn't bear them. Then she rounded a partition to see the only remaining one of a beautiful series of seascapes that had proved popular in the last proper exhibition he'd had, in a West End gallery in the early Nineties. He had been to stay for a few months on the Yorkshire coast near Whitby with his fishing friend, and these had been the result.

On another display board hung a cluster of portraits, not the one of Jamie, thank heavens, she never wanted him to sell those, but of people he'd encountered over the years, Jennifer, the actress who'd lived in the house for a bit, an odd-job man Leonie had employed occasionally, who had a very characterful face. These represented some of Peter's best work, she'd always thought, but the public never seemed to think so.

There were more, over a hundred in total, including a dozen mounted sketches. 'Well,' Leonie said, coming back to herself after they'd been round them all. 'It's astonishing seeing them all in place. Quite a body of work.' Indeed, it was as though Peter had taken his whole life and put it out for public view, and he'd done this for her, and for the house.

'Shall I fetch you a glass of wine?' Stef was before

her, forehead wrinkled with concern, and it occurred to Leonie that she must seem to be acting oddly.

'I think that might be a good idea, don't you?' Stef hurried off. Such a dear girl, she seemed so happy now. Only yesterday she'd heard from the college she'd applied for. They'd invited her in for an interview next week!

Leonie glanced about at the exhibition, content to be alone. She went back to the sketches and stood admiring Peter's sense of line in a series of London faces he'd captured.

The hall was filling up nicely with people now. She'd been aware in the last few weeks of Stef and Rick consulting with Will over the publicity, lots of murmuring about online this and that, lists left around the kitchen, but was amazed at the effect it had all had. The local paper was to send a photographer that morning, and Rick had shown her small previews about the exhibition on various websites. They'd really done Peter proud, she thought. And here was Stef back with a glass of wine and a tea plate of dainties. Bela and Hari had contributed to the event what they were good at, beautifully crafted pastry parcels of spiced vegetables, toasts decorated with seed, tiny fragile cups of coloured pâtés. 'Oh, how gorgeous, Stef, thank you!' She tasted one of the cups, and the flavour sparkled on her tongue, then sipped the chilly wine. Trudi had very generously supplied a dozen bottles of Prosecco, and, oh, here was Trudi now. At last, here was a hat to please Peter! Trudi wore a simple black fascinator in her silver-white hair that suited her timeless fine-boned elegance. Flanking her was a man Leonie recognized instantly. Not because she'd seen him before but because of Trudi's description of him. He was classically dressed in a tailored black suit and narrow tie. With his intelligent, weathered face and slicked-back iron-grey hair, he could only be Trudi's attentive ex-gangster. As Leonie hailed Trudi, his keen black eyes were already glancing round the room at the paintings, and he stopped to examine one, pushing on a pair of spectacles.

'Leonie, darling.' The friends kissed each other warmly, then stood back to admire each other. 'Here we are, two old model girls, still having fun.'

'Still beautiful, dear Trudi.'

'It takes a little longer than it did, but I try to keep the side up!'

Leonie laughed then became confiding. 'Am I right to ask if that's Tony?'

'It simply is! He insisted on coming. Not that I needed much persuasion to bring him.'

'He certainly looks interested in the paintings.' Tony seemed absorbed by the still lifes.

'He would be, Leonie. That's his job, though he's supposed to be retired.'

'Really? Should I introduce him to Peter?'

'Good idea. Where is Peter? I haven't seen him.'

'Hiding, I expect. There he is.' Stef was standing at the green-baize table, handing out booklets to the visitors. Peter hovered behind her, a mixed expression of pride and embarrassment on his face. He gave the impression that he was trying to keep out of the way.

Trudi went to fetch Tony whilst Leonie made polite conversation with a youngish, well-heeled-looking couple she recognized as close neighbours in Bellevue Gardens. Jimmy Hennings, that was the man's name. She'd never spoken to the woman. Jimmy was one of those fresh, open-faced men it was difficult to dislike, the type who went through life like an enthusiastic retriever dog, enjoying each new thing that came along.

'We are determined to buy a painting,' he said, a smile lighting his cherubic face. 'Jilly and I didn't know we had an artist living in Bellevue Gardens.'

Oh Lord, were they really called Jimmy and Jilly? 'Peter's very modest.' Leonie let the opportunity to mention her own artistic leanings go by. This was, after all, Peter's day.

Jilly, plump, dimpled, worried-looking, said, 'We're not sure whether to buy the bottles or the seashells. The colour scheme of our lounge is bright yellow, you see.'

'I should go for the one you like best,' Leonie said, thinking this a funny way to judge a painting.

'That's what I said,' Jimmy pronounced, delighted. 'The shells it is.'

They could always repaint the walls if it didn't match, was Leonie's naughty thought as she directed them to Stef, who would take their money.

She forgot the Henningses, for here were Rosa and Michal coming through the door, Michal still as wide-eyed and wary as a rescued puppy, but less skinny now, his face less pallid. Leonie went up to them at once and sent them over to get refreshments.

'Leonie, this is Tony.' She turned at Trudi's voice, which could only be described as purring. A hint of expensive cologne, those searching dark eyes, and Tony's grip was warm as he imprisoned Leonie's hand in his.

'Delighted to meet you at last,' he murmured. 'You are every bit as lovely as Trudi described.'

'Oh Tony, stop it at once,' Trudi scolded, but she was smiling, and Leonie realized that it must be a joke between them, Tony's ready charm.

'I'm afraid I'm glad to receive any compliments at my age,' Leonie said, beaming warmly at them both. After the Billy years she had learned to like games like this.

'Then I'm sure that you're often made to feel glad in that way,' he returned with the skill of a tennis player.

'Nicely put, Tony. Now, Leonie darling, Tony would like to meet Peter.'

'Then he shall!' Leonie caught Peter's attention and beckoned. He came over in a twinkling, trying his best to look friendly, but only managing wary, and Leonie introduced them to one another, explaining that Tony had been an art dealer.

'I simply wanted to congratulate the artist,' Tony said, and Peter hesitantly took the outstretched hand. 'You have a fine sense of colour in your work.'

'Thank you,' Peter managed to reply.

'There are one or two here that interest me, if I might have a private word.' Peter perked up at once, and the two men made their excuses and went to study one of the bigger landscapes.

'That's very, very kind of him,' Leonie said soberly to Trudi.

'No, I'm sure he's genuinely interested.'

'It would mean the world to Peter if he did buy something.' She broke off to greet Karina, who was out of breath, having presumably run up the hill from the café. Rosa elected to walk with her round the paintings, Michal trailing after them, looking somewhat bemused.

'Is that the boy who—?' Trudi whispered.

'Yes,' Leonie said. 'He's living with Rosa's friend Will for the moment. I don't think he knows yet what he wants to do longer term, stay in England or go home. I suppose it partly depends on Rosa. Their father's in prison here, I told you that, didn't I?'

'Yes, it's terrible.'

'So they may stay because of him. Rosa's a very loyal sort of girl. But there may be another factor involved.'

'Oh?' Trudi said, then glanced round, following the direction of Leonie's gaze to a lanky man with a mop of blue-black curls, who was lounging, one hand resting on the back of a chair, talking animatedly to Jamie, who was drinking beer from a bottle and throwing back his head to laugh. 'That's Will?' she whispered.

'Yes.'

'The one who helped find—?'

'That's the one.'

'And you think he and Rosa—?'

'Yes, but they don't seem to know it yet.'

'Ah, what it is to be young.'

'Indeed,' Leonie said, 'though I think I made a mess of it when it was my turn.'

'What it is to be old too.'

'Yes,' Leonie sighed. 'What is it they say? Oh to be young but with the wisdom of age, something like that.'

'I've always thought that sounded a bit dull and sensible. I'd have lost out on so much fun.'

'You're still having fun, Trudi, that's one of the things everybody loves about you.'

'Oh, thank you, darling. I just wish you had more. You deserve it. If only Guillaume—'

'No, Guillaume is in the past now and I'm perfectly happy. Anyway, I do have fun, Trudi, just a different kind from you.' She looked about, pleased to see all the dozens of folk who'd come to view Peter's paintings, and delighted to see Stef was putting up another *Sold* label, this time next to a bright-coloured meadowscape. It seemed mean to dwell on the inescapable truth. A truth that she must keep to herself, which was that even if every one of Peter's paintings sold at the prices he was offering today, they would only make a small fraction of the large amount of money she would need to renew the lease on 11 Bellevue Gardens.

By two o'clock the party was largely over and the crowd dispersing. Leonie helped Hari, Rick and Bela clear up and Jamie carried the small amount of leftovers, the crockery and wine glasses out to Blake's car, which he'd borrowed.

Trudi and Tony came into the kitchen to say goodbye,

and Leonie, who was tired by now, gladly accepted their offer of a lift home.

'No, we can manage,' the others chorused when she asked if it was all right to leave. 'You go, Leonie, put your feet up,' and she found herself gently and firmly propelled out of the kitchen. Peter was busy, speaking perhaps to a prospective customer, so she gave him a little wave and was escorted out to the church car park by Trudi and into the front passenger seat of Tony's glistening black saloon car.

When they reached Bellevue Gardens, she asked them in for tea. 'And cake. I made a fruitcake yesterday.'

'Have we got time, Tony?'

'I don't see why not, but are you sure, Leonie? You must be exhausted.'

'Not too exhausted to have a cup of tea with friends. And I'd like you to see the house that you might be helping to save. Look, there's a space further along there. Parking restrictions don't apply at weekends.'

Whilst Trudi took Tony out to see the garden, Leonie made the tea. The delightful spicy smell of the cake was comforting when she took the lid off the box. Cherries, currants, cinnamon. This recipe was her mother's and always made her think of her childhood, how magically these things had appeared once rationing ended. How everybody took things for granted these days, she thought, as the knife sank through the moist cake, releasing more of the delicious smell.

It had been a funny day, quite disconcerting to see all those paintings from Peter's past and hers, and knowing that some of them were going out into the world to adorn walls in other houses. It was pleasing to know that at least one wasn't going very far, to Jimmy and Jilly's up the road. Then, with a dive of spirits, she remembered that it would be she and Peter who would be moving away from it.

Footsteps, voices and shadows heralded Tony and Trudi's return from the garden.

'Let's go into my drawing room,' Leonie said. 'It'll be more comfortable there.' Tony insisted on carrying the tray and she went ahead to manage the doors.

'What a marvellous room,' Tony immediately said, once he'd put down the tray. He straightened and began to gaze around at the paintings, automatically feeling for the spectacles in his pocket. Leonie felt at once a cold sense of unease in realizing that she was exposing her private collection to his professional eye. He would judge her taste, maybe secretly price the paintings, and the bangles on her wrist tinkled together with nerves.

'Do make yourselves at home,' she murmured. 'I seem to have forgotten the napkins,' and she hurried out of the room, pausing to take down the work in progress from her easel – a pair of sleepy tortoiseshell cats – and prop it against a wall. She couldn't have a real professional evaluating her own humble attempts at art.

When she returned with some paper napkins a moment later, it was to find the pair of them standing in serious discussion in front of the bird picture George had bought her.

'Where did you get this, Leonie? I've forgotten,' Trudi asked.

'Haslemere in Surrey. It was a curio shop. I liked it and George bought it for me. I don't think he paid much for it, I wouldn't have let him do that.'

'Tony thinks it might be a Cotton.'

'I'm sorry?'

'Orlando Cotton. There's a retrospective of his work on at Tate Britain at the moment,' Tony said, stepping back and dipping his chin to frown at the painting.

'Is there?' She had a vague memory of someone mentioning it, Peter perhaps. She knew the name Cotton, of course. He'd been an English painter of the Thirties, his style what one might call surrealist or plain eccentric, depending on where you stood on these things. She looked hard at the picture, trying to see whatever it was that Tony was seeing in it. He'd taken out a tiny magnifying glass to examine it further. It didn't seem to be Cotton's usual style.

'The mark here,' he said, pointing to two tiny concentric rings in the bottom right-hand corner. 'I'm sure it's *OC*, Orlando Cotton.'

Leonie supposed that it might be, though the *C* was almost closed. She started to feel nervous again. Why was all this important? It was simply a painting she loved that meant a great deal to her.

'Leonie,' Trudi said, calmly taking her hand. 'Shall I pour the tea before it stews?'

'I can do that. Let's sit down, shall we?'

Tony selected an armchair from which he could still

see the bird painting and crossed one leg over the other in a languid fashion, the shiny leather of his polished shoes glinting expensively. 'It's an unusual subject,' he ruminated. 'The bird escaping. Cotton had a period in a mental asylum, you know. I wonder if it's connected to that at all. We'd need a specialist to study it, of course.'

'A specialist?' Leonie felt she was behind on something here.

'What Tony thinks,' Trudi said, with excitement in her eyes, 'is that this painting might be worth a few bob.'

'There's quite an interest in Cotton at the moment. Not just the Tate exhibition, but his pictures are fetching very good prices at auction.'

Leonie looked from one to the other, what they were saying slowly sinking in. 'What sort of prices?'

'Well, hundreds, some of them,' Tony said. 'The Americans like them.'

'Oh.' Hundreds was disappointing.

'Tony! These dealers and their jargon. He means hundreds of thousands.'

Leonie stared at her, not quite believing.

'The larger ones do,' Tony said, swallowing a mouthful of fruitcake. 'You know this cake really is very good. I couldn't say for sure about this particular painting, of course. It might be considered a minor work, but there is something very attractive about it, the bird, the way the artist draws you in, the floating girl and the sense of rapture.'

Hundreds of thousands. Even if it was tens of thousands that would help. But that little picture?

Leonie crumbled her piece of cake and dabbed a sultana into her mouth. The comforting spiciness of it soothed her. She took a mouthful of the strong tea, closed her eyes and felt calmer.

Her thoughts started to run ahead. She did not want this painting to go, never ever, but suppose, perhaps, it really was worth a great deal of money, enough to save the house, were she to sell it.

Just think, it might go to a museum and many more people would be able to look at it, study it, what would that mean?

'I can find somebody to examine it if you like,' Tony said. 'To establish if it really is a Cotton.'

'I suppose,' Leonie replied carefully, ' it would be the best thing to do.' Tony might be wrong. If he was then she wouldn't have to decide. Everything would simply be the same as before today. She didn't dare hope.

Rosa

Rosa hummed as she worked cleaning tables at the end of the day. She was so unaccustomed to feeling happy that she still had the pleasure of wondering at it, reminding herself of it as though happiness was a beautiful, fragile object that she took out every now and then to admire.

The terrible burden of worry about Michal was gone. He was safe and she saw him every day, delighting in the fact that he was getting better. At their reunion in the safe house she'd realized he was exhausted and traumatized by his experiences, and she'd seen the sense of him staying there for a few days to receive professional help. And he was eager to tell his story to the police.

Although Leonie had offered to squeeze Michal in somewhere at Number 11, at least for a short while, Rosa had been so grateful to Will when he'd offered his spare bedroom. Will was trained to help young men like Michal and she was touched by how her brother looked up to Will. Somehow they were managing to communicate despite the language difficulties. Michal was now taking English lessons every day and through the classes had found one or two companions of his own age, so he was keeping quite cheerful. He'd also gone with Rosa to visit their father, which he'd found very upsetting. He'd set his English father on something of a pedestal and felt he'd been badly let down. Rosa, who was used to feeling like this about their dad, was able to keep things in perspective for him.

She was happy, too, that Will seemed to care about Michal almost as much as she did. Will was such a loving person. She saw this in the way he guided Michal, teaching him how to cook and clean and change his bedsheets in a way that was kind but firm, to be responsible for himself and, crucially, to value himself, really building the boy's confidence. It was the way he was with all the young people he came across in his work. She'd been once or twice to help with a youth club at the church and appreciated how calm Will was, but strong, too, not putting up with nonsense. And she saw how the young people valued this, some of them so vulnerable and confused that it broke her heart. She wanted to help them, too.

As she cleaned, Rosa smiled to herself every time the picture caught her eye. It was a portrait of a woman with a cat sitting on her knee. A black cat, naturally. Karina had loved it as soon as she'd seen it at Peter's exhibition and had insisted on buying it, though it must have wiped out a week's profits.

'I'll claim it against tax,' she said grimly to Rosa, for she was feeling hard done by when it came to the authorities.

'It is part of the decoration,' Rosa agreed. The picture did indeed look well on the wall of the café, so that if you glanced to the right when you entered your eye was drawn to it, and several customers had commented favourably. Peter had actually received a commission from one of them as a result, so it was proving a good investment all round.

There was still much discussion at Bellevue Gardens about the success of the exhibition. When Rosa, Stef, Rick, Jamie, Hari and Bela had returned after the opening, they were all tired, of course, but elated by the atmosphere of the party, pleased by the hordes of people who'd turned up and by the fact that some of the paintings had been sold. As Rick said, since the exhibition was to continue into the following week, surely the success would continue. They assumed that Peter and Leonie would be very happy with the sales.

But then events had taken a peculiar turn.

'Where is Peter?' Bela had asked. She was laying out the remaining food so they could finish it up.

Nobody knew. Rosa had left Will and Michal to lock up.

Leonie had been in an odd mood. Her friends Trudi and Tony had brought her home, but had left soon after everyone else had come back. She was drifting around the house sighing and fiddling with things to no purpose. It was clear she had something on her mind, but nobody thought to ask if anything was the matter.

They'd all been sitting around the kitchen table with the drink and nibbles left over from the party and chatting quietly about the day's events when they heard the front door crash open. Leonie sprang to her feet as though a firework had gone off. The others all fell silent. Rick tipped his chair, reached for the door handle and when the door opened they craned their heads to look out into the hall.

They all experienced, rather than saw, the front door slamming shut. Rosa stood up and glimpsed Peter throwing his canvas shoulder bag down against the wall and staggering towards the kitchen. To see him clutching the door frame for support was to realize instantly that he was drunk, gloriously, famously so.

With a cross between a groan and a roar he half lurched, half fell down the kitchen steps. Rosa grabbed his arm while he steadied himself. Everyone stared at him in a silence tinged with horror and awe, and he stared back at them, a bewildered belligerence etched onto his face.

'Hope you're all satis … satisfied,' he mumbled as though on a stage addressing an audience.

'Satisfied with what, Peter?' Leonie replied gently.

Rick pulled out a chair, which after a failed attempt Peter sat down on.

'Pictures,' he said. 'Not good enough, Peter. Must be punished.' He brought his fist down on the table and everyone winced at the thud. Bela gave a little shriek.

Leonie said, 'Peter, no one knows what you're talking about.' She got up. 'Jamie, would you give me a hand?' She made a gesture towards the hall.

'Sure,' Jamie said, getting up in a rather uncertain fashion, but Peter brushed all hands aside.

'Never been any good. Useless. Like the old man said. "Peter, Peter, my boy, you're no good to anyone." Rubbish, that's what he called my paintings. "How you goin' to earn a living?" All he cared about was money, my dad.'

'Oh Peter. That was all a long, long time ago.' Leonie sighed sadly.

'Long time, yes. I've never been any good, though. Wanted to help. Wanted to pay my way with the house. Make a difference. Do something for you, Leonie. You've, you've … looked after me all these years, put up with me. That's what the show's for. Pay you back somehow. Save this place. But it's pathetic. Nobody wants the pictures. Nobody wants Peter's paintings.'

'You sold some today,' Stef was brave enough to put in. 'People liked them. Everyone said.'

'Good girl,' he said, grasping Stef's hand and patting

it. 'She's a good girl.' He smiled bashfully at her. 'She's done well today,' he announced to the generality. 'You've all helped. Wonderful. Sorry so useless.' His head sagged on his chest and he gave every appearance of being about to pass out.

'Jamie,' Leonie whispered. He came round the table and each of them took an arm, and gently persuaded Peter out of the room, slowly, slowly, then downstairs. Rosa got up and filled a jug of water at the tap, then followed them. In his gloomy bedroom, she and Leonie got him tucked under the covers, while Jamie stood back, embarrassed. Leonie got him to drink a little water then left a glass within reaching distance.

'I've never seen him like this before,' she whispered as they all returned to the kitchen. 'I suppose it's the pressure of the day.'

'But today was good,' Rosa said, puzzled.

'Peter would have found it quite stressful talking to people, seeing them judge his work. He's so private, usually.'

'He still went for it, though.' Jamie sounded impressed.

'He did. It was brave of him.'

'What was all that bad stuff about his dad?'

'He told me once, years and years ago. His dad was a bit like your great-grandpa the plumber,' she explained. 'Tough, overbearing. He saw Peter's artistic ambitions as an affront to his masculinity.'

'Peter's an old guy. Why would that affect him now?'

'You'd be surprised what old guys still feel. And old

ladies, too. Things that hurt us from long ago can be like grains of sand in an oyster. Some people cope. They coat the grains with mother-of-pearl and turn them into something beautiful, but not everybody manages to do this. Peter is one of those, I'm afraid.'

'You're not old, Grans. Not really. Just sort of mature.' He grinned at Rosa who shook her head at his bare-faced charm.

'Well, thank you,' Leonie said, pressing her lips into a firm line. 'I must say, I feel quite old today.'

Back in the kitchen they found everyone gathered so concerned for Peter that Leonie appeared close to tears. The fractious 'old guy' occupied a greater place in their affections, Rosa saw, than any of them had ever suspected.

By the next day, extraordinarily, Peter was right as rain, and the exhibition continued without further incident. At the end, after the paintings sold – which was most of them, in fact – had been wrapped up for dispersal to their new owners, Leonie broke the news to the household that once expenses had been covered, he'd made a sum touching five figures, which he was kindly putting towards the house. Rosa knew that this would not be enough to save it, but Leonie told them something else, too. One of the paintings in her drawing room was apparently more valuable than she'd believed, and she was going to take it to a specialist at one of the sales houses for assessment. 'But,' Leonie had said very clearly, 'there's absolutely no guarantee that it will be worth very much and, anyway, I haven't decided I want to sell it.' Still, the news generated a certain excitement in the house.

Rosa finished wiping the tables, dropped the cloth in the sink and reached for the broom to brush the floor. She worked quickly, with one eye on the clock, sweeping up the crumbs, then she rearranged the tables and chairs, deftly refilled the holders with sachets of sugar and sauce for the morning, then swapped her apron for her jacket and went to freshen up in the little cubicle at the back of the café.

After she'd painted kohl around her eyes, she studied her reflection in the scrap of mirror above the basin. Her expression was as solemn as ever, but it had shed its habitual burden of anxiety. Today her eyes were her own and shone back brightly at her, and her lips curved in a smile as secret as to be worthy of La Gioconda herself. That had been Eryk's pet name for her, 'Mona Lisa', because he said she looked so enigmatic. She felt a little pang thinking of Eryk, but it wasn't as painful as once it had been. She would carry the memory of him with her always, deep in her heart, but she found it was easier now.

She slipped her make-up into her bag and left, setting the shop alarm as she went, flicking out the lights and locking the door. However, instead of turning left for home, she crossed the road at the lights and started off the other way, up the hill towards the church.

It was a balmy evening and though the rush-hour traffic was heavy she chose instead to concentrate on the lushness of the grass verges and the golden sunlight shining through the trees, laying dappled shadows across the pavement.

All at once, a skidding of wheels and her heart leaped as a cyclist crossed her path out of nowhere.

'Oh, it's you, you gave me such a shock.'

'Sorry!' Will drew up beside her and leapt nimbly off his bike. 'I managed to get away early.' They stood together and smiled shyly at one another, hardly noticing that other people were having to veer past them. She was too intent on the way he held the bike perfectly balanced in the fingers of one hand, how he was removing his helmet with the other and shaking out his glossy hair. He was cultivating a modest beard now. It gave him a wilder, more piratical appearance, which she secretly liked.

She was dizzy with longing, but thought he'd never make the first move, sensed his shyness, what she could only call his respect for her and all that she'd endured. It would be down to her. It was difficult, though. She couldn't be sure and she was nervous of giving offence, of ruining this friendship.

He was busying himself looping the straps of his helmet over the handlebars, when he said without looking at her, 'Michal's going out tonight. He texted. It'll only be us this evening after all. Do you mind?'

'No,' Rosa replied, puzzled that Michal hadn't told her. He always told her things, but tonight he hadn't. So it would be her and Will, cooking supper together. That would be strange, but lovely.

They began to walk up the hill together, side by side, Will wheeling the bike. Once they brushed against each other, as if by accident, and Rosa felt herself shiver. After a few moments they reached the little memorial park where she and Stef still sometimes sat to eat lunch, and Will stopped.

'Listen, you don't have to come back, you know. I don't mind if you'd rather just go home . . .'

'Is that what you want me to do?' Rosa said in a low voice. She stretched out her hand and gave his arm the lightest of touches.

'No, of course not,' he whispered. 'Look, shall we . . . We can sit down and talk a minute.' And she found herself being led into the garden, where they sat down on the bench, the bike near by. They were holding hands and she leant in and kissed his cheek and he stared at her in wonder, then his mouth was on hers and his fingers stroking her face. At last, he pulled her into his arms.

'You don't . . .' he murmured, his lips against hers, 'mind . . .' He kissed her eyelids . . . 'This, do you?' Their mouths met once more.

'I don't mind at all,' she replied when they drew apart. She was smiling her solemn smile. This is what I want, she told herself fiercely as he cradled her against him and she closed her eyes. This lovely man who helps people, who helped me and Mik, who had been strong for her and helped her to be strong too.

She opened her eyes and saw aslant the creamy stone of the memorial, the names carved into it. There were English words, too, she didn't quite understand, at the top, a quotation.

'What does it say, up there?' she said, raising her head to point.

'*Their name liveth for evermore.* It's archaic. It means these soldiers live for ever in our memory.'

'For ever,' she nodded. With Will, now, she felt the possibilities of that word. For a long time after Eryk's death she'd closed up her heart in that way, had poured all the love she had to give into her family. But now, with Michal safe and happy, she felt her heart begin to open like a cold seed in the warming earth after winter.

So many strangers had helped her in London. Karina had given her a job and Leonie a home. She had friends, family, a community and now Will. In a way that she'd never expected she belonged here now. She was home.

Leonie

Leonie was in her bedroom, packing her favourite old suitcase that she'd used in her model days when travelling. Its bright blue satin lining had faded and worn thin, but she liked it and the soft creamy leather and the brass fastenings. It felt light and elegant to carry and today she felt light and elegant, too. A summer breeze blew through the open window. She was going away.

It would be her first proper holiday for years. Staying with friends in the country for weekends was lovely, but didn't count like abroad. She and Trudi were going to the Italian lakes together, just the pair of them, not Tony because Trudi said she and Tony weren't that type of close. Leonie needed the break, Trudi insisted, and

she, Trudi, was paying for it. Ten days in the most gor-
geous-looking hotel; Trudi had shown pictures on her
tablet thing. The hotel was right on the lakeside with
snow-capped mountains in the background. It would be
beautiful in June, and not too hot either. She was staying
at Trudi's tonight and they'd go to the airport early the
next morning.

She'd been through all her clothes and selected a
range of basics, then lots of accessories and several
dresses for evenings. She'd had to buy some trousers for
walking, and stout shoes, and a Panama hat that framed
her face nicely and didn't mind being folded. Trudi
had inspected these things, but looked alarmed at the
idea of walking gear. They'd never been on holiday like
this before, just the two of them, and Leonie privately
thought they'd be interested in different things, but she
was sure that there would be enough overlap and they
were old enough friends to agree to differ, so she hoped
it would be all right. It was a holiday in romantic Italy
and that was the important thing.

For she needed to get away, badly. The last year had
taken it out of her. It had felt like a great long journey
and it wasn't over yet. Jamie's departure, the shock of
finding out that she would lose the house, the vain
attempts to save it, the coming and going of tenants
with their hopes and dreams, their dramas and heart-
break, all this was exhausting. 'It's because you care so
much about them,' Trudi had told her, somewhat exasperated. 'You shouldn't try to live other people's lives
for them.'

'I know,' Leonie replied, a little crossly, because Trudi could be coldly cut-and-dried at times, 'but I can't help it. If they need my help I can hardly refuse it. It would be cruel.'

She withdrew a pretty, gauzy evening dress from the wardrobe. Trudi had made her buy it last week. It had cost far more than she would normally pay, but Trudi seemed sure there would be an occasion to wear it. She felt a little frisson of excitement at this idea and imagined handsome Italian *signori* in evening dress asking her and Trudi to dance.

The latest drama had been to do with the picture of the bird in flight. The expert at the auction house had made her sign a form that allowed him to take it to examine it. Last week he had written to her with his conclusions. The painting was indeed an Orlando Cotton, and it could be worth a good deal of money, definitely six figures, though he seemed reluctant to commit himself to exactly how much. He and his colleagues would be delighted to feature it in their autumn catalogue if she wished and they should discuss a reserve price. He would recommend an early sale though whilst there was plenty of interest in Cotton's work. So there was a huge unknown hanging over her. Even if she decided to sell it she couldn't be certain that the money raised would cover the cost of the lease.

And supposing it did, what then? She'd have saved the house, but for what? For so long she'd thought the house was everything. She'd kept it in memory of George and for Peter and for a certain kind of life. But the trouble was that things had a kind of way of changing and adapting when you weren't paying attention.

Some of the house's inhabitants had accepted the idea that they would have to leave and had made plans, or their lives had changed for other reasons not to do with the house and they recognized it was time to move on. Only yesterday, Bela had told her whilst they were cleaning the kitchen together that she and Hari had decided that they would go back to North India for a long visit to see what remained of their families. They could afford it, and because the local political situation there had shifted, Hari would no longer be in danger. They were looking forward to the trip. So much time had passed since they'd seen their brothers and sisters, and if they found they were happy there then they might retire there, with the help of money from Hari's wealthy brother, and not come back to Britain at all. That revelation had come as a bit of a shock, but it was a relief, too, that she need not feel responsible for the couple. Apart from Peter, they had been the tenants whose future she'd worried about most, and now she wouldn't have to.

Rosa would be staying for a while, but there was talk of her and Will getting married, so she would be moving on presumably. Jamie would be all right, she was certain of that now. He'd changed, loved his work and would do well at it. He and Blake were working on a television documentary about modern slavery with an independent production company and Jamie was hardly here he was so busy travelling round with the camera team, or on the research trail. Blake was getting him training as an investigative journalist, too, which meant evenings at college. One of his first commissioned assignments was an interview with Michal for an online news site. Yes, Jamie would be all right.

She laid a warm shawl for evenings across the top of her clothes in the case and pushed down the lid – then hearing laughter from the garden crossed the floor to glance out. There they were below, a honey-gold head and a sandy one, Stef and Rick, sitting on the grass together, just talking. She smiled to herself. They hadn't seen her yet.

She was not really worried about either of them, well, only a little. Stef's interview had gone well – the best portfolio the tutor had seen for a long while, Stef had been told – and she was waiting to hear formally from the college about a place for September. Rick had patiently applied for masses of jobs, but so far had only been offered a paid internship at a prestigious arts centre. Still, he seemed pleased with that as a start, so Leonie was too. Stef had explained to her how difficult it was these days and why the opening offered possibilities for Rick. He was busy with his story, too, she gathered, getting it ready for the publisher.

How shy he'd been when he'd arrived here first over a year ago, quiet, friendly, but a little distant. And look at him now, lazily tickling the back of Stef's neck with a long piece of grass, and laughing as she squealed and then turned and mock-wrestled him. As Leonie lowered the window sash they looked up and saw her and she smiled, and they both waved back.

And she thought how a lot of life was about getting your confidence back, learning how to fly again, to feel the air under your wings, to get the hang of living once more. She supposed that this was how they'd all done it over the years, the people who had lived in this house, and now she and Peter. If she sold the picture, they would have enough to get by. Whatever happened next, she would need to learn to let go. It was time to fly.

Acknowledgements

I would particularly like to thank Philippa Rudd of Cozens-Hardy Solicitors, Norwich, for her excellent advice on the knotty subject of freeholds and leases. Any blurring has been for the sake of the fictional situation and I hope that she is not too horrified. Thanks are due also to Felix Taylor, comics writer, for correcting some technical points in Rick's narrative, and to Judith Hurrell, whose account of a bird trapped in her chimney started me thinking.

My wonderful agent, Sheila Crowley, together with Rebecca Ritchie and the rest of the team at Curtis Brown, work very hard on my behalf. So do my brilliant publishers, Simon & Schuster UK, where especial thanks is due to Suzanne Baboneau, Clare Hey and Sam Evans, and freelance copyeditor Mary Tomlinson.

Reading Group Questions

1. *The House on Bellevue Gardens* is a novel of secrets and of hidden pasts and each character carries their own history with them. Whose story did you most connect with and why?

2. The residents of 11 Bellevue Gardens form a family of sorts. Each has their own trouble with their own family. What role does family play in the narrative?

3. *As she crossed the road towards Number 11 her heart gave a little jolt of satisfaction to see its bohemian tattiness; the house was like a louche Cinderella between more splendidly attired sisters. The neighbours – mostly young professionals who had snapped up the converted flats – might frown at its dilapidated paintwork and the weeds growing from its gutters, but she loved the house with all its faults. It had become her home at a time of crisis in her life and, in turn, she'd opened it to others who'd needed a safe place.*

   The house at the centre of *The House on Bellevue Gardens* is as much a character as anyone. How do you feel the author brought its character and history to life?

4. How do you think the theme of sanctuary runs through the novel? Who is providing sanctuary to whom? And is it always who you think it is?

5. Leonie's story is set over two very different time periods. How did the author evoke period in the novel and did you learn anything about the past that surprised you?

6. *Leonie sighed as she lay awake in the depths of the night. How clear her memories were of things that had happened fifty years ago.*

    What role does memory play in the story?

7. How do accidents and chance meetings move the plot along?

8. A bird becomes trapped in the chimney at 11 Bellevue Gardens. How does it represent the themes of the novel?

9. Leonie tells Stef: 'We're survivors, you and I. Rosa is another. What doesn't kill you makes you stronger, eh? We must live life bravely, Stef.' In a way many of the other characters are also survivors. Do they all overcome their problems? Are some more survivors than others?

10. What is the role of art and creativity in the novel? How does it link to the other themes of the narrative?